GONE
BEFORE

BOOKS BY SAM HEPBURN

Her Perfect Life

SAM HEPBURN

GONE BEFORE

bookouture

Published by Bookouture in 2020

An imprint of Storyfire Ltd.
Carmelite House
50 Victoria Embankment
London EC4Y 0DZ

www.bookouture.com

ISBN: 978-1-83888-831-2
eBook ISBN: 978-1-83888-830-5

For Aphra

CHAPTER ONE

I'm used to heat – the parched, yellow, bone-shrivelling kind that demands respect and keeps you careful. Not this all-colours-blazing, blowsy warmth that sneaks up and scorches your neck the minute you turn to admire the view. I flap my hands at my throat, push open the rusty gate and scramble on up the overgrown terraces. Another five minutes of hard climbing and I spot a ripple of roof tiles through the trees. A grey, startled bird takes off as I come around the ridge and ahead of me, just a few yards away, sits the Villa Rosa. I take in the open shutters, the red espadrilles kicked off on the step and the basket of courgettes – their buttery, star-shaped flowers still attached – and my legs give way, as if I'm going to hit the ground. Somehow I stay upright and keep walking, each step a little slower than the last until I reach the sun-bleached blue of the door. All I have to do is lift my fist and knock. I don't. I strain to make out the song pulsing faintly from an upstairs window, glance back at the spit of white rock thrusting into the electric glitter of the Mediterranean a few hundred feet below, and try to remember how to breathe.

Roz's voice snaps in my ear, sharp as the twigs underfoot. *Go on, kiddo. Don't bottle out now.* I curl my fingers, reach for the words I've been mouthing on the plane from London, the bus from Marseille and all the way up the zigzag road from Cassis, and rap out a sharp double knock that jolts the lazy hush of the hillside. The music stops. A long, hot silence. Then movement. The tentative scuff of footsteps. A darkening of the pinprick of light behind the spyhole. A bolt slides back. A latch lifts. The door opens a few inches, disturbing the air just enough to send a quiver through the overhanging tendrils of vine.

It's her. I feel it like an electric shock that leaves me seared and limp. She's older. Of course she is – nearly thirty-six by now, the spiky wild-child glamour of those early photos long gone. But who is it that her tired eyes are seeing as they stare out at me through that tumble of dark hair? A sweaty, suntanned stranger in cut-off shorts? Or the embodiment of fifteen years of guilt and hope, and fear and dreams?

'Yes?' The voice is wary.

'Kay Duncan?'

A twitch around the eyelids. 'Who are you?'

'My name is Phoebe Locklear.' I lick the salt from my lip. 'But I think I'm your daughter.'

An angry hiss shoots from her mouth. 'What are you after? Money? Publicity? A sick thrill?' She glances over my shoulder, as if she's expecting an accomplice to spring from the bushes. Her eyes jerk back to me. 'Leave. Right now. Or I'll call the police.'

'Please!' I slam my shoulder against the closing door and thrust my hands through the gap. The pressure eases when she sees what I'm holding: a child's yellow sou'wester, the chinstrap a grubby spiral of withered elastic. Slowly I turn back the brim and show her the name inked along the inside of the crown. *Maya Jane Duncan.*

'I was in Botswana.' The word seems unreal, out of place. 'On a nature reserve. That's why the police never found me.'

Her jaw moves. I shove the hat towards her. She takes it slowly, her eyes stuck fast to the smudge of lettering, her thumb pushing at the bumpy stitching along the seam. I stare at the big knobbly ring on her finger – a nugget of amber, golden and inviting as a lump of toffee.

The room is full. So much noise. So many people. I wriggle through their legs. She's lying on the sofa, smiling up at a man in a bright white shirt. I lean across her knees and drop my mouth onto her knuckle. A gritty clink of stone against my teeth. A stab of disappointment that her ring tastes of cold and nothing. The sound of laughter and the casual warmth of her hand on my forehead as she pushes me away.

'Where did you get this?' She's wagging the sou'wester in my face, eyes screwed up with what could be fury but feels more like fear.

What do I say? There's too much to tell. Two thirds of my life to unravel and explain. 'Roz… the woman who took me. She died. Cancer. Seven weeks ago. It was in a box of stuff she left me. And there was a letter.' I rummage in my duffel bag and push the folded sheet into her hand. 'Don't be upset by what she says… I don't blame you… not for any of it.' I've rehearsed that line so many times I almost believe it's true. *I don't blame you, Kay. Not for any of it.*

Her fingers – already tight on the paper – grow rigid as she takes in the words I've read a hundred times.

My Darling Girl,

What I am about to tell you will come as a shock. It might even make you hate me but I need you to understand that I always believed I did the right thing. Your mother is no cousin of mine – distant or otherwise. Her name isn't Locklear, it's Duncan, Kay Duncan, and she and your stepfather, David, are still alive. They lived in Kensington, in one of the big houses opposite a flat I used to rent on Stanford Street. As far as I know they're still there. He was something big in the music business and she was a party girl, with a drug habit she couldn't kick, who used to flit in and out at all hours then disappear for weeks on end.

It was seven months after I lost Phoebe in that terrible car crash in Malawi and the pain of losing my only child was still raw. My contract in Malawi had come to an end and I was back in

London for a few months preparing to come to Molokodi. I missed having animals around me so I used to walk a neighbour's dog – a wheezy old Alsatian with a torn ear. Perhaps you remember him.

I often used to see you in the park, always with a different au pair who'd be sitting on the bench yacking into her phone while you kicked around in the sandpit or hung off the monkey bars – such a sad, lonely little thing. Then one day I found you there on your own. Of course I marched you straight home – you were five years old for God's sake, far too young to be out by yourself. The girl who opened the door was contrite enough, but when I asked to speak to your mother she said she was away. A couple of weeks later it happened again. This time the house was full of people, most of them high or drunk and the ones who were sober enough to string two words together didn't seem to know who you were. One of them shouted upstairs and a man in a suit came down. He was older, more in control, maybe a lawyer or a PR man. He tried to charm his way out of it, ruffled your hair, thanked me for bringing back 'Kay's kid' and assured me it wouldn't happen again. But he didn't even know your name. I made some enquiries and found out that you'd spent time in care as a baby and I worried for you.

The morning I left for Botswana I was up just after six. I looked out of the window and saw you sloshing through the rain in your yellow mac and sou'wester. I ran downstairs and found you crying your little heart out. You said you were hungry and you couldn't get any of the grown-ups to wake up. You showed me a handful of coins, a few pence, and said you'd been to the shops to buy something to eat but none of them were open, and I thought, to hell with this. It was a spur of the moment decision but I've never regretted it. I still had Phoebe's passport and although she was a year or so older than you and had much fairer hair I was willing to take the risk. I don't know how much you remember of that day but I told you your mother was going away again *and she'd asked me to look after you. I booked you a ticket on my flight, cut off your hair, stuffed your yellow mac and sou'wester into my luggage and hurried you into a cab. I told you about the baby animals I was going to be looking after and said we had to pretend you were Phoebe so that you could come and help me. I made a game of it and said it would be our special secret that you used to be called Maya. I was worried you might kick up a fuss at the airport or on the flight. You didn't, of course. You were used to keeping quiet. When we landed in Gabarone I panicked. What had I done? This was madness. Then I checked the UK news. Your mother hadn't reported you missing until seven hours after you left the house. Seven hours! She was too busy sleeping off the excesses of the night before. So I decided to keep you. And later, when I told you that she and your stepfather had died in a fire and you'd be staying with me forever you barely seemed to remember who they were. And you've been happy, haven't you? And loved, and safe?*

The flat my parents left me in Fulham must be worth quite a bit by now and the investments should be enough to keep you comfortable. Be well, my darling. I hope that one day you will find it in your heart to forgive me. I did it for you and I would do it again.

Roz

Kay's head stays bent over the letter. I step a little closer. Her words fling me back. 'What the hell is this? Maya's dead.'

'No!' I thrust out a photo, a faded polaroid of a little girl, her thick dark hair chopped jaggedly close to her head. She's crossing a patch of scrubland, lugging a cheetah cub by its armpits. 'It's me,' I say. 'It must have been taken a few days after I arrived in Molokodi.' I hold it up against the shot the newspapers used in the 'Find Maya' campaign. A school photo of a little girl with a small serious face, framed by an overlong fringe and a wiry cascade of hair.

Her eyes lift, scour my features – my heavy ponytail spring-
ing from its clips, my twitching hands – and flick back to the
photographs. Something shifts in her expression, as if she knows
it's me but won't let herself believe it. I wait for a sob, a smile, an
exclamation. But she's shying away, her chest heaving, her lips
moving soundlessly. The kinder papers called her 'fragile', the
tabloids preferred 'junkie teen mum' or 'Crazy Kay', and I get
scared that I've snapped whatever flimsy threads have been holding
her together. 'I'm sorry… I should have written… or called…
but I thought…' *What? What had I thought – that she'd welcome
me with open arms? That I'd walk back into her life and make us
both complete? That she'd beg my forgiveness and all her guilt and my
resentment would just disappear?*

'I don't… I… I can't.' She backs against the wall, quivering
like a cornered dog.

I hold up my palms and say, gently as I can, 'I'm sorry. I'll get
a room in town and come back when you've had time to take
it in.' Eyes down, I hitch my duffel onto my shoulder and turn
away. Numb inside, I'm five or six paces down the path when she
calls after me.

'Don't go… please.'

I stop. Turn. She's bracing herself in the doorway. With a small
uncertain movement of her hand she stands back, leaving me to
step past her through a narrow hallway into the cool gloom of a
whitewashed sitting room. Slats of light seep through half-closed
shutters. A scarred flagstone floor. An easel and a table of paints in
one corner. A low sofa, sagging beneath a faded throw. She darts
ahead of me, a slight figure in loose cotton trousers, the ends of
her hair – still damp from the shower – streaking moisture across
the shoulders of her shirt. I follow her into the kitchen. A clutter
of bowls, plates and books on a painted dresser, dirty coffee cups
by the sink. She drops into a chair, sweeps aside a magazine and
lays the sou'wester, Roz's letter, the polaroid and the cutting on the

scrubbed wooden table, a shake in her fingers as she pushes back
her hair and inspects each one in turn. In the quiet I hear the buzz
of a small plane skimming low over the house and fading away
along the coast. I focus on the tiny lines around her mouth, the
fall of her hair – thick and dark but much softer than mine – the
empty piercings above the hoop of gold in her ear and the array
of possible futures unfolding before me.

She turns her head and looks at me. She is shivering, her breath
quick and rasping. Then with one sudden movement she's on her
feet, kicking back her chair, her eyes skidding wildly across the
surfaces. They land on a mobile phone. She snatches it up and
jabs it in a jittery arc, taking in the fridge and the rough wooden
shelves hung with jugs and mugs. 'Eat, drink, take whatever you
want I… I have to call David.'

'David? *Now?*' Heat flares along the backs of my hands. This
isn't about him. It's about me and Kay, trying to claw back what
we've lost, working things through.

Her eyes slide away, cowed and apologetic. She yanks open the
back door. 'I need a better signal.'

I catch a glimpse of a paved courtyard and a rocky slope topped
by wind-blasted pines before the door swings shut. Seconds later
it jolts on its hinges, as if she's slumped against it for support.
Emptiness settles on the kitchen. I have to give her time. It's seven
weeks since I first read that letter and I'm still dealing with the
fallout from what it said, still struggling to gather up the pieces
and match the Roz I'd trusted and adored with the depth of her
lies; her insistence that my real mother was dead, the reason why
I'd had to pretend I was her daughter, why, on the rare occasions
when she came back to the UK, I was never allowed to go with
her and why I'd been the only kid in my whole school forbidden
to go on any kind of social media. My belief in her had been so
complete that, even after her death, getting my own Instagram
and Facebook accounts had made me feel sneaky and disloyal.

I take a beer from the fridge, wander through to the sitting room and throw open the shutters, hoping I'll turn around and see some keepsake that Kay has hung on to; some reminder of me. The painting on the easel is a stormy seascape – drab swirls of brown, green and purple that look dull and oppressive beside the airy expanse of sky and sea framed by the window. The canvases stacked against the little table are just as gloomy, the only relief in the murk is a crimson 'K' daubed in the lower right-hand corner of each one. No child's face peers between the tree trunks, no shadowy figure runs through the swirling undergrowth. I run my finger over the brushes, unscrew the lid of one of the bottles and inhale a burst of linseed.

A slant of light through a dormer window. A messy jumble of paint tubes, a jar of brushes. Beyond them a blurry silhouette of Kay at her easel, singing along to the radio. I curl up small behind the old blue chair. It's cramped and dusty. I pinch my nose to hold back the sneeze because I know if she finds me she'll send me away.

I close my eyes, take a slow, steadying breath and let it go as I move on to the slab-stone mantelpiece. I pick through little piles of driftwood and shells that smell of the sea and study the framed photos. They are all of David, none of Kay. There's one of him at the Brit Awards, a proud smile on his bland, shiny face, another with his star act, Lila Mendez, towering above him in impossible heels as they hold up a platinum disc, and a more recent snap on the deck of a boat – wide grin, pastel polo shirt, pressed khaki shorts, dangling a gaping black fish half as big as he is. I climb the painted wooden stairs and move along the landing, pushing open doors. An unmade bed, magazines piled on the floorboards, a damp towel hanging from the bedpost, a spritz of deodorant lingering in the air, a guitar. No threadbare teddy hidden beneath her pillows, no child's shoe or snapshot of a skinny, dark-haired little girl in the bedside drawer, just a welcome pack from the rental agent and a tub of hand cream. I tiptoe on to a smaller, unused room; a brass bed, a wicker chair and a painted chest jammed beneath the slope of the ceiling. The third door opens onto a white-tiled bathroom.

Through the small square window I see her up by the pines, talking into her phone. She's moving around, picking at the bark and glancing back at the house, too agitated to stay still. Me too. I sit on the loo, rubbing my knees and scratching the insect bites on my arms. I pump the ancient cistern to make it flush, turn on a juddery tap and splash my face with water. I open the cabinet above the sink. Inside there's a blister pack of Xanax, a bottle of hair dye guaranteed to 'wash away the grey' and a jar of moisturiser. When I look out of the window again, Kay is off the phone, walking back to the house, her mouth still working. She stops halfway, sags against a ruined stretch of wall and dials again. She speaks urgently into the handset, beating the side of her fist against the stonework. Maybe it would be easier for us both if I just slipped away before she came back. For one weak, panicky moment I'm ready to do it but I'm still there, sitting at the kitchen table, finishing my beer when she pushes open the back door.

'He's coming,' she says, before she's fully inside.

'When?'

'As soon as he's rescheduled his meetings. He was about to leave for Dubai.' There's a slump to her body, as if speaking to David has softened her bones.

'Are you alright?'

'He's angry,' she says, her eyes on the flagstone floor. 'He says I shouldn't let you stay here. Not until we're sure.'

The heat is back, a rake of annoyance scraping my skin. I flex my fingers. 'I can understand why he's worried,' I say, brisk to hide the hurt. 'It's not a problem. Like I said, I'll get a room in town.'

'No! You're staying here!' She raises her eyes, aims them straight into mine. 'This time I don't need any more proof, and neither will he. Not... when he sees you.' Her jaw quivers, then out it comes, the question that must have gnawed at her, every moment of every day for the last fifteen years. 'Did she… hurt you?'

I feel a burst of unbearable sadness for her, for me, for all of it. 'The only person who got hurt was you,' I say. 'I was cared for, happy… loved.'

She presses her fingers into my flesh. '*I* loved you. That's what no one understands. Not the police or the papers, or the trolls who still tell me I didn't deserve to have a child. I was a mess. Ill, depressed. I couldn't cope.'

Crazy Kay in Suspected Overdose Drama
Kay Duncan Back in Rehab
Drug Mum Hits Back, 'It wasn't my fault'
Police interview Kay Duncan under caution
Cadaver dogs search Duncan home.

'I know,' I say softly.

She loosens her grip. 'You've been reading about me. Picking over the accusations.'

'Yes, but I don't believe the tabloids.' I don't tell her about the night Roz died, how I'd sat up devouring the huge file of cuttings she'd left me, reading all about the 'Find Maya' campaign, mesmerised by the blurred CCTV freeze-frame of a little girl in a too-big sou'wester that made the front page of every paper, and the shot of a traumatised, wild-haired, make-up-smeared Kay breaking down, unable to speak at the press appeal. Then I'd moved on to my laptop, raw and tearful with a box of tissues and a dusty bottle of rum and gorged myself on wobbly cam videos that claimed to reveal 'the truth about Maya', press reports of cruel hoaxes, false sightings, attempts at extortion, speculation about the identity, whereabouts and involvement of Maya's biological father, interviews with 'witnesses' whose hazy recall improved radically with time, and years of tabloid gossip.

Duncans given false hope by fake leads
Two prosecuted in Maya Duncan ransom scam
Kay Duncan in drug-fuelled sex romp
Is this the face of evil?

Eventually I'd staggered into the yard and passed out in a pool of my own vomit. Around dawn I'd managed to drag myself back inside, although no amount of face splashing and mouth rinsing could wash away the bile the world had spewed at her. 'Roz kept a file of articles about the investigation,' I say, as if character assassination is somehow less hurtful when it comes with a byline.

'So she could gloat about getting away with it?'

'She wasn't like that, she was—'

'What? What kind of woman steals someone else's child and keeps up the lie for *fifteen* years?'

'I don't know,' I say. I can't justify what Roz did. It seems mad to even try but there was a logic to it, a strange, Roz kind of logic that spins me away, even now, to a place of certainty where her very presence made everything clear and sharp. No fuzzy-edged compromises, no murky greys or hesitations, no room for questions, regrets or doubts; just rust-coloured soil, the hum of the water pump, lizards in the thatch, and Roz's pink determined face prickling with sweat as she hauls a sack of feed off the pickup.

'She was a… maverick,' I say. 'She didn't believe in other people's rules. She was independent, resourceful. She had to be to run a massive nature reserve single-handed.'

'So that makes it alright? You were a child. My child. Not some stray animal that was hers for the taking.'

'I know what she did was wrong, crazy, fucked-up, but she was grieving for her daughter and she thought…'

'Go on. Say it. That you needed rescuing, that being with her was better than staying with a mess like me.' Kay's mouth folds in, a dazed look on her face, like she can't even see me. 'Every night since the day I lost you I've dreamed that you came back to me and you're still a little kid and I get the chance to start over and make things right.'

'We can still make things right,' I say gently.

She blinks and refocuses, snapping back from wherever it was she'd drifted away to. 'No. Once the press find out there'll be reporters banging at the windows, hanging from the trees, dredging it all up again. Judging me.' She drums frantic fingertips on the table. 'Kay Duncan, the spoiled, self-obsessed junkie who took seven hours to notice her child was missing.'

'They won't. I haven't told anyone else who I am.'

Kay snatches up a pouch of tobacco and fumbles to roll a cigarette. 'Not even the police?'

'No.'

'But this woman, this *Roz*.' She spits out the name before running her tongue across the Rizla. 'Someone in her life must have known you weren't her real daughter.'

'It was always our secret.'

'Didn't she have a husband… a boyfriend?'

I laugh. I can't stop myself. 'Roz didn't have much time for human beings. Especially not men.'

'What about her kid's father?'

'If Roz knew who he was she never let on.'

Kay starts back, startled by the rev of a motorbike straining up the track to the house. 'Stay here.' She drops her half-rolled cigarette in a saucer and darts outside, slamming the door behind her. There's a crunch and grind of gravel as the bike pulls up. I cross to the window, hear the rumble of voices, and pull back quickly as the bike swings a noisy U-turn around the courtyard and roars away. Kay stays outside for what seems like an age after it's gone. When she finally comes back she's holding a white plastic carrier bag, thrusting it forward, a handle in each hand, like a child eager to please. 'Sardines,' she says. 'Straight from the sea.'

I'm looking down at the silvery fish packed on a bed of ice when she lets the bag drop, suddenly tearful again. 'When I heard that bike I thought the press hunt had started. They're going to make our lives hell when they find out. You know that, don't you? Every tabloid and every mindless troll falling over themselves to rake up the past.'

'Who cares what they say?'

Her lips quiver and turn down. 'You don't know what it's like to be vilified for every breath you've ever taken, accused of killing your own kid, spat at in the street, despised as a woman, a mother, a human being.'

'No, I don't. But now we can tell the world the truth and put an end to it.'

'They'll make you hate me.'

'No one can do that.'

She takes my hand and clasps it between both of hers. 'Can't it stay our secret? Please, just for a few more days. So we can get to know each other before they turn you against me?'

'If that's what you want,' I say, as gently as I can, though from the moment I read Roz's letter I've been longing to end the hazy lie of being Phoebe and reclaim the sharp reality of being Maya, however fraught and painful that transition might turn out to be.

She hears my disappointment and draws back to look me in the eye. 'You've sold your story to the papers.'

Her accusation cuts deep. 'I swear. I haven't told anyone.'

'I wouldn't blame you. You could get a book deal, sell the film rights, make thousands.'

'No!' I hate that she thinks I might be lying, and it hits home that she doesn't know me at all – at least not the grown-up me. 'I don't need money. You read Roz's letter. She left me everything she had.' A wave of grief burns through my chest and comes out in a sob.

Kay's face grows still. 'You loved her.'

'I'm sorry.' I look at the floor, try to hold back the tears, but they won't stop coming. 'She was all I had for so long and she... she was good to me.'

This admission was never part of the careful homecoming speeches I'd rehearsed in my head and I look up, afraid that I've hurt her, surprised when she says quietly, 'I know. And somewhere under all the anger there's a part of me that's grateful to her for keeping you safe. But when this story gets out I won't be the only bad guy. The press will tear her memory apart and paint her as a deranged child-snatcher. I don't think you're ready for that.' I shake my head, dumb and grateful. 'So let's buy ourselves some time. Time for you to grieve, time for me to deal with my feelings about Roz, and most important of all, time for us to get to know each other.' I sniff hard and nod. She's right. Of course she's right. 'And you'll stay here?' she says. 'Just you and me.'

'And David,' I say, unable to keep the sulky edge out of my voice.

'He won't be here long. He just wants to make sure that I'm not' – she lowers her head – 'seeing what I want to see.'

Why am I being so churlish? After everything she's been through I can't begrudge him wanting to protect her. 'Of course I'll stay,' I say. 'For as long as you want. But right now what I need more than anything in the world is a shower.' Gently, I try to pull my hand from hers. She just goes on looking at me and doesn't let go. 'What is it?' I say.

'Your voice. I imagined you in so many ways – taller, shorter, darker, fairer – but never with an accent.'

'And never this sweaty.'

She breaks into a smile and releases my hand. 'Bathroom's upstairs. Towels in the cupboard on the landing. Shall I show you?'

'It's fine.'

'Alright. I'll get these on the grill. You must be starving.' She picks up the bag of sardines.

I sling my duffel onto my shoulder and turn as I reach the door. She's watching me, expressionless, though anything but calm – her grip on the bag has turned her knuckles pale beneath her tan.

Upstairs I turn on the taps, pull off my dusty shorts and T-shirt and stand with my hands pressed against the tiles, groaning out loud as the scalding water sluices my skin. Still naked, I rub the steam from the mirror above the sink and study my reflection. This dark-haired, green-eyed girl with a freckled tan is no longer Phoebe Locklear. Phoebe Locklear is dead, killed sixteen years ago in a car crash in Malawi. This girl is Maya Duncan.

CHAPTER TWO

When I come back down in a clean shirt and jeans, Kay is in the kitchen slicing tomatoes. She looks up, swings back her hair. 'Have another beer.'

'Thanks.' I take a bottle from the fridge and indulge myself a little, play the game that we're just an ordinary mother and daughter taking time out in our chic little holiday hideaway instead of two wary strangers linked only by blood and loss. The fantasy doesn't last.

Her phone buzzes and she's edgy again, checking the screen. 'It's David,' she says, slipping it into her back pocket. 'He's catching the first flight to Marseille on Monday.'

'So soon?' I lean back against the counter and hide my disappointment beneath a show of opening the beer. 'What's the deal with you and him?'

'Deal?'

'You're here. He's in London.'

Her hands grow still and she closes her eyes as if to hold back pain. 'I had a bit of a relapse last year. I… I needed to get away for a while, clear my head.'

'So you're still together?'

'Of course! He comes over whenever he can get away.'

She sees the look on my face. 'He's a good man, Maya. I won't pretend we haven't had our rocky patches but living with me can't have been easy. There have been plenty of times when…' She winces at a memory she's not ready to share and purses her lips.

'The truth is I wouldn't still be here if it wasn't for him.' She nods to herself and goes back to her slicing.

> *David Duncan flies in from the US to stand by distraught wife after stepdaughter goes missing*
> *Kay Duncan was revived by her husband, who gave her mouth-to-mouth resuscitation while he waited for the emergency services to arrive*
> *Duncan slams hoax sightings of missing Maya*
> *Duncan threatens to sue ex-cop for slander*

'Are you going to pick him up?'

'He keeps a car at the airport.'

I wave my beer at the slope of pines through the window. 'What does he do with himself when he's here?'

She slips the knife into another tomato and tips her head towards the sea. 'Fishes mainly, takes diving lessons and fiddles around with his boat.'

I tell myself not to be childish about sharing her and force a smile. 'Maybe he can take us for a trip around the creeks; everyone says they're amazing.'

The knife drops. 'Damn!' Her finger flies to her mouth.

'Here, let me see.'

The cut is deep. I pull her towards the sink, shove the wound under the tap and hold the back of my hand to my nose to stave off the smoke drifting through the open door.

'The sardines!' Kay wails. A text pings. Her eyes dart to her phone.

'Don't move!' I tell her. 'Keep your hand in the water.' I rush outside to the grill and flip the wire rack. Blackened fish skin clings to the mesh at the bottom while the tops of the sardines are still raw. 'It's alright,' I call. 'I like them crispy.'

Back inside, I find her pressing the cut with a piece of kitchen towel, half laughing, half tearful. 'What a bloody disaster! I spend fifteen years dreaming of cooking you a homecoming supper and what do you get? Charred fish!'

I catch at wisps of memory, searching for a glimpse of Kay in the kitchen at Stanford Street, the touch of her hand as she sets a plate of food in front of my childhood self. All I see is hearty, capable Roz slinging up twenty yards of electric fence between digging a fire pit and roasting enough corn cobs to feed half a dozen hungry rangers.

'Where do you keep the plasters?' I say.

'It's alright. I'll find one.' She hurries to the door, snatching up her phone on the way.

While she's gone I finish my beer, make the salad, find half a baguette and do my best to rescue the sardines. Kay takes a bottle of white wine from the fridge and we carry the food out to the little metal table at the front of the house. We sit on wobbly chairs facing the sea, surrounded by the shriek of crickets. The sun is sinking, a big fiery ball dripping gold across the water. Beneath it, the dark bob of a fishing boat heads for the glimmer of lights at the far end of the bay.

'It's beautiful,' I say. 'But doesn't it get lonely up here on your own?'

'I like lonely.' She pulls at the plaster on her finger. 'That's why I came to Provence. To get away.'

'From what?'

'Guilt. Memories. Being Kay Duncan.'

It's risky but I dip a toe into the murky waters of her past. 'You were just a kid when you had me,' I say, carefully. 'No wonder you couldn't cope.'

She gazes out at the sunset. 'Fifteen when I fell pregnant. Sixteen when you were born.' She's breathing oddly, as if trying to get control.

'How did your parents take it?'

'I thought my father was going to kill me.' Her gaze shifts to the blackened outlines of the pines.

'Did he want you to have an abortion?'

'*Abortion?* Oh, no. Never.' She drags her eyes from the trees and pours the wine. 'That would have gone against *Pastor* George Burney's "Christian" values. Much better to pack me off to a mother and baby home till the kid was born, then have it adopted.'

'What happened?'

'I told him where he could stick his adoption, so he threw me out.'

'What kind of father does that?'

She shrugs. 'One who thinks he'll go to hell if he gets contaminated by his daughter's sin.'

'You're kidding?'

'Nope. All that fire and brimstone was as real to my father as the numbers in his account books.'

'What about your mother? Didn't she try to get in touch with you after you left?'

'She wouldn't have dared.'

'Not even when I… went missing?'

'She died the year before it happened. Strange really – seeing as my father was the one who was ill. But he hung on despite the odds.'

'Till when?'

'Last year.' She tosses her head as if to shake off the memory.

'Oh,' I say, surprised. 'I thought both your parents died way back.'

'That's what I used to tell people.' She picks at the rusted edge of the table. 'It wasn't exactly a lie. The day he threw me out he told me I was dead to him. I just kind of returned the favour.'

'And the press never tracked him down?'

'They'd have got pretty short shrift if they had. Everyone at his crackpot church thinks the media are instruments of the devil.' She pulls a sour little smile. 'At least they're right about something.'

'Did you ever speak to him again?'

An uncomfortable pause before she speaks. 'He got bladder cancer. Survived the op but never really got back on his feet, so right at the end I went to see him.'

'What happened?'

'I went through the motions of asking him to forgive the sins of my misspent youth. It meant he died happy.' Her voice is flat, as if the thought of her father has severed all connection between her words and her feelings.

'It's sad you never got a chance to say goodbye to your mother,' I say, quietly. 'What was her name?'

'Mum's?' She stays silent for a few seconds, a dip and rise of her throat before she answers. 'Ruth.'

Ruth. I say the name in my head. I had a grandmother called Ruth. 'Do you have a photo of her?'

The question seems to trouble her, as if keeping a photo of her mother is somehow shameful.

'Please.'

She stands up slowly and heads into the house. By the time she gets back I'm halfway through the wine. She hands me a small, vinyl-covered album, opened at a photo of a pale, fair-haired young woman in a shapeless cotton dress holding a baby to her chest. I turn through the pictures, half of them askew, the rest long gone, leaving ghostly squares on the rubbed grey ribs of the pages. 'Is that your father?' I say, sliding the album towards her.

She nods and looks down into her glass. I take back the album and study the photo – thin-lipped George Burney in rimless glasses speaking at an event for a company called J. P. Dutton & Co.

'Is that where he worked?'

'Kept their books for thirty years.' Scorn rises in her voice. 'A company man through and through.'

I turn the page: George with his mousey, much younger wife and toddler daughter outside a shabby, tin-shack church – not a smile between them; a class photo from St Mark's Primary in Northampton, showing a pasty Kay in an oversized grey skirt and jumper, easy to pick out among the princesses in pink with their perky ribbons and cherry cheeks. According to the names printed beneath the doubtful motto – 'The Best is Yet to Be' – she was Kaitlin back then.

'How did you get on with the other kids?' I say.

'They thought I was weird. Even when their mothers took pity on me and made them invite me to their parties, I was never allowed to go.'

My throat closes in. 'What did you do when your father threw you out?'

'Waited till they'd gone to church, broke into the house and took everything I thought I could sell – not that there was much. *Pastor* George had penny pinching down to an art form.' She shivers slightly, though the night is still hot.

'Then what?'

'I went to London – where else – moved into a squat with a load of wannabe musicians, dyed my hair black, started calling myself Kay and tried – and failed, to make it as a singer.'

'What was that like?' I say. The tabloids had painted a lurid picture of sex and drugs but I want to hear her side of it.

'Nowhere near as bad as the press made out,' she says, as if she's plucked the thought from my mind. She starts to roll a cigarette. 'It was in a big old house in Deptford, probably worth a fortune by now, and there were a couple of earth mother types living there who looked after me when they weren't too stoned.'

'What did you do for money?'

'Busking mainly, a bit of shoplifting. A couple of the girls made decent money pole dancing but the clubs weren't exactly queuing up to take on underage, pregnant runaways.'

We sit in silence while she gazes away into the shadows. I pour the last of the wine into our glasses and feel around for something to say to bring her back. 'What did you do about scans and stuff?' I say. It's clumsy but it does the trick.

'Not much. I gave birth squatting on a carpet in one of the upstairs rooms – candlelight, a few joss sticks and a whole lot of chanting. The kind of thing you'd pay thousands for at a holistic birthing retreat.'

'We were just kids but it was a beautiful experience,' fellow squatter 'Suki' recalled. 'Like totally real and natural. The only painkillers Kay had were a few puffs of weed and when the baby came out we cut the cord with a sheath knife we'd passed through a candle flame.'

'How did you cope once I was born?'

'It wasn't that hard. You were a pretty good baby and in a place like that there was always someone around to pick you up if you cried or keep an eye on you if I wanted to go out. I managed to keep on top of things till about a year after you were born.'

I know what's coming.

'Then one night I took something my so-called boyfriend brought round and I ended up in hospital. The police raided the house and the authorities took you into care.' Kay lights her roll-up and takes a long drag. 'But I'm sure you read all about that. All those social workers lining up to tell the world how selfish and irresponsible I was. Every loser who'd ever crashed in that house trying to make a few quid out of my pain.'

'How did you get me back?' I say gently.

'That was all down to David. When I met him he'd just launched Lila Mendez.' She throws me a look to see if I recognise the name. I nod. Mendez was big when I was growing up. Even in Botswana. 'She took his label to the next level. He expanded, bought the house in Stanford Street – we got married and suddenly there I was, living in one of the smartest parts of Kensington with a beautiful home and more money than I knew what to do with. So I used it to fight the care order. As soon as we got you back, we changed your name to Duncan – David's idea, not mine – and I did my best to make a home for you, a family. But I was weak and screwed up and, as the world never ceases to remind me, my best wasn't anywhere near good enough.' She summons a bitter, half-there smile, and it's as if the whole past we never had is distilled into this moment; soothed tantrums, favourite stories, new shoes, rainy afternoons, grazed knees, the brush of her finger on my cheek as I slept.

She looks into her wine glass. 'What about you? What are your plans for the future?'

'I had a place at the University of the Witwatersrand to read veterinary science.'

'*Had?*'

'I deferred it.'

'Because of Roz's cancer?'

I nod carefully.

'It's OK,' she says, thumbnail working the rust again. 'That woman was your life for fifteen years. I have to get used to it.'

'She got her diagnosis a few weeks before the start of term.'

'So you stayed home to nurse her.'

'God no. She was far too proud for that. In fact, she was furious about the deferral and insisted that the doctors were all idiots and she had no intention of dying. So I made out I wanted to take a year out to work on our breeding programme.

'But seeing her like that, and feeling so helpless, got me thinking about changing to medicine – maybe going into research.'

'Good for you. Though God knows where you get your brains from.'

I take a breath and blink to ease the pulse behind my eye. 'Did my dad go to university?'

'Your dad?' She seems startled by the question and sucks hard on her roll-up.

Jesus, she's not making this easy. 'Who was he?'

Another silence. Followed by a shrug. 'I have no idea.' This news unsteadies me, another loss I'm not ready for. 'Look, I'm not proud of it but I was fifteen, miserable and desperate for my first taste of freedom, so I used to sneak out when my parents were asleep and hang out with anyone who'd buy me a drink or a spliff. A couple of times I staggered home in the small hours with no idea where I'd been or who I'd been with, so clearly some lowlife took advantage.' She drops the butt onto the ground and grinds it out beneath her foot. 'Sorry if that disappoints you.'

'No… I was just, you know… curious.' I stare out to sea and let go of another piece of the dream. 'I'm thinking of applying to a British med school,' I say after a bit. 'I think my grades are good enough.'

'That's great,' she says absently.

'And I want to spend a bit of time exploring the UK. Maybe we could go together,' I say tentatively. 'It would give us a chance to… you know, get to know each other. You could take me back to your hometown and show me my roots.'

A pause that lasts so long it scares me, then she lets out a strange little laugh. 'Let's do it. Thelma and Louise eat your hearts out.' She raises her glass and I raise mine, though I haven't got a clue who she's talking about.

'How was growing up in Botswana?' she says.

I worry that this is going to take us to places she won't want to go, but if we're going to build any kind of relationship she needs to know everything about me, just like I need to break through her twitchy reserve and find out everything about her. 'Roz home-schooled me to begin with,' I tell her. 'Four hours of lessons every morning. The rest of the time I got to help with the animals.'

'Sounds like a pretty lonely life for a kid.'

'It was fine.' How can I tell her that I'd loved every magical second of it? 'Roz taught a couple of the rangers' children as well. But when I was twelve she sent me off to the International School in Gabarone to get some GCSEs.'

'I suppose by that time she was sure no one would recognise you.'

The thought nips my nerves. I'd always assumed the home-schooling had been so Roz could save me from the horrors of eating meat, and teach me 'proper' things like poetry, decent punctuation and how to sex a pangolin. Now I'm not so sure.

Her ring clinks against her glass. 'Did you ever tell anyone you'd had another life before Roz?'

'Never. She said it had to stay our secret.'

She nods, picks up the bottle and glasses. 'Let's go inside. I'm getting bitten to death.'

I carry the plates into the kitchen and stop by the dresser. There's a photo I hadn't noticed before, peeking from behind a blue enamel jug. I put down the plates – wonder for a moment if she put it there when she came in for the album – and ease it out. It's a torn snapshot of a serious, dark-haired child of three or four trailing a plastic spade across a beach and reaching for an ice cream held out by a woman whose face and body has been ripped away. Only her fingers are visible, small and neat, red painted nails and a big amber ring.

I run towards her. Hot sand burns my feet and rubs between my toes. Sunlight stings my eyes. My shoulders throb where the sun has turned them red and raw. But I keep on running because she is laughing, laughing, laughing and the sound is like the drip of melted ice cream cooling all the places where it hurts.

Kay has stolen across the flagstones.

'Why did you tear yourself out of the picture?' I say.

Our eyes meet for a long, still moment. 'I… I don't like to be reminded of who I was,' she says, and surprises us both by bursting into tears.

CHAPTER THREE

I flop into bed hot and a little drunk, toss and flail between tattered snatches of sleep and tip into a dream that feels sharper than reality. I see Roz. She's standing on Kay's terrace with her back to me, looking out to sea. Not the Roz who stole Kay's child and lied to me for fifteen years, but steady upright Roz who had gone from my life like an oak tree felled by a storm. My heart leaps. I run towards her. She turns. It's not Roz at all, but cowed little Ruth Burney in her cheap cotton dress shushing a crying baby wrapped in a brightly coloured shawl. She looks up and sees me. Her face hardens and she hurls the bundle into the air. For a moment I watch it twist and turn then I lurch forward and catch at nothing. Her baby is just a roll of rags that swirl and flutter in my face. I open my eyes, a feeling of loss as sharp as the night Roz died spreading through my chest. But I am not alone. I sense a presence, even before I lift my head and see Kay beside me, her back against the bedhead, her knees pulled up a little.

'How long have you been here?' I say.

'A while. Sorry.'

'Don't be.' I loosen the tangled sheet and cover her naked legs.

We lie in the still, quiet heat of the night, silent and not touching. Slowly I close my eyes, aware of the rise and fall of Kay's breath and the yawning gulf of darkness between us.

*

I wake to the sound of curtain rings rattling along the rod and sunlight flooding the room. Kay, dressed in a white linen sundress, turns from the window. 'Fancy a swim?'

'What's the time?'

'Six. If we're quick we'll have the beach to ourselves.'

'Give me five minutes.'

She's waiting for me by the back door, floppy hat pulled low on her head, blue-and-white striped bag hooked over her shoulder. I fight the urge to reach for her hand, to be a child again, skipping by her side as we head off to the beach. We cross the courtyard to a wooden lean-to that serves as a garage. Inside it sits a squat little convertible with its top down. I can see from the curve of the bonnet, the goggle headlights and the pits and dents in the chrome that it's ancient. What holds me, though, is the colour. Baby blue. Kay's favourite.

I've drawn a picture of her on a piece of card, spindly legs and sticky-out hair and tried to write 'Happy Birthday Mummy' at the top in rainbow letters. But it doesn't look right and I'm worried she won't like it. I pick through my caterpillar pencil case. If I can find the right shade of blue to colour her dress it won't matter about the writing. A rush of happiness when I find the crayon I'm looking for. But it's blunt. I empty out the whole pencil case looking for my sharpener and start to cry when I realise it's not there.

Which of her birthdays was that? Her twentieth? Her twenty-first?

I can't imagine having a child at my age, let alone one old enough to write.

'Jump in.' She's leaning across to open the door, her big square sunglasses catching my reflection. I pick the dried leaves from a tear in the leather seat and settle myself beside her.

'Nice car.'

She pats the old-fashioned steering wheel. 'I bought it with the money from the first paintings I ever sold.'

She manoeuvres the car across the bumpy ground and out onto the top of the track. Her driving is surprisingly fast and competent. As we careen downhill I crane round to look at her front gate – the rusty barrier between my past and my present. She accelerates smoothly onto the coast road and I lean back and let the wind pull my hair. Terraces rear up as she swings past the pillared entrance to a vineyard, passes a burned-out shepherd's hut, swerves expertly around a ribbon of bends and pulls up in a narrow parking area at the top of the cliff. I get out and follow her to the edge. The view drops away to a spear of emerald water, capped by a triangle of sand; and she was right, it is totally deserted.

She pulls off her amber ring, threads it onto the narrow gold chain she wears around her neck and throws her hair forward so I can do up the fastener. Then we clamber down the hillside, tripping and skidding as we pick our way through the bent pines that have somehow managed to root themselves in the tumble of stone. Ducking beneath the branches, we tear off our clothes, and plunge laughing into the glorious chill of the sea. I yelp and shiver but the cold soon turns to smooth, silky warmth. I flip onto my back and gaze up at the pale morning sky, a pang of regret for all the years Kay spent battling her demons while Roz and I made happy memories: stopping the jeep to release an injured wildcat I'd nursed back to life; taking turns with my new binoculars to watch a baby rhino totter after its mother.

I flip over. Kay surfaces just ahead of me, a flash of scarlet and white in her stripy one-piece. 'Race you to the rocks!' She points to a jag of white peeping above the surface and dives beneath the glassy sheen of the sea. I strike out after her, pull myself up onto the rock beside her and sit hugging my knees. We look back at the strange rugged coastline; its sheer cliffs – dark along the waterline – rising like stained teeth, rotten at the root.

We dive back into the water and swim to the shore. Taking my cue from Kay, I ignore the questions simmering beneath our smiles and put on a show of ease. It's tricky but in some ways a relief to lay out my towel beside hers and make-believe, just for today, that this bizarre situation is normal.

Our lazy morning on the beach rolls into a bread and cheese lunch on the terrace, and when we've eaten Kay suggests spending the afternoon on the sun loungers. As we drag them across the courtyard a whirring sound catches my ear – low and somehow comforting. I stop to listen.

'You alright?' Kay asks.

'It's that noise. It reminds of the pump we had in Botswana.'

Kay listens for a moment, then looks away. She's very quiet as we set out the loungers and I kick myself for breaking the spell and allowing the past to intrude.

'You draw?' she says as I get out my sketchpad and pencils.

'Not very well. I seem to have inherited the urge, but not the talent.'

Wary of asking her outright if she'll fetch her things and sketch with me, I nudge the conversation around to her painting and ask her how it's going.

'Not so well,' she says restlessly. 'I thought this amazing landscape would inspire me but it's all been a bit… overwhelming.'

'When did you take up art?'

'The first time I went into rehab.' A swift wry smile. 'It was either that or basket weaving.'

She reaches for her magazine and I sketch alone, trying to capture the startling beauty of this place, but the cliffs come out blocky and stark, and on paper the still, smooth sea looks lifeless as a puddle. In the end I give up and we lie side by side watching the sparkling white yachts heading for the hazy rim of the horizon.

'I'm impressed you want to do medicine,' Kay says, after a while, massaging a blob of sun cream into her face.

'That's the plan, though it's tough to get a place.'

'You seem pretty smart to me.' Her mouth twists. 'Though what would I know? Want some?'

I turn to take the bottle and catch a faded tattoo, just discernible at the top of her bare brown arm. It's a looped capital D about the size of a fifty-pence piece, garlanded with thorn twigs hung with tiny droplets of blood, picked out in rusting red.

She's asleep face down, her thick dark hair spilling across the snowy white of the pillow. I trace the magic D with the tip of my finger, careful not to touch the prickles because I know about the thorn trees growing around Sleeping Beauty's castle. I lean closer and whisper 'Mummy' but my new au pair is calling, telling me it's time to go to school. I run downstairs and worry all day that my princess mummy will sleep for a hundred years.

'I used to think your tattoo was a magic symbol,' I say.

She peers down at her shoulder. 'Hardly. It was definitely amateur hour the night we got those done.'

'D for Doxettes.'

There's a sudden edge in the air. She looks at me hard. 'You *have* done your homework. Worst name for a girl band ever.'

'Who came up with it?'

'Vicky.'

'That's Vicky… Bunce?'

She nods. 'She was so pleased with it I've never had the heart to tell her how much I hated it.'

'Do you still see her?'

A slight, uneasy pause. 'Haven't for a while. But she's a good person. And there aren't many of those around.'

'So it was you, Vicky Bunce and the lead singer, Chrissie…?' I grope for her surname, 'Was it, Mullen…?' Kay doesn't help me out. 'Anyway, I read about the band in that interview she gave after I… went missing. But I couldn't find out much else about it.'

She reaches for a cigarette. 'That's because we never got beyond playing the pub circuit. Grubby back rooms and drunken punters were about as glamorous as it got.'

'But you were good enough to get an audition with David Duncan,' I keep going. 'Especially you – you're the only one he signed up.'

She flips open her Zippo and eyes me over the flame. 'I never even got to record a single, so let's not kid ourselves it was my voice he was after.'

I laugh. 'If I remember rightly, Chrissie said the exact same thing, only a lot less politely.'

Kay doesn't laugh. 'She was the one with the dreams,' she says, softly, 'and that audition with David was her one big chance to make them come true. Then I sneaked in and snatched it away. I should have realised how much that hurt her.'

'Did she ever forgive you?' I say.

She snaps out angrily. 'Why the big interest in Chrissie? I haven't seen her for years.'

Her sharpness is so sudden and so unexpected I flinch away. There's a silence. It lengthens. Unsure how to fill it, I pick up my sketchbook and pretend to draw. After a few prickly minutes she leans up on her elbow and looks at me, strained and serious. 'I want you to promise me something.'

'OK.'

'Don't ever give anyone the power to destroy you. It doesn't matter how much they hurt you. If someone fucks you over just block them out and walk away.'

She turns to stare at the sky and I think about the nameless dead-beat who fathered me, the parents who threw her out, the boyfriend whose drugs nearly killed her, the conmen who took advantage of her loss, the journalists who still hound her, the trolls who taunt her. Moments later her hand brushes mine. The shock of her touch disorients me but as she lifts her fingers away her words stick with me. *If someone fucks you over just block them out and walk away.*

CHAPTER FOUR

Sunlight burns my eyelids. Voices seep through the floorboards. A woman's, high and tearful. 'I told you, this changes everything!' And a man's, low and controlled – 'For God's sake, calm down.'

Mummy and David are arguing again. He gets cross when she won't eat or take her medicine. I pull the pillow over my head but I can't block out the sound. Will she start crying? Will doors slam and shake the house? I hate it when that happens but it's better than when Mummy goes quiet and locks herself in her room.

I lie for a while, looking up at the sun-dappled slope of the ceiling before I find the strength to get up and go downstairs. The voices break off as I open the kitchen door. A man sits at the table, a mug of coffee, the sou'wester and Roz's letter on the table in front of him. Kay – her hand on his arm – glances up. He pushes back his chair and moves slowly towards me, blocking my view of her. I take in the slight cleft in the bulbous tip of his nose, the full cheeks and rounded, slightly protruding chin. He's paunchier than in the photos in the sitting room, his hair, although still fair, is receding and he's got heavy circles under his eyes, as if he hasn't slept for days, though there's nothing dull or sluggish about the way he's studying my face, my hair and my restless hands. 'Well,' he says as I hurriedly drop them to my side. 'I suppose you look the part.'

'You see,' Kay says.

'Alright, Kay, come on,' he says crisply. 'You know what we agreed.'

'But—'

'Please.' He looks at me, half apologetic, half businesslike. 'I know this isn't what you or Kay want to hear, but given the way she's been hurt in the past it would be irresponsible of me not to do everything I can to verify your story.'

'Of course,' I say. 'You've got every right to be suspicious.'

'Too damn right,' he says, without rancour. 'After fifteen years of nutters and con artists turning up on our doorstep with "irrefutable proof" of Maya's whereabouts I don't even trust myself.'

'I've made coffee,' Kay says, 'and there's eggs and toast coming up. Why don't we eat while we talk?'

David turns back to the table and holds up the cafetière. I nod, desperate for caffeine, and scrape back the chair opposite him as he pours. 'Please, ask me anything you want.' Kay darts a nervous look at me over his shoulder and goes back to cracking eggs into a bowl.

'Alright.' He settles back and as he taps his thumbs together the steely focus of the hard-nosed music magnate descends. 'How did you find out that Kay was here?'

I tip milk into my mug. 'Your housekeeper in London told me.'

He frowns, groping to put a name to the woman who irons his shirts and mops his floors. He finds it eventually. 'Lenka? The new girl? Why would she speak to you? Our staff have strict instructions about confidentiality.'

'I told her I was Kay's cousin, in Europe on a gap year.'

His gaze sharpens. 'She doesn't know Kay's address.'

'Yes, she does, doesn't she, Kay?' I look up at her, expecting an easy nod of confirmation, but she has turned away to unhook a whisk from the wall.

His eyes on mine, David says firmly, 'Don't involve Kay. I'd like to hear this from you.'

'Before she left London she asked Lenka to forward her mail to the poste restante in town,' I say.

He turns to look at Kay. 'Darling, there was no need for that, I told you I'd bring it when I came.'

Kay – hesitant for a moment – clatters the whisk against the bowl.

'You're always so busy, I thought it would be easier for you.'

He turns back to me. A slight lift of one eyebrow invites me to go on. 'Lenka said Kay was using the name Burney, not Duncan, so I went to the post office and asked if anyone knew where Madame Burney was staying.' David twitches with alarm. 'Don't worry,' I say quickly. 'I gave them the cousin story as well.'

'Was that to protect Kay or to protect this woman?' His face darkens. 'This… *Roz*.'

'To protect us all,' I reply, a childlike glow inside when he nods approval.

'Do you remember being called Maya?'

'No,' I say, bluntly, hoping honesty will work in my favour. Surely in this instance a liar would have lied.

'What did Roz call you?'

'Kiddo, usually.' I attempt a smile.

'Have you got a photo of her?'

I open my duffel and take out a shot of Roz I've always loved. I push it across the table and for one unsteady moment I see her with his eyes – a frowsy, sun-weathered woman, with a frizz of blonde-grey hair escaping from beneath a khaki baseball cap, at the wheel of a dented jeep; a woman who stole his stepchild and ripped a gaping hole in his wife's heart. He stares at it for a moment, a dawning horror on his face, then he tips back in his chair, holding it up so that Kay can see. 'Look, Kay. She didn't age well but it's that busybody from across the road.'

Kay turns slowly, as if she can't bear to put a face to the woman who took her child.

Her eyes drop to the photo. 'Oh,' she says, quietly, and turns away.

'You knew her?' I say, suddenly confused.

'Oh, *yes*.' David's voice is scathing. 'We knew her. Though I'd forgotten her name. She was always sniffing around, knocking on the door to tell me I'd left my car lights on or we'd put our bins out on the wrong day or she'd seen someone suspicious in the alley. I thought she was harmless. Christ.' He rakes a hand through his thinning hair. 'I even gave her a bloody key to the house.'

It's Kay who looks startled now. 'What on earth for?'

'To keep an eye on the place, that time we went to Berlin. You know, water the plants, turn on the lights. In exchange I made a donation to one of her charities – rhinos I think it was. Or donkeys. God, if only we'd known.'

I'm still trying to process this revelation when he gestures to the folder I've pulled from my bag. 'What else have you got in there?'

'Phoebe Locklear's birth certificate.'

He runs a quick eye across the details and drops it onto the table. 'What about her death certificate?'

'I couldn't find it.' I feel the chill of his stare. 'She died in Malawi, in a car accident. I'm not sure exactly what happened. Roz didn't like to talk about it.'

His eyes linger on mine for a long, penetrating moment then slide away to the folder in my hand. I push it across the table. 'Here. Help yourself.'

I watch him pull out the bulging envelope of cuttings. He glances at me then tips them onto the desk and shuffles through them. 'Where did you get these?' There's a hardening in his voice, a growing distance.

'They were in the box with the letter and the sou'wester. Roz gave it to me just before she died. She told me not to open it till after she'd gone. I think she'd been getting them sent over from an agency.'

'And you never saw them when she was alive?'

'Never.'

He works his jaw, eyeing me closely. 'You and she hadn't been poring over them for months, picking through the facts so you could cook up this story about you being Maya?' He lifts and drops the sou'wester. 'The clothes she was wearing when she went missing, the au pairs who told the press she was always wandering off on her own, the timings on the CCTV sightings the day she disappeared? Facts you could spice up with a few colourful details Roz gleaned about our lives when she was snooping around our house?'

Kay is watching me but doesn't speak.

'Why would I make it up?' I drop the deeds to Roz's flat and her share certificates onto the table. 'I don't need anything from you. Roz had family money. You can see for yourself that she left me more than enough.'

He glances at the figures on the documents, raises an eyebrow but says evenly. 'No amount of money is ever *enough*, and none of this tells me anything about *you*.'

'What do you need?'

'How about your plane ticket from Botswana or… your acceptance to university in South Africa?'

I tap my phone, flustered by his stare. I don't like the way he's making me feel, the way he's studying my face, the way his doubts are gathering momentum. Isn't there some lie-detection system that analyses micro expressions? Fleeting tightenings and dilations, giveaways of stress you can't control? If so, what message is my dry-lipped, heart-pounding panic sending out? I hold out the phone. 'This is my boarding pass and if you swipe—'

'Email them to me. I'll get my people to check them out.' He tosses me his business card. 'While they're at it they can do a search for Phoebe Locklear's death certificate. It doesn't matter if she died abroad. As a British citizen her death would have to have been registered in the UK.'

I try to hold his gaze and keep my voice level. 'Knowing how Roz felt about bureaucracy, it's quite possible she never reported the death.'

An overlong pause, then he leans back in his chair, a dismissive sweep of his hand that takes in everything on the table. 'You see my problem, Phoebe? Even if you find the missing death certificate there's nothing conclusive about anything you've told me. In fact, you could say that while the evidence I need is conveniently unavailable, the evidence you *have* provided is all a bit *too* neat. A letter you can flash around instead of a deathbed confession, the photos of you in Botswana, a kid's sou'wester, the legacy that appears to make you independently wealthy. None of it's actual proof that you're Kay's daughter and without—'

I cut him off mid-flow. 'I'll take a DNA test.'

He tips his head to one side. 'You'd be willing to do that?'

'Of course.'

'David!' Kay's hands flail in front of her.

'It would settle any doubts once and for all,' he says. 'Then we could all rest easy.'

'You're right,' I say. 'It's the best way.' I reach for my phone. 'There must be somewhere online who'll send us a kit.' I scroll quickly. 'Yes. Look, there's a place in Lyon.'

'How long does it take to get the results?'

'Forty-eight hours from the time they get the samples back.'

'I'm not waiting that long.' He plucks the phone from my fingers and scrolls down the screen. 'There's a lab outside Toulon that's got an appointments service.'

'Wait.' Kay pulls at his arm. 'What if someone sees us and puts two and two together before we're ready to go public?'

'That's true,' I say, anxious to make this as painless for her as I can.

'Let's order a kit.'

'No,' David says, firmly. 'Kits can be tampered with. I want this done professionally, with legally certified results.' He studies the screen. 'It says here this place in Toulon guarantees complete confidentiality. If we apply online you don't even have to go in together.'

Kay shakes her head, still uncertain.

'David's right,' I say. 'We have to do this properly.' I look from her to him, keen to show that I'm fine with taking a test. He takes his laptop from the dresser and logs on, his plump fingers moving efficiently over the keys before he turns the screen to me.

'You fill in your half then I'll do Kay's.'

The 'I' jars. Why can't Kay fill out her own damn form?

I cast an eye down the options, listed in French, English and Arabic, a world of stories unfolding in my head – tales of lost and found, love and hate, anger and regret.

Paternity DNA Test
Maternity DNA Test
Sibling DNA Test
Y Chromosome DNA Test
Aunt/Uncle DNA Test
Grandparent DNA Test
Complex Relationship DNA Testing

A spike of excitement as I select the box marked 'maternity' and a bittersweet mixture of sadness and elation as I fill in Phoebe Locklear's name and date of birth – this will probably be the last time I ever use them. I add my email address and pass the laptop back to David. He types quickly, pausing only to take out his wallet. 'Call them,' he says as he adds his credit card details. 'See if we can get an appointment this morning.' His voice is imperious, as if I am one of his 'people' standing by to do his bidding, though all I say is, 'What time shall I book for?'

'Here to Toulon takes fifty minutes, maximum an hour, so any time after eleven will be fine.'

I'm keying the number into my phone when David's hand drops firmly over mine. 'You won't get a decent signal in here. I'll walk you up the hill.'

Kay swings round, pan and spoon in her hands. 'What about your eggs?'

'Hold them till we get back.' David pulls open the back door.

Once outside, he strides ahead until we're out of earshot then he stops and takes me by the shoulders. I smell the coffee on his breath. When I look up, his eyes, although ringed with exhaustion, are crinkling a little, along with his mouth.

'I don't know if it's the hair, or the smile, but you've got such a look of Kay when I first met her.'

A sob swells in my throat. 'For a moment back there I thought…'

He makes an exasperated noise. 'I'm sorry about the third degree. You've seen the way Kay is. Some days she can barely hold it together and every time there's a false lead the disappointment nearly destroys her. For her sake, I have to make one hundred per cent sure.'

I hear the concern in his voice. 'Of course,' I say. 'You have to protect her.'

He starts walking again, only slower this time so I can keep up. 'She was fine, better than she's been for ages, then about eighteen months ago she… had a setback.'

'What happened?'

'Some conwoman contacted her while I was away, telling her she knew where Maya was and – for a price – she'd take her to her. She seemed much more plausible than any of the others and by the time I found out about it Kay had parted with God knows how much money and convinced herself it was the real thing. When it turned out to be yet another bloody scam she came crashing down so hard she...' He stops and looks away to the sea. 'Well, let's just say I'm not going to let it happen again.' He turns to me, his face intense, almost pleading. 'So if this is some elaborate hoax I'm going to give you the chance to walk away right now before you do her any permanent damage. No fuss. No police. No prosecution.'

'It's not a hoax, David.'

'If it's money you're after, I'll pay you not to hurt her.'

'I promise you, I don't want your money and I would never hurt her.'

'What if that bitch Roz Locklear made it all up? Planted all this stuff in your head. She was obviously unhinged.'

I hate that he's so vicious about Roz. I can't blame him though, not after the wrong she's done him. 'All these memories are coming back, of you, of Kay, of our lives in Stanford Street. She couldn't have planted those.'

'You think? What if she's been drip-feeding you little details for years, all part of some demented plan to provide for you once she was dead?'

I panic for a moment, reaching for pieces of the past I don't have: memories of the morning Roz took me, crying as I slosh down the road in my gumboots, walking upstairs to her flat, standing in the bathroom while she shears off my hair, sitting in a plane. 'Why would she?' I say quickly. 'She had plenty of money of her own. And anyway, how could she know that... that you love cucumber... or can't stand the squeak of polystyrene.' *Or that I used to hide under the bed with my head stuffed in a pillow when you and Kay were arguing?*

He gives me a swift, penetrating look. 'Alright. But for Kay's sake, I'm going to go on voicing doubts until we get the test results. OK?'

'Sure.'

'Till then, if anyone asks who you are we stick to the story that you're Kay's cousin visiting from abroad, then as soon as we've got the results I'll get my PR people to work out a strategy for dealing with the press.'

He's really thought this through. No wonder he hasn't slept.

He walks at my side, so close I can smell his aftershave. The ground is uneven and he reaches out a protective hand to steady me as I key in the passcode to my phone. 'Best place to get a signal is up by the trees,' he says. 'Do you want to make the call or shall I?'

'I'll do it,' I say. 'Might as well get some use out of all those dreary afternoons in double French.'

CHAPTER FIVE

David's silver Mercedes skims us along the coast road in a cocoon of air-conditioned comfort. The road ahead is so hot it shimmers like the landscape in a dream, and the sea I glimpse through the window is a never-ending expanse of crystalline blue. Music streams from the CD; a demo tape of some throaty-voiced kid David insists is going to be the next big thing. Kay hums along, glancing round every now and then to throw me a small, searching smile. I don't say much. I just inhale the smell of leather and trace the outline of their bodies with my eyes; Kay's swamp of dark hair spilling out over the headrest, David's gold watch glinting on his wrist as he changes gear.

I'm hot and I feel sick and trapped but he's cross and going too fast and they won't stop arguing and I keep saying I need to do a wee but they're not listening and I know they'll be even crosser if I make a mess on the seat. Mummy's always telling me I'm a big girl now but I don't feel big and I really, really need a wee.

The lab – a shiny tower of steel and glass – sits on a sweep of lush green turf. I wait in the car park for ten long minutes, watching the turning arcs of the sprinklers before I follow Kay and David through the glass doors. I take a numbered ticket and walk past them to the other end of the gleaming white waiting room. According to the leaflet I take from the rack this place offers diagnostic services in haematology, serology, microbiology, pathology, allergy and molecular biology as well as genetics. I pass the next five minutes wondering what sort of answers the other people in the room – two couples, one with a thin restless baby they pass between them, and a hawk-faced elderly man – are hoping their bodies will provide.

'*Numero dix-sept!*' A red seventeen flashes on the screen above the reception area. David stands and ushers Kay – her face well hidden beneath her favourite straw hat and sunglasses – over to the desk. She whispers to the receptionist. The woman searches through a file of printouts, and hands one to Kay. She signs it, returns the form and gives me a tiny forbidden smile on her way to the swing doors.

I wait on in the sterile quiet. A clench of adrenaline when my number is called. I sign the form quickly and look up to see David watching me. Soon it's my turn to sit in a tiny cubicle and open my mouth like a hungry fledgling while a brisk, blonde technician takes a swab of my cheek cells, then I'm outside again, blinking into the sunshine. I glance at the time. Almost midday. A little clock starts ticking in my head, counting down the promised twenty-four hours until we get the results. David and Kay are waiting by the car. He's fussing over her, asking if she's alright. She bats him away, all smiles. When he sees me he smacks his hands together in a job done kind of way, declares he's starving, and suggests lunch at a seafood place a bit further down the coast.

'Hey.' I lean in, holding up my phone, and snap a selfie of the three of us. Kay's smile vanishes and her hand flies to her face as if I've slapped her. I pull back. 'I – I'm sorry. I just wanted to remember this moment.'

David flings a jovial arm around her shoulder. 'Quite right too. Kay's got a bit allergic to cameras over the past few years, haven't you, darling? Here. Let me take a couple of the two of you.'

Kay nods and forces a smile as he pulls out his phone. She relaxes a little on the drive to the restaurant and swings round excitedly to point down a side street to a strip of brightly coloured awnings. 'Quick, David, go back. Find somewhere to park.'

My muscles tense, braced for the snappy refusal of a hungry man. But he's rolling his eyes, looking for somewhere to turn the car around and rubbing her knee with his hand, smiling indulgently when she looks up at him.

The market is rich with colours, smells and the chatter of families in their holiday best threading their way through stalls piled high with fat, sun-ripened fruits, cooked chickens, bread, cheeses, dried herbs and spices. Kay fills a freshly bought basket with tubs of paella and ratatouille, insisting that she's going to spare me any more of her culinary disasters. Even David joins in, picking over pots of honey and bunches of herbs, laughing when I add a cucumber to the pile of salad stuff in Kay's basket. For one surreal moment the tensions between us dissolve and it's as if I'm watching the scene from afar, seeing us the way the other shoppers see us – an ordinary family without a care in the world.

The restaurant David's picked is a sort of casually elegant hut with a canopied terrace jutting out onto the Mediterranean. He chooses a table set a little apart from the rest, right on the water's edge. My eyes slide away to a portly man eating alone at the next table. There's something faintly disgusting about the napkin tucked into his collar, the pudgy fingers delicately working a silver pick into the claws of a huge lobster and the shine of butter on his lips.

Kay follows my gaze and smiles. 'You want to try some? They get it flown in from Boston.'

'What's wrong with the local lobster?'

'All fished out years ago, like most of the seafood round here.'

'That's terrible.'

I turn down the imported lobster. Kay and I order squid and shrimp and David chooses a thick fish stew. Afternoon sunlight shimmers off the water and slices through the wine glasses, casting dancing ovals onto the wooden table, and the conversation is all food and wine and 'try this' and '*mmm* that's so good' until the waiter takes away our plates and brings cheese.

David pokes a knife into a little pat of something pale and creamy, wrapped in straw, and says in a low voice, 'We've got twenty-four hours to decide. Either we try to keep this quiet for as long as we can and run the risk of the press finding out, or we take the initiative straight away and make sure the story gets told our way.'

'Oh, David, let's not spoil this lovely lunch,' Kay murmurs.

'You're the one who's going to take the brunt of the attacks,' I say. 'So it's fine with me if you want to delay.'

David pulls a dismissive face. 'With you the age you are, looking the way you do and turning up out of the blue it's only a matter of time before someone guesses the truth. For all our sakes I think a managed announcement as soon as we get the results is the only way to go.'

Kay's looking down at her plate, shaking her head.

'Don't worry.' He takes her hand but stays looking at me. 'My people know exactly how to handle the press.'

I balk at the way he's taking control again, treating us like one of his acts who's been caught fiddling their taxes or peddling porn, but deep down I think he might be right. 'What would this "managed announcement" entail?' I say.

He leans in to the table. 'They'd probably offer an exclusive to one of the quality Sundays with photos and interviews in exchange for a sensitive piece that played down the problems Kay was having at the time – and played up Roz's grief over losing her kid – present the snatching of you as a one-off act of madness of a bereaved mother, one she blocked out as soon as she got you to Botswana.' I nod, grateful he's not planning to throw Roz to the wolves. 'They'd get a quote from Kay, explaining that as a mother who knows the agony of losing a child she can understand why Roz did what she did, even if she can never forgive her. Then, if you could cope, they'd probably want to back that up with a couple of hand-picked broadcast interviews – maybe you and Kay smiling on the couch of one of the softer TV breakfast shows and you on your own on the radio, maybe *Woman's Hour* for a bit of soul bearing. If we give them enough photo ops and useable quotes and they think we've got nothing to hide the rest of the press should be happy enough to regurgitate what's out there.' His eyes drill into mine. 'We *don't* have anything to hide, do we?'

'No.'

'Good.' He refills our glasses and raises a toast. 'To the future,' he says.

I drink the wine and when the waiter offers us a tray of liqueurs I take one and down the strong, numbing liquid in one go.

CHAPTER SIX

It's mid-afternoon by the time we get back. David changes into jeans and a mucky old T-shirt and drives off in Kay's car to get a part for his boat while Kay and I spend what's left of the day on the loungers. She reads and dozes and shows no inclination to talk and I tell myself that it's good that we can be quiet together. It gives us time to absorb the enormity of what we've lost and to prepare ourselves for the media onslaught ahead.

That night she warms up the ratatouille she bought in the market and David picks out some fancy wine from the special stash he keeps locked in the outhouse. While we eat it's mainly him who talks. He can't see that I couldn't care less about the temperature sensor he's had installed to keep his wine collection in tip-top condition or the state-of-the-art generator that kicks in if there's a power cut. He's so wrapped up in his lecture he doesn't notice Kay murmuring that it must have been the hum of the generator that had reminded me of the pump at Molokodi. I smile at her, touched that she remembered, saddened that the reference might have hurt her.

'Kay says you renovated your boat yourself,' I say, when David starts up about a priceless crate of Chateau Margaux he picked up at auction. 'What's she called?'

'*Serenity*,' he says, thrown – but only momentarily, before he embraces what's clearly his second favourite topic. 'I got her for almost nothing about five years ago.'

'So you didn't buy her here?'

He laughs. 'No chance of a foreigner getting a bargain like that on this coast. No, I bought her from a friend in Brighton and sailed her down here when Kay rented this place.'

Kay, who had been smoothing her lighter with her thumb, lets it drop onto the table. 'I'll make some coffee.'

'You know, you've really impressed me,' David says when we're alone. 'In my business I meet a lot of twenty-year-olds and I don't think any of them could have dealt with all this the way you have. Flying over here on your own, tracking Kay down, coping with the emotion.'

I shrug, feeling embarrassed. 'I suppose I was brought up to be practical and self-sufficient. If you live in the middle of nowhere it's the only way to survive. Though sometimes it makes it tough to ask for help or to let other people in.'

'Well, you're not on your own anymore. You've got us.'

I look up at him and smile. He doesn't smile back, just looks at me thoughtfully.

By the time we've gathered up the plates and followed Kay inside, David is making plans to take us on a tour of the creeks tomorrow afternoon. I dry while he washes and as he hands me the dripping dishes I try to push this sunburned man in his crumpled T-shirt and oil-stained jeans into the dapper, grey-suited David Duncan-shaped space in my mind. He reaches down the coffee jar. 'So which med schools are you applying to?' Pathetic, I know, but it gives me another little buzz of pleasure that Kay's been telling him about my plans.

'Not sure yet. I need to do some research.'

'My lawyer's wife's a consultant at St Thomas's. Nice people. When we get back to London I'll get them over for dinner so you can pick her brains.'

'That'd be great.'

He drinks his coffee then shuts himself away upstairs to work while I get out my laptop and look for something to watch with

Kay. I skip over the kind of detective series Roz and I used to binge on – secrets, lies, and old, cold cases waiting to be solved – and go for *Victoria*, reckoning that the problems of nineteenth-century royalty are about as far away from our own family drama as I'm going to get.

Around ten o'clock David comes down to open another bottle of wine. Stooping to refill our glasses, he tells us he's booked himself on a flight back to London tomorrow night and suggests that we stay on in Cassis for a couple of days. That way, we'll give his PR team a chance to fine-tune their press strategy before we join him for the announcement. I watch him go upstairs with the bottle in his hand and steady a swoop of excitement. Fourteen hours and I'll have proof of who I am. Twenty-four and I'll have Kay all to myself.

David's pouring himself a coffee when I come down the next morning, a tingle of anticipation running through my limbs. 'Here.' He hands me his mug and fetches down another. I glance at the laptop sitting open on the table and check the time – ten thirty. 'Where's Kay?'

'Still asleep.' He upends a bag of croissants onto a plate. 'First time she's slept in for years, so I thought I'd leave her to it and drive into town to pick up breakfast. I can't believe the difference in her. It's like she's snapped out of a trance.' He crumples the greasy bag in his fist and turns to look at me, a little embarrassed. 'We never gave up on you, you know that, don't you? Even on our darkest days we always believed you'd come back to us.'

I look away, ashamed that I've barely spared a thought for this man or his feelings since I found out what Roz had done.

'You and Kay seem… good together,' I say.

'Better than we used to be, you mean?'

I shrug a little and blink away.

'How much do you remember?'

'Arguments… Kay crying… you both getting angry.'

'I *was* angry. Nearly all the time. It's not easy to see someone you love trying to destroy themselves.' He picks out knives and plates from the crockery stacked beside the sink. 'I was too pig-headed to accept that addiction is an illness. I thought if I kept up the pressure I could force her to put her crappy childhood behind her and move on.' He unwraps a brick of snow-white butter and drops it into an earthenware dish. 'She was doing alright, coming off the drugs, going to therapy, putting on a bit of weight. And then… then we lost you. When I flew in from LA that night and saw the state she was in I honestly thought she wouldn't survive the guilt. But it wasn't just her who was to blame.' I stay quiet as he stares into the sunlight. 'I won't even pretend I was a great stepdad – we both know I was crap. But I was young, ambitious, away half the time and determined to make it big. What did I know about kids? I thought those au pairs we hired would do the job just fine until Kay got well enough to do it herself. So it wasn't fair that she was the one the press turned on.' He drops into a chair and stretches out his legs. 'The shock of losing you was a real wake-up call for me. I started to rethink my priorities and go along to her counselling sessions to learn how to help her to help herself.' He dips his croissant into his coffee and bites off the softened end. 'But no amount of therapy could achieve what you coming back has done. And the great thing is it's not too late. She's still young enough to make a new life, maybe have another baby. She was always too frightened before. It's a chance for us all to start over.'

Another baby? The bruised child in me hates the idea. The curious adult is intrigued by the thought of a sibling.

'Did you ever meet her father?' I say.

'I drove her up to see him before he died. I'm glad she went – closure – isn't that what they call it?'

'What was he like?'

'Old, frail, missing a few marbles.' He takes a long sip of coffee. 'I've been thinking, as soon as I get back to London I'll have a word with Martin about the legal side of switching your identity back and getting you a new passport.'

'Martin?'

'My lawyer. He's a bit old school but totally reliable and, most important, utterly discreet.'

Seeing the sense in talking to a lawyer doesn't stop me resenting David's need to take charge all the time. 'I've been thinking too,' I say, 'about our plans for going public.'

'And?'

'I think we should do the press interviews a couple of days before the announcement, then insist on an embargo so that Kay and I can get away somewhere before it all kicks off.'

He looks me dead in the eye and chews thoughtfully. I wait, ready to fight my case. 'That's not a bad idea,' he says. 'If there's a far-flung place you've always wanted to see – Samoa, Machu Pichu, Mauritius – let me know.'

'Who's going to Mauritius?' Kay stands in the doorway, hair piled up, flicks of eyeliner, blood-red lips, slender brown legs in strappy sandals.

I feel hot and confused. Is it Sasha or Gail who's picking me up today? I can't see either of them and Mrs Hopgood's looking at me with her cross face because she'll have to stay behind again until one of them comes. I hear my name. I turn around. It's Mummy pushing through the gate in a short red dress with her hair puffed up and her eyes all big and dark and her arms outstretched. She's so pretty it makes me shiver and I don't care that I haven't seen her for weeks and weeks and weeks.

'You two,' David says. 'I thought I'd pack you off to a luxury spa.'

'Why not?' Kay comes over and lays her hand on my shoulder – kneading it a little as if to reassure herself that I'm real. Close up there's pink around her painted eyes, though her voice is cheerful enough. 'While you're feeling generous let's go somewhere really nice for an early dinner before you leave for the airport.'

'I've got us a table at Chez Phillipe,' David says.

She pours herself a coffee – strong and black. 'How on earth did you manage that?'

'I told him it was a *very* special occasion.' He smiles at Kay then at me. 'So what about this flat you've inherited,' he says, brightly. 'Where is it exactly?'

'Fulham.'

He seems impressed. 'Habitable?'

'Not really. It's been rented out for years. I'll have to get someone in to sort it out.'

David laughs. 'If you need any advice on interior decoration, Kay's your woman.'

Kay, who's been staring into her coffee cup, looks up and frowns at him.

'Come on, darling,' he says. 'You're brilliant at that kind of thing.'

She turns hesitant eyes on me. 'Maybe Phoebe has her own ideas about what she wants.'

'Not at all,' I say quickly. 'I'd love some help.'

'What kind of look do you want to go for?' she says, still reticent.

'I don't know – something clean, simple, airy.' I wave a vague hand. 'A bit like this.'

'Alright.' Relaxing a little, Kay reaches for her laptop. 'Let's make you a mood board. How many bedrooms?'

'Three. I thought I'd use the smallest as an office and get a flat-mate in for the other one. I don't think I want to live on my own.'

'You won't be on your own,' David says. 'We'll only be ten minutes away.'

'Don't badger her,' Kay says. 'She'll want to be with people her own age – not old fogeys like us.' She glances at me and says softly, 'But you can't blame us for wanting to make up for lost time.'

David smiles indulgently and heads to the door with his coffee and newspaper, calling over his shoulder, 'If you need any structural work done we've got a great builder. He did our kitchen and all of our bathrooms.'

Kay goes back to her mood board and I can't stop looking at her. Her concentration as she makes her choices, the way she glances up to gauge my reaction to a sink or a sofa. It feels like we're finally starting to make a proper connection. As the screen fills with images I even dare to picture the two of us trotting into department stores, swatches in hand, poring over cushions, ordering blinds, pausing to kick off our shoes and gulp down cups of coffee before ploughing on to look at taps and tiles. I'm so deep in my reverie I hardly notice David come back for more coffee. An email alert pings me back to the screen. Everything grows still. Even the breeze through the window. It's here. The message from the clinic. Nobody moves. I feel sick inside, like the day of my A-level results. I look at Kay. 'Aren't you going to open it?'

She shunts her chair aside so I can reach the keyboard. 'You do it.'

I look up at David. He's on my left, nodding approval, his hand pressed reassuringly into the centre of my back as he leans into the screen. Kay is on my right, sitting so close I can smell the fruity scent of her shampoo.

I asked for a party and a puppy and a dinosaur cake. But they've got me a toy poodle with a flappy red tongue, and a square cake with hard pink icing because David forgot to order the dinosaur one and he says Mummy's not well enough to cope with a real dog or a house full of children. The collar on my dress is itchy and I'm not allowed to blow out the candles because the photographer isn't ready, and they're squeezing into me so hard they're squashing me and now David is telling me to hold up the knife and smile for the camera because the picture is going to be in a magazine and we have to look happy.

I click on the email, knowing that this too is a moment I will remember for ever. A flash of white and an endless wait while the pitifully slow WiFi draws three columns of figures down through cyberspace. Instinctively the scientist in me flicks across the digits, trying to make sense of the readings. Kay nudges me, impatient. 'Scroll down.'

I slide my fingers down the mouse pad, My eyes fasten on the conclusion at the bottom of the page:

Phoebe Jane Locklear is excluded from being the child of Kaitlin Ruth Duncan. The exclusion is based on the fact that she does not show the genetic markers, which must be present in the biological child at multiple DNA systems. Therefore it is practically proven that she is not the daughter of Kaitlin Ruth Duncan.

The silence grows heavy, unfillable.

I hit the mouse again, go back to the markers, my eyes zigzagging between 5.9s and 6.2s in a fevered attempt to find an error I can point to and laugh and say, *These people! What the hell are they playing at?* But the digits dance and swim in a meaningless blur. Kay sits shaking her head like an overwound doll, her mouth, as she looks at me, puckering into a quivering hole. 'She's dead, isn't she? My Maya's dead. Why did you lie to me?'

'I didn't lie. I swear to you!' I reach for her hand.

She shudders away, her voice rising high. 'Don't touch me. Don't ever touch me!'

David throws himself between us, his face contorted, his voice breaking as he speaks. 'Why? Why would you do this?'

'It's a mistake. It has to be… there'll be some genetic anomaly that's affected the readings…'

'So that's why the bullshit about med school.' His lips pull down at the corners as if the sight of me disgusts him. 'What were you going to do, fake up another test of your own, blind us with science?'

'No! I'm as shocked as you are. How would I know all that stuff about you and Kay and our lives at Stanford Street if I wasn't Maya?'

'Because that sick bitch Roz Locklear told you what to say!'

'No. She wouldn't, she wasn't like that.'

'I believed you. You know that?' He's sweaty, deadly pale, trying to catch his breath. 'We both did, every single word that came out of your lying mouth.'

'I wasn't lying. I swear I thought it was true.'

A sudden fury breaks through his anguish. 'Save it for the police.' He rams me back into the chair, holding me down with one hand, while he pulls out his phone.

'David, No!' Kay darts forward and claws at his arm. For a second I think – hope – she believes me. 'I can't face the police,' she sobs. 'Not now, not after—'

'It's fraud, Kay.'

'I don't care. Don't you see? It's punishment for what I did.' She throws back her head, squirming and rocking like she's in physical pain. 'And I'm going to go on being punished until the day I die.'

He hesitates, as if to go to her, but pulls me up by my shoulder instead, and drags me to the door. I buck against him and yell back into the kitchen. 'Please, Kay, I'd never lie to you. I'd never want to hurt you!'

He pushes me into the sitting room and slams the door. Sputtering his words, he jabs his finger into my chest. 'I gave you every chance to back off and walk away. I even offered you money. But no. You went on and on. Lie after lie. God knows if Kay will ever recover from this. If I had my way the police would be here right now and if you speak to the press or say one word about this to *anyone* I *will* have you arrested. Now get your stuff and get the fuck out of my house.' He pushes me towards the stairs. 'You've got five minutes before I throw you out.' Limp and defeated, he presses his hands to his face and turns back to the kitchen. Kay's sobs seep up through the floorboards, hot in my ears as I run to my room and shove my things into my duffel bag.

A confused mess of misery, I run out through the front door and stumble down the terraces, falling and smashing my shin against a heap of rocks; a bizarre reversal of the hope and trepidation that had carried me up this overgrown hillside just three days before.

CHAPTER SEVEN

I feel flimsy and unattached, as if my mind has slipped free from my body. I need Roz's voice in my head to hold me down and explain what just happened. In Botswana, I'd felt her presence everywhere; in every jeep, every fly-blown fruit and dusty street but here, among these shuttered buildings, rigid rows of masts and screeching seagulls, it's as if the woman I'd loved and trusted was an illusion, all trace of her whisked away by the breeze from the sea.

I push through the crowd on the quayside and limp into the first bar I come to. What I need is hydration. What I crave is oblivion. Ignoring the pavement tables crammed between jauntily striped tarpaulins, I make for the dim interior of the Café du Port, pull myself onto a bar stool and order a large cognac. Above me, on the wall-mounted television, a troupe of long-haired, long-limbed girls gyrate in tasselled shorts to a silent song. I stare at their fixed pouts, perfect breasts and painted faces while I gulp down the brandy. I order another and dab a paper napkin at the blood oozing from the wound on my shin. It's deep, though I barely register the pain. My brain's too taken up with the shock of the test results, shining a wavery torch down dark pathways of possibility. Did the sheath knife they used to cut Maya's cord see more action in that squat than anyone was admitting? Was there some other runaway holed up in that house, giving birth around the same time? Two teenagers too doped up to notice whose baby was whose?

I knock back my drink. Wouldn't some hint of that have come out by now? The papers had interviewed dozens of former squatters eager to outdo each other's squalid tales of Kay's life in Deptford. Not one of them had mentioned another baby in the house. So maybe the swap happened in foster care – some social services screw up. I wave at the barman and gaze at the sticky brown liquor he pours into my glass, vaguely aware of the comings and goings around me, regulars greeting each other in the kind of quick-grunted French I'll never understand. Some of them watch me openly – squat boatmen in grimy T-shirts, and bored boys in aviator shades, downing espressos and staring at the foreign girl getting pissed on her own. Others are more subtle about it. But they're staring all the same.

Somewhere around the fourth or fifth cognac I dare to face the possibility that David was right about Roz and that everything she said in her letter really was a sick, manipulative lie. I raise my head, see her staring at me – stern and disapproving – across the crowded bar. She folds her arms. I look away and wave to the barman again. A slurred voice that must be mine asks if he's got a vacant room. He tosses a key onto the counter, patently relieved that I'll have somewhere other than the floor of his bar to pass out.

I grip the tarnished brass tag, press the metal corners into my palm – pain to keep my brain awake. Did Kay make up her pregnancy to upset her father, a lie that in a drug-addled fug drove her to take a baby from another woman? But where does that leave the eyewitness they interviewed in the papers – the one who played midwife? And for any kid to get snatched once in a lifetime is rare enough. But twice? Come on. Even this pissed I'm not buying it. My arm drops heavily off the bar and sends my glass crashing to the floor. I stagger outside and weave along the quayside. The only person who can help me unravel this is Kay, and David won't let me anywhere near her. I lurch to the edge of the quay, wrap my arms around a metal bollard and vomit into the water.

Still bent, I wipe the back of my hand across my mouth. There's a boat in my outer vision, the white stripe running its length rising and dipping along the waterline, just out of sync with my heaving stomach. I retch again and drag my head up, embarrassed that a blurry figure is looking down at me from the deck. I move away, fogged with misery, totter back towards the bar and catch my reflection in the glass as I thump against the door. A question hits my brain and burns through my body like a squirt of acid. If I'm not Phoebe Locklear and I'm not Maya Duncan, then who the hell am I?

Pain takes a jackhammer to my skull and jolts me, blow by bone-splitting blow, towards consciousness. There's light on the outside, burning my eyelids. A blanket of darkness on the inside, muffling my memory. I run tentative fingers down my body. I'm dressed. I flap out a hand. Hit sheets and pillows. No rough, bony elbows. No hot, heavy legs. I'm alone. In a bed. God knows whose it is or how I got here. I force my eyes open. Ginger. The walls, the curtains, the shiny bedspread, the tatty rug – all shades of the same sickly brown. An attic bedroom with a low-beamed ceiling and a narrow iron balcony. My duffel bag sits on the chest of drawers. I slither off the bed and rip off my clothes, cringing at the crust of sick on my T-shirt as I stagger into the tiny shower and turn on the water. The effort exhausts me. I vomit into the toilet bowl, scrape myself upright and throw back my head to let the tepid water rinse the bile from my chin. What am I doing here? Slowly, it comes back to me, images rising to the surface like blobs of fat. Me, Kay, David. *Oh God.* I sink to my knees and throw up all over again. I emerge from the shower and dig through my bag for something clean to put on. My fingers catch the thin fabric of a rumpled T-shirt, a spatter of dried blood staining the hem. I hold onto the towel rail, searching through the snowstorm in my head for the moment I was injured. Slowly it seeps back. It wasn't me who got hurt. It was Kay, cutting herself on a kitchen knife.

Through the blur I see my hand holding hers high as I lead her
to the sink, a trickle of blood rolling down my arm.

'Hey!'

Damn. It's the barman from last night – mid-thirties, eyes the
colour of slate, a capable hand wiping the counter with a chequered
cloth. There's something in the tilt of his head that suggests a jaded
amusement with the world, or maybe it's just me he finds funny. I
squeeze past a pair of narrow-hipped boys with slick-backed hair
and face him down. 'Who put me to bed?'

'My sister.'

I drop my bag and slump against the bar. 'You have a sister?'

'No.'

I feel myself blushing. 'Did I pass out?'

'Only after you threw up on my shoes.'

I look away to avoid his smile. 'Is this your place?'

'My father's. Remy *fils* earns the money. Remy *père* gambles it
away.' He nods benignly towards a table of sun-wizened old men
playing cards. 'You want coffee?'

'Yes. And water. Lots and lots of water.'

'I'm assuming you have money?' He turns and reaches down a
cup. 'You owe me for half a bottle of cognac, a broken glass and the
room. Though you can have that cheap. It's one we use for staff.'

I smile weakly and toss my credit card onto the bar. He glances
at the name and then at me. 'Him or you, Phoebe?'

'Him or me, what?'

'Who was unfaithful?'

'It wasn't about a relationship.' I look away. 'Not that kind
anyway.' He shrugs. 'There *are* other reasons to get blind drunk,'
I say, haughtily.

Clearly not in Remy's world. He pulls a sceptical face and shoves
my card into the reader. 'How many nights?'

'One more,' I say, unable to face the thought of throwing up in a train or a plane.

'You want to eat?'

'Never, ever, again.'

The chatter in the bar is bad enough but the grinding, thumping and hissing now going on behind it is unbearable. How can making one cup of coffee be so damn noisy? It's nearly midday. Twenty-six hours since my world fell apart for the second time in as many months. Beyond the tables outside the café the fishermen are selling off the last of their meagre catches, sloshing out their plastic trays and scrubbing down their stalls. Sturdy women in aprons propel small children along the waterfront, tourists in baseball caps point and turn, raising cameras to catch the clifftop castle in their grinning selfies, watermen jump between boats, lugging nets and coils of rope, a boy and a girl bend in to each other, murmuring as they walk. A constant ripple of activity that leaves me feeling stalled and hollow.

'Here.' Remy sets the cup of coffee in front of me, a blister pack of aspirin tucked beneath the handle.

'Thanks.' I snap out a couple of tablets, swallow them down and wince into the sunlight as my attention pulls towards the quayside. A clot of people is forming at the water's edge, eyes and bodies turned towards the far side of the harbour. I crane my neck and catch the red and black of a powered dinghy scudding across the water. The watermen are shouting to each other, a frisson of concern, a darkening of faces that jars against the backdrop of sunny sky and blue, translucent water.

'What's happening?' I say to Remy.

He looks up, a glass and tea towel in his hands. 'It's the *marins pompiers*, the… lifeboat.' He wipes the glass and stacks it on the shelf above the bar. 'Probably a tourist. They hire boats without a clue what they're doing then they're surprised when they get into trouble.'

The lifeboat disappears around the headland. The crowd hovers and mutters for a moment before splintering in every direction. I sink back into my thoughts, digging deep for any kind of reason why a woman as down to earth as Roz might have lied about the death of her own child and concocted a fantasy about Kay's. One memory catches in me like a chip of swallowed glass. We're out riding, me on my pony, Missy, Roz on faithful old Sheba, and I ask her straight out about Phoebe's father. 'Who was he, Roz?' The look she gives me – so cold and angry – before she turns and gallops home. I never ask again. The chip of suspicion burrows deeper, turning Roz's mistrust of all men into something sinister. Am I the product of a rape she was desperate to forget? A pawn in a story she made up to remove the taint of my conception and allow herself to love me?

I type 'imposter' into my laptop and scroll through a piece about the fluidity of identity before the advent of DNA testing. Live newborns whisked into aristocratic birthing chambers in warming pans, dead ones smuggled out the same way. Martin Guerre, whose life was lived by another, kinder man. Lambert Simnel, Perkin Warbeck and the long line of crazily named pretenders whose lust for the crowns of Europe brought them death. How many more were there who knowingly or unknowingly got away with it? Shams who ruled from stolen thrones? Cuckoos living in the homes of ordinary families whose yearning to believe their lost loved ones had returned was enough to silence their doubts? If Kay and I hadn't had the test would our need to believe that we were mother and daughter have been enough to heal the gaping wounds in our lives? Or would the cracks in our shared delusion have gradually begun to show? Small suspicions that festered and grew until one of us accepted that we were living a lie?

'Christophe!'

I look up from the screen. Remy is greeting a rangy blonde man crossing to the bar. I just about make out that he's asking him about the lifeboat, though Christophe's gruff response is incomprehensible.

'What is it?' I say.

Remy's eyes drift over my shoulder to the sea. 'They're looking for a woman. A man walking his dog found a pile of clothes and a note on the beach at St Vincent.'

I take a swallow of coffee, savour the hit of caffeine. 'Who was she?'

Christophe rolls a careless shoulder. '*Une dame Anglaise.*'

Fingers of fear tap against my skull. 'You know her name?'

He shakes his head. There must be thousands of British women staying along this coast, so why are the taps turning into a drumbeat? I pick up my phone. Put it down. I don't have Kay's number. Or David's. I don't even know the name of the beach where she swims. I'm running out of the bar, knocking into the pavement tables, cutting across the cobbles to a cab parked on the wharf. The driver's leaning against the bonnet, smoking. He turns lazily as I jump in the back and flicks away his cigarette as I say breathlessly, 'The beach at St Vincent!'

I curse the tourists sauntering down the middle of the street and sit forward on my seat as we hit the coast road, immune to the beauty of the bone-white cliffs falling away to the water on one side and the hillside etched with green and purple rearing up on the other. I twist round as we pass the track to the Villa Rosa as if, if I stare hard enough, I'll see Kay bombing down the hillside in her little blue car. The cab swerves on, the queasy sway of my insides mirroring the bends in the road. I recognise a pair of pillared gates, the strips of earth showing between the vines like flesh between cornrow braids, and bite down on my lip as we pass the ruined shepherd's hut perched on the hill. I will the driver to keep driving, to take me to a beach that Kay never goes to, a beach where a woman I've never met has chosen to walk into the sea, but he's slowing down, pulling into the parking area. A sunlit flash of baby blue strikes me like a body blow. Kay's car is parked on the gravel, a police car beside it.

My mind spins a story – she's heard about the missing woman and come to the beach to help with the search. I tell the driver to wait, and run to the cliff edge. David is down by the water talking to a policewoman, his body bent forward like one of the wind-blasted trees on the hill. I crumple against the fence. Other cars are pulling up behind me. People getting out, capturing the scene on their phones. I stumble back to the cab, ready to tell the driver to take me straight to the airport so I can get away from this hellish thing that I've done. I stop with my fingers on the door handle and turn to look back at the sea. I can't leave Cassis. Not yet. Not until they find Kay's body and extinguish every last shred of hope.

CHAPTER EIGHT

The Café du Port is packed. I sit in a corner, the smell from the bowl of onion soup congealing beside my laptop turns my stomach. But lifting the spoon, prodding the sodden bread and shreds of rubbery cheese, shakes the numbness and helps me to pretend that I'm a functioning human being. My head's too heavy to move but my gaze drifts across the room – shapes and sounds distorting as if I am the one who is floating beneath the waters of the Mediterranean. A couple of faces I half remember from last night; regulars who saw me drink myself into a stupor. Others are total strangers – boatmen, tourists in fresh-off-the-peg Breton T-shirts, pensioner cronies of Remy *père*, a lean dark-haired man hunched over the bar, unshaven, morose, drinking on his own.

Kay Duncan. The name rises through the babble and fades back into the murmur of fast-flowing French coming from the table beside me. I turn slowly to look at the well-dressed, heavily made up woman and her skinny male companion, intent on their plates of steak frites. 'Did you know her?' I ask. The woman glances up warily. 'She... she knew my parents,' I say, astounded that I've found the strength to speak, let alone the wit to lie. 'I... I was planning on visiting her while I was here.'

'Ah.' Pacified, the woman drops into English. 'It is very sad when something like this happens.'

'Did you know her?' I say again.

She waggles her carefully lacquered head. 'A little. My shop delivered groceries to the Villa Rosa, but she called herself Madame

Burney so I did not know she was the one who lost her little girl. She was always so polite when she phoned in her order, so pleasant.' She nods to herself, losing interest in me.

My eyes slide back to my laptop as the news breaks on screen – *Kay Duncan, mother of missing Maya, in suspected suicide drowning* – accompanied by long lens paparazzi shots of Kay emerging hunched and head down from a rehab centre, and then make-up slicked and tumble haired from the days when she first met David. Within seconds the story is gathering speculation like a beetle balling up dung – tweets asking if it was guilt, new evidence that she killed Maya, or an imminent divorce that made her do it. Mobile phone footage of the beach at St Vincent appears, hastily assembled packages raking over the story of Kay's life: the drugs, the marriage to David, the rehab, the depression, the five-year-old daughter who went missing wearing a yellow mac and sou'wester.

Maya Duncan's disappearance remains one of the most famous missing person cases in UK history…
No arrests have ever been made…
Kay Duncan has always been a person of interest in the case…

No mention of the latest fraudster who threw her a lifeline of hope then snatched it away, but I don't need tweets and trolls to press home my guilt. The leaden heave of my stomach, the weight of my limbs and the flutter of images rattling through my head are doing a fine enough job of that already.

A shot of Maya in a blue velvet dress with a lace collar appears in the BBC news feed. I press pause. There she stands, squashed between Kay and David, knife in hand ready to cut her birthday cake, just as I'd pictured the scene. Is that all it takes? A photograph and a bit of subtle suggestion to trick an unsuspecting mind into creating a memory, reversing the image so the outsider looking in thinks they're an insider looking out? Is memory really so unreliable? Reality so malleable? Information so easy to plant in the human mind? Tapping 'false memory' into my laptop throws up article after article that seems to indicate that it is. I stare into my soup bowl, its pale slithers of onion floating like jellyfish in the dark broth. Is David right? Is that how Roz did it? Filled my head with the stuff of memories culled from her collection of cuttings, drip, drip over fifteen years, shaping pictures in her head and mine, as vivid as the images we shared of Pooh Corner, Hogwarts and her all-time favourite, the dorms of St Trinian's, until I think I really do remember being Maya? Were the yellow sou'wester and the deathbed letter clever, real-world touches to cement the lies?

I let out a cry – frustration shot with loss. I left the letter and the sou'wester with David Duncan. He's probably burned them by now. I spool on through the sting of tears. The news packages about Kay don't tell me anything I haven't read before, only this time I'm coming at the facts with new eyes, searching – shamefully – for snagged threads I can pick at to unravel an explanation for Roz's deception and shift this suffocating sense of guilt.

Remy switches the bar's TV to the local news and turns up the sound. For a moment the energy in the room diverts to the images on screen, but the possible suicide of *une dame Anglaise* is of little interest to the locals – the dark-haired man at the bar lifts his head for barely a moment before lowering it and continuing to drink with steady determination – or to the Germans and Americans downing coffees and making loud plans for the afternoon. It's the Brits who react – a whole table of them. They've lived with Maya Duncan's face staring out from their TVs and newspapers for the last fifteen years, forever frozen in time as the dark-eyed, thin-cheeked child she was when she vanished, alongside snatched shots of petite, brown-haired Kay in dark glasses, ducking away from the cameras – two players in an iconic mystery made so much more piquant by the involvement of the man who created chart-topping singer Lila Mendez. The women in the group can hardly believe their luck. A snippet of celebrity trauma to spice up their Facebook posts while they're here; a dusting of tarnished stardust to make them shine when they get home. Their voices rise loud and knowing above the clatter of crockery… *after all this time… guilt catching up… always knew she killed that kiddy… I mean, who takes seven hours to notice their five-year-old's gone missing?*

'Kiddy.' The word sets me on edge, a sure tell for faked concern for a child. I want to slap their smug red faces and tell them it's not frail, damaged Kay who was a killer. It's me. The girl with no name who drove a broken-hearted woman to suicide.

The TV cuts from a shot of the beach at St Vincent to the rusty green gate leading up to the Villa Rosa and I imagine David pacing back and forth across those worn stone tiles, consumed with grief for Kay and hatred for me. I click open the email from the clinic. Even as I reread the damning words – *Phoebe Jane Locklear is excluded from being the child of Kaitlin Ruth Duncan* – I'm searching for reasons to exonerate Roz. Across the bar the coffee machine hisses and splutters. What if someone lied to her about who I am? Someone close to Kay. Someone who had their own motives for pretending I was Maya? I pull myself upright and forward the sequence of DNA markers to bald, bluff Rob McClennan, who runs the breeding programme at Molokodi, and add a hasty note of my own.

Hey Rob,

Just wondering if you could do me a huge favour and take a look at these DNA test results. It's for a friend I met on my travels. As you can see, they came back negative for mother/daughter but she's keen to know if the two of them could be related in any other way. I told her if there's any kind of link you're the man to find

*it. I'm also going to send you fresh samples of their DNA in case
you need to run your own tests to be sure.*

I owe you big time!
Phoebe x

Half an hour later I set off for the post office with a brown
paper parcel. Inside it, carefully wrapped and sealed in separate
plastic bags, are the white T-shirt stained with Kay's blood and a
handful of my hairs – coarse dark strands ripped out at the root.
I send the parcel by the fastest method possible.

CHAPTER NINE

I spend the evening hunched in a corner of the bar, flicking through the newsfeeds in the hope that by some miracle Kay has been found alive. When the last customer has staggered into the night I offer to help Remy clear up. He tolerates my presence – out of pity, I assume, for what he thinks is my broken heart. Once we've stacked the last chair and collected the last glass, and I can't put off the pain of being alone any longer, I climb the stairs to my attic room and sit at the window looking out over the harbour wall to the open sea. Is Kay out there in the black water, hair splayed out beneath the sprinkle of stars, or has she sunk to where there's nothing but darkness? As if what I did to her isn't heinous enough, as the night wears on my guilt takes on new and ever more disquieting shapes. What if, in some tragic outburst of infantile anger, I killed Maya Duncan and Roz whisked me away to Botswana to keep my identity and my crime from the world? What if pretending I was Maya and sending me to Kay was a distorted deathbed attempt to right an impossible wrong and bring her comfort through pretence? I dash the idea away, dismissing it as absurd, irrational, illogical, but it doesn't ease the panic rising in my throat.

The next morning, Kay's disappearance is making headlines on every news site. I pick through the stories word by word.

> … *A cyclist reported seeing a woman answering Kay Duncan's description leave her distinctive pale-blue convertible at around 6.30 yesterday morning before heading down the path to the beach…*

*David Duncan's claim that he was at home from 6 a.m. until
10 a.m. hosting a series of conference calls has been corroborated
by a property developer in Dubai and four US-based financiers
involved in the discussions...*

The BBC has an exclusive interview with the dog walker who
found Kay's clothes and towel on the beach; a stocky, red-faced
man in his sixties. At first I don't take in what he's saying, and then
I do. He's talking about the note she left. My gaze moves from his
rough red fingers weighing a handful of air to demonstrate the
size of the rock she'd used to hold down the paper, to his thin lips
shaping the words she'd written:

'*This time it was too much to bear.*'

The message was meant for me and it finds its mark. I am the
straw that broke her, the weight that tipped the balance of her
grief. I fold in on myself, my eyes burning and wet. I wipe them
with the back of my hand and force myself to scroll on, lingering
over the reports of Kay's previous drug overdoses that unnamed
'friends' are now presenting as suicide attempts.

I wander out into the hot sunshine and up the cobbled lanes,
between higgledy-piggledy rows of narrow buildings – cafés,
restaurants and shops crammed with local delicacies, ceramics,
baskets and hand-painted kaftans. The bright offerings mock the
drab grey guilt I feel inside, the merry calls of *mademoiselle!* strike
a jarring note in my ears, driving home the realisation that I have
no more idea of my own name than these beckoning shopkeepers.
I have no roots, no identity, no family. The past I believed was
mine was a lie, the woman who brought me up was a manipulative
fantasist, the woman I thought was my mother was a stranger.
And now, because of me, she's dead.

I stumble into the cool of a white stucco church and sit on a
polished pew at the back. A middle-aged couple come in to light
candles and say a prayer. I envy them. Roz, with her militant

atheism and paranoid distrust of authority, has even stripped me of the solace of religion. An elderly woman shuffles into the confessional and pulls the little curtain shut. Minutes later she comes out, her sins forgiven, her guilt washed clean. I resist the urge to follow her into the tiny box. Even if my French were up to it, what would I say? That I told a hurt, troubled woman I was her long-lost daughter and drove her to suicide? Do they dole out dispensation for telling deadly lies that you thought were truths?

I close my eyes and sift through the disconnected images I'd always taken for memories. I focus in on the blanks and gaps. I still can't picture the school I went to in London or the friends I'd had. When I turned up at Stanford Street a week ago and spoke to the Duncans' housekeeper, I hadn't recognised any of the surrounding buildings or the park at the end of the street. Is that normal? Or is it simply that Roz omitted to describe them to me? I look around me at the painted saints, the chubby Jesus in his mother's arms, the sunlight streaming through the stained-glass windows, the splashes of coloured light streaking the marble floor. How much does anyone remember of their early childhood? The priest comes hurrying down the aisle, feet tapping, hands clasped in front. He is young and fresh faced, with deep-set dark eyes that flit towards me as he passes, as if he has sniffed out my crimes. I look away until he's walked past me then I slip out into the little piazza, whose centrepiece is a marble obelisk dribbling water into a shell-shaped bowl.

In need of coffee, I search among the crowded tables of the nearest café for an empty seat, dithering between joining a morose old man nursing a glass of wine or squeezing in beside two whispering girls poking spoons into green glass flutes of ice cream. I go for the girls and I'm making my way to their table when a woman in her twenties, wearing jeans and a crumpled white shirt, plonks herself down opposite the old man and pulls the strap of a heavy canvas bag over her short reddish hair. She leans forward to pick up the menu. Her gaze skims the faces around her and hovers for a moment on mine. Red letters leap from the pass swinging from her neck. Press. My heart bangs. *She's a journalist. She knows I was staying at the Villa Rosa. Someone saw us at the clinic in Toulon. She's followed me here to grill me about my connection to Kay.* A headline rings in my ears: *Botswanan backpacker arrested in attempted Maya Duncan scam.*

I break into a sweat, ready to run away across the slippery cobbles. *Calm down!* She can't actually *know* anything. But if someone's been gossiping about me wouldn't it be better to find out exactly what they've said? Heart still thudding, I change direction and move towards her table. 'Mind if I sit down?'

'Sure.' She doesn't look up from her phone.

Besieged, the old man grunts, drains his wine and gets up to go. I sit down, smile at the approaching waiter and order a coffee.

'Same,' my companion says, mid-text.

'You're a journalist,' I say, tilting my chin in defiance.

'Yep.' She pulls the menu towards her and runs her eyes down the page. 'And a croque monsieur.'

I gaze down the sloping street to the sparkling slice of harbour visible between the buildings. 'Are you covering Kay Duncan's suicide?'

'Yes.'

'What have you found out?'

'Nothing.' She lays down her phone and hooks her elbows over the back of her chair. 'So now I'm just hanging around with the rest of the press pack waiting for them to find the body.'

She has no idea who I am. My heart steadies for a moment then speeds up. 'How come it hasn't washed up yet?'

'It won't surface till it fills with gas. In water this warm that shouldn't take long, but on the way up it could easily get caught in the propellers of one of the big yachts.' She sees me flinch and shrugs. 'It happens. But the coastguard tells me they usually find something identifiable within four to seven days.'

I don't say anything. I stare at a crack in the flat shiny cobbles.

'My paper wants a picture of the life she was living down here but there's nothing to tell. She was practically a recluse, hardly showed her face.'

'Did you interview her husband?' I say.

'Yes, but he's in pieces, blames himself for letting her come here in the first place. He's been out in his boat searching for her, says he can't rest until they find her, but by all accounts she was a strong swimmer so God knows how far out she went.'

I play with one of the sachets of sugar in the bowl in front of us. Lift. Drop. Lift. Drop. 'Did he… say why she did it?'

She shakes her head. 'Didn't have to. To be honest I'm surprised she waited this long. Imagine losing your kid, then being subjected to years of abuse. Some of the filth the tabloids made up about her makes me ashamed of my profession.'

The waiter brings her croque monsieur and our coffees. I rip open the sugar and pour it into my cup. She eats quickly, sinking small white teeth into her sandwich and firing off questions between bites. 'What are you doing here?'

'Gap year.'

'On your own?'

'Best way to travel.'

'You're not British.'

Who knows what the hell I am? I go for, 'Brought up in Botswana.' I must remember that line. It's just about the only truth I can tell.

'I've heard it's beautiful.'

'It is. Very.'

'I'm Laurel. Laurel Myers.' She offers me her hand.

I hesitate then take it. 'Phoe—' I falter, choking on my dwindling sense of self. 'Phoebe Locklear.'

Another few bites and she's licking her fingers, calling to the waiter for her bill. Then she's up and off, swinging her bag onto her shoulder. 'See you, Phoebe.'

I drink a second cup of coffee and wonder how I'm going to fill the long empty days and hot, guilt-soaked nights until the coast guard finds 'something identifiable'.

CHAPTER TEN

It's almost dawn when I fall into a sweaty half sleep, only to dream of five-year-old Maya Duncan incarcerated in a bricked-up room, her hand reaching out through a slit in the wall, her small, frightened voice begging me to set her free. It's dark. I creep closer. Her voice drops to a whisper. She's telling me who I am – words I long to hear but can't make out.

The sound stays with me as I pull on my running things and set off along the coast road, punishing my body for three hours, relishing the fire in my lungs and the agonising wrench of my ankle when I trip on a dip in the path – pain to dull the gnawing sense of helplessness. I stop to catch my breath. I'm panting, head down, hands on thighs when I see David shuffling along the quayside like a sleepwalker. He's stooped and unshaven, a denim cap pulled low over his forehead, a bottle of water in his hand. I tell myself I'm not following him, just heading the same way, but when he walks on past Remy's café so do I. He keeps going, away from the shirt-sleeved waiters raising the shutters on the bars and restaurants and the boatmen setting out their pavement signs offering diving trips and sightseeing tours of the creeks, to where the road forks. Shoulders slumped, he follows an overgrown track that drops steeply to the sea.

I glance over my shoulder. There's no one in sight. Unable to stop myself I call out, 'David!'

Slowly he turns, dazed and trembling, his face pouched with misery.

'Get away from me.' He lowers his head and starts walking again.

I hurry after him, 'I know what I did is beyond forgiving... but we have to talk. Please, just for a minute...'

He pivots round, his face stiffened by fury. 'You've some gall. Back off or I'll call the police!'

'I thought it was true. You have to believe me.' Tears blur my vision. 'Roz would never have wanted it to turn out like this.'

'No? Then what did she want?'

'I... I don't know.' I slump back against the rock wall and slither to the ground, my voice clogged with snot and tears. 'All I can think is that somehow Maya and I got swapped as babies. If that is what happened, maybe the swap was tied up with her disappearance.' The words tumble out, shaping possibilities as they come. 'If we worked together, pooled our knowledge... there's a chance we could find her, or at least find out what happened to her and...' I look up at him, desperate to salvage something from this horror. 'And clear Kay's name.'

He shakes his head, a weary exhale. 'God, you're good. But whatever game you're playing you can stop it. Right now.'

'If I'd been trying to con you what could I gain by talking to you?'

'Maybe you're short of a quote for some tacky news story. *My days with Crazy Kay*, or how about *David Duncan shares his grief?*' His voice rises, raw and rasping. 'Or you're doing it for kicks. God knows, you wouldn't be the first.'

'No!' I leap up as he turns away. 'I know I can never make this right but I swear I thought I was Maya.'

'Then it has to be what this Roz woman *wanted* you to believe, filling your head with lies – conning you like she tried to con us.'

'It's not just images that I remember, it's sounds, voices – you and Kay together – clear as anything.'

His head sways as if it's coming loose from his neck. 'I remembered something last night. That time I asked her to keep an eye on the house I went downstairs the morning after we got back and she was in our living room, looking through Kay's photo albums. She gave me some bullshit about forgetting which day we were coming home but who knows how long she'd been in the house, sneaking around, watching us, listening through keyholes, collecting tiny details of our conversations to flesh out her lies.'

This picture of Roz is so disturbing I hardly know how to respond. 'Why would she want to deceive us?'

'I don't know and I don't care. All I do know is that Maya is dead, and now, because of you, so is Kay.'

'You don't know that Maya's dead.' My voice is harsh, sharpened by a sudden fear that the key to who I am died with her.

He stares at me with a sort of grieved exhaustion. 'Let me tell you something I've never told anyone before. Ten years ago a friend in the Met told me that despite all the public avowals to the contrary they were downgrading the investigation because they were convinced that Maya had been killed within hours of her disappearance. He thought if I could find a way to break it to Kay it might help her to move on. I told him to forget it, that we'd never give up hope. But now she's gone I have to face the truth. Maya is dead and there's nothing anyone can do to bring her back. So please, have some damned compassion and leave me alone.'

He walks away, unsteady old-man steps, and disappears through the overhang of trees. I climb back to the road. At the top I look back at the shimmer of the Mediterranean showing through the belt of pines, their stems dark and gnarled against the blue. As I stand there, *Serenity* noses out into the creek with David at the helm. He chugs slowly towards the open sea. Grief throws a low punch into my belly as I picture him out there scanning the water for his wife's bloated, gas-filled body.

*

Who knew that guilt could feel so physical? It smothers everything, like the ashy aftermath of an explosion; the food in my mouth, the air in my lungs, the thoughts in my head. I can't read. I can't watch a movie or even think about med school applications. All I can do is scour the internet for updates on the search for Kay's body or wander the town in the hope that one of the slight, dark-haired tourists who set my heart jumping will look up and it'll be her, running towards me, tossing back her head and shouting that it's all been a stupid mistake. I wander out along the clifftop road and sit as near to the edge as I dare. My gaze drifts from the lone climber dangling from an invisible thread on the opposite cliff to a white pleasure cruiser gliding across the open water, at its stern a ripple of dark bumps. Are they dolphins? I rummage in my bag for my binoculars – the pair that had once been Roz's – and let my ten-year-old fingers trace the engraving on the brass.

Happy birthday to my darling girl, R xx

It's true. For fifteen blissful years I *was* her darling girl. So how could someone so practical and straightforward, someone who'd loved a child the way she'd loved me, have concocted this destructive web of lies? Or was that the point? It had always been just Roz and me, safe in the world she'd created for us at the conservancy. No stories about her childhood, no birthday cards from her family, no old friends coming out to stay, no photos of the real Phoebe tucked away in a book or a drawer. It's only now that it strikes me as strange that I know almost nothing about Roz's past – only that she lost elderly parents young and spent a large chunk of her youth and inheritance campaigning for animal rights.

I raise the binoculars to my eyes and scan the water. The bumps disappoint. They're ripples, not dolphins, and the motor launch is moving on. I shuffle a little closer to the cliff edge and stare down the craggy drop to the spatter of rocks a hundred feet below. It shocks me that if I threw myself onto them there would be no one to mourn me, no one to search for my body or lie awake at night wondering what they could have done to make me want to live.

Forty-eight empty hours later I'm passing the terrace of a tapas restaurant hung with fairy lights when a voice shouts, 'Hey, Phoebe!'

It's Laurel Myers, the journalist, beckoning me over to a crowded table. I recognise a couple of her companions from the TV news – a gathering of reporters waiting, like me, for Kay's body to be found; raucous, drunk and hungry for information about her life and her death. I press my tongue to the top of my mouth, ready to call 'No thanks', but I'm so lonely I could scream so I raise a shaky hand and squeeze through the tables to join them. A glass appears in front of me, someone fills it, slopping red wine onto the white tablecloth. I gulp it down. Voices close over me, rambling stories of drunken colleagues and over-sexed politicians, punchlines met with backslaps and throaty roars. I'm slugging back my third glass of wine, laughing with the laughter, cramming strips of sticky, forbidden red meat into my mouth when one of the women, a sharp-faced brunette, waves towards the entrance and calls, 'Will, over here!'

A new arrival – floppy fair hair, squished half-smile – shunts along the bench towards me and reaches for the wine. He greets the people around the table, picking them off by name, before turning curious and not quite matching brown eyes on me. 'Hi, Will Betteridge.'

'Phoebe Locklear,' I fluster.

'Good to meet you, Phoebe. Who are you with?'

'I'm not press. I'm… on a gap year.' I wince at how pathetic that sounds.

'Touring Europe?'

'Erm… not really. Just staying in Cassis for a couple of days then back to London.'

He screws up his eyes. 'What's the accent?'

'I was… brought up in Botswana.' His eyes widen. 'On a nature reserve,' I add, foolishly.

'Lucky you. I was brought up in Guildford. On a cul de sac.'

'I'm guessing the head count of endangered wildlife was lower.'

'Don't you believe it. The survival of Surrey's middle classes is definitely under threat. Have you seen the price of organic quinoa?'

I laugh uncertainly and tell him I know nothing about Surrey. He launches into a description of a childhood so different to mine he might as well be describing life on Mars, tearing into his parents' dreams and politics with a mixture of affection and despair. Then he asks me about growing up in the bush. Even as I warn myself to be careful, that this man is a reporter trained to pick and probe and squeeze out other people's secrets, I feel myself drinking in the closeness of another human being – warm male flesh pushing against mine, an arm flung carelessly along the back of my chair as I describe the joys of growing up at Molokodi with a relative who 'took me in when my parents died'. More people arrive and squeeze onto the bench, pressing us closer. I don't resist. Neither does Will. Around us a noisy quarrel about the rights and wrongs of a recent libel action vies with an animated discussion of the merits of 'fritos' versus 'en su tinta' when it comes to calamari.

'Come on, Will.' The voice of the brunette, who everyone is calling Sally, cuts through the clamour. 'You're the expert. After everything Kay Duncan's been through, why top herself now? Was it really guilt catching up with her or was there something else?'

I feel my veins unravelling, spilling out through my skin and floating around me in a throbbing sea of red. I press the tip of my knife into my palm and stare at my plate, convinced that Will's going to haul me to my feet and denounce me as the culprit.

'God knows,' I hear him say. 'I've been trawling through every conspiracy site, chat room and gossip blog I can find and I can't see anything that might have tipped her over edge. The Met are just as confused. There haven't been any new threats or accusations against her, and the last false sighting of Maya was at least six months ago.'

'Well, you know how it is,' Sally says, suddenly acid, 'if someone dicks you around it can take a while to deal with the hurt.'

Will turns away and acts as if the barb shot straight past him, but close up I see the downturn of his mouth.

'So you're an expert on Kay Duncan?' I say, my voice hollow.

He shrugs. 'I did a big piece for the ten-year anniversary of Maya's abduction and I've kept on top of the story ever since.'

'What do you think happened to her?'

'I've always had a feeling she's alive, but I've got sod all to back it up.'

'I heard the police downgraded the investigation a while ago.'

'Who told you that?'

'Oh…' I mumble, feeling cornered. 'Someone I met.'

'Well they're wrong.' He reaches for the wine and fills our glasses. 'Every new Met commissioner pumps in more funds, hoping the mystery is going to get solved on their watch.'

'Do you think it ever will?'

'God knows. There's plenty of people convinced that Kay did it – you know, the kid eats some of her tablets thinking they're sweets and David Duncan throws money at making the body disappear – and plenty more with a vested interest in keeping the mystery unsolved. And it's not just the conspiracy cranks. Maya Duncan's face sells papers. Put the mystery to bed and a lot of news outlets kiss goodbye to a cash cow.'

'Including yours.'

'Including mine.' I catch his smile and think how good he is to look at. 'But I'd give anything to discover the truth. Can you imagine what it would be like to find her alive, break the story and get the bastard who took her sent down?'

I'm deep in a drunken fantasy of tracking down Maya and earning his undying adoration by handing him the scoop of a lifetime when I see Sally glaring at us. Her eyes, proprietorially narrowed, stay fixed on Will as she turns and murmurs to her neighbour. The dark spicy smell of his tapas-laden breath, the prickle of stubble against my face, as he leans closer and whispers, 'Let's get out of here.'

He pulls me to my feet and I put a steadying hand against his chest. 'What's with you and Sally?' I say as we stumble into the street.

'We used to work together. She wanted more.'

'You didn't?'

'I was married. So was she.'

'Was?'

'My wife left me.'

I leave it at that. Who am I to question someone else's truths?

In his room he tips me onto the bed and kisses me, first gently, and then, when I pull him closer, he pushes his tongue hard into my mouth. I run my hands down his spine, sober enough – just about – to know how risky this is. Drunk enough and lonely enough not to care.

I wake up late, troubled by the band of pain closing around my forehead and pressing down behind my eyes. I didn't drink *that* much last night but it feels worse than any hangover I've ever had. I turn over. Will has gone, leaving a note on his pillow with his number and an instruction to call him. I creep out of his hotel and trudge through the pines to the road that leads down to the harbour. A brush of chill, gritty wind brings up the goose bumps on my arms and invades my eyes. Above the sea the sky is turning the colour of piss and along the quayside the wind is shunting the boats around, creaking the guy ropes. When I get back to the Café du Port the lunchtime regulars are hunkered down beneath the flapping awning muttering to each other.

It's Remy's day off, his place taken by a birdlike woman who scowls and pretends not to understand my French when I try to order something to eat. I stab my finger at the menu and glare at her, though when my food finally arrives it's as much as I can do to force down a few bites of lettuce. I push away the plate and sit shivering over a cup of coffee, watching the yellow sky darken through ochre to black, and flipping between ghosting Will Betteridge forever, and texting him there and then. I drag myself up to my room and distract myself from thoughts of Will and the jittery cold in my bones by watching back-to-back episodes of *Friends* – a childhood comfort permitted only on the very sickest of sick days.

Eventually I crawl into bed, and lie there rocked by waves of foreboding that rise and fall with the crash and groan of the storm outside. Around midnight I take a sleeping pill and fall into a thin, restless sleep.

CHAPTER ELEVEN

The morning dawns bright and storm-washed and my brain feels strangely crisp inside my skull. I hurry downstairs, keen to go for a run. It's Remy who tells me the news; a throwaway, over-the-shoulder update as he bends into the dishwasher. 'They've found a woman's body in one of the creeks. It must have got washed up by the storm.'

I push away from the bar. Vaguely aware of Remy's eyes on my back, I stumble across the worn wooden floor, down a window-less corridor of textured brown walls lumpy as porridge, past the kitchen and storerooms until I can finally slam a door behind me and sob into the sink. When I've stopped crying and splashed my face with water I slink back to the bar. Remy juts his chin to the place along the quayside where the press pack are gathering. I see Will, adjusting his shirt in front of a TV camera operated by an overweight man in headphones. I slip outside and hover with the gathering crowd as he turns to look into the lens.

'The body of Kay Duncan, missing wife of music mogul David Duncan, was found by a boatman early this morning lodged in the rocks along the coast beyond Port-Mieux, and has been taken to the morgue in Marseille. Despite the condition of the body, Mr Duncan was able to make a positive identification using her clothes and jewellery. He has also provided a toothbrush for DNA testing to confirm the identification. A spokesman for Duncan Entertainment has asked the press and public to respect his privacy at this difficult time.' He turns to the tall dark-haired man at his side. 'With me is Capitaine Arno Segal, head of the team who recovered the body.'

I thought I was ready for this, but I'm not. It's official. Kay is dead. And I'm the one who killed her, as surely as if I'd tied a weight to her slim brown legs and tipped her into the sea. I take small trembling steps back to the café and I'm staring blankly at the news feeds when Will plops down on the seat opposite me. He taps his phone on the table to get my attention. 'You didn't call.'

'Sorry. Hangover.'

He sighs and turns impatiently towards the bar. 'God, I need coffee.'

'What's wrong?'

He runs his hand through his hair. 'It's this story. Sally was right. Why would Kay Duncan kill herself now? What am I missing?'

Remy appears behind him, giving me a cock-eyed look of curiosity as he places a cup of coffee in front of Will. I glare him away.

'What did you mean about the state of the body?' I say, carefully. 'It can't have decomposed that much in six days.'

'Water's pretty warm round here and predators are attracted by rotting flesh. Plus the storm pounded what was left of her to mush against the rocks. Though the desk in London was too squeamish to let me put that in.' He glances round, clicks the buttons on his phone and holds up the screen. My brain stalls, refusing to process the broken, eyeless mess – smashed skull, teeth protruding through a lipless mouth, witchy hair hanging from a floating flap of scalp. 'Can you believe it? The kid who found her took this and about half a dozen other shots and sent them to his mates.'

I lift my hand to shield my eyes and pull away. 'I don't want to see it.'

But the image has seared itself into my brain.

Will pockets his phone and reaches for my hand. 'Sorry. I thought you medics were made of sterner stuff.'

I gulp down a mouthful of orange juice – lips pressed hard against the glass. 'Are they absolutely certain it's her?' I whisper when I've clawed back control.

'Hundred per cent. The swimsuit, the ring on a chain round her neck, the faded tattoo.'

When I refocus, Will is moving his lips, saying words I can't process. I cut him off. 'When did I tell you I was applying for med school?'

'Erm, maybe the only other time we've met?'

'What else did I say?' My voice, gripped by panic, comes out higher than I'd planned.

He studies me for a moment, then grins. 'As far as I remember, baring our souls wasn't exactly high on the agenda.' He swallows his coffee and stands up. 'Sorry. Got to do a two-way with London.' He drops a hand onto my shoulder. His touch has a steadying warmth. 'Do you want to meet up later? Go for a walk, maybe have a swim?'

'Shouldn't you be working?'

He laughs. 'I'm always working. It'll be a chance to pick up some colour for a background piece I'm doing for one of the Sundays. We can pick up some wine and have a picnic on the beach.'

I stare up at him and tell myself – sternly but without conviction – that getting drunk and loose-lipped with this man for a second time is a bad, bad idea and anyway, I should be jumping on a plane and starting the search for who I am.

'Sure,' I hear myself say. 'Come find me.' I tip back my glass and crunch down the ice so fast a spear of pain slices through my brain. *It'll be fine. I won't drink and I'll watch every word I say.*

When he's gone I gaze out at the sea and close my eyes, yellow burning my eyelids. I yearn to roll back time and bring Kay back to life, but I can't do that. I want Roz to wrap me in her arms and tell me the truth about my past, but the woman I loved and thought I knew is more than dead – it looks like she never existed.

Yet somewhere in the deepest most unshakeable part of myself I still can't believe that sending me to Kay was just a random act of crazy. There has to be a reason, an overlap, a moment in their pasts when their troubled lives converged. In a sudden blaze of purpose I book a seat on the next cheap flight to London then hurry out of the café and up the cobbled streets until I find a stationer's tucked away down a whitewashed alleyway. I take my time inspecting the selection of notebooks, settling finally on a thick maroon one with black endpapers and a soft leather cover. Holding it in my hands, imagining the smooth blank pages filled with notes about Kay and Roz, seems to knock a little shape into my shapelessness.

Back in my attic, I sit cross-legged on the bed and on the first page write Roz, Kay, Maya and Phoebe, setting out the names as four points on a needleless compass. North, South – Kay and Roz. Two mothers, two enigmas, two damaged women who each lost a child. East, West – Phoebe and Maya. Two little girls, both gone before their time. I circle each name, then at the point where the four circles meet, the point where I hope to find myself, I draw a thick black question mark. Realising I'm holding my breath, I let out a slow exhale, turn the page and write down everything I thought I knew about Roz and everything I've found out about Kay. What began as an orderly list of bullet points quickly turns into an outpouring of hurt and confusion, scrawled with angry underlinings and blotched with tears.

CHAPTER TWELVE

I can't pretend I've had many actual boyfriends but I have had quite a lot of sex with quite a lot of people – six years at a mixed international boarding school saw to that. Apart from getting drunk on cheap beer or trying to sneak into the downtown casino that advertised itself with the enticing tagline 'The more you weigh, the more we pay', what else was there to do in term-time Gabarone? But on the whole the boys I've been with bored me, which made things easy. Being with Will isn't easy. For one thing, he's not a boy. According to his Wikipedia page – which I happened to glance at – he's twenty-eight. For another I'm petrified he'll work out that I'm the reason Kay killed herself and, most worrying of all, just watching him weave his way across the café with his eyes locked on his phone makes me feel breathless and out of control.

'Hey,' he says.

'Has something happened?'

He takes my arm, still thumbing the screen as he guides me outside. 'Let's hope Duncan's got the sense not to look on Twitter.'

'What are they saying?'

'Now Kay's out of the picture the trolls are turning on him, poor sod, saying the abduction was his fault for swanning off to the States and leaving his "cokehead" wife at home with her own kid. Really vile, some of it. The more I think about it the more certain I am that one of these creeps did something to push her over the edge. A letter, a phone call, a knock at the door.'

The rap of my knuckles on Kay's door sounds in my head as we climb the steep cobbled streets. With quick tripping steps I hurry past the crowded pavement cafés, convinced the laughing diners can see through my clothing to my guilt. Bell-shaped wine bottles, coiled conch shells, tiny alleyways, racks of postcards twirling in the breeze, a family of fun seekers heaped with snorkels, plastic buckets and a flamingo-shaped inflatable whose lolling head pecks at the back of their youngest child's knees. It feels unreal, as if I'm seeing it all from a long way away. We stop at a deli to buy our picnic. I fake interest in the vast spread of cheeses and hams and even manage a smile when the assistant applauds our choice. Will's phone buzzes as we reach the till. He studies the screen with the look of professional focus that I'm starting to dread. 'What now?' I say.

He stuffs the food into his bag and shifts it onto his shoulder. 'Laurel says someone's scrawled graffiti over Duncan's boathouse. Mind if we take a look?'

A rattle of panic. 'What if we bump into Duncan? I… I wouldn't know what to say to him.'

'It's OK. She says he's down at the town hall sorting out the death certificate.'

I stumble when we reach the turning, toppled by the memory of David's grief-ravaged face glaring down into mine and the angry words spewing from his mouth. Will kicks a path through the thorn bushes surrounding the padlocked gate and holds back the brambles to let me through. We walk on for twenty yards or so to a wooded bank of pines with glimpses of sea beyond. My hands sweat as we turn the corner. There below us, jutting into the water, sits the boathouse, the scrawl of white graffiti standing out harsh and accusing against the black of the wooden walls – 'Tueur', 'Justice pour Maya' and, in case he didn't quite get the message, 'Baby Kiler' in smudged, misspelled English.

'Bastards,' Will murmurs. Sickened yet fascinated, I leave him taking photos, edge down the steep pathway and reach up to touch the 'r' of 'Kiler'. The paint is still tacky. I step back and circle the boardwalk. The newly installed double doors at the back are fastened by another heavy padlock but the chain on the smaller side door has been cut through and the padlock is swinging free. 'Someone's broken in,' I call.

Will pockets his phone, comes slithering down the path and pokes his head inside. 'Hello!'

There's no answer. No scuffling, no whispering, just silence. He pushes the door wide.

I grab his arm. 'You can't go in.'

'Why not? I'm just making sure the vandals didn't damage the boat.' His grin disappears as he steps inside.

With a nervous glance up the track, I follow him into the cool gloom of the boathouse. Duncan's boat is a beautiful thing – a clinker-built fishing boat suspended above the water by a sling and a metal winch, the name plate at the bow etched in elaborate gold lettering.

There's a sharp smell of varnish and patches of new wood on the hull. I look around me, surprised to see Duncan's silver Mercedes parked inside the double doors at the back. I switch my gaze to Will, who is trying the handle of the store in the corner. It's locked, secured by a heavy mortice. With calm efficiency he works the tip of a penknife around a knot in the wood, levers it out and peers through the hole.

'What's inside?'

'Not much. Take a look.'

I crouch down and put my eye to the hole.

The store is swept clean, nothing in it but a trio of fuel cans and a large wire cage propped against the far wall.

'What's that wire thing?'

'Looks like an old lobster trap. Come on.'

I turn around. He's on the winch ladder, scrambling onto the boat. I pull myself up after him and pause at the top, picturing the trip we'd planned along the creeks – me, Kay and David. I make my way down the narrow stairs to the lower deck where Will is unlatching cupboards, opening drawers, running his hands over oversized waterproofs and racks of fishing gear.

'What are you doing?'

'Trying to get a sense of Duncan.'

'And?'

'He's organised, meticulous and this is definitely his domain; none of this stuff is Kay's. And he's pretty serious about his fishing.' He lifts the lid of a big chest freezer and sniffs. 'Even this is for storing catch.' I look inside. The cavity has been scrubbed out but beneath the musty smell of disconnected fridges there's still an indelible undertow of fish.

'Judging by the way everything's been packed away, he's not planning on taking any more trips for a while.'

As we move on through the cabins, I spot a shelf of CDs and demo tapes all in alphabetical order. A whole section dedicated to Lila Mendez. I can't stop my eyes flitting to the Ds or my heart fluttering with disappointment that there's nothing marked 'Doxettes'. In the wheelhouse the instruments are shined and polished, the charts well used and neatly stored. I lean against Will, breathing in the smell of him as he opens the logbook and leafs through the record of *Serenity's* runs. I notice how careful and clean David's writing is. Will's eyes meet mine and linger. 'We should go,' I say simply.

Will looks thoughtful as we pick our way along the shoreline and doesn't speak as he leads me down to a little strip of beach, shielded from the world by a curve of rock. I watch him check his phone and then slump onto the sand with his back to the cliff. 'I just don't get it. Duncan's just lost his wife and he wasn't even in the country when Maya went missing, but some jerk goes to all the trouble of lugging pots of paint down that cliff path so they can accuse him of killing her. What's the point? And of course all those horror show photos of her body are already on the internet. He's got lawyers trying to get them taken down, and mainstream outlets are unlikely to use them, but they're still out there, still attracting vile comments.' He turns to look at the sea and the sunlight catches his hair. 'Maybe that's what I should write about. The power of the hate campaign that didn't even stop with Kay's death.'

I squeeze in beside him and take his hand. We sit in silence for a while, watching the sunlight shimmer on the water, and then he turns and pushes a strand of hair from my face. 'Have you got a boyfriend back in Botswana?'

'No.'

'No ripped eco warrior pining for you in the bush?'

'Just a couple of Chacma baboons who found it tough saying goodbye. What about you? I guess you pick up a new girl on every story.'

He regards me in silence. 'Almost never.'

'Why not?'

'I rarely come across anyone I can be myself with.'

Touched but a little unnerved, I slide my fingers into his hair and pull his lips to mine.

That night he takes me to a restaurant perched high on the hill and we choose a table with a fabulous view of the harbour. The sky is a dense dark purple, streaked with orange where it meets the black of the water. Our afternoon on the beach has eased the bleakness and left me calm, hopeful even, but when I pick up the menu a rush of guilt flings me back to the sunlit meal in Toulon when Kay was happy and alive and convinced that the girl who had come knocking on her door was her long-lost daughter. What the hell is wrong with me? How can I smile and eat and have sex when I should be finding out why Roz sent me to Kay with a cruel destructive lie? How can I look Will in the eye when I'm the culprit he's looking for?

'Hey,' he says. 'You're miles away.'

I look up and all I want is to confess that I'm her; the key to Kay's death. Instead I scrabble for something to say. 'Did you know this coast is so overfished they have to import half the seafood?'

He nods. 'I tried to do a story on it once. Not sexy enough, apparently.'

My fingers aren't working properly and I have to use two hands to sip from my glass of sparkling water, my clumsiness made worse by his anecdotes about stories that *did* count as 'sexy' – the criminals he's unmasked, the liars he's exposed.

Our food comes. Misery in my mouth, the smell and taste of it in every bite. I drop my fork. 'What's the trick to finding out the truth?'

He laughs. 'My first editor used to say forget the facts, it's the spaces between them you want to look at. He was a pompous old twat but it wasn't bad advice.'

'What does that even mean, "the spaces between them"?'

He rocks back in his chair and studies me with an intensity that makes me look away. 'Well, take you for instance. This lovely, mysterious girl, all alone in Cassis. She says she's on her gap year, staying here for a few days before going back to London. OK, so if I were looking at the spaces between I'd ask why she picked Cassis when she's got the whole of Europe to explore, and why she came all the way here just for a few days.' He's smiling but his eyes are shrewd, probing.

'I was planning on seeing more of France,' I say quickly, 'but a problem's come up with my foster mother's will.' I look away, dumbfounded by the slickness of my lie. 'That's why I need to get back.'

'Are you abandoning me?'

'Yep. I've got to see her lawyer.'

He reaches for my hand. I tuck it away.

'Shame. I was hoping I could entice you to come with me to Brussels.'

A quick, darting movement in the corner of my eye. I raise my head. To my right, on the far edge of the bay, a fizz of sparks. I watch it drift and die in a plume of smoke that twists grey and ragged against the dark of the sky. 'There's a fire,' I say, craning up from my seat.

Will – glass in hand – turns lazily to look down the hillside. A spurt of flame shoots above the rooftops and lights up the shoreline. I follow the curve of the road leading down to the blaze. A shock of certainty. 'It's David Duncan's boathouse.'

Will is on his feet, tossing his credit card onto the table, calling to the waiter that he'll be back for it tomorrow. 'Phoebe, come on.' He's out the door, running down the cobbles, pushing through the crowds, his phone pressed to his ear, shouting at someone to get his arse in gear and meet him on the jetty. On the quayside, faces lift towards the band of brightness. Will shouts, 'Hey, Steve!' and veers away to join his cameraman. Surprisingly nimble for his size, Steve holds his camera on his shoulder, filming as he runs. We follow the coast road to the turn-off and clamber over the gate, choked by gusts of acrid smoke. Below us the boathouse is a bright ball of flame that floats – disconcertingly – on the water. Confusion. Excitement. A group of drunken teenagers cheers and jostles for a better view as the emergency fireboat speeds around the headland, churning lines of white in the water.

I watch the fire lick along the edge of the doors and run swiftly over the walls, devouring the graffiti. In a few seconds the whole structure is a giant brazier, belching torrents of black smoke into the night. A scream of excitement as the fuel cans explode in a burst of crimson flame. The crowd lurches back, raising their arms to shield their faces as a blazing roof beam smashes onto the deck of *Serenity*.

Will taps notes into his phone and Steve rushes around taking shots from every angle as the firefighters bring the blaze under control. Up on the track, an empty ambulance backs up and speeds away from the sodden mass of scorched wood and twisted metal, while the deflated onlookers drift back to the bars and restaurants. Will – flushed and excited – is interviewing a policeman, who refuses to be drawn by his questions about a link to Kay's suicide – the possibility that the trolls now aiming their venom at David have taken their attacks to the next level. But to me it makes a hideous sort of sense that all this chaos and destruction was sparked by what I did to Kay.

CHAPTER THIRTEEN

I wake up the next morning with an emptiness inside. Then I realise why. Will isn't here. I left him at the waterfront arguing on the phone with his producer and dragged myself, depressed and dead tired, back to Remy's attic. How could I stay when I felt responsible for the carnage we had witnessed? How can I hope to stop the spiral of destruction if I don't know why it started? How can I even think about having a relationship or moving on with my life if I don't know who I am? I take a shower to wash the smell of smoke out of my hair, fetch a coffee from the bar and ring the cuttings agency Roz used for her dossier on Kay. If some obscure magazine mentions something new about Kay's past, I need to know about it. I explain to the woman who answers the phone that I am the daughter and executor of Roz Locklear – only half a lie – and ask if I can transfer her account to my name.

'One moment please.' She taps and tuts. 'Sorry, that account has been closed.'

'Who by?'

'Ms Locklear.'

'When?'

'Let me check.' She makes a hissy little whistling noise. 'Here we are. Nearly three months ago.'

'Oh… right,' I say after a beat of confusion. 'Can I set up one of my own then? I'm looking for anything new on Kay Duncan and the disappearance of Maya Duncan.'

'Hard copies or scans?'

'Both. If that's OK.'

'Fine. We can start that today. Did you want Ms Locklear's file sent on?'

'Oh, no,' I start, then change my mind. 'Actually, yes please.' She takes my details and I hang up, picturing Roz in the final pain-wracked days of her life, too weak to discuss even the most pressing problems to do with the running of Molokodi, struggling to sit up or even speak, and try to square that with her finding the will and the strength to cancel her account with a cuttings agency.

Still bemused, I open my notebook and try to draw up a list of people I can talk to from her past. The page stays blank. She didn't have any family left – at least none she was admitting to, and there's no one at Molokodi who knew her before she moved to Botswana. I switch to Kay. No parents, no sense of any friends or extended family flying out to visit her in France. In fact, the only person she'd spoken about with any warmth was her old bandmate Vicky Bunce. Might Vicky be able to throw some light on a possible mix-up of babies after Kay gave birth?

Finding Vicky is surprisingly easy – she's a hairdresser now and, according to her website, runs a 'premier South London salon'. I send her a friend request and flick through her Facebook photos, stopping at a blurry 'throwback Thursday' snap of her as a teenager all dressed up in ripped leather and thigh-length boots. Had she been on her way to meet Kay?

Heartened by this small victory, I spread out the cuttings, searching for people and places that might link Kay to Roz. But it's hard not to get sidetracked. Up until now I've completely ignored the press speculation about the seven hours between the last sighting of Maya on the CCTV camera at the corner of Stanford Street and Kay's panicked phone call to the police. Now, I'm riveted by every snippet of information, every half-baked theory: the Belgian paedophile who entered the country the day before; the analysis of Kay's speech patterns that said she was lying when she called the police; the two blonde men – never identified – seen in the corner of the last CCTV image of Maya. Why had they never come forward?

I unfold a profile of 'The Man Who Created Lila Mendez'. There in the middle of the page are Kay and David helping Maya to cut her birthday cake – the scene I'd thought I'd seen from the inside looking out. Unlike the other cuttings, this isn't a photocopy but an original centre-spread, ripped from a gossip magazine that's been folded for so long the creases have scored white lines across the photos. I study Maya's face. The eyes, the chin, the tight little mouth I'd thought were mine. I take in Kay's extravagant hair spilling across her face, her eyes lowered as if weighed down by the heavy sweeps of black eyeliner, her wistful lips slicked crimson, the nugget of amber on her finger, David's steady gaze, the rigid icing on the shop-bought cake, the candle glow reflected in the knife blade.

Unease snakes up my arms. Four flames. *Four* pink candles. Maya Duncan's *fourth* birthday. I scramble to read the date printed along the bottom of the page. Dizzy, I throw out a hand to steady myself against the wall. Maya Duncan went missing when she was five. This feature was printed fourteen months before her disappearance. *Calm down!* The agency must have sent Roz a backdated article from their archive. I smooth the pages flat and check front and back for an agency label. There isn't one. Not even a staple mark. I sift on through the cuttings, checking the dates, breathing faster as I turn up three more articles from before the abduction. One's a gossip piece with a photo of Kay and David all dressed up at a charity fundraiser, the second is headlined *Music Mogul's Wife in Overdose Scare*, the third is the much-used shot of Kay looking frail and shabby in her trademark shades and an oversized man's coat leaving rehab, all of them labelled by the agency. My brain rebels, refusing to accept what this means. But there is no other explanation. Over a year before Maya's abduction and six months before she rented the flat in Stanford Street, Roz had been stalking Kay, gathering cuttings about her before she'd even left Malawi.

'Roz!' I call out her name the way I did as a kid when I woke to the gauzy touch of a ghost, but she's not here to switch on the light, snatch the mosquito netting from my face and hush away my fears. I have to tell David. However much he loathes me he's the only person left alive who can help me find out why. I tear a page from my notebook and try to find words to break through his pain, a cry for help I can push into his hand or under his door. Reluctantly, I slip the note into my bag and get a cab to the Villa Rosa. I can't stomach the thought of knocking on that front door and having David slam it in my face so I go around to the back of the house. A small red Citroen sits on the gravel. A woman's voice calls out, sharp and commanding. I take a swig from my water bottle and inch along the line of trees until I can see into the courtyard. The door of the outhouse hangs open and a scrawny figure in a short black dress is leaning inside shouting orders in English. 'For God's sake, be careful with that wine.'

I wince and pull back as a man in shorts comes out carrying a crate of David's precious Chateau Margaux and dumps it on the ground. Gravel crunches beneath my trainer. The woman snaps round and shouts, '*Qui est la?*'

I step from the trees and call out. 'I've got a letter for David Duncan. Is he here?'

Blonde with a leathery tan, she flicks me away with heavily ringed fingers.

'Get off this property. You people make me sick.'

'I'm… not a journalist.'

'I don't care who you are. You're trespassing. Go away.'

'It's to say I'm sorry about his wife.' I wave the envelope. 'Can I leave it in the house?'

'For God's sake. You people will try anything.'

I pull out my phone and walk towards her, holding up the picture I took of Kay with David and me in Toulon, the one I haven't had the heart to look at since the DNA result came through. 'I knew her. I visited her and David a couple of weeks ago.'

She takes the phone, studies the photo carefully, then gives it back and fingers the white enamel necklace at her throat. 'He's not here. He's in Marseille.'

'Any idea when he'll be back?'

She sighs heavily. 'He's not coming back. He's gone to a hotel and left me to clear the house. Not something I'd usually do for a client, but under the circumstances…'

'Are you the owner?'

'Sadly not. It belongs to an Italian couple who never get time to use it.' She offers me her hand. 'Shelley Morton. And you are?'

'Phoebe. Kay… was an old friend of my mother's.' The lie feels claggy on my tongue.

An eagerness appears in her eye, a kind of coy excitement. 'Poor woman. I've only just found out who she was.'

I slip the phone back into my pocket. 'My mother was really shocked when she heard what happened.'

'She's not the only one.' She's about to say more when a van turns into the courtyard and pulls up in front of the outhouse. 'Oh, Mick, you're a life saver,' she trills, hurrying over to greet the driver. 'I couldn't think who else to call.'

A muscular man with the craggy skin of a dedicated smoker jumps onto the gravel. 'No problem. I've got a buyer for the generator and the freezer if you're still selling.'

'The freezer's gone.' Shelley says. 'David must have sold it, but tell them they're welcome to the generator. Could you take over on the wine? He wants it all out of the coolers and crated up.'

The man moves past me and I turn back to Shelley. 'Did you see much of Kay when she was here?'

'Almost nothing.'

'But when you did, how did she seem?'

'Quiet, polite, withdrawn.'

'Depressed?'

'I wouldn't have said so, though of course now I keep thinking I should have persuaded her to stick with the other place. It can't have been good for her living up here all on her own.'

'Other place?'

'An artist's studio I found for her right on the quayside. It was all arranged. Fantastic light, decent-sized living accommodation and, considering the location, a very reasonable rent.'

'What happened?'

'I don't know. It was all a bit strange. A few days before she was due to move in she emailed me saying she'd seen the Villa Rosa on my website and decided that something away from the crowds would suit her better.'

I have a flash of Kay thinking she was coping with the aftermath of the last hoaxer, believing she was tough enough to face the eyes of a small town, then tumbling back into the depression that David had described. Guilt pricks at my edges.

'I know David was worried about her being so cut off,' I say.

'Poor man, he's falling apart. I can't get him out of the lease for this place. But he doesn't care about the money.' She flings out her hands. 'He just wants rid of everything that reminds him of what happened. Once the funeral's over he says he never wants to set foot in France again.'

'When is it?'

'As soon as they've done the autopsy. And if I know our town council they'll be rushing that through as fast as they can. Suicides play havoc with the tourist trade.'

'Will the funeral be held in that little church on the square?'

'Oh no, far too public. David's asked me to arrange a private cremation in Marseille. He says his French isn't good enough to deal with the bureaucracy. Frankly, on top of disposing all of Kay's things and sorting out the insurance for the boathouse, it's a hassle I could do without.'

'Can you tell me which hotel he's in?'

'Sorry. He wants to be left alone.'

'Alright but… would you give him this?'

She takes my letter, raises a languid hand – half goodbye, half dismissal – and goes back inside the house. I retreat across the courtyard feeling burned-out and hollow, as if the hot-scented wind gusting up through the terraces could blow me apart. The doors of the lean-to are open, a glint of chrome and baby blue flash a memory of Kay at the wheel, her head flung back, a smile on her sun-kissed face. In a heartbeat I'm running back to the house. 'Shelley!'

She comes out onto the back step, her painted eyebrows rising as high as her Botoxed brow will allow.

'Kay's car. Are you selling that too?'

'Oh God, I'd forgotten about the bloody car.'

'Is it for sale?'

'Yes, the whole lot's got to go. Why?' – an eager smile – 'Do you want to buy it? You can have it dirt cheap if you take it off my hands.'

'Yes. I… I want to drive back to London.' What am I doing? This is madness. I've got a flight booked for tomorrow and I've never driven on the right in my life.

She names a paltry price and smiles again when I accept. 'I don't suppose you're interested in the wine coolers or the generator? All top quality and less than two years old?'

'Sorry.'

I follow her back to the house. The kitchen is stark, stripped, empty of Kay. Her books and magazines, even the smell of her perfume, have gone.

'How long will the paperwork take? I'd like to leave first thing tomorrow.'

'No problem. I'll sort it out this afternoon. Where are you staying?'

'The Café du Port.'

She lets out a sigh. 'Alright. I'll get the car to you tonight and leave the key with Remy.'

I take down the details for the bank transfer, waiting all the while for Roz to protest in my ear at the ridiculousness of this purchase. She doesn't say a word.

That night, as Will packs for Brussels, I tell him I saw the Healey advertised in town and bought it on a whim before I discovered who it had belonged to. A beat of surprise, then he pulls me close and says, 'Better you than some ghoul collecting memorabilia.'

If only he knew.

Remy kisses me on both cheeks in that odd French way that feels so detached yet so intimate – Roz was never one for kissing strangers. I throw my bag in the back of the Healey and run my hands around the wheel. The car's interior is neat and compact – all piped leather and walnut wood – nothing like the ripped vinyl and chipped plastic of Roz's rattletrap jeeps. I study the knobs and switches, kick off my shoes, try my bare feet on the pedals, close my eyes and see Kay laughing as she pushes a hand through her hair, a wink of sunlight bouncing off her ring. I spring my eyelids apart and rummage in the glovebox, pull out a satnav, a lipstick, a pair of big square-framed sunglasses and a leaky tube of ointment, which leaves a smell of tar on my fingers. I wipe the stickiness from my hands, pull the top off the lipstick and look in the mirror as I run the dome of crimson across my lips and put on the glasses. I shove everything back, stick the satnav to the windscreen with a lick of spit and, with a rush of trepidation, punch in the Fulham address. I slip into first, flick on the windscreen wipers instead of the indicator and in a fluster flick again, doubling their speed before I manage to turn them off. I tell myself to settle down. I try the other lever, get it right this time and hit the accelerator. The car leaps and stalls. I take a breath. Only 1,350 kilometres to go.

CHAPTER FOURTEEN

It's nearly eleven o'clock the following evening when I get to Fulham. I realise with a pang that it's not even two weeks since I arrived in Cassis. I park the car and approach the house, hoping to be greeted by the cheery lights of new neighbours in the downstairs flat but the 'To Let' board is still up and the whole building is in darkness. With a jaw that aches from grinding my teeth and a heart that feels like lead I drag myself up the stairs and slip my key into the door of my 'three-bedroom Victorian duplex', which the property websites tell me is worth an astonishing amount of money. Bought by Roz's parents in the seventies, it's been rented out for years and the furniture has boiled down to a lumpy sofa, a dining table with bulbous legs, six chairs with cracked leather seats, a set of mahogany bookshelves and three beds: one double, one single and one somewhere in between, which the moist-lipped elderly agent – leaning in a little too close – described as 'a gentleman's occasional'. Exhausted, I drop my bags on the stained carpet and curl up fully dressed on the sofa, cradling one of the cracked cups from the kitchen and a bottle of wine I picked up from a garage on the way.

I blink into daylight, heave myself off the sofa and throw open the window, grateful for the dullness of the sky and the backwash of diesel from the passing lorries. No heart-crushing reminders of the Côte d'Azur, no hints of the dusty dry of Molokodi. I turn back and look around the room, overwhelmed by the ugliness of the striped wallpaper and the green velvet curtains, faded to grimy yellow along the folds. This is my home now, the only docking point in my newly untethered existence. I close my eyes, pierced by the memory of Kay making me a mood board in the light-filled kitchen of the Villa Rosa. The sudden feeling of connection as she glanced up from her laptop to gauge my reaction to a selection of wall tiles, the brush of her hand that sent a quiver up my arm. The sound of David's voice, '*You're not on your own anymore. You've got us.*'

Loss breaks in jagged waves. I wander around the flat banging open drawers and musty cupboards, making a mental list of necessities – teaspoons, sink plugs, vodka. I try the balcony doors. The lock is loose but the frames are so rotten I'm scared to open them in case they fall apart. My phone beeps. It's a selfie of Will sitting all alone in a swanky hotel bedroom.

Why are you there when you could be here? xx

Because I did something terrible, Will, and I don't know who I am. I hide the truth behind a glum face and a shiny pink heart emoji, retrieve the half-full bottle of wine from beneath the sofa and gaze too long at the liquid inside before I throw it down, grab my phone and search for a local builder. I don't have a clue about dealing with workmen or decorating houses but seeing as there's no one to help me I'm going to have to learn.

I'm not sure whether to be pleased or alarmed when the builder I pick at random says he can come round in a couple of hours; time I spend going over my list of questions for former Doxette Vicky Bunce and wading through the mail piled up in the hall. Correspondence about shares, pension plans and endowment policies; all the bureaucracy of Roz's life rendered pointless by her death, all the wealth she left me, tainted by her lies. I slit open final demands for rates, house insurance and boiler cover; arrears explained by the letter from her bank telling me that they've cancelled all 'the deceased's' direct debits and standing orders. Glad of the distraction I log into her account and start listing the payments so I can set up accounts in my own name. The start of my new, lonely life. My eyes sting when I find a donation of £100 a month to cancer research. Tears drop onto the keyboard when I see she set it up two years before she told me she was ill. I work on down the list and stop on a standing order of a thousand pounds paid out every three months to Western Union. Curiosity turns to something darker when I see she cancelled it the same day she cancelled her account with the cuttings agency. Dying Roz had been even busier than I'd thought.

The bank informs me that the payments were set up before their system was digitised, so I'll have to apply in writing if I want more details. A Scot at Western Union, who finds my accent as troublesome as I do his, says the payee is untraceable, since the money was arranged to be paid out on presentation of a password. I hang up, shaken by a new and disturbing possibility.

Was someone blackmailing you, Roz?

Someone who knows who I am?

Was it my mother?

The buzz of the doorbell startles me back. The builder, who introduces himself as Tomas, is a big man, middle-aged and handsome in his way with cropped grey hair and silver half glasses hanging reassuringly from a chain around his neck. His sidekick, Lukas, is young and wide-shouldered with pale brown hair that flips down over his eyes. I traipse after them as they go from room to room shaking pipes, rolling their eyes and muttering to each other. I like them. I like their bulk, their throaty eastern European accents, their earthy sense of practicality and the way they fill the flat with life.

'Where is fuse box?' Tomas asks as he opens the airing cupboard.

'I've no idea,' I say, a stranger in my home as well as my skin.

'So, new kitchen, new bathroom upstairs, new toilet downstairs, new boiler, new electrics and paint all walls and woodwork – yes?' he says when he's finished his tour.

'Yes,' I say. 'When can you start?'

He glances at Lukas. 'Maybe tomorrow. We will fit you around our other job. I will send you quotation.'

'Fine,' I say.

'We need key,' Tomas says. 'You have spare key?'

I hand it over, meek and obedient.

The emptiness when they've gone leaves me gasping.

The air is sticky the next morning, threatening rain, and I drive with the roof closed, the black vinyl stretched taut as a bat's wing over the metal struts. Even so, every time another driver looks my way or a biker draws parallel at traffic lights and turns his visored head, I feel watched and exposed. I pull on Kay's dark glasses, shake my hair forward and tell myself it's the car. It's a classic; a curiosity. Of course it attracts attention.

I make for Stanford Street and park near the corner where Maya was last caught on CCTV, mentally squaring up the grainy image of that little girl in her oversized sou'wester against the edge of the railings before I walk down to the Duncans' white-pillared house. It's easy to spot; it's the only one protected by a high stucco wall. I stand on the opposite pavement and crane my neck to see through the barred metal gate. Despite the carefully tended window boxes and neatly clipped bay trees on either side of the door, a desolation has descended on the place, its lifelessness heightened by the drawn curtains, the empty driveway and the browning bunch of cellophane-wrapped flowers hanging from the gate. Two middle-aged women – cagouls, flat shoes, backpacks – stop to raise their phones and snap a selfie, their perky day-tripper smiles carefully adjusted to 'sombre'.

'*There are always tourists taking photos outside number fifteen,*' *the Duncan's long-time neighbour, Emma Peat, says wearily. 'They find some ghastly attraction in being pictured at the spot where a little girl was abducted. But of course Kay refuses to move out, just in case Maya ever manages to find her way home.*'

I turn away and muster the courage to look up at the red-brick mansion block behind me. Unless Roz lied about that too, one of these sets of windows belongs to the flat she rented the year Maya was abducted. A man in a linen suit pushes out through the swing doors. I catch a glimpse of polished brass, dark wood and crimson carpet. Do I remember a glow of warmth and safety, a stepping in from the wet, or is it merely hope playing tricks with my head? I make my way back to the car unable to shake the sense that someone is watching me, though no furtive figure scurries into a side street, sinks behind a newspaper or drops low in the seat of their car as I unlock the Healey. I tap the postcode of Vicky Bunce's salon into the satnav and head towards Streatham. As London flashes past, its tower blocks and overpasses, chicken shops and ice cream vans, I pray that Kay's former bandmate will be able to give me at least some of the answers I crave.

CHAPTER FIFTEEN

Vicky Bunce scrapes shellacked fingernails up my neck and tugs them through my hair. 'Oh, dear God, when did you last get it cut?'

'It's been a while.'

'You've not been using conditioner, have you?'

I admit, suitably penitent, that I may have been a little slack in that department.

'So what are we doing today?' She clamps my head between her palms and jerks my face to the gilded mirror, forcing me to look at myself, which right now is a form of torture. I stare at the creature in front of me. I don't know who she is, this girl who picks through a catalogue of hedged bets and half-truths every time she opens her mouth. Today she's Phoebe Jones, Kay's cousin from Botswana trying to make sense of Kay's life – and her death – for elderly relatives back home – at least that's what I told Vicky when I rang to make the appointment. Tomorrow – who knows? Booking a haircut had been a way to put Vicky at ease while I got her talking about Kay, but now I'm here all I want to do is slough off Phoebe Locklear, blank out Maya Duncan and lose myself in this glittery world of flock wallpaper, smoky-eyed portraits in fancy frames and purple towels – rolled and stacked like ancient scrolls in diamond-shaped racks.

'Something radical,' I say.

She separates a hank and inspects the ends. 'For starters you could do with some intensive conditioning, then I'll give it some shape. Show off those lovely eyes.'

Roz appears in the mirror, a look of amused scorn on her face. A scowl sends her packing.

'What you need is one of our deep hydration treatments. It'll smooth out the frizz and give you a deep shine that will last for weeks. If you want I've got a great deal going on a facial and makeover package. I promise you, you won't know yourself when I've finished.'

'Great,' I say, uncertainly. A whole new look for the new, nameless me.

My eyes lift from my own reflection to settle on Vicky's. The skinny teenager pictured in her Facebook album has fleshed out into a curvy upgrade of womanhood – precision enhanced breasts, lashes, lips and hair, chunky gold at her ears and throat, every inch of skin sprayed to a tawny gloss. The edges of her faded Doxettes tattoo – just visible beneath the cap sleeve of her tightly fitting top – the only reminder of her raunchy younger self.

'Thanks for fitting me in at such short notice,' I say.

'My other stylist is off today so you were lucky I had a cancellation.' She slides her hands into my hair and flounces it into the kind of wild bush that made me want to weep as a kid. 'Did you have any trouble finding the salon?'

'Not really. Though it's going to take me awhile to get used to driving in London.'

'Where did you say you're from?'

'Botswana.'

She's looking at me in the mirror, separating out strands of my hair as if she's working out how to cut it, but I can tell it's me she's sussing out. 'I'm not even sure where that is,' she says.

'Squashed between Zimbabwe and South Africa.'

'Oh, right. What brought you to the UK?'

'My mum died.'

She softens a little. 'I'm sorry.'

'The family thought it would do me good to get away for a while. So I came to London.' My throat grows dry, as if I've swallowed a puff of dust. 'Then I took a trip to France and, like I said on the phone, while I was there I dropped in on Kay and ended up staying at her villa for a couple of days.'

'When was this?'

'A couple of weeks ago.' I feel my face burn. 'Just before she died.'

Vicky presses her hand to her mouth. 'How did she seem?'

'Fine. That's why it was such a shock when—'

She cuts me off, her eyes narrowing. 'She never mentioned she had relatives in Africa.'

I say quickly, 'Our families lost touch a while back. That's why they asked me to find out everything I can about her. They want to get a sense of the woman behind all those horrible headlines.'

She holds my gaze. 'How do I know this isn't a crock of lies?'

I fight the urge to come clean and tell her what I did and why I'm here. But she'd hate me. Nearly as much as I hate myself. So I say nothing and instead show her the photo I took of the three of us in Toulon. She takes my phone. I hold my breath like an escaped POW presenting stolen papers at a checkpoint while she strokes the screen to enlarge the shot. After a couple of beats she walks away and stands by the window, gazing down at the screen. I wait for her to find her way back.

'You wouldn't believe the number of people I get in here pretending they want a haircut when what they're really after is dirt on Kay.'

'When did you last speak to her?'

'About eighteen months ago. She'd sent me one of her paintings – totally out of the blue – and I called her to tell her how much I loved it.'

I look up at her, surprised and a little confused. From the way Kay had talked I'd had no idea that she and Vicky had stayed so close.

'To be honest, I couldn't stomach the miserable stuff she used to do, all sludgy browns and blacks. Horrible. But this one was gorgeous. She said she was done with the past and that experimenting with colour was all part of moving on. No more drugs. No more rehab.' She bites down on her lower lip, unable to stop it quivering.

Her grief is electric. Her need to make sense of Kay's death as overwhelming as my own. My eyes smart. Horrified by my sudden loss of control I squeeze them shut but the tears seep through.

Vicky sniffs hard and glances at me in the mirror. 'Hey, are you OK?'

'Sorry,' I say, helplessly. 'I know I'd only just met Kay but the shock of her killing herself so soon after losing my mum… it's really got to me.' The detail might be shaky but the emotion is real and the sobs come in waves.

'Tell me about it,' she says, softly. 'I lost my gran last year and I honestly thought I was getting over it. But Kay dying has ripped off the scab and brought it all back like it was yesterday.' She passes me a tissue and dabs her own eyes with another and even though I'm a fraud, grieving for a woman who lied to me and the dashed dream of a mother who wasn't mine, sharing our pain brings me the first glimmer of comfort I've felt in days. After a minute, she blows her nose. 'Honestly, what are we like?'

'This must be hard for you,' I say. 'I totally understand if you'd rather not talk about Kay.'

Caught between sniffs, she tries for a smile. 'It's alright. I've been bottling it up for so long it'll do me good to talk to someone who actually cared about her. Believe you me, they're few and far between.' She bins the tissue and stares down at the photo on my phone. 'Look at her, all covered up in that stupid hat and shades. Imagine having to hide your face every time you went out in case you got spat at by a stranger. Still, at least she's smiling.' She hands back my phone. 'Would you mind sending me that photo?'

My fingers freeze. Vicky sees me hesitate and seems pleased that I'm wary. 'Don't worry. It's just for me. I'd never let the world get its hands on a new photo of Kay.'

Still reluctant, I send the photo. How can I refuse?

'Thanks,' she says, getting teary again. 'It's no wonder she was so up and down. Every time she managed to scrape herself together some bastard would throw dog muck over her fence or print a load of lies in the papers.' She lifts my hair and drapes a towel around my shoulders. 'They're saying that's probably what happened this time. Some bullshit from out of the blue pushing her over the edge. For all his faults, David always did his best to protect her from that kind of stuff, but there's only so much he could do.'

'I heard his lawyers tried to get those horrible photos of her body taken down, but they're still out there.'

'What photos?'

'Didn't you see them? The kid who found her took them.'

'That's awful,' she murmurs, shaking her head in disgust.

She leads me over to the sink. I wait until I'm settled in the chair, head thrown back, throat exposed, warm water dousing my head. 'It's great that you stayed friends all this time. Did you see much of her after the band split?'

'On and off. She'd either be bombarding me with drunken texts – she'd broken up with David, she was moving in with him, she hated him, they were off to Hawaii to get married – or I'd hear nothing for months. Water not too hot for you?'

'It's fine.'

'Then I got married and moved up north and she went from sleeping in a squat to living the high life in London. David's acts in and out of the house the whole time, drugs, drink, parties, rehab. I'd try to catch up with her whenever I visited my mum and dad, but she wasn't easy to pin down.'

'What about when Maya went missing?'

'I rushed down to see her as soon as I heard. Why the hell the police forced her to make that car crash of a press appeal I'll never know. She was heavily sedated, but of course the papers made out she was stoned. I offered to stay on and look after her but she was in such a state David got in a professional nurse. After that it was a spiral of depression, drugs and rehab that went on for years. Sometimes she'd be alright for a few weeks or months but the pain was always there. That's why I was so amazed the last time I spoke to her. She was like a different person. Calm and happy, telling me about going to France to concentrate on her art. She said she'd get me and my son, Danny, over for a holiday as soon as she'd settled in. He was really excited about it.' The squirt, squirt of the pump action dispenser stops abruptly with her sigh. 'But once she got there she stopped answering my calls, the texts petered out, the holiday never happened and I never spoke to her again. And now I can't even go to the funeral.'

'Why not?'

'David's keeping it private. Given the way the press has been trashing her for the last fifteen years I suppose I can't blame him. And to give him his due, he did send me his private number so he could put his lawyers onto it if I got any hassle from the media.' The pump starts up again. 'Do you know, that's how I found out Maya had gone missing? A pair of reporters knocking at my door less than an hour after the police got the call. Offering me money, asking what Kay was really like. *Tell us about the drugs. Do you think she killed Maya?* Bloody cheek. I told them to take a hike.' Her fingers dig into my scalp.

'Chrissie Miller didn't seem to have any qualms about telling them exactly what they wanted to hear.'

'I know. And it's no excuse, but she was still bitter about Kay and David.'

'After all that time? That's pathetic.'

'Yes, but for Chrissie it wasn't just about Kay getting a solo deal and breaking up the band.' She pauses, as if she's not sure how the old folks back in Botswana are going to take this. 'It was Kay's relationship with David. She saw it as a personal betrayal.'

'Was she... in love with Kay?'

'I don't know about love; they were both screwing pretty much anyone who came their way. But neither of them had family. Kay had run away from home and Chrissie had been in care for years, so till David came along they'd sort of looked out for each other, shared each other's secrets, worn each other's clothes – Kay and Chrissie against the world.'

'What about you?'

She laughs. 'I went through my fair share of drugs and boys but girls never did it for me.'

'What happened to Chrissie?'

'She tried going solo for a while, got a small part in a West End musical that closed after a couple of months, then there was some kind of trouble; cheques, credit cards – I don't know the ins and outs but she got off with probation. She's a cruise ship entertainer now, a bit of cabaret, a bit of stand-up. Sounds glamorous but I wouldn't fancy it.'

'She got a partner?'

'Chrissie?' Vicky snorts. 'There's someone new every time I see her.'

'Kids?' I glance up into her immaculately made-up eyes.

'She's not the motherly type.'

'Like that's ever stopped anyone.'

'True, and she wasn't always as careful as she should have been, but she made damn sure she never ended up pushing a pram.'

I close my eyes, feel the pulse in my neck. 'What do you mean?'

'She'd had two abortions before I even met her.'

'She never... gave a kid up for adoption?'

'No way. Too worried about her figure to ever go through with a pregnancy.'

I stay quiet for a moment, taking that in. 'Why had she been in care?'

'Her mother was au pairing in some posh house in Knights-
bridge and got pregnant by her boss. He refused to admit it was
his so she dumped the baby and buggered off back to Germany.'

'How do you know?'

'Chrissie tracked her down as soon as she turned eighteen. Kay
and I were with her when she made the call. It was heart-breaking.
Her mother had a new family and didn't want to know. To be
honest, I think that's what made Chrissie the way she is. She even
stopped spelling her name the German way because she hated
being reminded of her mum.'

I glance away to the window. A passing shopper manoeuvres
a buggy over the kerb, another grips the hand of a stumbling
toddler. The bond between mother and child – so primal, so
precious, until it snaps.

'Are the two of you still close?'

She laughs. 'To be honest I'm probably the only friend she's got
left. All that pent-up resentment pisses people off. So I'm the one
she turns to when things go wrong and as soon as she gets back
to the UK she's usually straight down here to get her hair done;
blonde, auburn, pink, black, highlights, extensions. You name
it. She'll try it. A different look every time. But it's been a while.'

'Why's that?'

'I don't know.' The water keeps running but her hands grow
still. 'Even after everything that happened I thought she'd get in
touch as soon as she heard about Kay. I messaged her straight away
but she never got back to me.' The taps go off and she wrings the
excess water from my hair. 'Still, the minute she needs me I'm
sure she'll come running.'

'Do you think she'd speak to me?'

'She hasn't seen Kay for years.'

'I meant about the past.' I keep my tone breezy, almost
throwaway. 'You know, tell me all those teenage secrets she and
Kay used to share.'

She shrugs. 'You could try. She's usually back for a few weeks over the summer.'

'Could you give me her number?'

'I'm not sure. She might not—'

'Could *you* call her then, and ask her to call me? Please, Vicky. She can always say no.'

With a little sigh, she wipes her hands and takes out her phone. She dials, listens and holds the speaker to my ear. A fizz of frustration as a recorded voice declares that the number is 'temporarily unavailable'.

'She must still be abroad,' Vicky says.

'Could you keep trying her over the next week or so?' I pull a wheedling face. 'I'd *really, really* like to talk to her.'

'Oh, for heaven's sake,' she says, half laughing, half exasperated. 'Here. Do it yourself.' She pings a contact card onto my phone. 'But don't blame me if she tells you to get lost.'

I smile, grateful, and glance down at Chrissie's details. Unsure if Vicky realises she sent me her address as well as her number, I press save and quickly close the screen. 'If you hear from her can you ask her to call me anyway?'

'I wouldn't hold your breath.' She flips me forward, wraps a thick towel turban-style around my head and leads me back to the mirror. 'She's often away for months at a time. Makes a fortune renting out her flat.'

I watch her as she sets to with a comb, working some kind of serum through my hair. 'So how's life treated you since the band split up?' I say.

'Oh, you know. Me and my ex moved back to London five years ago, he found someone younger, we got divorced...'

I look up at her and frown sympathy.

'It's fine. My mum and dad were brilliant and helped me buy this place. Salon downstairs, decent-sized maisonette upstairs. What more could a girl want?' Her upbeat smile falters. 'My only regret is that I never had more kids. My Danny's the best thing that ever happened to me but I had a bit of trouble getting pregnant and at one stage I thought I might never be a mother.'

I look down at my hands. 'How old is he?'

'Fifteen.' She shows me a holiday snap of a gangly, freckled boy with blonde hair and flappy elbows. 'He took the divorce pretty hard but we've worked it out so he stays with me in the week and goes to his dad at weekends and for half the holidays. To be honest we're much closer now that it's just the two of us, more like best mates than mother and son.'

'Is he musical?'

She smiles. 'You could call it that – he plays the drums.'

'What about you? Are you still singing?'

'A bit of karaoke down the pub.' Her giggle, as she bends across me, makes her golden cleavage wobble. 'It's a laugh. You should come along one night.'

The offer warms me and I realise how much I like her. Another life flickers through my mind. A positive DNA test, Kay reunited with Vicky, me laughing and cheering as they down their drinks and get up on stage to perform. Outside, the storm breaks, fat raindrops coming at the window from a suddenly leaden sky. I take a breath and nudge the conversation back to the early days of the band.

'What was Kay's squat like?' I say.

She shrugs. 'Pretty much like any other house share. Rows over whose turn it was to get toilet paper and do the washing-up. I don't know why the media made such a big deal about it.'

'Did you ever live there?'

'I liked my home comforts too much, but Chrissie used to stay there on and off.'

'And that's where she was living when Maya was born?'

'That's right. She was just a few months old when I first met Kay. Honestly, she was the best behaved baby. Hardly ever cried.'

She dips her head. 'Poor little mite. I still lie awake at night thinking about her.'

I clasp my hands tight to stop them shaking and for a moment neither of us speak. Then I just go for it. 'Were there any other babies in that house?'

'Babies? God no.'

'Anyone else who got pregnant?'

'Not that I know of. Why?'

'I just wondered.' Disappointed, I change tack. 'How did Kay feel about Maya being taken into care?'

'She was devastated. She adored that kid. But she knew she was better off in care till she got herself sorted out.'

My throat closes up and I have to make myself breathe. 'How was she when she got Maya back?'

'Happy, scared, angry. Things were never simple with Kay.'

'And she never doubted that…'

Vicky eyes me steadily, head tipped to one side. 'That what?'

'That they gave her back the right baby?'

'*Are you joking?*'

'It was just' – I look away from her incredulous face to voice the lie – 'something my aunt said…'

'Why would anyone even *think* something like that?'

'She just wondered if that could be why Kay had problems with… mothering Maya.'

'No way! It's not like Maya was a newborn; she was a toddler when Kay got her back. A proper little person.'

'If Kay hadn't seen her for over a year she might not—'

'She *did* see her. Two hours every Saturday, supervised by a woman from social services. Kay said they were the worst and the best moments of her week.'

A mix-up in foster care – the solution I'd been counting on – shrivels and dies. It takes a few moments before I can speak.

'Did Kay ever tell you who Maya's father was?'

Vicky gives a harsh little grunt. 'She couldn't even remember sleeping with him, let alone who he was.' She turns away. I'm worried I've pushed her too far but she's taking a photo from the little drawer in the table under the mirror. She drops it into my lap. 'I dug it out after you rang. Us in all our deluded glory. We thought we were going to be bigger than the Spice Girls. As it was, we never even got to play a proper venue. You can keep it if you want. I've got loads.'

It's a signed photo of the Doxettes screaming out a song – a whirl of light, flesh and metal-studded leather. Vicky a little taller, a little curvier; the other two, angrier and slighter – identical dyed black hair, identical bright-red lips, identical black slashes around their eyes. I want to skip through time and be there in that crowded pub – drunk, stoned, punching at the sky. Determined not to start crying again, I say, 'That's got to be you in the boots.'

'Yep.'

'So which is which out of the other two?'

She leans over my shoulder and points a pink fingernail. 'That's Chrissie on guitar and that's Kay at the end.'

'How did anyone tell them apart?'

She laughs. 'Peas in a pod, my dad used to call them. But Kay was always the wild one, up for anything, didn't give a damn.' A sad pull to her shiny lips. 'It's funny, all that stuff people come out with when someone dies young – *she was so full of life, I can't believe she's gone* – I used to think it was crap. But that's exactly what Kay was, a fiery ball of anger and energy.'

I stare hard at a point above Vicky's head – a mismatched join in the black rose wallpaper – till my hand steadies enough to thumb through the pictures on my phone and hold up a shot of Roz. 'My aunt thought I should try and speak to this woman while I was here – Roz Locklear?' I say the name with a tentative upswing. 'She thinks she and Kay might have been close at some point.' I shiver at the crassness of the lie. 'Did you ever come across her?'

Vicky studies the image. 'Who is she? Some kind of counsellor?'

'I don't know. It was just… a name that came up.'

She shakes her head. 'Sorry, I don't remember the name or the face.'

'If you think of anyone else who knew Kay, would you let me know?'

'Sure.' She calls over her shoulder to the sullen teenager picking her nails by the till, 'Marilyn, can you bring Phoebe a coffee and some magazines' – and then to me as she adjusts the towel around my shoulders – 'You relax with that on for twenty minutes and I'll get the treatment room ready for your facial.'

Lulled by whale song and cocooned in a fleecy white towel, I stare up at the ceiling while Vicky homes in on my eyebrows with a pair of tweezers. 'Was David good to Kay?' I say.

'He wanted to fix her.'

'How did she feel about him?'

'To be honest, I've no idea. She was messed up when it came to men. Who wouldn't have been with a father like hers?' Her voice is uneasy. 'Sorry, was he your uncle or something?'

'God no. I'm related… on her mother's side,' I say hurriedly. 'I know he was religious.'

'He was a bully who liked hurting people.' Her voice drops, her cheeks throb crimson. 'Hypocritical old bastard. He should have gone to prison for what he did to Kay.'

'Did he… hit her?'

'And the rest.'

A prickle of revulsion, like I've tripped over a stone and kicked loose a slither of black things. 'What do you mean?'

'Oh God.' She stops plucking and turns up the volume on the speaker. 'I couldn't say anything out there, not with Marilyn around.' Pan pipes chime in with the whale song, dreamy ethereal notes that jar with the anger in her voice. 'He used to drag her down to the cellar, strip her naked and beat her. And you want to know the best part? He used to yell at her while he was doing it, telling her it was the only way to save her from eternal damnation. It started the day he found an invitation to a make-up party in her school bag. She was nine years old.'

Her words grab my guts and twist them tight. Are these the memories Kay spent her whole life trying to obliterate with drugs? The pain she'd been struggling to numb?

'It's like life had it in for her right from the start.' Vicky clams up for a few seconds, holding back the tears, and I lie there gazing through the grimy window she's opened into Kay's past. I take a long breath.

'You... don't think it was her father who got her pregnant?' I say.

'I asked her once. But she said it was the beatings he got off on – making her suffer.'

'Why didn't her mother stop him?'

'Too frightened. He was beating her too. All in the name of God.'

A flash image of the mousey little woman in Kay's album, so insubstantial she looks ready to fade away.

'Someone must have realised what was going on, a neighbour, a teacher?'

'Of course they didn't. People see what they want to see and he came across as a normal, respectable man; did his job, paid his bills, mowed his lawn, went to church and made sure he never left any marks where it showed.'

A jarring, off-centre memory of Kay talking as if this monster had been redeemable, as if the way he'd treated her had been no big deal.

'Right at the end I went to see him... I went through the motions of asking him to forgive the sins of my misspent youth. It meant he died happy.'

If that's what years of therapy does for you I'd rather keep hold of the anger.

'You know she made her peace with him at the end,' I say.

'Bollocks she did.'

'I promise you.'

'Who told you that?'

'She did. David went with her. He said it gave her some kind of "closure".'

'What about the court case?'

The whale song rises to a mournful moan, a desultory prayer bell dings a response. 'What court case?'

'I'd been telling her for years she should prosecute the old bastard before it was too late, and the last time I spoke to her she said she'd been talking to a support group about going to the police. She asked me if I'd be willing to testify that she'd told me about the abuse twenty years ago. Of course I said I'd do anything I could to help.' She stares down at me. 'Why would she change her mind?'

'I don't know, Vicky,' I say, and despite the warmth of the room a chill ripples through me.

CHAPTER SIXTEEN

Vicky's assistant goes to fetch my jacket while Vicky sips a coffee and takes a moment to relax on one of the padded velvet chairs in the waiting area. She looks up from her phone. 'I'll let you know if I think of anyone else you can talk to, and don't worry about that lovely photo you sent me. It's safe, I promise.' She glances down at her screen, and I see she's made the mistake of googling the images of Kay's body. 'It helps to block out these horrific ones. I can't believe that kid took so many. He even turned her over – look. What on earth was he thinking?'

'I'd rather not look at them, Vicky. And you shouldn't either. Focus on the one of her smiling.' I blush as I say this, knowing that even that snatched moment of happiness had been based on a lie.

She swipes her phone and zooms in, gazing intently at the screen.

Marylin comes back with my jacket. I pay with my card and take a last look at my smooth, glossy hair in the mirror. 'Thanks for the chat, Vicky. It was so lovely to meet you and you've done a brilliant job with my hair.' I pick up my bag and lean in to give her a hug. Her body is stiff and unresponsive.

She claps her phone to her chest and looks up. Beneath her make-up her face is ashen and her eyes wide. 'Oh my God,' she murmurs. 'Oh my God.' She stands up shakily. 'Marilyn, can you cancel the rest of my appointments?'

'I'm so sorry,' I say. 'I'm an idiot. I should never have mentioned those disgusting photos.'

She brushes past me. 'It's not your fault... I... I just need to go upstairs.'

'Will you be alright?'

She pushes open the door and hurries along the pavement. I run out after her. 'Vicky, do you want me to come with you?'

She turns briefly, shakes her head and disappears down an alleyway at the end of the row of shops.

Furious with myself, I get in the car and slam the door. What's the matter with me? Vicky opened her heart to me and all I managed to do was upset her. I pull out into the slow-moving traffic and cut through streets of downbeat shops selling discount brooms and buckets, cheap loans and overripe fruit piled high in plastic bowls, my anger turning to confusion as I try to process her revelations about George Burney. Why hadn't Kay gone ahead and prosecuted him? Had she been afraid of the backlash? The trolls and haters calling her a liar, the tabloid press taking the word of a dying old man against that of 'the most hated woman in Britain'?

I drag my thoughts back to the rest of what Vicky had told me; I'm not hers or Chrissie's, that's for sure, and I'm not even the offspring of some junkie who was too zonked-out to remember she'd left her kid at the squat. Most disappointing of all, the baby that social services took from Kay was the one she got back. As I pull up outside my flat I fall back on the only certainty I have – that there has to be more to link Roz to Kay than a letter full of lies and a bundle of press clippings.

The front door jams on a padded envelope. I wiggle it free, take it upstairs and step into a moonscape of stripped plaster, exposed pipes and loose electrical wiring that shivers to the screech of power tools and the beat of hammers. *These guys aren't messing around.* Lukas – barely recognisable behind a white mouth mask and wraparound goggles – waves frantically as I make for the downstairs loo and shouts, 'No water!'

I pick my way upstairs, edge around the loft ladder, duck through the puffs of grit floating down through the open hatch and open the door to my tiny box room; my whole world shrunk down to a microwave perched on a chest of drawers, a single bed and a dust-caked kettle. I take out the signed photo of the Doxettes Vicky gave me. Smiling a little, I pin it to the wall, eyes still drinking in the manic energy of their set as I rip open the package and pull out a slim brown folder. A compliments slip drifts to the floor. It's from the cuttings agency:

R Locklear, archived files as requested.

I drop onto the bed. For a long time I sit very still, praying that I'd been wrong about Roz stalking Kay for over a year before Maya's abduction. I open the file. Pent-up breath bursts from my lungs when I see the first entry. Roz opened her account with the agency six years before Maya disappeared but the person she'd wanted to keep tabs on wasn't Kay. It was a man called Jonas Parks. I dip into the darkening uncertainty of life with Roz, searching for mention of a specialist vet, a visiting conservationist or a foreign donor called Parks. I draw a blank. Dry-mouthed, I turn the page. And there it is, in neat square script. A request for cuttings on Kay and David, dated fourteen months before Maya disappeared. My mind grapples for an explanation; Roz in the tedious heat of some expat doctor's waiting room, flicking through a pile of imported magazines – a newly bereaved mother in need of antidepressants to survive the pain of Phoebe's death, stumbling across the photo of Maya's birthday in the feature about David Duncan, the picture of this 'lovely family' triggering a fixation in her grief-crazed mind. A phone call to the agency to order cuttings about the Duncans, another to a rental agency to find her a flat in Stanford Street so she could watch their real-time comings and goings. Is that how it was, Roz? Did you kill Maya in a fit of deranged jealousy and concoct the pretence that I was her to ease your conscience? A snort of derision and a toss of Roz's head send the threads of this theory tumbling into a knotty heap.

I go over the long slow days leading up to her death, the novels I'd read to her, my voice battling the silence long after she'd drifted into a drug-induced sleep, the spikes of bougainvillea I'd arranged in vases all around the room, the injured shrew I'd smuggled in to show her when the nurse was on a break, her trembling hand creeping towards mine as the sun burned gold in the compound and she finally accepted that she was going to die. The same hand that somehow, just hours before the end, had summoned enough strength to pick up her phone, close her account with the cuttings agency and cancel her payments to Western Union.

With a rapidly beating heart, I cross-reference the dates she was sent cuttings with a Google search for Jonas Parks. The hits are mainly trial reports from the *Leicester Herald*. It seems that in the nineties Parks set up some kind of commune at Rickman's Farm near a village called Horton-on-the-Water, and the prosecution claimed that what went on there was a whole lot creepier than an experiment in alternative living.

> *It's alleged that Jonas Parks exulted in his power over his followers and used it to gain money and sexual gratification…*

I click on a photo of a youthful Parks – dark hair, slack mouth, pasty skin, half-closed eyes gazing knowingly at the camera through square, thick-framed glasses.

> *… A number of his followers came forward to vehemently dismiss these allegations, claiming that Delphine Lomas, the woman who*

*made them, was a former acolyte who had become embittered by
Parks' refusal to admit her to his inner circle.*

I read on through a clutch of interviews with his supporters,
who seemed to think that allowing some deluded fantasist to
control when they ate, slept and peed was their ticket to Nirvana.

*'Jonas has a way with him that makes you sit up when he speaks and
this uncanny ability to make you feel he can see right inside you.'*

Parks ended up going to jail for unlawfully entering the parental
homes of some of his younger, richer devotees and helping himself
to whatever he could find. His defence – that the girls had invited
him in and handed over the family silver as a gift – hadn't washed
with the jury or the judge, who had given him nine months.
There's another photo, this one of a couple of his older followers
demonstrating outside the courthouse. There's something deeply
sad about their frumpy, limp-haired desperation and hastily
painted 'Jonas Parks is Innocent' placards, when it's clear from
the coverage that their self-proclaimed leader was only interested
in 'enlightening' the younger, more nubile members of his flock.

For God's sake, Roz, who was this creep to you?

I slam down the lid of my laptop and call Will. It's ridiculous, I
barely know him but right now the only thing that will make me
feel better is the sound of his voice. He doesn't pick up. Hollow
and hungry, I go out in search of food and working plumbing.

When I get back the builders have left, leaving a silence more
penetrating than the noise of their tools. I'm sitting on the stairs,
spooning tepid yellow curry from a polystyrene container, when
I catch the sound of my ringtone. A delicious wave of happiness
as I dash up to my room and kick through the chaos on the bed.
When I finally retrieve the phone it's stopped ringing. Disappointment gives way to a flutter of adrenaline. The caller wasn't Will.

It was Vicky. Has she remembered someone from Kay's past? I hit voicemail.

'Phoebe, it's Vicky, there's a—'

I press replay. That's it. Five breathless words.

I call her back.

The number you have dialled is currently unavailable. Please try again later.

I do try the number again. Again and again. I'm still trying it twenty minutes later when I reach for my keys and hurry down to my car. Once I reach Streatham High Street, I park in a side road and start to run. The lights are on in the betting shop, the shabby little bistro and the flat above the salon. I slow down, feeling foolish. Vicky probably changed her mind about calling me then switched off her phone to get a bit of peace and quiet. I stare up at her window and replay her message. The tension in her voice and the abruptness of the cut-off send me on down the dim alleyway and out into a car park at the back of the shops. I look around, conscious of a movement; a sound, a feeling. A fox slinks from behind a row of bins and limps away. I hurry up the steps to the walkway that runs along the flats. A figure in a leather jacket turns at the scrape of my feet, a belligerent swagger as he comes towards me. I pull back. He's just a kid, but he's tall and bulky.

'You Vicky?'

'No. Why?'

'She ordered a special and now she's not answering her door.'

I slip past him and try Vicky's bell. The sound is loud and jarring. I push my face to the frosted door panel, cupping my eyes with my hands. In the glare of the hall light I make out something dark humped on the carpet. Blood hits my face, sweat breaks out on my skin. I drop down and push open the letterbox. Vicky is lying wedged against the bottom of the stairs, face down in a silky crumple of black, chestnut highlights glinting, one immaculately manicured hand stretched out as if to grasp something that isn't there. I shout her name and then scream at the delivery boy to call an ambulance. He fumbles for his phone, all the swagger knocked out of him, and I stagger on rubber legs along the walkway. I beat at the neighbour's door, flat hands at first, then clenched fists when no one comes. Finally a growl from inside. 'Alright, alright!'

A man in boxers, fat belly bloating out a grubby white T-shirt, pulls open the door. 'Who the hell are you?'

'Vicky's had an accident. We've got to break into her flat.'

Canned laughter erupts from a distant TV. The man stands motionless, beer can in hand, fleshy mouth loosening. A movement behind him, a woman in pink joggers appears, hair scraped back off of a thin careworn face, 'Fuck's sake, Colin. Where's your toolbox?'

'In the van,' he says, helplessly.

The woman darts away, comes back and ducks under the man's arm with a trophy in her hand – a brass football on a twisted column – and scuffs along the walkway, her feet rammed into green monster slippers complete with shiny black claws. She grasps the trophy, swings back sinewy arms and slams the ball against the wired glass. The panel shatters and bends but doesn't break. The delivery boy moves her aside and kicks at the dent with the heel of his boot, opening up a hole big enough for me to reach my hand inside and open the latch. The door opens a few inches then jams against Vicky's body. A siren screeches through the silence. The woman slithers to her knees and pats Vicky's hip through the gap, the way Roz used to comfort caged animals in the clinic at Molokodi. 'Don't worry, Vick.' She murmurs. 'You'll be alright, girl.' I stand looking down at her with a numbed face and a growing sense of unreality.

I take the mug of strong, sweet tea that Pat of the monster slippers hands me, my mind replaying images in random flashes – faces strobing in the circling blue light, the stillness of the body on the gurney, Vicky's son's wobbling chin as he runs into Pat's kitchen, Vicky's ex behind him, hovering clumsily in the doorway, the scar on the cheek of the paramedic who pronounced her dead, the chip on the lid of Pat's big brown teapot – and all the time the cogs in my brain click against the broken ratchet of Vicky's voicemail. 'Phoebe, it's Vicky, there's a—' There's a what? Something she forgot to tell me about Kay? A karaoke night coming up at the pub? A jinx on all the Doxettes?

'Can I have your name, please?'

I look up into the questioning eyes of the policewoman called in by the ambulance crew, convinced, for one panic-stricken moment, that she'll check on her system and discover that the real Phoebe Locklear is dead and I am an imposter. But what other name can I give?

'Phoebe Locklear,' I say, calm as I can.

She writes it down and flips the page of her notebook. 'Were you a friend of Miss Bunce's?'

'Kind of… well, more of a client.'

'Why were you at her flat?'

'She rang me.'

'Why?'

'I don't know. I missed the call. I rang back but her phone was switched off so I… popped round.'

Vicky's son Danny looks up at me, his blue eyes seeming to focus for the first time since he arrived.

'What time did she call you?' the policewoman says.

I pull up the log and show her the screen. 'Eight seventeen.'

Danny's eyes stay fixed on mine as she makes a note, takes my address and turns her attention to the delivery boy. After twenty minutes she and her sidekick leave, satisfied that Vicky's death is non-suspicious – that she tripped on her kimono and fell awkwardly down the stairs, but they'll get in touch if they need to.

When they've gone, Vicky's ex, Roger, a big, blank-faced man who has said and done very little since he arrived, grasps gruffly at practicalities, telling Dan to fetch some more clothes from his room and muttering that he'd better board up the broken glass on Vicky's door. Pat's husband – who has donned a pair of greasy trousers – offers to help him and the two of them disappear, leaving Danny sitting shocked and shivery at the kitchen table.

'Shall I go with you to get your stuff?' I say, gently.

He nods without looking up. I lay my hand on his shoulder and for one hot shaming moment I envy him the purity of his grief. He has lost the mother he knew, loved and understood and right now his pain is unbearable. But untainted by guilt and uncertainty, he will, eventually, find a way to sleep and breathe and live.

'Mum never turned her phone off when I wasn't home,' he says when we get outside.

My skin prickles beneath the sweat. 'Maybe it ran out of charge.'

He pushes open Vicky's front door – his knobbly white wrist protruding from the cuff of his rugby shirt, a crunch of glass as we step inside. His head jerks away as if he can't bear to look at the place where Vicky fell, and he runs into the immaculate kitchen and snatches up the end of the charger plugged into the socket above the counter. He throws it down and pounces on the squishy designer bag sitting on the chair, tugs at the zip and tips out a shower of purse, wallet, lipsticks, pens, loose coins that bounce across the tiles and a plastic cash bag stuffed full of banknotes. He gazes up at me, his mouth drooping with a sort of dazed bewilderment, then he gets out his own phone, makes a call and stands with it pressed to his ear, eyes darting unseeing as we strain for a ringtone to sound somewhere in the silence. His brows pucker when the recorded message kicks in.

He dashes into the sitting room and stops for a moment, casting around as if he might see Vicky with her feet up reading a magazine or reaching for the remote. In a sudden frenzy he pulls the sofa from the wall, throws the cushions onto the floor and drags aside the armchairs, all the energy of his grief exploding into this need to find her phone. He turns and runs up the stairs. I go after him, stopped on the top step by the vast canvas hanging on the wall in front of me. It's a field of poppies; jaunty, in-your-face bursts of black-eyed red, sharp against a windswept dazzle of yellow corn and blazing blue sky. In the bottom right-hand corner there's signature; a little red 'K'.

I'm startled, speechless, overcome with envy. I want this painting so badly I feel like ripping it off the wall and running to the car – a blast of joy to excise all this death. I lift it down. There's a date on the back. Kay painted it nineteen months ago, when she was feeling upbeat and full of plans to go to France. I hang it back on the hook and hurry after Danny. I find him in Vicky's bedroom, which is as spick and spotless as the rest of her home, frilly edged cushions arranged just so on the blue satin bedcover, not a comb or lipstick out of place. He approaches the dressing table, lifts the lid of a jewellery box and runs his fingers through the beads and bangles. He searches beneath the bed, pulls out the night table and a little padded chair, grunting breathlessly when I offer to help. Together we open the wardrobe, working through the pockets of every garment, then we start on her shoes, shaking them out – even the fur-lined boots she can't have worn for months. I move away to poke through Vicky's drawers, lifting the neatly folded bras and freshly ironed tops now destined for some high-street charity shop. Danny slams the wardrobe doors and drops onto the bed, 'She must have had it when she ordered a takeaway and when she called you. So where is it?'

'Maybe someone took it when we were at Pat's. A shitty thing to do, but it happens.'

He scowls at me as if I'm an idiot. 'Who's going to nick a two-year-old phone and leave the takings from the salon?'

There's a silence after he speaks. I want to fill it with words that will answer his question and quiet the pounding in my ears. Nothing springs to mind.

I realise too late that I'm too shaken up to drive but I take it slowly; headlights floating up out of the dark, half-lit figures spilling out of pubs, kids jostling and yelling on street corners, a feeling of being viewed through a distant lens. It's past midnight when I get home. I pour myself a large vodka and crawl into bed, hoping the alcohol will dull my whirring brain but the image of Vicky's body only gets sharper. I try to block it out by visualising Kay's wonderful poppy painting, only instead of losing myself in glorious swirls of red, blue and yellow I find myself back at the Villa Rosa, staring at the dry brushes and the gloomy, untouched canvas on Kay's easel. My heart stumbles. It's not just that Kay hadn't been painting in colour; from what I'd seen she hadn't been painting at all. I knock back the last of the vodka feeling as if I've snatched at something in the dark, felt the shape and firmness of it in my palm and run into the light to find that my hand is empty.

CHAPTER SEVENTEEN

The horror of Vicky's death floods back the moment I wake up. Was it my fault? Am I jinxed? Fated to bring death wherever I go? Misery slithers towards me, jaws pulled wide. I just want to let it swallow me up. I turn my head into the pillow and sob and sob, not just for Roz and Kay and Vicky but also for me and for Maya. How long I lie there I don't know but after a while the pillow is soaked and I'm too drained to cry anymore. I shuffle to the bathroom, stumbling through the ripped-out wreckage of my flat, slurp water from the tap and shuffle back to bed with a box of cereal, telling myself I'll get up when the builders arrive.

I sleep and wake and sleep again; thick, stale sleep, where dreams lurk like rotting weeds waiting to reach out and drag me down. The day drifts on. No one comes. Even the builders have abandoned me. Just like everybody else. It's dark again and then it's dawn. Another day that I can't face. And then another. I try not to think but thoughts come at me from all directions, scratching at the inside of my skull, crawling around my mind. Death. Lies. Deception. It's easier when the fog descends. A dreary eternity of grey that seeps into every crevice of my brain and fades very slowly to black. It's light again, a pink sky outside my window, a faint tapping sound. A face peers round my door. Smiling, boyish. For a moment I'm baffled. Who is he?

'Lukas?' I say, blearily. 'Where have you been?'

'Another job,' he says simply. He looks at me curiously then shifts his eyes around the room. 'Are you sick?'

'No,' I say, shamefaced.

'You look sick.'

He dumps a pile of catalogues on the end of my bed and retreats. I reach out and pick one up. It's for kitchen cabinets. The others are for bathroom fittings and tiles. Tears prick the back of my eyes. I want to pull the duvet over my head and sink back into oblivion. I mustn't do it. Somehow I have to get up, clear the fug from my head and get on with making a new life. One that isn't built on lies. One where the thought of choosing furnishings for my flat doesn't fling me back to that last sunlit morning at the Villa Rosa and smother me in icy waves of grief. One where I know who I am.

Stiff and leaden, I swallow two aspirin with a mug of black coffee, force down the last of the dry cereal and rummage in the mess for my laptop. Still certain that the key to my past must somehow lie in Kay's, I hit the internet, snatching at facts and making notes to stop myself from sinking back into despair.

A couple of hours later, showered but still wobbly, I'm heading to Northampton. A grey unrolling of motorway, my notebook beside me, open at a list of Kay's childhood haunts, the addresses gleaned from the electoral register, phone listings and various property platforms. Ahead of me a slat-sided truck packed with sheep, lurching between lanes.

George Burney's bungalow is still unsold, and turns out to be even less appealing than Kay described – stained pebbledash, brown paintwork, beige curtains blocking the windows like cataracts and a coating of brick dust from the block of flats they're demolishing next door. The agent is waiting for me beside a banana-yellow Kia with *Hartwell Homes, The Key to Good Living* splashed across the side. She teeters towards me – high heels, tight navy skirt. 'Hi, I'm Jody.' Her eyes drift down my stained T-shirt, take in my torn shorts and flit back to my face, which I'm guessing looks as ravaged as I feel. With a nothing-fazes-the-agents-of-Hartwell-Homes smile she turns and hurries ahead, hugging her clipboard. I scan the property details she's handed me, take a breath and follow her inside. The interior is chill, uninviting, and still furnished. A *Mary Celeste* of misery. No pictures, no television, no books save for a linen-covered bible, placed at an angle in the middle of a cheap wooden dining table.

'Think of it as a blank canvas,' Jody chirps. 'Ready to make your own but if you're into vintage I'm sure the previous owner's estate would be open to offers on the contents.'

We move on to the kitchen. China sink, cracked wall tiles, scuffed lino buckled at the edges. I see nine-year-old Kay at the table, dreaming of the heady delights of her classmate's make-up party, unaware of the terrible punishment to come. I pull open the drawers one by one: cheap cutlery, stained wooden spoons, a bundle of pamphlets bound with an elastic band. I work one loose: *Welcome! Learn more about the Breakaway Brethren and what family and faith mean to us.*

I turn it over. There's an address stamped on the back. I slip the pamphlet into my pocket and turn back to Jody, who has lifted a corner of the greying net curtains and is busy extolling the potential of the overgrown back garden.

'Does this place have a cellar?' I ask.

'I think so.' She trots down the hall, throws back a bolt on a door in the hallway and feels for a light switch. I leave her burbling by the door – 'Perfect for a utility room' – and count the creaking steps, fingers skimming the brick wall as I descend into what's clearly a coal hole. Loose plaster patters in my eyes and settles on my skin.

A half-moon and a starry sky above the terrace of the Villa Rosa, Kay gazing at the burning tip of her cigarette as I ask her to take me back to where she grew up. A pause that lasts so long it scares me then she lets out a strange little laugh.

I swing round and knock into the dangling light bulb. Pale circles of light sway and bounce, sooty smears rear up from the blistered whitewash, generating uneasy flickers of sound and shadow that rush in faster than I can block them out. I run back up the stairs and stand in the doorway, gasping.

Jody's smile never wavers. 'Would you like to see the bedrooms?' We find them down a stunted corridor. One double. One single. Bare floorboards throughout and a bathroom with a chipped enamel bath scarred blue and brown beneath the taps. No mirrors, pictures, rugs or colour to break the unutterable drabness or muffle the clack of Jody's heels. 'How long's it been on the market?' I ask.

'Just over a year. All it needs is the right buyer to see its potential.' She glances around her, the chirpiness of her sales pitch dampened by the dreariness of what she sees. 'Still, if you're after something a bit more modern, we have some charming newer properties I can show you.'

'I'll bear that in mind.'

I stand at the front gate, trying to blink away the images writhing before my eyes as I wait for Jody to drive away. The bungalow next door is boarded up and there's nobody home in three of the four boxy townhouses opposite. When I try the bell of the last one a tiny girl in spangly leggings and a My Little Pony crop top opens the door. She fixes her eyes on the teddy in her hands when I ask if her mummy is home. We stay like that for a couple of minutes before a heavily pregnant woman in denim dungarees appears behind her. 'Hello, can I help you?'

'Hi, I'm sorry to trouble you. I'm enquiring about George Burney.'

'Who?'

'The old man who used to live at number fourteen.'

'Sorry. I didn't really know him. He was an invalid, wasn't he? Kept himself to himself.' She glances down at her daughter, who is walking her teddy along the top step.

'Is there anyone in the street who might remember his wife, or maybe knew him before he got ill?'

'I'm not sure.' Her face takes on an eager, helpful expression. 'There used to be an old lady at number eighteen but she moved out last year and the rest of us are all pretty new here.'

'That's a shame. You see, I was a friend of his daughter's,' I say, hoping for some sympathy for a woman who'd lost a child not much older than her own. 'I'm writing an article about her. Trying to set the record straight.'

Curiosity piqued, she leans against the side of the door. 'Ooh, was she famous?'

'She was… Kay Duncan.'

Her smile withers. '*Maya* Duncan's mother?'

I nod.

A short, nasty silence. Then she jerks her daughter inside and slams the door so hard it clatters the knocker. The sound turns my stomach; a swill of something sour and oily. So this is how it felt to be Kay.

I'd been kicking myself for not taking pictures of Kay's family snaps when I was in France, but I don't need a photograph to know that this gleaming white building with its freshly painted 'Gospel Hall of the Breakaway Brethren' sign is a far cry from the tin-shack chapel I saw in her album. I drive on a few yards and park on the rutted verge. It's very quiet, the only traffic a lone biker throttling down to take the corner as I cross the freshly tarmacked car park. The red-painted doors stand slightly ajar. I slip my fingers through the gap and take a peek inside. White walls totally bare, save for a single banner proclaiming 'Jesus Christ is Lord' fixed across the far wall. The pale wooden pews and parquet floor are new and the place smells soulless – a mixture of fresh paint and the harsh disinfectant that a group of women in headscarves are using to mop the floor.

'I'm sorry to trouble you.' My voice echoes off the hard surfaces. 'I'd like to talk to someone about George Burney.' The women lift their heads and turn in unison. It takes me a moment to realise they're glaring not at my face, but at my shorts.

One of them – a heavy-boned woman in a crumpled blue dress – comes towards me. Angry eyes in a joyless face. 'This is a house of God. You can't come in here dressed like that.' Her hand darts forward and for the second time in as many hours a door slams in my face.

I stagger back and stand for a moment, shaken by the force of the woman's anger. Still a little stunned, I circle the building in search of a gardener or a caretaker. There's no one around so I thumb through the 'Welcome' pamphlet I took from the bungalow: plenty of dewy-eyed couples skipping across sunlit lawns and scrubbed youths in button-down shirts holding hands in prayer, but only one contact number which, when I call it, is out of service. Back at the porch, I find the door firmly shut. Undeterred, I inspect the information board – prayer meetings, bible study, outreach. My eyes drop to a shiny little plaque screwed into the wall. Bile rises in my throat.

This hall was erected by the Circle Trust in Loving Memory of Pastor George Burney, an exemplary leader, whose compassion, generosity and love were as boundless as his faith.

I squat down to take a photo of it, wondering just how deluded the directors of this trust had to be. As I lean in with my phone I catch the reflection of my newly sleek hair in the polished brass and relive the shock of Vicky's death. *Why did you phone me, Vicky? Why didn't you finish your message or pick up when I called you back?* A car door slams behind me. I swing round and stand up slowly. A man is striding across the car park. Somewhere in his mid-forties, his pallid skin, grey trousers and white shirtsleeves smack of someone summoned hastily from the meeting rooms of middle management to deal with a problem. 'John Didcot, church elder,' he says without extending his hand. 'And you are?'

'Phoebe Locklear.'

'Well, Miss Locklear, I'm sorry if Sister Judith was abrasive but we insist on certain standards of modesty for anybody entering these premises.'

'Sorry, I didn't mean to offend anyone.'

'I understand you were asking about George Burney.' His eyes are flat and grey, rimmed with stumpy, fair-tipped lashes, his gaze unswerving.

'Yes, and I just noticed this plaque' – cordial smile – 'that's quite a dedication.'

Didcot draws breath. 'Brother George was a fine man who did his duty to God in all things, but I'm afraid I objected to the erection of that plaque. Our focus should be on simplicity and humility, not on the glorification of any one individual, no matter how generous their contribution to the life of our community. Unfortunately I was overruled. May I ask what your interest is in Brother George?'

'I was a friend of his daughter's.'

He's still controlled but I can see he's unnerved. 'Brother George had no daughter.'

'Just because he disowned her doesn't mean she didn't exist,' I say evenly.

He exhales. A long hard gust. 'Miss Locklear. You have to understand, Brother George had no choice but to separate himself and the rest of our community from evil to prevent contamination.'

'Oh, right, so wearing shorts in church is a sin, but abusing your kid gets you a memorial plaque and a free pass to Heaven?' *So much for my attempt at cordiality.*

He purses his mouth. 'I suggest you refrain from making wild accusations.'

Wild? Really? Then why don't you look the least bit surprised? I bite down hard on my lip and take a breath. Anger's not going to get me what I need. 'Look, I'm writing an extended obituary of Kay, trying to set the record straight about her life, and I just want to talk to anyone who may have kept in touch with her after she left Northampton.'

'Then your mission is futile. When a member of our community has been shunned we erase them from our hearts and minds.'

'*Shunned?* She was a child, fifteen years old, pregnant and frightened. What she needed was love and support and you all turned your backs on her. Even her own mother! Who *are* you people?'

'As I said, Miss Locklear, there can be no place for unrepentant sinners in our community.'

'But plenty of room for perverts like George Burney!'

The word hangs between us, twisting for a moment in the silence.

'I suggest you think very carefully before you repeat these unsubstantiated accusations.' He looks me up and down and I realise, with a shiver, that he's memorising my face.

'Is that a threat, Mr Didcot?'

'God strikes the heads of his enemies, Miss Locklear, and protects the righteous with his righteous hand.'

I can't believe this man's for real. 'A God who protects child abusers?'

He spins away, takes a couple of steps and turns back. 'Perhaps you should look to the state of your own eternal soul, Miss Locklear. Bearers of false witness are an abomination to the Lord.' He strides back to his brand-new Toyota Land Cruiser – chrome-plated simplicity and turbo-charged humility all built in. I walk back to my own car, and watch him roar past, so angry I can hardly suck in enough air to breathe. When he's gone I sit there holding the steering wheel, skin crawling with anger and disgust. They knew!

The whole community knew what a sick bastard George Burney was. Which means his wife did too. Did Ruth Burney lie awake at night, grieving for her lost daughter and imagining the grandchild she would never see, or did her self-righteous certainties mean she slept the sleep of the blameless?

'Miss Locklear.'

I swivel round. A furtive face is peering at me through the passenger window. No make-up, bad skin. She could be thirty? Forty? It's hard to tell. I lean over and unlock the door. 'Who are you?'

'My name's Esther. I have to be quick.' The woman holds up a can of furniture polish. 'I told Sister Judith I was fetching this from the car.' She drops onto the seat, and tugs her headscarf low over her forehead. 'It's not true that Kaitlin's mother didn't care about her.'

'How do you know?' I say, slightly thrown by her use of Kay's birth name.

She throws a jittery glance at the chapel. 'Ruth was my aunt. I promise you it broke her heart when Brother George cut Kaitlin off.'

'Then why didn't she expose him for the bastard he was and do something to help her pregnant daughter?'

'Because he forbade our whole community from even mentioning Kaitlin's name. We had to act as if she never existed or risk being shunned ourselves.' She looks nervously over her shoulder. There's no one around, just the biker I saw earlier parked down the lane, looking at his phone like he's lost. 'My mum was the only person Ruth dared to talk to about her. And now she blames herself for Kaitlin's suicide. If she'd had family to support her maybe she'd have had the strength to cope with losing Maya.'

I don't trust myself to respond to this, but she's too jumpy to notice.

'When did you last see Kaitlin?' she says eagerly.

'Earlier this summer.'

That seems to please her. 'Would you visit my mother, Miss Locklear? She tried to get in touch with Kaitlin's husband when she heard the news but he refused to take her calls.'

'Can you blame him?'

Silence. The bark of a distant dog. The smell of honeysuckle from the hedge. She twists the lid of her spray can. 'Mum's not well. She probably hasn't got long. It would mean so much to her to talk to someone who'd been Kaitlin's friend.'

Her pale, earnest eyes search my face. I look away, afraid of what she might find. 'What's her address?'

'Here.' She hands me a scrap of paper and opens the passenger door. 'Her name's Alice Foreman. My niece is with her today. I'll tell them you're coming. If anyone turns up while you're there just say you arrived unannounced and then leave.' Before I can speak she's hurrying across the road. I watch her go. Kay's dowdy, put-upon cousin, a can of furniture polish gripped tightly in her hand.

CHAPTER EIGHTEEN

I'd been expecting Alice Foreman's home to be as drab and lifeless as George Burney's bungalow, so it's a surprise when I arrive at a newly built block of flats surrounded by flower beds and neatly mown strips of lawn. I take the lift to the first floor, arrange my face into a smile of sorts and ring the bell. A plain-faced woman in her twenties answers the door. 'Hello,' I say, brightly. 'Esther sent me. I've come to see Alice.'

She gazes at me for a minute then leads me down an unadorned hallway into a bedroom whose pristine plainness is alleviated by a jug of fat brassy sunflowers sitting on the windowsill and a jumble of framed photos cluttering the top of the chest of drawers. 'She's here, Gran.' She leans in to me on her way out and whispers, 'Try not to tire her out.'

Kay's aunt is already tired out; a delicate, heavy-lidded doll held upright by a drift of pillows. She's probably somewhere in her seventies, her grey-streaked hair, although lustreless, still thick, the rest of her reduced and withered as if she's been starved. She drops a disc of crotchet onto the bedcover and holds out a fleshless hand. 'I prayed you would come.'

I move awkwardly towards the vinyl-covered chair at her bedside and search her face for a resemblance to Kay. All I see is age and pain. 'Mrs Foreman—'

'Alice, please.'

I sit down, perching on one hip. 'Alice, I'm not sure what you want from me.'

'Esther says you were Kaitlin's friend.' My throat flushes hot. 'I want to hear about her from someone who actually knew her. Not that filth they wrote in the papers.' She smiles. 'How did you meet her?'

I feel the colour creep up my face and reach hurriedly for a tissue from the box by her bed. She pats my hand and says gently, 'Not if it upsets you,' which makes me feel even more of a fraud.

I blow my nose hard before I can manage the lie. 'We met at an art class.'

She tips her head to one side. 'You're not English.'

'I was brought up in Botswana. But I live in London now.' Keen to divert the conversation back to Kay, I say quickly, 'Your daughter said that you and Kay's mother were close.'

'Very. Even though I was twelve years older.' She looks away to the window. 'But Ruth was taken first. I don't care what the doctors said – she died of a broken heart.' She turns back to me, pink eyelids blinking unhappily. 'After I lost her there was no one I could even speak my niece's name to. As for Maya, I used to pray every day that Kaitlin would live to see her again. Now all I can do is pray that they've both found peace.'

Her pain seems real but I say nothing. Maybe clinging to my anger with the brethren is easier than dealing with my own crimes against Kay. With trembling hands she takes a plastic pill organiser from her table, lifts away the tray of tablets and slides out a photograph. 'Ruth found this hidden under Kaitlin's mattress after she left,' she says.

I take it from her hands – a faded polaroid with a sickly yellow tinge, and stare at it, rigid with sadness. A young girl, barely more than a child, peers through a curtain of brown hair. She's wearing ripped fishnets, a grungy leather jacket and combat boots but her smudged make-up and narrow frame make her look like a kid playing dress up.

'Where did she get the clothes and make-up?'

'Stealing from shops, borrowing from friends, who knows? She must have been creeping out of the house and putting them on when George was asleep.' Alice shakes her head. 'When you think of the punishment she was risking…'

'Did Ruth have any idea who Kay was meeting or who might have got her pregnant?'

'None,' she says, forlorn.

I hold up my phone. 'May I?'

'Of course.'

I take a photo of the Polaroid then prop it against the box of tissues, barely able to tear my eyes from the image. 'She was fifteen and pregnant. I just don't understand why you and Ruth didn't do anything to help her.'

'We were weak, I know that, and I'll regret it till the day I die. But by that time I was widowed with two young children and almost as dependent on George as Ruth was. So we faced a terrible choice: give up everything – our beliefs, our homes, our church, our families – or reach out to a child who had lost her way.' Her voice, already breathy, is fading. 'We tried to help her in secret, we even scraped up the money to pay a private investigator to look for her, but George found out, and when he confronted us we gave in and my sister died not knowing what had happened to her child.' Her hands move restlessly on the bedcover. 'It was only when Maya was taken and my daughter, Esther, saw Kay Duncan making that heart-breaking appeal for her return that we realised it was Kaitlin. It wasn't the way she looked; she'd changed so much. It was something in her voice. I went to George immediately and asked his permission to contact her.'

'What happened?'

'He refused to even let me say her name. But I wrote to her anyway.'

'Did she reply?'

'No. And I completely understand why. After that, Esther used to smuggle in newspapers so we could read about the search for Maya, then we'd burn them so that George wouldn't find out.'

'Why on earth did Ruth marry a man like Burney? Apart from anything else, he must have been at least fifteen years older than her.'

'He was a leader. Revered, looked up to. When he started courting her my parents felt honoured, and for a while so did she. But once they were married I don't think she knew a day's happiness.'

'Not even when she had Kay?'

'George had set his heart on having a son and he made her feel like a failure for producing a girl. We used to say to her, don't worry, Ruthie, maybe next time. Only there never was a next time.'

She's sick and frail but the memory of the cellar at Burney's bungalow is too fresh in my head to let this go. 'You know he used to beat Kay?' I say, quietly. 'Abuse her and tell her he was doing it to drive out her sin?' Her fingers flutter to her crotchet then sink back onto the bedspread. 'It started when she was nine years old, and your sister just stood by and let it happen.'

'He was violent to her too.'

'She should have gone to the police.'

'When you're trapped like that it's easy to convince yourself that it's your fault and you're being punished for your own good.'

Her voice cracks. My eyes flit across the photos on the chest. Plenty of children and grandchildren but no sign of Alice's husband, and I wonder if she's speaking from her own experience. 'Was George the only elder abusing his power?'

'No.' Then, after a bleak pause, 'And he wasn't the worst of them.'

I wait for her to go on but her lips tighten.

'They should be prosecuted,' I say.

'Our community prefers to deal with these things internally.'

'You mean hush them up.'

Her watery eyes find mine. 'About ten years ago there was a problem at one of our sister congregations. Two of their elders went to prison and the church was forced to pay out a hefty compensation to their victims. After that, our leaders brought in new rules about punishments.' She runs a thumb over her blue-veined knuckles. 'The terrible thing is, most people in our community are still convinced that men like George Burney are superior beings whose mission to protect the righteous puts their actions beyond reproach.'

'Kay had been thinking about going to the police,' I say, making it sound as if it had been me, not Vicky she'd confided in. 'She'd even talked to a support group for victims of abuse, then she changed her mind and decided to forgive him.'

She looks up, genuinely surprised.

'She went to see him before he died,' I say. 'Didn't you know?'

Her brow furrows and she shakes her head. 'That man didn't deserve her forgiveness.'

'Perhaps he mellowed at the end,' I say.

'Don't you believe it. He was handing out judgements right up until the day he died, tearing families apart without an ounce of compassion and making the rest of the world dance to his tune. He had my daughters at his beck and call and the way he treated his carers was shameful. At least two of them walked out and the last one must have been a saint to put up with it.' She twitches her head as if to shake off the image and puts a speckled hand over mine. 'Let's not waste time talking about George Burney. Tell me about Kaitlin. Did she ever find any happiness in her life?'

For a moment I say nothing. 'She loved to paint,' I manage at last. 'And her husband was very… protective. But losing her kid – I don't think she ever got over it.'

Her voice dips and trembles. 'Did her friends stand by her?'

'One of them just died,' I blurt out, too abruptly. 'A girl from a band she used to be in. She fell down the stairs. Isn't that terrible? Kay and her best friend gone within weeks of each other.'

Alice looks at me strangely, a look which seems to crystallise all the unnerving thoughts in my head. 'Poor woman,' she says uncertainly.

Emotion has brightened her jaundiced eyes but exhausted her. I hold a glass of water to her lips and lift her slightly so she can drink, the way I used to with Roz – the same sharp bones beneath her flower-sprigged nightdress, the same feeble tremor as she breathes. I ease her back onto the pillow and imagine, for a moment, that I am family, taking my turn to care for a beloved great-aunt. I close my eyes while I navigate back to why I'm here, then take a breath and open them again.

'Alice,' I say gently, not sure if she's asleep or awake. 'Did you or Ruth ever come across a couple called Locklear? They had a daughter called Rosalyn.'

A long silence, then her lips move. 'No Locklears among our community.'

'You're sure? Not even twenty years ago?'

'Certain. All our families know each other. Half of us are related, at least by marriage.' A wheezy rattle of a sigh. 'That's what makes it so difficult to leave.'

Her granddaughter pokes her head around the door. 'Gran, Esther just called. Brother John's on his way.' I can see she's panicked but Alice stays serene.

'He'll be coming to warn me not to tarnish my soul by speaking to outsiders.' She finds my hand again. 'You must go. But bless you for coming. Talking to you has done me so much good.'

'Goodbye, Alice,' I say, stirred by the terrible affinity I feel for this gentle, dying woman, who is also haunted by regrets, and if onlys, and the devastating wrong she did to Kay.

'Goodbye, my dear,' Alice says. 'And please be careful. Men like John Didcot will do almost anything to protect their own.'

I look back at her from the doorway and see her slip Kay's photo back into its hiding place.

I drive away, angry with George Burney, with Kay, with this whole damn mess. It's getting muggy, grey-tinged clouds blotting out the blue. In the distance a pair of chimney stacks rise above the roofline of a red-brick factory, the faded name of the company – when I crane my head – just visible above the trees. J. P. Dutton & Co. A flash memory of a photo in Kay's album. George Burney, drab and unsmiling, at a Dutton's event. Before I know it I'm making a detour, curious to see the place where Kay's father had spent his working life.

The old industrial estate is silent. Nothing moves. Nothing makes a sound apart from me; my footsteps echoing on the cracked concrete. I stop outside the derelict factory and stand looking up at the 'J. P. Dutton & and Co' sign stencilled in ten-foot high letters above a row of small barred windows. I imagine George Burney grinding figures all day in one of those poky offices, and going home each night to beat out his frustrations on his lonely wife and unwanted daughter. The same George Burney who'd been memorialised on that plaque at the gospel hall as *an exemplary leader, whose compassion, generosity and love were as boundless as his faith.* I grope for the name of the organisation who had built the hall and commissioned that toadying dedication. *The Circle Trust.* A cold creep of unease. What was this trust exactly? Was it funding some kind of cover-up for the crimes of the Breakaway Brethren elders?

I walk back to the car and ring Tim Edgecombe, Roz's long-time broker and the other executor of her will. He's a busy man but he takes my call straight away. No surprises there. He's been dealing with the mountain of paperwork for weeks and I haven't even been opening his emails.

'Phoebe,' he says. 'You're a hard woman to get hold of. Have you signed that last lot of documents I sent you?'

I picture him in his leather swivel chair, a snappy dresser: striped shirt, shiny shoes, spotted bow tie.

'Sorry, Mr Edgecombe, I'll get on to it today.'

'How are you holding up?'

'Oh, you know…' My voice cracks a little.

'So,' he says gently. 'What can I do for you?'

'I know it's a bit random, but I was wondering if there's anyone in your office who could look into something called the Circle Trust for me. I think it's some kind of financial institution.'

'Any particular reason?'

'It's… for a friend,' I say. *How lame is that?*

'I see,' he says. 'Any more information?'

'Only that it funded the building of a gospel hall in Northamptonshire and dedicated it to a man called George Burney. He was an elder in a sect called the Breakaway Brethren.'

'Is that it?'

'I'm afraid so.'

'Let me see what I can do.'

I feel my spirits lift. Maybe I should ask for help more often. 'Thanks, Mr Edgecombe.'

'Is there anything else I can do for you?'

'Actually, while you're there, you don't happen to know anything about the payments Roz used to make via Western Union? The payee was anonymous and I'm curious to find out who it was and what the money was for.'

Silence. But I know he's still there. I can hear the click of his pen.

'Mr Edgecombe?'

'Look,' he says, his voice suddenly formal. 'As Roz's heir and co-executor you're technically entitled to scrutinise, and indeed veto, any transaction made on behalf of her estate. However, we both know she was in denial about the severity of her illness.'

'I don't understand. What are you saying?'

'I'm saying that if she'd had more time she would have made a confidential arrangement about certain aspects of her finances.'

'Well, she didn't,' I say, more curtly than I should. 'So please, tell me exactly what you know.'

'Just before she died she called me. She could barely speak but she instructed me to put aside a number of shares and use the dividends to keep up those Western Union payments. She also asked me to bury the transactions so they slipped beneath your radar. I told her I wasn't happy about it but I would do my best.'

'Why didn't she want me to know?'

'She didn't say, and it wasn't my place to ask.'

'Who was the payee?'

'She didn't tell me that either.'

'Are there any other *arrangements* you're not telling me about?'

'No.'

'I'm sorry. I didn't mean to sound rude.'

'Don't worry. This a difficult time for you. If there's anything else you need, just ask.'

I say goodbye and hang up, confused but mainly upset. No, not upset: devastated that I've caught Roz out in yet another deathbed deception.

I start the car and check the mirror. I'm not alone. A white van is nosing around the corner. It stops mid-turn, backs up with a crunch of gears and disappears. My phone beeps. It's a text from Will.

CHAPTER NINETEEN

I look around me at the crowded restaurant – mud-green walls, dark floorboards, everything from the chairs to the painted candlesticks artfully distressed – and for one scarily desolate moment I think Will has stood me up. Then, with a shudder of relief, I see him at the back, attended by a hovering, punk-haired waitress – clearly a fan – who flounces away when I kiss him hard on the mouth.

'Like the hair,' he says.

Faces around me tremble, candle flames shimmer, voices slow and distort.

He knows about Vicky. He's going to ask why I went to see her, why I've been poking around in Kay's past.

I stare into his warm, smiling face and the world around me steadies.

I drop into the chair opposite him. 'Thanks. What happened to yours, you get nits?'

He runs sheepish fingers over his brown-ish crop. 'Ah. The golden locks. A leftover from my ground-breaking investigation – *Is life better for blonde men too?*'

'And was it?' I load butter onto a hunk of bread.

'Clearly not. You abandoned me.'

'Sorry. Things to do.' My face flushes hot. I look away. Two women brush past us, deep in conversation as they follow a waiter to their table. I watch their easy intimacy, groomed blondes so alike there could never be a second's doubt that they are mother and daughter. I turn back to Will. 'How was Brussels?'

'Dull. The only excitement was seeing David Duncan at Marseille airport on the way out. He looked terrible. It can't help that on top of everything else he's being sued by Lila Mendez.'

The waitress reappears, rocking on her toes. Unlike Will, who seems entranced by her recitation of tonight's chalkboard specials, I order quickly and without interest from the menu. 'Sued?' I bite into my bread, careful not to show more than a passing interest. 'What for?'

'Back revenue. She was a minor when he signed her up and that lowlife she married last year – what's his name… Ricky West – is claiming Duncan took advantage of her.'

'How?'

'Locked her into a deal that West's lawyers claim was less than "fair and reasonable".'

'How much are they asking for?'

'Millions, I should think. Plus a reversion of copyright.'

'Did Duncan really screw her over?'

He shrugs. 'Maybe. And maybe he thought he was doing her a favour taking a punt on her in the first place. That's his thing – the master manipulator, shaping unknowns into the people he wants them to be, creating the whole package. When he stops pulling the strings they usually fall flat on their faces. Though that's probably not the way the judge will see it, and from all accounts West's out for everything he can get.'

How have I missed this? I've set Google alerts for David – not to mention Kay and Maya – and I haven't seen a word about any lawsuit. 'Has this been on the news?' I say, eyes on the crumbs I'm pushing around my plate.

'He got an injunction.'

'So how come you know so much about it?'

'I have my sources.' He leans back so the waitress can set a bowl of moules in front of him, his 'thank you' rewarded with a freshly lipsticked pout and an unnecessary amount of eye contact. 'Apparently it's been rumbling on for a while.'

Our waitress slaps my starter on the table, a plate of sprats – wide-eyed and open mouthed – arranged around a blob of horseradish.

'Are they going to court?'

'Not if Duncan can help it – he's got his lawyers thrashing out some kind of back-room deal.'

I sit there appalled at the thought of David losing his wife and his major act within weeks of each other.

'My editor's such a sick bastard, he's had our researchers checking to see if Kay had life insurance – how's that for faith in humankind?'

I chew my bread for a little longer than necessary before I swallow it down.

'Did she?'

'What?'

'Have life insurance?'

'Not a penny. Anyway, they don't pay out for suicides.'

I'm unsettled and he senses it – looking at me oddly in the wavery candlelight. To divert his attention I blurt out the first thing that comes into my head – or rather the thing that's been rattling around in there since the moment I found out he'd been married. 'Why did your wife leave you? Did you cheat on her?'

His smile closes down and he draws his thumb across the tablecloth. 'Actually, she cheated on me and discovered she preferred the other guy.'

I touch the tips of his fingers. 'Sorry… I shouldn't have asked.'

'We met in the final year of university. The golden couple. The envy of all our friends. We got married three years after graduation and I thought I was the luckiest man alive. Two years later she left me.'

'I'm so sorry,' I say.

His expression flickers between anger and pain, settling on neither as he tries for flippant. 'Her new bloke's a professional golfer. How could a hack like me compete with that kind of glamour? What about you? Any traumatic heart-breaks I should know about?'

I force a smile. 'Apart from the Nigerian diplomat's son who took my virginity in the back of an armoured Toyota and the volunteer who seduced me with his knowledge of the drivers for raptor decline, my past relationships have left my heart pretty much intact.' *Not this time, though, Will. I can't see myself getting out of this one unscathed.* Without warning, tears sting my eyes. I blink hard and take a sip from my glass.

A flash of concern crosses his face.

I say quickly, 'So, what are you working on now you're back from Brussels?'

He hesitates but takes the hint. 'Usual stuff – expenses scandals, drug gangs in rural Scotland, trying to impress this girl I met in Cassis.'

'I've heard you're doing just fine on that front.'

'Good to know.'

'Don't let it go to your head.'

'Did you sort out the problem with your foster mother's will?'

I stare at the battered watch on his wrist. 'I'm... working on it.'

His duck breast arrives with yet more flouncing from the waitress. I have turbot, the accompanying herb butter slopping a little when the plate hits the table. A shared moment of amusement as Will catches my eye and I find myself thinking how good we could be together.

It's not until we've got a cab back to his tiny flat in Spitalfields – stripped beams, naked brick, leather and steel – and he's fetching our second bottle of wine that I scrape up the courage to ask him, 'Have you got any contacts in the police?'

He looks at me over his shoulder, backlit by the glow from the open fridge.

'A few.' He frowns a little. 'Why?'

'Could they check someone out for me?'

'Depends. Who is it?'

I hesitate, still weighing up the risks, scared of what he might find out about Roz, scared of what he might find out about me.

A sideways smile. 'I *knew* there was something you weren't telling me.'

'Oh, forget it!' The words fly out. Too harsh and too loud.

He puts down the bottle and comes towards me, surprised and concerned.

'Hey, what's wrong? Do you want to talk about it?'

Yes, more than anything in the world. But I can't admit the damage that Roz and her lies have done, not to anyone, but especially not to you, Will.

'Whatever it is, you know I'll do anything to help. I mean it, Phoebe.' He runs a knuckle down my cheek and as he kisses my throat I push aside my fears and, just for a moment, allow myself to imagine a future with this man; one where I trusted him enough to tell him my secrets, and he loved me enough to keep them.

CHAPTER TWENTY

When I wake up it's almost nine and I'm naked and alone, a mug of coffee cooling on the bedside table alongside a note – *Back Thursday night. I'll cook you dinner.* Light-headed, I pull on one of Will's shirts, pad into his living room and make fresh coffee with his fancy beans in his fancy machine. The smell mingles with the sunshine and the memories of last night and when I catch my reflection in the floor-length window there's a shadow of a smile on my face. I move over to his desk. Half fearful, half hopeful that I'll find something that will bring me back to earth, I shuffle through the piles of papers, open a box of business cards – Will Betteridge, Roving Correspondent – and pull open the top drawer. Guiltily, I lift out a wad of car brochures. Underneath them there's a framed photo, face down. I turn it over. It's Will on his wedding day, cheek to cheek with a slim blonde bride on a shiny dance floor, the two of them smiling at the camera; a spotlit whirl of hope and expectation. How long was it before her lies began? Or had her deceit set in before she'd even said her vows, the whole wedding a sham from pearl-studded start to acrimonious finish?

I trail a fingertip across Will's face. He knows exactly how it feels to be betrayed by someone you love, to wake up one day and discover that you never really knew them at all. Something shifts deep inside. Before I lose my nerve I fire off a text asking him if his police contact could run checks on Roz – 'because her past's turning out to be a bit of a mystery' – and on Jonas Parks – because 'I think she might have known him and he's a creep'. I add Roz's details and a link to the reports of Parks' trial, hesitate and press send, though anxiety still tingles my thumbs at the thought of involving Will in any part of this. Still, no going back now. I open up a new page in my notebook and write Parks and Roz's names in heavy capitals across the top. What's their connection? It's not something that's likely to be revealed by their police records and since I can't ask Roz, I'll have to ask Parks. My nerves crackle at the thought, though whether it's fear of facing a man like Parks in the flesh or fear of what he might tell me about Roz I'm not sure. Exorcising my dread with sips of Will's overpriced coffee, I search for an address for Rickman's Farm, and wonder how on earth you're supposed to pronounce Lei-cest-er-shire.

The downbeat Englishness of Horton-on-the-Water is like something you can inhale. A shallow stream, which presumably gave the place its name, a squat stone church, a pub – the Blue Boar – slung with plastic bunting, a half-boarded-up takeaway and a post office cum corner shop with a rack of newspapers and sacks of charcoal lined up beneath the window. The satnav sends me on through the village, the day hotting up as I flip between asking Parks straight out why Roz was keeping tabs on him and just floating her name and seeing how he reacts. I'm at a crossroads, turning onto the main road, when the signpost catches my attention. Northampton, eighteen miles. My foot hits the brake. A lorry thunders out of nowhere, swerves to avoid me and lets out a mournful bellow of reproach. Shaken, I drive on.

As I take a turning into the woods I'm still debating whether, in a country as small as this one, a distance of twenty or so miles between Jonas Parks' commune and Kay's hometown could mean something or nothing at all. The road narrows to a track, crowded on either side with trees that scrape their branches along the sides of the car. After about half a mile of bumping over ruts and peering through gaps in the green I glimpse a brick wall swamped by brambles and saplings. I park and, a few yards further on, find a sign that says 'Rickman's Farm' nailed to a tree and a set of padlocked metal gates hung with a 'For Sale or To Let' board. *Damn!* I breathe through the burn of frustration and take a photo of the board – it's so weathered I can hardly make out the agent's name.

Turning away, I retreat into the trees, marvelling at how cool and dark it is. After a while I hit a narrow pathway – barely more than a line in the dirt – and follow it uphill. I move quickly, unnerved by the earthiness of the English woodland; the snappings and rustlings, the sudden caw and flutter of a bird disturbed by something or somebody unseen. I stand quite still and glance back through needled branches to a huge fallen tree trunk, its splayed roots and shadowed branches crusted with mud. The rustling stops. I step quickly off the path and push through the undergrowth to a spot where the fencing gives way to a skimpy hedge. I squeeze through a gap and see the farm strung out like an afterthought along the banks of the river. I take more photos – zooming in, click, click, click – fields of brown straggly stems, an empty trailer abandoned beside a water trough. A text pops up on screen: *My contact's checking those names. You looked so lovely when I left I was tempted to miss my flight xxx*

My hands sweat as I slip the phone back in my jeans and make my way along the edge of the fields. There's a drowsy desolation about the farmyard, shed doors hanging off their hinges, a twisted dishcloth dried out in the mud, a couple of clapped-out cars rusting in front of an iron sheet barn with an off-kilter weathervane perched on the gable top. I peek through blackened windows into a narrow storeroom and make out a stained mattress and a yellow plastic bowl fuzzed with cobwebs. I climb rickety steps to an empty hayloft, check out a tool store and slip through the half-open doors of the barn. It's dark and dusty inside, bales of hay piled in the empty stalls, a musty smell of dried cow dung. I walk on to the house itself. It's a plain, square building, the kind children draw, with five boarded-up windows across the upper storey, two either side of the front door and a steep grey roof badly in need of repair, with a red-brick chimney in the middle. I pick up a fallen rake and slash a path through the weeds to the back of the house. There's a wooden water butt against the wall, above it a small broken window with a spiral of bindweed creeping through the hole in the glass. I scramble onto the water butt, prise open the window, wriggle through it and drop down into a musty little storeroom. Blinking into the half dark, I cross a hallway and push open the door to a long, low sitting room. There's a fireplace at one end and a ratty, beaten-up sofa just about visible in the gloom. I take out my phone and search for the words of the girls interviewed by the local paper, the followers who bought into Jonas's two-bit version of Paradise.

> *I sat in the dark and spewed vitriol at my father. There was worse for my mother. We'd been doing this stuff for three days, late into the night. Not eating, not sleeping and I swear I saw the two of them sitting right in front of me. Cold and judgemental. There were about a dozen other women sat around me all shouting at their families. Arsehole! I fucking hate you! Bitch! Bastard! The noise was deafening and Jonas was shouting, 'Tell them what they did to you! Tell them how it hurt!' I started sobbing until I was bent over, head down, retching and sweating. Then he said, 'Picture them dead.' I'll always remember that. 'Picture them dead.' I knew it was fantasy but somewhere deep inside it felt real. And you know what? It felt good. 'Now leave them,' he said. 'Walk away. They can't hurt you now.' He laid his hands on my head and a buzz of energy zapped all the pain that had been backing up inside me for years and for the first time in my life I felt free.*

I move on upstairs. Four bedrooms, each one crammed with iron bed frames, give it the air of a deserted boarding school. The room at the end is slightly larger with just one double bed in it and a dark wood bureau angled in one corner.

Jonas needs children. Golden offspring who will bring guidance to our broken world. He says if we're not chosen to bear them we can still serve him by seeking out other girls who might prove worthy of that honour.

Vomit in my throat, I turn my back on the bed and bang open the top drawer of the bureau. It's lined with dusty sheets of newspaper that disintegrate as I pat my hand around inside. I bring out a green plastic comb and a wadded-up chewing gum wrapper. The next one rattles as I open it. I push aside a collection of dried-out biros, the curled metal spring from a spiral notebook and an empty can of deodorant and lift out a snapshot of a smiling, blue-eyed baby girl peering up from a buggy. I lay it to one side and take out a sheet of stiff paper on which someone has drawn a version of the same photo in sickly pastels, distorting the eyes so they're huge and staring, pinking up the lips and cheeks, adding an awkwardly drawn hand held high as if in benediction and replacing the buggy with a circle of yellow shading, giving the image the otherworldly glow of a tacky icon.

There's something almost, but not quite, childlike about the way it's been done – amateurish yet at the same time knowing. Next comes a photo of Jonas Parks and a dozen or so women, lazing around beside the river, sharing a picnic. Some of the women are smiling, some eating, some toasting the camera with paper cups, some lie stretched out enjoying the sunshine. An idyllic image. Except for one thing. Someone has taken an indelible marker to one of the women and very, very carefully blacked her out. I gaze at the angry blob of black, ambushed by memories of Roz's crinkly blonde hair, the clean soapy smell of her scrubbed hands, the way she used to push up on her elbows and tilt back her head to drink in the sun, the sharp familiar shape of her. I have to leave. I walk away, first slowly, then I break into a run and scramble out of the farmhouse the way I got in.

*

The clang of a bell and the smell of damp and old biscuits as I enter the village shop. The elderly man behind the counter looks up from his newspaper, pencil stub poised above a crossword as if irked by the interruption.

'Hi.' I push a couple of chocolate bars across the counter. He rings them up and pulls a face when I hand him a ten-pound note.

'Nothing smaller?'

'Sorry.' I slip the chocolate into my bag and say lightly, 'I don't suppose you know where Jonas Parks moved to after he left Rickman's Farm?'

He looks me up and down. 'What would you be wanting with Parks?'

I offer him today's lie. 'I'm writing a thesis on the dynamics of personality based communes.'

'Are you now?' – a sly smile – 'Well, once he'd bled Amy Rickman dry and let her farm go to blazes he got her to rent him a place somewhere the other side of Milton Keynes. Far as I know he took his whole harem with him.'

'I thought Parks owned the farm.'

He lets out a scornful bark. 'You must be joking. That's been Rickman land for generations. Amy's dad would be spinning in his grave if he could see what she's done with it.'

I push harder, feeling around for any kind of link between Rickman's Farm and abused, unhappy teenage Kay.

'Did Parks' followers, you know… ever hang out in the village, maybe get the bus to Northampton?'

'There is no bus to Northampton and they never came into the village. As far as I know he kept the lot of them penned up like sheep.' His liver-coloured lips turn down with a mixture of relish and disdain. 'Lord knows what went on behind those gates.'

CHAPTER TWENTY-ONE

Glad to be back in Fulham, I push open the front door and grab the roll of flyers jammed in the letterbox. As I wrestle with takeaway menus and offers on wine and dry cleaning I notice that the door to the downstairs flat is open. Not by much – just a couple of inches. Thrilled that I've finally got neighbours, I tap the door with my fingertips and call, 'Hello?'

No answer. I stick my head inside. In the spill of light from the hallway I make out polished floorboards and striped wallpaper. 'Hello!' I shout. 'Anybody there? I'm Phoebe, I live upstairs.'

A rush of bulk slams me against the wall. Sweat, weed, muscle. My phone skitters across the floor. My palms skim flesh. Filled with fury I claw at stubble, searching instinctively for the soft wet of mouth, nose and eyes and jerk up my knee. With an umph of pain he throws me off, jabs me hard with his elbow and makes a dash across the hall and out through the front door, a fast-moving figure – black beanie hat and dark hoodie – he darts behind a lorry and disappears in a spray of muddy grey. Gasping for air, I swing round and inspect the locks on the flat and the main entrance. They're both intact. He must have had keys.

I run up the stairs and unlock my door. Once inside I slam it shut, turn on the light and sink back against the wall. A few seconds of relief and then, beneath the thump of my heart, I hear a sound, somewhere between a swish and a crackle. I dip down to take a hammer from the toolbox on the floor, shift along the wall and crane my head to see who's there. The room is in darkness but the balcony doors are open and the edges of the plastic sheeting draped around the table and chairs are lifting on the breeze. I raise the hammer with both hands, move silently forward and step out into the rain. I swing left, then right. It's empty. Feeling foolish, I peer over the iron railing into the garden below. The feeling of foolishness ebbs as my eyes follow the heavy ropes of wisteria twining up from the patio to form a natural ladder to my balcony. Had the intruder been in my flat? Had he heard me open the front door and tried to make a hasty escape the way he'd got in?

I run back inside, close the French doors and wiggle the rusty bolt until it creaks into place. I stare at my fear-struck face in the glass. What if he wasn't alone? Slowly I shift my eyes to the reflection of the room behind me. I turn slowly. Keeping my shoulders to the wall I shuffle up the stairs and kick open the doors to the bedrooms and bathroom, crashing them back on their hinges. Empty. With a shuddery breath I let the hammer drop.

Roz would have been proud of the way I'd defended myself – *Always fight back, kiddo* – but the police call handler is less than impressed. No, I didn't get the owner's permission to enter the downstairs property, yes, it's possible it was my builders who left my balcony door open, no, I couldn't give a description of the man, not really, and no, as far as I could see nothing was stolen from my flat but I had everything of value with me. I glance down at my laptop and notebook sticking out of my bag; all the information I've gathered in my search for who I am.

As if I'm an idiot the call handler witters on about upgrading all the locks in the building and advises me to call the non-emergency 101 number if I'm still concerned. Concerned? Of course I'm still bloody concerned. If I hadn't come back when I did the intruder could have sneaked in and out of my flat without me suspecting a thing. I look around me at the chaos of my tiny box room. Has he been here before? Going through my things, watching me while I sleep? I sit trembling in the dust and silence reliving my encounter with John Didcot. *Be careful*, Alice had said, *men like John Didcot will do almost anything to protect their own.* At the time I'd dismissed her warning. But I feel it now. A ripple of threat.

I shove the chest of drawers across the door, slip the hammer under my pillow and crawl, fully dressed, beneath the sheets. I lie in the stifling gloom and think of Maya vanished into nowhere, Kay floating alone in the dark waters of the creek and Vicky lying face down at the bottom of her stairs, her hand stretched out in front of her, perfectly manicured, perfectly still.

In the morning I leave an angry message for the agent managing the downstairs flat, telling him to sharpen up his key security, and one for Tomas asking him to install the heaviest locks he can find on all my doors and windows and to make sure the whole place is secure before his workmen leave. Then I call Alice Foreman to get the name of the agency that supplied George Burney's carers. It's a long shot but still a possibility that Burney might have got garrulous at the end and opened up about Kay's childhood and what the brethren had to hide. By eight o'clock I'm back on the motorway heading for the Laurels, a private nursing home on the outskirts of Northampton. Despite the lush green lawns, the kids' drawings of 'My Nana' pinned to the noticeboard, the vases of bright flowers and my Roz-instilled distrust of religion, all I can think is, *Please God, don't let me die in a place like this.* The faint tang of urine, sharp beneath a sickly overlay of air freshener, the ungainly wing-backed chairs, the shuffling silence and stooped pink heads ringed by haloes of bone-white hair. I follow the receptionist's directions to where Lewis Graham – early thirties, freckled face, good teeth – is handing out cups of milky tea to a row of bundled-up figures propped in chairs. Seemingly unperturbed by all this death in waiting he smiles sadly when I tell him I'm a friend of Kay Duncan's and flash the selfie of us in Toulon.

He glances at the photo and shakes his head. 'I couldn't believe it when I saw the news. I didn't know her well but she seemed like a lovely woman.'

'She was,' I say.

'So what can I do for you?'

'I'm writing an extended obituary of her – trying to set the record straight about her life.'

'Who do you work for?'

'I'm not a journalist, just a friend. But I'm hoping one of the broadsheets will take it. Maybe *The Guardian*.' More lies, but they work.

'Good for you. No one deserves the kind of kicking she got from the tabloids.'

'If you have a minute, could we have a quick chat about her father?'

'Oh, I don't know. I'm not supposed to—'

'Totally off the record. I know he gave her a tough time as a kid and I just want to get a sense of the kind of man he was.'

'Well, as long as you promise to keep my name out of it.' He wheels the tea trolley over to the wall. 'I'm just about finished here and I'm due a break.'

I catch the watery eye of a man shunting determinedly towards us on a Zimmer frame. 'Is there somewhere a bit more private?'

'Through here.' He leads me down a corridor into a messy little staffroom furnished with squat blue chairs – snagged upholstery, orange pine arms – arranged around a muted television tuned to a shopping channel. 'When I started caring for George I had no idea he even had a daughter. It was only after a few months that he started mentioning her, but he always called her Kaitlin so it came as a bit of a shock when I found out who she was.'

'I heard he was… difficult.'

Lewis grins. 'Not the easiest of patients, that's for sure. You expect it when they've got dementia but George was firing on all cylinders right up until the end. Can I get you a coffee?' He flicks on the kettle and offers me a biscuit from a tartan tin. 'Sorry, I didn't catch your name.'

'Phoebe.' It feels more alien every time I say it. I take a biscuit and snap it in half. 'How long were you with him?'

'About a year. I covered most of the day shifts and there were a couple of students who came in to do the nights.'

'Did he tell you he threw Kay out when she was fifteen and pregnant?'

'Yes. He was totally open about it, though he used some strange word for it.'

'Shunned?'

'That's it. He said he'd been forced to shun her because she'd been corrupted by evil. Shocking, but unfortunately telling my patients what I think about their parenting skills isn't part of the job.'

'Did he have many visitors?' I nibble my custard cream.

'Not really. Some old guy he'd known for years used to come round every Friday to give him a game of chess.'

'What did they talk about?'

'The old days, mainly. They'd both worked at Dutton's and it was a big deal when it closed down. I was only a kid but I remember the workers standing outside with placards. People like George Burney, who'd been there all their working lives, made redundant overnight with little or no hope of getting another job. Really sad.'

'What did they make?'

'Some kind of machine parts I think.'

I look down and flick a couple of imaginary crumbs from my lap. 'What about the elders from his church? Did you ever see a man called John Didcot?'

'Sandy hair? Ten-foot stick up his backside?'

'That's the one.'

'Yes, he dropped in a couple of times to discuss church business.'

'What kind of church business?'

'They were having problems with the architect designing their new chapel.'

'You never got the sense they were worried about outsiders investigating the brethren?' I say, my voice thin beneath the blood in my ears.

'What do you mean?'

'Kay had been talking to a support group for victims of abuse.'

'Christ.' He runs his hands through his hair. 'No, they never mentioned anything like that, at least not in my hearing.'

'Never talked about the elders at their sister church being prosecuted?'

He stares at me, clearly horrified. 'I had no idea.'

I crunch down the rest of my biscuit and picture George Burney, crotchety and demanding, playing out his role as a blameless man of God right up until the end. 'Anyone else?'

'A couple of his nieces used to come in and read to him.'

'I'm guessing it wasn't the latest Jackie Collins.'

He laughs and hands me a mug of instant coffee. 'Sadly not. I have to say it cheered things up no end when Kay finally gave in and bombed up in that sporty little car of hers.'

My eyes pull nervously to the bonnet of the Austin-Healey visible through the window and cut back to Lewis before he looks up from spooning sugar into his coffee.

'Sorry, what do you mean, *gave in?*'

'She'd been refusing to see him for months. George had been dictating letters to me two or three times a week telling her if she didn't "kneel before him and seek repentance for her life of sin" he'd leave everything he'd got to the church. When that didn't work he told her he didn't want to die knowing his only daughter was going to rot in hell. Not exactly a master of subtle persuasion.'

'Did she write back?'

'Just once. She said if he left her anything she'd shove it in his shitty bungalow and set fire to the lot and if there was any justice in the world he's the one who'd be rotting in hell.'

I shift forward in my seat. 'Who talked her round?'

'Her husband.'

'David? Did he even *know* George?'

'Oh, yes. He'd been dealing with the old man's care decisions for a while.'

I'm struggling here, but David Duncan is clearly a man who likes to surprise. Lewis sees the look on my face and shrugs. 'Once Kay told social services she didn't want to know I suppose he didn't have much choice. Anyway, he came up a couple of years ago to see about moving George into a place like this and selling the bungalow to pay for it. According to George, the two of them hit it off and when he decided he wanted to be cared for at home I think it must have been David who picked up the tab, because twenty-four-hour home care doesn't come cheap.' I realise I'm gaping and quickly shut my mouth. 'Anyway, when George got nowhere with Kay he started putting pressure on David, telling him it was a woman's duty to obey her husband and a husband's duty to keep his wife on the righteous path.'

'You're joking.'

'Nope. George had pretty unreconstructed views about most things, but he was in a class of his own when it came to anything to do with gender. He had his own page on his church's website and every week he'd dictate a sermon to me and get me to upload it.'

'Can you send me the link?'

'If you want, but they're like something out of the dark ages – Lucifer waging a war of depravity on the righteous, a world saturated with sin and abomination.' He swings his legs onto the pile of magazines on the coffee table and dunks a biscuit into his mug. 'He'd have snuffed it on the spot if he'd known I went home to a husband and two kids every night.'

He laughs and I laugh too, distracted – momentarily – from the confusion inside. The reprieve doesn't last. 'How did David manage to talk Kay round?' I say as the dull, dirty ache seeps back.

'I have no idea. But it was a bloody miracle.'

'When she turned up did Burney, you know… apologise to her?'

'Apologise? No way. "Sorry" wasn't a word in his vocabulary.'

I hadn't expected to hear that George Burney had grovelled and begged, but I'd assumed she'd stormed in to tell him what she thought of him and some hint of contrition on his part had softened her anger. 'So what happened?' I say, utterly bewildered.

'Well, she didn't kneel in front of him but she sat by his bed with her head bowed, took his hand and asked him straight out to forgive her.'

This picture sets my nerves shrieking so badly I want to punch my fist through the plate glass window.

'From then on every time she came they used to spend at least ten minutes praying together.'

I stare at him, incredulous. 'She visited him more than once?'

'It must have been six, maybe seven times.'

My eyes stinging, I look away to the TV screen where a shiny presenter mouths the attractions of a china shepherdess spinning slowly on a velvet plinth – milky skin and high round breasts pushing up coyly from a painted bodice, mine for only £9.99. Six or seven visits? How is that 'going through the motions'? Maybe that's the way it works with blood family, all crimes forgiven in the downhill rush to death.

'She and David used to bring him newspapers and fruit, stay for an hour or so chatting about the weather and whenever George got worried about bills or paperwork, David would sit down with him and sort it out.'

'Did Kay go to his funeral?' I say, my voice unsteady.

'George told her not to. He said he might have found it in his heart to see her but he wasn't going to let one of the shunned contaminate the rest of the Brethren. And David didn't want anyone even knowing she'd started visiting him in case the paparazzi found out and tried to snap photos of her at the old man's deathbed.'

I take another bite of biscuit. The crumbs sit dry in my mouth.

'Did she ever talk to him about Maya, or the abduction?'

'Not in front of me.'

'Did the name Roz Locklear ever come up when you were with him?'

He sips his coffee and shakes his head. 'Sorry.'

I stare down at my mug. The chirpy *It ain't lost till Mum can't find it* caption on the side rings a little hollow when it's your mum you're looking for.

'I haven't been much use to you, have I?' Lewis says.

'Actually this has been really…' I reach for a word that's suitably bland '… informative. I'll leave you my number, in case you think of anything else.'

Outside in the car, I drop my head on the wheel. So much for Will's advice.

How am I supposed to concentrate on the spaces between the facts if the facts keep shifting? My phone beeps. It's a text from Lewis: *Call if there's anything else you need*, and a link to the Breakaway Brethren website. Not even sure I can bear to read this stuff, I click it open. Clearly set up a while ago, the pages are full of the same low-res images of gloopy adolescents they'd used in their leaflets, only this time they've been spiced up with faux marble banners announcing the weakness of mankind and the reality of Hell. George Burney's page, while big on exclamation marks and denunciations of lust, also offers handy tips on ways to avoid God's wrath, most of which involve giving up 'stubbornness' and following the word of George. Other pages give guidance on home, family and ways to avoid contamination by the sins of others, but the general thrust is the same – do as you're told or face the flaming pits of hell.

The archived obituaries are more interesting, giving a strangely fascinating insight into the Brethren's history. Alongside mono-chrome studio portraits of grim-faced men with stiff collars and wayward eyebrows there are snapshots from the 1940s of women and children in pinafores and clumpy boots lined up outside the doors of the old gospel hall, and pictures, spanning five decades, of preachers and leafleteers on the streets of Northampton. One from the 1970s shows a crowd of brethren gazing devotedly at a man holding forth in the market square. I zoom in and realise with a jolt of disgust that the object of their rapture is a young George Burney.

CHAPTER TWENTY-TWO

Hushed murmurs and echoey coughs as the mourners file down the aisle of St John the Divine. They're mostly female; some young – shuffling in short skirts and teetering heels – some elderly – wide-fit black shoes and frumpy little hats dusted off for the occasion – some Vicky's age – crying and hugging each other. The ones on their own, looking a little lost and uncomfortable, are probably clients like me, invited by the mass email sent out by Vicky's sister. I only saw it at the last minute and I spent the whole of yesterday wandering up and down Oxford Street in search of something to wear. I've never cared much about clothes but for Vicky's sake I'd braved a smiley, overeager sales assistant asking 'what's the occasion?' and bought a black silk shift dress and some low-heeled leather pumps. Then I sat on the tube back to Fulham, with my parcels on my lap and tears sliding down my face and dribbling into my mouth.

I cast up and down the rows in search of Chrissie. She has to have flown back for her best friend's funeral, but I have no idea what she looks like now. Pat, tight-lipped in navy, turns and gives me a nod. I nod back and as I slide into a seat at the back I spot Vicky's ex staring stonily at the floor and Marilyn from the salon pushing a balled fist against her mouth.

'Quite a turnout,' the woman beside me whispers approvingly to no one in particular. I glance towards the entrance, worried for a moment that Will's editor might have been tempted to make something of the death of two Doxettes within weeks of each other and ordered him back from his assignment in Scotland to cover the funeral. *That's ridiculous. Of course the press aren't here. Vicky's death was an accident. A terrible, terrible accident that had nothing to do with Roz's lies, Kay's suicide or a half-baked girl band that never even cut a single.* My neighbour throws me a searching look, as if I've said the words aloud and failed to convince her.

The South London church is a squat Victorian structure; raw, red-brick columns and narrow, leaded windows. An organ squeals out the strains of 'Abide With Me' while Vicky, tanned and smiling, stares up at me from the cover of the order of service. I turn as the coffin arrives at the door carried by four pallbearers in black suits and spit-shine shoes. It glides past me, glossy white and heaped with pink roses. I picture her inside, smooth and tanned on a bed of purple satin, not a hair out of place. Behind it come her parents – her mother, small and dark, sobbing into a hanky and clinging to her grey, upright husband. Danny walks behind them, skinny and bewildered in a stiff new suit, beside him a blonde woman who stares straight ahead. I guess she's Vicky's sister. I murmur my way through hymns I don't know and entreat a God I don't believe in to give us comfort in our grief, blindsided by a tearful swell of emotion when I think of Roz's wicker casket buried – at her own insistence – without ceremony beneath the Mopane trees at Molokodi, and Kay's lonely cremation in Marseille with no one there but David to say goodbye.

We emerge from the church into bright morning sunshine and I see Danny scuffing the dirt by the church wall, his freshly clipped head bent low on his chest.

'Hey,' I say softly. 'You did really well back there.'

'I didn't want to come.'

'They say it helps.'

'How? It's shit.'

'Seeing all the people who loved her. Saying a proper goodbye.' The clichés make me wince.

'Yeah, well she and Dad weren't even talking, Nan and Grandad have still got Aunty Liz and who the fuck are the rest of them?'

'It's not about how well people knew her. I was just a client but I really wanted to be here.' I feel rotten but – eyes wandering across the mourners – I ask quickly, 'Did Chrissie Miller come?'

A sullen shake of his head. 'She texted Nan saying she couldn't get a flight.' Then his head jerks up. 'How do you know Chrissie?'

'I don't but... your mum mentioned her when she was telling me about the band she used to be in.'

He stares at me as if he's trying to bring me into focus. 'It was you.'

'What?' I say, timidly.

'Mum had her old photos out that morning. She was looking for a picture of the band to give to a client.'

'Oh, yes,' I say. 'That was me.'

'Why?'

'I... my mother saw the Doxettes play way back. She wanted a souvenir.'

He blinks at me so sharply I think I'm about to be outed as a liar by a fifteen-year-old. 'How many photos did she give you?'

This wasn't the response I'd anticipated. Unsure where this is going, I tell the truth. 'Just one.'

'What happened to the rest of them?'

'What do you mean?'

'Dad found the empty box shoved in the sideboard. All her Doxettes memorabilia gone. Photos, demo CDs, the lot.'

I shiver at this image and my heart beats hard. 'Maybe she had a clear-out,' I say, aware of how feeble this sounds.

He shakes his head, quick and agitated. 'Not of that stuff.'

I dig my nails into my palm and look away to where his grandfather is shaking hands with the vicar and an orderly line of women – handbags clutched tight – wait in turn to give Vicky's mother a hug.

'You were one of the last people she contacted,' Danny says, unexpectedly.

'Oh,' I say. 'You found her phone.'

'No. I checked her bill against the contacts in her computer. That afternoon she called a mobile and talked for nearly half an hour. A bit later she called it again, then she called the takeaway, then she called you.'

'Can you give me the mobile number she called?'

'Sure, but I tried it like fifty times. It's been disconnected. Dad thinks it was some new boyfriend. But it wasn't.'

'How do you know?'

'Me and Mum had a deal. She always told me when she'd met a new bloke. Even if it was just casual.'

I want to be alone with this information so I can pick it over and work out why it feels so wrong, so it's a relief when I see his aunt beckoning him to join the ribbon of people making their way to the graveside. 'Come on,' I say. He pushes himself off the wall. I squeeze his shoulder and stay back as the family clusters around the grave. Something snags. A figure loitering at the far edge of the crowd. Certain I hadn't noticed any denim among the respectfully dressed congregation in the church, I crane to get a look at his face. The man swivels and slouches away, hands in his pockets. Just a gawper, I think angrily, getting a morbid kick out of watching the burial of a stranger.

Later, when the mourners have gone, I add a single white rose to the tributes and stand looking down at the grave. Whose mobile did you call, Vicky? Who cut you off when you called me? If it's the person who took your phone and your old photos what is it they didn't want the world to know? I try Chrissie Miller's number for the hundredth time. It's still 'unavailable'. A wave of helplessness swells inside me. Death, deception and unanswered questions wherever I go. I have to start finding answers or my sanity will shatter. Back in the car I fumble for my notebook and stare blurrily at the dwindling list of names I've gathered from Kay and Roz's pasts. I stop at Delphine Lomas, the woman who appeared for the prosecution in Jonas Parks' trial. I inhale, then exhale slowly and reach for my phone. According to her LinkedIn profile Delphine now runs *Finty Lomas Organics*, a cruelty free cosmetics store with an address in Covent Garden.

CHAPTER TWENTY-THREE

Once, when I was six or seven, I pestered our cook Evangeline into taking me with her on her weekly trip to the market. Of course, as soon as we arrived I got bored with all the haggling and gossiping and wandered off after a dog or a goat or something far more interesting than the price of mangoes or the birth of Kiki Molefe's twins. I was sure I'd only gone a few yards but when I looked up Evangeline had disappeared and all I could see was a sea of strangers closing in. I remember the smells, the fear, the voices. Every time I moved I hit a dead end or a wall of legs so I sat down in the dirt and howled out her name. Like magic, a man stepped out of the crush, the tallest man I'd ever seen, and he swung me up onto his shoulders and twirled me around, shouting, 'Can you see her? Can you see her?'

It felt like I was flying and I looked out across the maze of stalls and there, on the far side of the market, was Evangeline running up and down accosting passers-by. I waved at her and she looked up and saw me and came stomping back to get me. Sometimes when I'm panicked it helps to remember the glorious relief of that moment. Right now, it chills me to think that if I hit any more dead ends I could be left howling in the dirt forever.

I see Delphine Lomas through the panes of the old-fashioned bow window of her shop on Mercer Street; a slim blonde in a flimsy cotton dress instantly recognisable from her website photo. She's delving into a cardboard carton she's balancing against her hip. I push open the door. The air inside is tart and citrussy, a fruity tingle of scents. She glances up. Late thirties, understated make-up, smooth hair softly pinned, jade drop earrings. She offers me a quick businesslike nod and goes back to building a pyramid of coarse-cut hunks of soap, leaving me to browse the displays of glass bottles – emerald, sapphire, crimson – trimmed with smart italic labels, charcoal grey on cream. I unstopper a jar of bath oil, hold it to my nose and start at the fragrant bolt of home – jasmine-scented sunsets, the whoop and chatter of the bush at dusk, a flash of headlamps as Roz bumps her pickup through the gates of the compound. I wait for the assistant to go to the rescue of a floundering gift-pack buyer, then I make my move.

'How much is this?'

Delphine's head flicks round. 'Nineteen pounds seventy. Seems a lot I know, but you only need a couple of drops for each bath.'

Her accent is clipped and very English – echoes of the gloved and hatted heroines in the black and white movies that Roz always wanted me to watch.

'Great. I love this smell.' I follow her over to the till. 'Finty, that's short for Delphine?'

'That's right.' She angles the jar on a bed of sea green tissue, flicks up a couple of sheets with a briskly licked thumb and rolls them around the glass.

'I love your shop.' I finger the edges of my credit card and look around at the elegantly arranged shelves.

'Thank you. Where did you hear about us?'

I pause, nervous now. 'I saw your name in the reports of Jonas Parks' trial.'

She straightens up, one hand pressed hard on the half-wrapped package. 'That's not something I'm interested in discussing.'

'I…' I falter under the fixity of her gaze, but can't afford to lose momentum. I say quickly. 'I want to talk about Roz Locklear.'

Fleeting surprise on her face – suppressed almost the moment I see it. Her fingers, moving mechanically, snap off a length of straw from a metal-toothed dispenser.

I press her. 'Roz died three months ago. I'm trying to find out about her past.'

A tiny pause as she secures the package, a slight fumbling as she drops it into a paper carrier bag and thrusts it at me. 'Who are you?'

'Phoebe. Roz's daughter.' It works. She's shocked – more than shocked – there's no hiding it this time. I hold out my open passport. She studies the name and the photo and then looks up at me. I see her confusion in how intensely she's searching my face, how frantically she's groping around for what to say.

'I thought Phoebe was dead.' Her voice is hollow.

'Me too,' I hold her gaze. 'That's kind of why I'm here.'

Her eyes drop and she tips forward, gripping the edge of the counter. I lay the group shot I found at Rickman's Farm in front of her.

She starts back. 'Where did you get that?'

'I went to the farm. Please,' I say, 'talk to me.'

The doorbell jangles behind me – a scurry of customers enters the shop.

'Not here,' she says, low and quick.

'Where?'

She scribbles a note on the back of a gift card, drops it into the bag and with a crisp, 'Enjoy your purchase,' she pivots round and disappears through the 'Staff Only' swing door.

CHAPTER TWENTY-FOUR

Just got back. Got something for you. Can you come over? Xxx

I spend the next hour looking at Will's text, sipping a coffee and resisting the urge to text him back and tell him I'll be there as soon as I can. Once I've talked to Delphine I may need time alone. I wander out into the streets of Covent Garden, and stop to watch a silver-sprayed mime artist held horizontal in mid-air by the tip of an umbrella and a red-faced beat boxer freestyling a frenzy of percussion with his lips; slick illusions that strike sourly with my need for truth. Still ten minutes early for our meeting, I push my way out of the sunshine into the gloom of the Hand in Hand. So much for the olde worlde charm of London's pubs – a sweaty throng of lunchtime drinkers, swirly carpet, dark mismatched furniture, a flashing row of fruit machines and a fake jukebox, playing Lila Mendez through a speaker. If the music's an omen I can't even guess if it's good or bad. I check Delphine's note – this is the place. And I get why she picked it. She doesn't want to bump into anyone she knows. I squeeze my way to the bar and see her at a corner table, staring into an almost empty glass. Maybe she likes to be punctual. Maybe she needed a drink before we talked. No greeting when I slide in across from her with another glass and an opened bottle of South African red. Her head stays low, her eyes fix on my hands as I set them down, her lips barely move as she speaks. 'Why are you using a dead girl's identity?'

'OK.' I spread my fingers flat on the table, raising and lowering the tips as I speak, half to calm her, half to stop myself stumbling from my carefully filleted version of the truth. 'Roz brought me up believing that Phoebe died in a car accident in Malawi. She said my mother was her distant relative and when my parents died she took me in because there was no one else.' *Slow down – don't let her see this is rehearsed.* 'She was about to start a new job in Botswana and she said the only way she'd been able to take me with her was by pretending I was Phoebe. So the truth had to stay "our secret".'

'Didn't that seem odd?'

I see Roz sitting across from me, arms folded, head cocked. 'Not really. When I was little she was my world and I'd have said or done anything to make sure I stayed with her. Then, as I grew older the whole secrecy thing just seemed to fit with her aversion to bureaucracy and, in a way, I kind of liked the idea that I was at least a year younger than everyone else in my class but still managed to keep up.'

'Didn't you ever ask for photos of your mother and father?'

'She said all their possessions were destroyed in the fire that killed them. But after she died I did some digging and found out that everything she'd told me was a lie.' A slug of wine – sharp and vinegary. 'If I'm ever going to find my parents I need to know who Roz really was and why she lied.'

'I never met her. She left before my time.'

Another blow. But she's holding something back. Why else would she bring me here? I slide the group photo across the table and tap the blacked-out figure.

'You knew this was her. I saw it in your face. Why would anyone do that to a photo? It's like something out of Soviet Russia.'

She turns away, sickly pale, and gazes at the slashed backrest of the empty seat between us, a gape of something grey and grubby visible through the slit. 'Because that's exactly how it was. Roz was the object of our collective hatred.'

'Why?'

'We were jealous.'

'Of her and Jonas?'

'Oh, no.' A sour little smile. 'He spread his attentions pretty liberally.'

'Then why?'

'Because we were nuts. All of us.'

'Including you?'

'*Especially* me.'

'How long did she live at Rickman's Farm?'

'Nearly two years.'

It's hot in the bar, a close stagnant heat that defies the listless fan above our heads. 'I don't get it. She'd have hated living by someone else's rules, especially someone as controlling as Parks.'

Delphine swallows her wine and brings both hands to rest on the stem of her glass. 'She wasn't there by choice. She needed somewhere to hide.'

'Who from?' I wait for her to go on, my heart thumping, my eyes on the fake jukebox, which has shuffled from Mendez to Madonna and is now playing Tina Turner's 'What's Love Got To Do With It?'.

Delphine glances around then drops her head. 'The police.'

The police? Roz? A splinter of terror slides into my chest. 'What had she done?'

'Only Jonas knew that and that's the way he liked to keep it. Other people's secrets are power and God knows we've all got them.' Her eyes come looking for mine and bore into me as if she knows what I did to Kay. I look away.

'What about you, Delphine?' I say, defiant. 'Why were you at Rickman's Farm?'

'I was a lost soul and Jonas Parks was a magnet for girls like me – the confused, the lonely, the rejected. He offered us what we thought was love, and answered questions that we didn't even know we'd asked.' She reaches for the bottle and fills her glass. 'Once we'd let him into our heads and handed over everything we owned he did everything in his power to cut us off from the outside world. He called it unchaining us from our "toxic pasts". And of course he convinced us – and maybe even himself – that what he was doing wasn't about sex or money or power but about helping humanity.'

'How?'

She's looking at me, the mockery in her raised eyebrow belied by the pain in her voice. 'By *allowing* us to bear his "Golden Children", offspring who would carry on his "superior" line and bring guidance to a broken world. Only there was a major flaw in his plan.' A blurt of mirthless laughter. 'No one was getting pregnant.'

'Parks had a problem?'

'Seems obvious now, but dodgy sperm didn't exactly fit with his superman image. So he blamed us. He said that only the truly worthy would be chosen to bear his wonder children and we had to make up for it by bringing him younger, better, worthier vessels.'

'*Vessels?*'

A bitter smile. 'Believe me, in these situations the jargon is key. The more biblical the better.'

'And you bought into this crap?'

'Hundred per cent.'

'Why didn't someone tell him he was shooting blanks?'

She shrugs. 'That's how it works in a place like that. The leader blames you for anything that goes wrong then uses that guilt to control you. Of course it helps if the conditioning is backed up by punishments. In our case food and showers denied if you questioned something Jonas said. If you *really* displeased him he'd confine you to one of the sheds without food or heating.'

'Locked you in?'

'Sometimes. But psychological locks can be just as powerful as physical ones, especially if you think you deserve the punishment.'

I think queasily of the stained mattress and cobwebbed bowl in the storeroom at Rickman's Farm.

'Was he violent?'

'Occasionally. Sometimes he'd use sex to debase us, force us to do things we didn't want to, but he preferred to let us punish each other – slaps, silence, bullying.' Her lip quivers. 'And there was always the circling finger.' She extends her forefinger and draws a small circle in the air, level with a spot between my breasts.

'What was it? Some kind of hypnosis?'

'Hypnosis, conditioning… call it what you like. But it made your whole body tingle. He'd look you in the eye while he did it and tell you he was calming your bad energies, quieting your unhealthy doubts, drawing out the real you. Making you just that little bit worthier.'

I flop back in my chair. 'Why didn't you just walk out?'

She gazes unseeing at her glass. 'I was frightened. I thought I wouldn't be able to function without him, or that place, or those people.'

I see Alice Foreman, pale against her pillows.

We faced a terrible choice: give up everything – our homes, our church, the rest of our families – or reach out to a child who had lost her way.

'But you're smart, independent, successful.'

'Only after years of therapy. If my godmother hadn't left me her business I might never have got back on my feet.' She drops her eyes like a guilty child. 'When I heard I'd inherited it my first thought was to sell up and give the money to Jonas.'

'That's terrible.'

'Sure, but plenty of his victims are still with him, handing over every penny they can lay their hands on.'

'They must have seen through him when he went to prison.'

'You're kidding? They saw him as a martyr and me as his persecutor in chief.'

'That must have been tough.'

She worries the edge of a beer mat with her nail. 'I saw it as part of my recovery process – I thought if I could get him sent down for rape and false imprisonment as well as breaking and entering I could prevent him from destroying any more lives. I spent weeks tracking down his former followers but half of them didn't reply and the ones who did refused to testify. In fact they all lined up to call me a liar. So all he got was nine months. He was out after four.'

My head jerks up, one of those involuntary responses to a stare from a stranger. I run my eyes across the red-faced boys at the bar to some guy with a stumpy ponytail and a black baseball cap who thinks it's cool to keep his shades on in a darkened pub. I catch the eye of a sleazy suit with a skinny blonde hanging off his arm. He winks. I scowl and flick back to ponytail guy. Something about the hunch of his shoulders and the tilt of his head takes me back to Cassis. Is it someone at Remy's bar he reminds me of? I look away and turn back to Delphine. 'Sorry, can we go back a bit. Why did everyone hate Roz?'

She leans back, twisting the stem of her glass.

'Please. I need to know.'

She nods very slowly. 'It turned out that one in a million of Jonas's pathetic sperm was live and it just so happened that Roz was the "blessed recipient".'

I sit motionless for a second, feel the pulse beat in my temple. 'Parks was Phoebe's father?'

She nods again.

'Are you sure?'

'Roz never denied it, even when things turned nasty.'

My pulse speeds up. 'What kind of nasty?'

'Parks decided that Phoebe should be brought up collectively with no single mother figure in her life, and since he alone shared her superior genes he alone would be allowed to show her affection.'

'That's monstrous.'

'It gets worse. He wouldn't let her leave the farm – even to see a doctor – because of the dark forces bent on destroying his golden children.'

'And people believed him?'

'Of course. Textbook cult dynamics – make it all about us and them. Roz stuck it out for a few months after Phoebe was born, I assume because she needed to stay in hiding. Then one morning she got up before dawn and walked out, taking the baby with her. To save face Jonas said she'd been "corrupted by the forces of darkness" and he turned her into a figure of hate. The evil transgressor who had disobeyed his rules and – horror of horrors – stolen away his golden child. So there was a kind of mass desperation to give him another one. But when nobody got pregnant, Parks upped Phoebe's mythical status and made her out to be this irreplaceable, all seeing, all knowing specimen of super-humanity and turned finding her into a quasi-religious quest.'

I take out the photo and the idealised drawing of the child I stole from Rickman's Farm. 'Is this her?'

An involuntary shudder comes with her nod. 'Imagine what they'd have done to that poor kid if Roz hadn't got her out of there.'

I stare at the two images – the plain, straight-haired toddler and the haloed, cherubic doll. 'That's why she was keeping tabs on Jonas after she left the farm. She knew he wanted Phoebe back.'

She downs more wine. 'By the time I arrived at Rickman's Farm, finding Jonas's golden child was all anyone was talking about. He'd bought a couple of laptops and handpicked a group of us to devote every waking hour to searching for Roz. She'd been ultra-careful about leaving any kind of footprint but eventually, after nearly two years we…' She tips forward, screwing up her eyes as if pressed down by an unbearable weight '*I*… found an R. Locklear on the staff list of a small private nature conservancy in Malawi. I made a call to the trust that ran it and they confirmed it was Roz.'

I shunt forward a little on my seat. 'And then?'

'Jonas and that mad old bat Amy Rickman flew out there, promising to bring Phoebe home. His plan was to snatch her, take her to the British Embassy and denounce Roz for this crime she'd committed. It was something bad, I know that, because he was banking on the Brits getting her extradited to stand trial in the UK.'

A jangle of memories: the times I got up in the night and found Roz sitting alone in the dark, the bouts of insomnia that left her drawn and irritable, the rattle of the bottle of pills she kept on the top shelf of the bathroom cabinet. I tune back into Delphine. 'If he had any problem getting custody of Phoebe, Amy was going to put up the money for a top lawyer.'

'What happened?'

'I only know Jonas's version – he used to tell it over and over like some ancient hero recounting a battle – but as far as I can work out he pitched up at Roz's lodge in the middle of the bush, threw Phoebe into his car and drove off. Roz jumped into her jeep and gave chase but it was dark and he wasn't used to the winding dirt roads. He lost control, the car swerved off the road, tipped into a dry riverbed and caught fire. It was Roz who scrambled down and pulled them out. He and Amy were badly injured but Phoebe…' She pushes her hand to her mouth. 'Phoebe was killed instantly. Five years old.'

The horror comes in waves but I snatch at a thread of hope. 'What if Phoebe survived? What if Roz just pretended she was dead to get Parks off her back?' I look down at the pictures on the table in front of me and my skin goes cold beneath the sweat. 'What if I'm really her?'

Delphine reaches over and pins my forearms to the table. Her eyes drill into mine. 'When you walked into the shop and showed me your passport I wanted to believe exactly that – that you were Phoebe and I'd be able to sleep properly for the first time in seventeen years.' She drops her eyes. 'You're not.'

'Babies' hair and eye colour can change as they get older.'

'You're not scarred.'

'Maybe Roz managed to pull me out of the wreckage unharmed.'

'Not just from the crash. The little finger on Phoebe's left hand was shorter than it should have been, and semi-fused to the next one. Jonas said it was a sign of her superior status – a flaw in her outer being to shield her inner perfection from the forces of darkness.' She cuts her eyes to the portrait's clumsily drawn hand. 'Even if it had been operated on it would have left a mark.' She lifts my left hand and separates out my little finger – full sized, straight and unscarred. 'See?' She lets my hand drop. I slide it beneath the table and watch her reach for the wine bottle. Another woman with death on her conscience, trying to numb her guilt. She fills our glasses. 'Parks was badly injured in the crash. He spent weeks in hospital in Lilongwe and when he got back the scars and the walking stick added to the martyrdom and helped him to whip up more hatred against Roz.'

'Why didn't you challenge him?'

She's shaking, holding back tears. 'You don't get it, do you? By then I'd almost lost the ability to think for myself and I couldn't confide in anyone because I was scared they'd start hating me the way they hated Roz.'

'I'm sorry… I didn't mean… it's just from the outside it's difficult.'

'Finding the strength to leave was the hardest thing I've ever done. My own family was a total mess and I was giving up on a dream of belonging.' She pushes a tissue to her nose and shakes her head while I sit in silence, looking to see how I might fit in to these new realities of Roz.

After a while I say, 'I need to see Parks.'

'No. You don't.'

'I need to know why Roz was hiding from the police.'

'Let it go. She's dead.'

'This crime she committed could be the key to who I am, the reason she lied to me about my parents.' *The reason she lied about Kay.*

'You have to keep away from him.'

'Why?'

She glares at me. 'Because you're exactly the kind of victim he goes for – young, vulnerable, looking for answers.'

'I'll be careful.'

'Oh, for God's sake! You've got no idea what he's like. You'll think you're on your guard and all the time he'll be reading you, finding your weak spot so he can make you do and say and be exactly what he wants.'

I want to yell at her that I'm far too smart to get manipulated by a creep like Parks. But her concern is real and it touches me. She slumps forward, cradling her face in her hands and asks, 'Did Roz ever have any more children of her own?'

'No,' I say, surprised how hurtful a word like 'own' can feel, a word Roz never used to describe the child she'd lost – *You and me, kiddo, that's all that matters.*

I feel eyes on me again. I look back at the bar. The blonde guy has gone and ponytail man is on his phone, head bent, his back to the room, one finger pressed to his ear.

CHAPTER TWENTY-FIVE

I leave Delphine and walk down to the river, heartsick at the thought of Roz chasing through the bush to rescue Phoebe from her psychotic father, swerving to a stop as his car plunged into the ravine and scrabbling down the bank to tear her dying daughter from the flames. No wonder she'd tried to drop off the radar as soon as she'd escaped from Rickman's Farm. But why carry the grief alone for all these years? And why go to so much trouble to keep me from even knowing Parks' name? Looking around at the passing ferry boats, the sunlight hitting the water and the sweaty tourists nibbling ice creams, I imagine Roz's secrets festering inside her, corroding every thought, every relationship, every chance of happiness. I walk on down the Embankment. Even before I get to the station I know that for my own sanity I can't bottle this up much longer. At some point I'll have to smash the silence and share at least this part of her past with Will. A weight shifts, my step lightens. Maybe, when I find out how her story first touched mine, I'll find the courage to risk everything and tell him the rest.

'Smells good!' I say as I walk into his flat.

He grins and glances up from the pan he's stirring. 'You wait. A couple of hours in the oven and it'll be nectar of the gods.' He scoops up a spoonful of sauce and leans in to taste it. 'Good news on Roz's police check,' he says, rolling the sauce around his mouth. 'Not so much as a speeding ticket.'

I give him a nervous smile, drop my bag on the counter and stretch up to kiss him.

He stops stirring and kisses me back. 'Your Mr Parks, on the other hand…'

'What about him?'

'Turns out the police took those sexual exploitation allegations seriously. They even put out an appeal for victims and witnesses.'

I pull away and help myself to a beer. 'Any takers?'

'Just one. A witness. Unfortunately she couldn't name the victim and refused to appear in court because she didn't want her husband knowing she'd been in a cult. I managed to get you a copy of her statement, though.' He nods towards a large white envelope propped on the counter. 'I warn you, it makes pretty grim reading.'

I reach for the envelope, pull up a stool and slide out three photocopied sheets. The text is scabbed with blocks of black. I look up at him.

'The police promised the witness anonymity *and* there's a rape involved, so my contact redacted everything that could identify her or the victim.'

I snap the cap off my beer, take a sip and start to read.

STATEMENT OF [REDACTED]

Between 1997 and 2000 I was a member of a commune led by Jonas Parks based at Rickman's Farm outside Horton-on-the-Water in Leicestershire. I make this witness statement in support of the charges against him of assault, false imprisonment and the rape of a minor.

I joined the commune of my own free will. I was 24, estranged from my family and feeling lost and unhappy. There were sixteen women living there when I arrived, ranging in age from 19 to 35. Jonas Parks had rules for every aspect of our existence. We were punished if we disobeyed them. Having sex with him was seen as an honour and a duty. Nobody ever refused him. The sex was partly for his gratification and partly because he wanted children. At the time I was there he only had one. A daughter called [REDACTED]. Her mother was a woman I knew only as [REDACTED], who ran the farm.

I shift uncomfortably. I don't need to see the originals to tell me that this woman is Roz; her blacked-out name a disturbing echo of her blacked-out image in the photo I stole from the farm.

Jonas acted as if his daughter was his property, to do with exactly as he wanted.

He made rules about how she should be brought up and he rationed the amount of time her mother was allowed to spend with her. He wouldn't even let her sleep in the same room as the baby and he made one of us take the child back to the nursery as soon as [REDACTED] finished feeding her.

A sickening flash of Parks alone with Phoebe, pouring his crackpot poison into her head, making plans for their future – two 'superior beings' in a world of his own making, untrammelled by the norms of lesser mortals.

[REDACTED] was upset and angry about it but Parks had some kind of hold over her so she kept quiet. Parks had done a deal with the bikers from the Hillside estate. He supplied them with home-grown cannabis. In exchange they picked up girls from nearby towns and brought them to the farm. Parks got the rest of us to ply these girls with food, alcohol, weed and, worst of all, kindness to get them to stay. He told us we were offering them the chance of enlightenment.

The rape of a minor took place on the night of 5 November 1999. I know this because it was Jonas's fortieth birthday and we were having a bonfire party to celebrate. He had been wound up all day, ranting about righting the crooked scales of justice and restoring harmony. One of the bikers, a small-time drug dealer called Keith Sharplin, known as 'Sharpie', turned up that night with a girl we'd never seen before. I think he must have given her a spiked drink before she got there because by the time she arrived she was so out of it she could hardly stand up. Jonas homed in on her the minute she staggered in. He paraded her around like a prize and told everyone she was his special girl and when she passed out completely he picked her up and took her off to the barn.

Images bump around in my head; a teenage girl, doped senseless, being dragged across the dirty concrete floor of the barn at Rickman's Farm, the sliding metal doors rumbling shut, leaving her alone with Jonas Parks.

Next morning it was my turn to help [REDACTED] with the milking. Around 5.30 a.m. we entered the barn. We found this girl lying in one of the stalls, half naked and totally out of it. She was curled up on her jacket. We went through the pockets trying to find out who she was. I found her school bus pass. It was rubbed and crumpled and had a flower doodled in biro in one corner. Under all that make-up she was just a kid. Judging by the blood on her thighs she'd been a virgin before Jonas raped her.

'See what I mean about grim?'

I look up at the sound of Will's voice. Half attentive, he is scraping a handful of chopped herbs into the pan. I don't speak. I can't.

We cleaned her up as best we could but she was semi-conscious and couldn't even say her own name. We were desperate to get her to a doctor before Jonas woke up. We couldn't call an ambulance because he made anyone who had a mobile surrender it on arrival and the only phone at the farm was locked in his office. We decided to get the girl to the road and try to flag down a car to take her to A&E. But Jonas had a rule that nobody could leave the farm without his permission and after a couple of hundred yards I froze. It sounds insane I know but I just couldn't go any further. So [REDACTED] did it on her own, half carrying, half dragging this girl through the woods.

I ache inside. This was my Roz, the Roz I'd loved and admired, at her angry fuck-it-all best, risking everything to save a stranger.

Jonas went mad when he discovered the girl had gone and he sent Sharpie out to find her. Then he called everybody into the house and questioned us one by one. [REDACTED] warned me to keep my mouth shut but Jonas used to do this thing with his finger, circling it just between your breasts. There was a new girl there. I think her real name was [REDACTED] but we called her Mouse. When he pointed his finger at her she immediately started crying and told him she'd seen [REDACTED] dragging the girl off to the woods. She begged him to forgive her for not raising the alarm. Then he did it to me and I broke down and told him everything. He said the dark forces that had entered us had to be cleansed and he locked all three of us in separate sheds without food. I can't remember how long we were there. After a couple of days you get confused but it was at least four.

About six weeks later Sharpie turned up again. He said he'd asked around about Jonas's 'special girl' and the word on the street was that she was pregnant and that her dad, who was some kind of preacher, had thrown her out.

I pretend not to hear a hundred broken fragments clatter into place, pretend not to see the neon finger tracing 'It's her' across the inside of my skull. Aware of Will's eyes on my back, I snatch up my bag and make my unsteady way to the bathroom. Unsure whether to feel angry, vindicated or confused, I lean over the sink and press my forehead against the cool of the mirror.

This is it.

The tie that bound Roz's life to Kay's. Their daughters – one dead, one missing – were half-sisters, fathered by the same arrogant monster of a man. I shake open my notebook to the page where I set out Roz, Kay, Phoebe and Maya as points on a needleless compass. At the place where the circled names meet – the overlap where I'd been sure I would find myself – I write 'Jonas Parks'. I stare at it for a long time and then, glazed and trembling, I splash my face with cold water, stuff my notebook back into my bag and walk slowly back to the living room.

'Do you mind if put on the news?' Will is leaning back against the sink, pointing the remote at the television. 'I want to catch the headlines.'

'Go ahead,' I say. Glad of anything that will keep his questioning gaze from me, I go back to the witness statement.

We all sat there in silence waiting for Jonas to explode. But he stayed very cold and calm and told Sharpie he'd give him a hundred pounds to find the girl and another thousand if he brought her back to the farm. Then he turned the full force of his fury on [REDACTED]. He dragged her to her feet, started shaking her and accused her of getting rid of his special girl out of jealousy because she'd recognised her as another 'chosen vessel' and she wanted to keep that honour to herself. He ranted about the forces of evil being out to deny the world his golden children and warned us to be on our guard against the darkness in our midst. Then he made us swear to stop [REDACTED] having any more contact with her baby. He said her malign presence would corrupt the light in his golden daughter.

About a week later Keith Sharplin came back to the farm. He said he'd found the girl living rough in London but she'd miscarried the baby.

Miscarried? The word trips me up and leaves me flailing. Baffled, I lift my head and watch a square-faced politician with saggy jowls defending arms sales to Saudi Arabia.

When he heard this, Jonas pulled [REDACTED] to her feet and struck her hard across the face. She fell to the floor. He dragged her up again and hit her repeatedly until she collapsed. I had never seen him so violent or so angry but to my shame none of us did anything to help her. That night, when everyone was asleep, [REDACTED] broke into the nursery, took her baby and left the farm. I left a few weeks later. I do not know what happened to [REDACTED] or to the schoolgirl who Jonas raped.

I do the maths again, re-counting the weeks from 5 November to Maya's birth the following August. This 'special' girl *has* to be Kay, but why would a scumbag like Sharplin lie about her having a miscarriage, when it meant giving up the chance of Jonas's thousand pounds? I have to get out of here. I have to think. I glance up. Will is speaking.

'Sorry?' I say.

'I said, do you think your foster mother spent time at Parks' farm?'

'Maybe.' I pick up my bag and try to slip past him.

'Where are you going?'

'Chemist.' That usually shuts men up. Not Will. He takes me by the shoulders and holds me firm. 'What's going on?'

'Nothing.'

'Oh, come on, I'm not an idiot. Let me help.'

'I... I won't be long.' I slip past him and hurry out into the streets of Spitalfields. I keep walking, past brick-lined shops selling artisan tofu and handmade shoes, and lose myself in the stream of shoppers pouring towards Petticoat Lane. I weave in and out of the crowds feeling like an actor hired to play the lead in my own story, only to find that I'm a bit player in the biopic of someone else's life, sound-tracked by snatches of music drifting from shop doorways; a nameless walk-on stumbling blindly through a storyline that makes no sense, peopled with characters who shunt in and out of focus. Roz, the saviour turned destroyer; Maya who was lost, then found, then lost again; and Kay, the mother whose child was supposedly never born. I spin around. Litter and ice creams, screaming toddlers, tattooed flesh, scorched concrete, a helmeted biker pulling up on the kerbside, the sickly sweetness of candied peanuts, and the hot sweaty sensation that although this story isn't mine, someone watching the drama has eyes only for me.

Will is contrite when I get back and keeps apologising for giving me a hard time but even as I curl up beside him on the sofa, slide my hands beneath his shirt and whisper that I'm sorry I know his journalistic instincts are still on high alert.

That night I can think of nothing but the vicious punishment Parks inflicted on Roz for saving Kay and the lengths she went to to protect Phoebe from his pernicious influence, starting awake every time I drift off. Then later, as Will shifts and murmurs beside me, all lanky limbs and flailing arms, I drift into the recurring dream of five-year-old Maya calling to me from a bricked-up cell, the sound distorting and dissolving as she whispers who I am and begs me to save her. This time her prison is in darkness, the only light a twisting shaft of blue slanting through a slit in the wall. Her abductor is moving towards me through the shadows. His silhouette looms closer to the beam, the light creeps up his legs, his torso, his throat, his chin and then, in a flash of blinding brightness, it illuminates the face of Jonas Parks. I jolt upright.

Will turns in his sleep. 'What's wrong?'

'Sorry,' I whisper. 'Bad dream.'

His hand finds my thigh, steadying my nerves as I try to think through what my gut is screaming at me. Parks was obsessed with the idea of producing golden offspring. After years of believing that Phoebe's death had left him childless he could easily have seen the feature about David Duncan and worked out that Maya was his. So he snatched her from the street – or got one of his followers to do it – and had her brought up collectively at Rickman's Farm, hidden from prying eyes.

Will is sleeping soundly when I slip out of bed and tiptoe into the sitting room. I huddle on the sofa with my notebook and the witness report of Kay's rape, testing my theory against every scrap of information I've collected. It makes heart-stopping sense, but leaves out one vital piece of the puzzle – me.

I leave a note on Will's pillow:

I need some space to get this Roz thing sorted in my head. I'll call you. Promise. xxx.

CHAPTER TWENTY-SIX

'Keith? Bottom of aisle three.'

My phone pings – another text from Will which I ignore like all the others. *Where are you? Let me help. Why don't you trust me?* I follow the direction of the till girl's thumb until I spot Keith Sharplin, Renton's Discount Homestore's white-coated king of paints and varnishes. I walk towards him, down an aisle littered with stray taps, kicked-in crates of wall tiles and stacks of boxed toilets 'priced to go'. He's lifting five litre tubs of own-brand emulsion onto metal shelves, a grunt with every bend.

'Mr Sharplin?'

'That's me,' he says without looking round.

'I'd like to ask you a few questions.'

'Oh, yeah? What about?'

'Someone you used to work for.'

His shoulders stiffen for a moment then he turns to look at me. Rangy, sandy-haired, rat-faced; it's not hard to picture his glory days as biker, drug pusher and procurer of vulnerable girls. 'Who might that be?'

I drop a print out of the trial report from the *Leicester Herald* on the counter and point to the photo. 'Jonas Parks.'

A moment of silence while we both examine the police mugshot of Parks. My eyes slide from his stark unignorable gaze to the narrow line of his nose and the self-satisfied curl of his lips. I hear the sharp intake of my own breath and steady myself against the edge of the counter. Sharplin is the first to speak. 'Don't know him.'

'Please don't lie to me, Mr Sharplin,' I say, my voice scratchy and uneven. 'I know you were a frequent visitor to Rickman's Farm.'

'Who are you?'

I breathe through the lie. 'I work with Will Betteridge on the breakfast news.'

Vanity tweaked, Sharplin wipes his hands down the front of his dustcoat and plucks Will's card from my outstretched fingers. He studies it carefully.

'How did you find me?'

'I dropped in on the only Sharplins still living on the Hillside estate. Seems your grandmother's quite a fan of Will's work.'

'Why should I talk to you?'

'If you don't, we'll assume you've got something to hide. If you do, we might pay you for an interview.'

He tucks the card into his top pocket. 'How much?'

'Depends how forthcoming you are.'

'What does that mean?'

A couple rattles towards us pushing a bag of cement and some wobbly lengths of piping on a flatbed trolley. They hover and pass on.

'It means that I sound you out then report back to Will. If he thinks you're worth putting on camera, I'll be in touch to negotiate a fee. Of course' – delicate look away to a bin of half price paint rollers – 'if you wanted to protect your anonymity we could always shoot you in silhouette.'

His gaze shifts from my face. I follow his eyeline to a man with a badge and a bad suit over by the racks of knobs and knockers who's looking in our direction. Sharplin – with a conspiratorial wink at me – plucks a colour chart from the shelf, spreads it on the counter and stabs a nail etched with grime at the 'Inspiration' range of 'sunset reds and rich magentas'. Reluctantly I move in a little closer. There's a mustiness about him, the smell of dirty clothes left too long in a heap. I switch my phone to record and lay it down next to the chart. Sharplin gives a little smirk, 'So what's Parks been up to now?'

'Tell me about Kaitlin Burney, Mr Sharplin.'

The smirk falters. 'Who?'

'Kaitlin Burney.'

'Never heard of her.'

'Jonas's "special girl".' I tap the buttons on my phone and swipe – in what I hope is a researcher-like way – to the picture of Kay as skinny goth girl that Alice Foreman kept hidden beneath her pills. 'You took her to Rickman's Farm twenty years ago on the night of his fortieth birthday.'

His eyes slide to the photo and flick quickly away. 'I took a lot of girls to Rickman's Farm.'

'In exchange for a steady supply of Jonas's home-grown cannabis.'

'It wasn't like that.'

'What was it like?'

He picks up a stapler, flips back the handle, puts it down again. 'I had connections. I'd tell Jonas about the girls I met in town, if he liked the sound of them I'd take them to meet him. No harm in that.'

'Why Kaitlin Burney? What was so "special" about her?'

'Jonas liked them young.' He grins. I hold his gaze.

'We both know there was more to it than that.'

I'm fishing but he bites and hunches forward. 'This is off the record, right?'

'Right.'

'Jonas wanted to piss her old man off. He was some kind of religious nut and he and Jonas had this beef going way back.'

'So let me get this right,' I say after a long pause, 'Parks told you to bring this girl to the farm and you went right ahead and did it, even though you knew she was underage and that he was going to rape her to get back at her father.'

'I don't know about any rape.' He glances over at the man with the badge. 'I met her in town, then I her took her to Rickman's Farm.'

'Did you tell her that's where you were taking her?'

'I said there was a party and I'd take her if she wanted. She was totally up for it.'

'Then why did you spike her drink before you set off?'

'I never.'

'What was it, Rohypnol?'

A shifty shrug. 'Not my fault she couldn't hold her drink.'

A kick of disgust jolts my gut. I swallow hard.

'Did you see her the next day?'

'Nah, by the time I woke up she'd gone.'

'What did Jonas have to say about that?'

'He was pissed off.'

'Did you see her in town again?'

'No. I heard her dad had her on lockdown.' His top lip draws back from his nicotine-stained teeth. 'Punishment for being a naughty girl.'

Lockdown? Not an image I want to dwell on.

'Then what happened?'

'What do you mean?'

'You heard she was pregnant.'

'Oh, yeah.' He shrugs again. 'Some bloke in the caff told me her dad went apeshit when he found out and he threw her out.'

'And you told Jonas.'

'Yeah.'

'How did he react?'

'He got excited. He said it was his duty to humanity to' – another smirk – '*procreate*.'

'Did he offer you money to find her?'

'Yeah. He said to tell her to forget about her family because she and her kid could come and live at the farm.'

'Did you find her?'

'Yeah.' He pushes the sides of his palms to his jaw, cracks his neck, first one side, then the other. *Snip. Snap.* 'She was in London, living rough, into all sorts. By the time I got to her she'd lost the kid. I told her she could still come back to the farm but she didn't want to know.'

I lean in. 'Why are you lying? You never even looked for her.' I catch a gust of stagnant breath and flinch away.

He turns the page of the colour chart and fixes a twitchy eye on the 'cool blues and classic teals'. 'Why would I give up the chance of a grand?'

'I'm guessing someone made you a better offer.'

Very suddenly, he pushes away from the counter. 'I've got work to do.'

'Fifteen hundred, maybe two thousand upfront to top what Parks was offering. Then Western Union transfers of four thousand a year for the last twenty years to stop you telling him Kaitlin Burney gave birth to his daughter.'

'How the hell…?'

'Deal's off, Mr Sharplin.'

That freezes him. 'What?'

'Roz Locklear is dead.' What's left of his cockiness evaporates. 'She died three months ago. Her executors have decided to stop the payments.'

'Shit.' He drops his weight back onto the counter as if Roz's handouts had been the only thing keeping him upright. 'You sure about that?'

'Certain.'

'Shit,' he says again, shaking his head.

'Did she tell you why she wanted you to lie about the miscarriage?'

His head grows still and he turns to look at me, no doubt calculating how much cash he can squeeze out of me to make up his losses. 'She said Jonas was a sick bastard who'd destroy that kid's life if he ever found out she existed.'

'Were the follow-up payments your idea or hers?'

He eyes me steadily. 'Like I said. We had an agreement. She wired the money, I kept my mouth shut.'

'You never thought of asking her for more?'

'Course I did. Only the transfers were anonymous – no name, no address, no way of contacting her.'

Smart move, Roz.

'Hey,' a man's voice calls from across the aisle. 'Got any primer?'

Sharplin half turns and points. 'Top shelf.'

'Mr Sharplin, did Jonas Parks ever try and track Kaitlin down after that?'

'Don't ask me. Once I'd done the deal I never went back to the farm.'

'And you've no idea what happened to her?'

'Why would I?'

Sharplin's a chancer, a petty extortionist and a liar, but as one hardcore phoney listening to another this feels like the truth.

I gather up my phone and the newspaper report on Parks' trial. 'Thank you, Mr Sharplin. We'll be in touch.'

'When?'

'Soon.' I turn to go.

'Hang on, you haven't got my number.'

I snatch up the colour chart, rip out a page and toss him the pen hanging from a string nailed to the counter. He writes slowly in awkward capitals.

'Thanks.' I turn away and blunder into the street, scrunching Keith Sharplin's address and number into a murky palette of shit browns and slime greens. Behind me harsh laughter and the scrape of metal on stone as two boys kick a can along the kerb. Breathing fast, I pull up the Breakaway Brethren website on my phone and thumb to the 1970s shot of George Burney preaching on the street. I spread my thumb and forefinger to zoom in on a single face among the crowd of adoring faithful. A mixture of horror and exhilaration as I compare the picture on the screen to the mugshot of Jonas Parks.

CHAPTER TWENTY-SEVEN

I spin the car around and head across Northampton, weaving fast through the midday traffic and clipping the kerb as I pull up outside Alice's flat. It's Esther who lets me in. With barely a hello, I squeeze past her and push open the door to Alice's bedroom.

'Phoebe!' Alice blinks up at me from her sea of pillows.

I thrust the photo from the brethren website at her and point to the teenage boy standing behind George Burney. 'Who is he?'

She fumbles for her glasses, peers at the photo and says quietly, 'He's one of the shunned. It happened a long time ago. His name was Jonas.'

The silence in the room grows deep, punctured only by the tick of the clock on the chest of drawers. Slowly I drop into the seat beside her bed. 'Did you know he set up a cult?'

'Officially we weren't allowed to speak about him, but yes, I knew. To be honest, I wasn't surprised. Even as a boy he had a calling to leadership and a wonderful way with words.' Her brow puckers. 'But there was always something troubling about him; a deep insecurity coupled with arrogance.'

'He's Maya's father.'

Totally unprepared for this, Alice's mouth forms a trembling circle. She struggles to sit up.

'He raped Kay to get back at her father,' I say, wondering too late whether I should have spared her the full horror of Parks' crimes. 'Why, Alice? What happened between him and George Burney?'

She presses her knuckles to her mouth like a skeletal child trying not to cry. 'George was his mentor. He stepped in when Jonas's father died because his mother was too grief-stricken to cope.' I squeeze the arms of the chair, padded vinyl against my sweaty palms, and wait for her to go on. Her face grows very still. 'George made him his protégé and groomed him for great things.' She's speaking slowly, as if every word is causing her pain. 'He used to call him his golden boy. The son he'd always longed for but never had, and for a while Jonas practically lived at the bungalow.' She drops her head as if in shame. 'Ruth had just had Kaitlin. She was lonely. George was hardly a hands-on father and when he *was* around he seemed bent on squeezing every drop of joy out of her life. And there was Jonas. A lonely lad, not that much younger than she was. Someone for her to talk to; someone to keep her company; someone to take the baby off her hands now and then and give her a break. Two young, unhappy people starved of love.'

A terrible pause, though I can guess what's coming. 'They became close. Too close. George found out. Ruth swore that nothing had happened between them but George denounced Jonas as a demon. He cut him off from our community and made Ruth pay for those few snatched moments of happiness for the rest of her life.' She takes a tissue from the box beside her bed and holds it to one eye, then the other. 'Jonas Parks was added to the list of names we weren't allowed to speak and Judith Parks became yet another mother severed from her child.'

Her words summon a flushed face, a furious shout, '*You can't come in here dressed like that!*' and the cold, unapologetic eyes of John Didcot: '*I'm sorry if Sister Judith was abrasive.*'

'I think she's the one who threw me out of the gospel hall,' I say.

'Most probably,' Alice says. 'These days she channels her unspent love into polishing up those shiny new pews – trying to scrub away the taint of her son's sin.' She closes her eyes and shakes her head. 'That poor, poor girl. I know it nearly destroyed Jonas when

George cast him out, but how could he do that to an innocent child?' Her eyes spring open and her voice sharpens. 'Did he know Maya was his daughter?'

'Not at first. But there were pictures of her fourth birthday party in a magazine profile of David Duncan. If he saw them and recognised Kay it wouldn't have been difficult to work out.'

She looks down at the photo again, a complicated distress in her face. 'You think he's the one who abducted her?'

'It would make a lot of sense.'

She nods slowly. 'Are you going to the police?'

I lower my eyes. 'I… I… need to talk to him first.'

'Why?'

'I need to ask him about someone who lived on his commune for a while. He knows things about her that she never told anyone else. Things I need to know.'

'Wouldn't it be more honest to ask her yourself?'

'She's dead.'

'Was this woman good to you?'

'Yes,' I say quietly.

She squeezes my fingers. 'Then why not let her secrets die with her?'

I pull my hand away and stand up to go. 'They're not hers to keep.'

I stand on the pavement outside the flats, trying to decide what to do. Is Alice right? Should I go to the police station right now? Walk in off the street and tell the desk sergeant I've got a new theory about Maya Duncan and not much more than a hunch to back it up? While my head says, *Yes – it's the sensible thing to do, Parks is deranged and dangerous and I can't rescue Maya on my own*, my heart screams, *No! – they'll discover I'm the reason Kay killed herself and I'll lose the opportunity to confront Parks about Roz's past and my identity.*

I leave the car and start walking, hoping the air will clear my head, but the arguments won't stop battering my brain and it doesn't help that I haven't eaten since last night. Dizzy and confused, I walk into the first café I come to. It's an uninviting world of grease and steam, offering a selection of all-day breakfasts pictured above the counter in bleached-out technicolour. I order a coffee at the counter, pick a wedge of apple pie from a scratched Perspex display case, and carry my plate and slopping mug over to a table at the back. I take a bite of pie. It's sweet and so stodgy it sticks to my teeth. I wash it down with a swig of powdery coffee and feel my blood buzz as the carbs and caffeine hit my brain. I work on through the pie, sip the coffee and squeeze my throbbing skull. *What are you going to do? Come on. Make up your mind!* The answer springs at me. I stop eating, the last fragment of pastry halfway to my mouth.

I can't involve the police, not yet. Not because I'm frightened of exposure – although I am – or because I need information from Parks – although I do – but because this is my one chance to make some sort of peace with Kay. I stare out across the café. I can't undo what I did to her but if I get this right I can rescue her daughter and clear her name.

I fetch another coffee, search for the photo of the 'For Sale' sign outside Rickman's Farm and flick back through my notes. According to the shopkeeper at Horton-on-the-Water Amy Rickman was renting a house for Parks 'somewhere the other side of Milton Keynes'. This snippet of information, combined with a flaky story about being a relative visiting from abroad who's lost the rest of Amy's address, and some dubious phone flirting with a trainee in the estate agent's office, elicits the information I need.

I follow the satnav past a cluster of abandoned industrial units – big grey sheds and lonely brown silos scrawled with graffiti – then comes a disused petrol station, chained-up pumps and grass stalks pushing up through slabs of litter-blown concrete. I slow right down and a few yards further on, I see Oak Bank. Charged with the task of offloading Rickman's Farm, the agency had obviously decided to dump Amy Rickman with the second most undesirable property on their books. Set back from the road, it's a solitary, yellow brick chalet; a show home for a development that never got built. It's not nearly as secluded as Rickman's Farm but isolated enough to keep a brainwashed captive hidden from the world. I look down. My hands are shaking. It's cold hard fear. I feel it tightening my muscles, loosening my gut.

I turn the car around and park out of sight behind the kiosk of the petrol station. I sit there wavering. Can I really do this? Yes. I have to. I get out of the car, climb onto what's left of a rotten bench and grab the top of the wall. The broken brickwork rips my palms but I haul myself up and take a look at the back of the house. A dust-coloured cat slinks through half-open French windows and pauses to stare at me before it disappears beneath a stained tarpaulin. I shift along a little, peer through a gap between the sheets pegged out on the washing line and glimpse a bunker-like shed, partially screened by trees, squatting at the far end of a long, battered lawn. I stare at it for a long time. Nerves deadened by a surge of anger, I jump from the bench, turn off my phone and lock it in the boot with the rest of my stuff. It's both a wrench and a relief to silence the steady pulse of texts and calls from Will, but I tell myself it won't be for long.

Wiping my scratched palms on my jeans I walk around to the front of the house and stand at the gate, taking in the net curtains pulled across the plate glass windows, and the double garage, its open roller door slightly askew, topped by a flat-roofed extension. A woman comes out of the garage swinging a black bin bag. She drops it into a wheelie bin and looks up, shielding her eyes against the sun as I open the gate. She's in her late thirties, a roll of pale flesh – the sort that never tans – peeping between the top of her shorts and the bottom of the man's shirt knotted low on her waist. 'Can I help you?' she says.

I pull out the cheap burner phone I bought en route and waggle it vaguely at the road behind me. 'My car's broken down and I need to phone a garage' – embarrassed wince – 'but I've run out of credit.'

The woman studies me, a placid smile on her lips. I hold my breath. 'Come in,' she says after what feels like a beat too long.

I cross the crazy paving and walk through the garage into a small utility room being used as a boot store. I turn as the door clicks shut behind me and note the keypad above the knob that locks the door from the inside. I follow her through into a kitchen that's as tired and shabby as the rest of the place – chipped edges on the laminate units, a trickle of brown down the side of the swing bin, a floor-to-ceiling cupboard crammed with packets of tea, budget tins of tomatoes and bags of toilet roll. In the middle there's a long table covered in a chequered oilcloth, one end of it set out with mixing bowls, baking trays and a bag of flour. Between the sink and the fridge there's a glass door that gives straight onto the back garden.

'You must be hot,' she says. 'Can I get you a drink? Tea, coffee, something cold?'

'Something cold would be great,' I say.

'I'm Hannah, by the way.' She offers me her hand.

'Clara de Jaeger,' I say, giving her a name stolen from a class-mate who had once announced loudly – and, it turns out, with uncharacteristic perception – that I was 'nobody'. Not *a* nobody – that's the part that had stung my lumpy, fifteen-year-old self the sharpest. I was a creature so far beneath the beautiful Clara's bud-lipped, blow-dried contempt that I didn't even merit an indefinite article. Hannah takes my proffered hand, but instead of shaking it, she takes the other one too, turns them both palm upwards and inspects the cuts and scratches. There's something intrusive about her touch that causes me – instinctively – to pull away.

'What did you do?'

'I… tripped and fell.'

She goes to the fridge, pours a tumbler of something from a plastic jug and sets it down in front of me, placid smile still in place. 'Homemade lemonade.'

I smile back at her and take a long gulp. The liquid is sweet and fragrant.

'I'm trying to place your accent. Are you South African?'

'I was brought up in Botswana.'

'Botswana?' She stares at me, blank-eyed and smiley. 'Gosh, you're a long way from home. Do you have family over here?'

I shake my head.

'All in Botswana?'

'Not… anymore.' I give it a couple of beats. 'My mother died a few weeks ago.'

Hannah drops her head in sympathy but not before I see the shine of interest in her eyes. Delphine's warning glows hotly in my head: *You're exactly the kind of victim Jonas goes for – young, vulnerable, looking for answers.* Which is what I'm counting on.

'I'm so sorry,' she says. 'What did she do out there?'

'Worked for a charity.'

'And your father?'

'He was never part of my life.' *Good line – one I should use again.*

'I'm sorry. I know how hard it can be to have no one, especially when you're young.'

I look away to the brown and white floor tiles. 'Yeah, the last few months haven't been great.'

Her voice drops to a sympathetic murmur. 'I think it's your pain that drew you to us, Clara.'

If I really had just broken down in the middle of nowhere and come to this house to use a phone, this is the point where I'd be making my excuses and getting the hell out of here. But I'm totally prepared for the game she's playing and she has no idea about mine. 'Drew me?' I give a shy little shrug. 'I don't know about that. I went to an open day at the university and took the wrong turning off the bypass.' And now I smile. 'So, is there a phone I could use?'

'Jonas has one, but he's resting right now.'

'Jonas?' For all my careful preparation my voice comes out stiff and unnatural.

'Our teacher.' She eyes me steadily. 'He guides our community.'

I keep up the feigned surprise. 'Is this some kind of commune?'

'It's a place of peace.'

'Will he be long?'

'He'll be down for lunch.'

I glance at the orange plastic clock above the worktop. Just gone midday. 'Is it OK if I wait?'

'Of course.' She stretches up and takes a small basket from the top of one of the cabinets. 'But you'll have to put your phone in here.'

The basket is full of crystals – milky purple, pale green and pink. Even though I'm prepared for the no phone rule and the cheap burner was bought to hand over, I still feel a prickle of fear. This is how it starts. The stripping away of outside contact; the precursor to the stripping away of self. I force a little laugh. 'Whatever for?'

'To block the electromagnetic rays.'

'No need,' I say, putting up a show of resistance. 'It's switched off.'

'It's still toxic,' she says, shoving the basket a little nearer, like an exasperated teacher demanding the surrender of a wad of gum. I drop the phone onto the crystals. She hurries to the door. 'I'll just pop it somewhere safe.'

I watch through the window as she walks down to the shed. With a quick glance back at the house she unlocks the door. A slice of black appears and disappears as she slips inside. I take my bearings. From what I can see the garden is huge but completely enclosed by the high brick wall. That means the only way out of here is through the locked utility room or the front door, which I'm guessing is also kept locked. Phoneless and on edge, I swirl the inch of cloudy liquid left at the bottom of my glass and wonder if I should have gone for tap water. As I watch, another woman emerges from the shed – a slim, serious-looking blonde in her late thirties – carrying a cardboard box. She heads towards the French windows further along the back wall. Moments later I hear footsteps on the stairs. Has she come to warn the others to prepare for a visitor?

'How come Jonas has a mobile if he thinks they're so dangerous?' I say when Hannah gets back.

She's slightly flushed and circles of sweat have appeared under her arms. 'His aura is strong enough to withstand the contamination,' she says, placid smile back in place. 'Now, let's do something about those cuts.' She tosses me a tea towel. 'Give your hands a good scrub and dry them on that.'

I hesitate then move obediently to the sink. 'What about computers?'

She takes a bottle of iodine and a box of plasters from a drawer. 'Jonas keeps a couple of laptops in his office but we only use them if we're helping with his research.'

I think, with a shudder, of Delphine's three-year cyber hunt for Roz.

'What kind of research?'

'For his writings. We send his word all over the world.'

'Do you get to read magazines and newspapers?'

'Why would we darken Jonas's light with lies?'

'What about TV and radio?'

She tuts, as if I'm a child who should know better. 'I told you. This is a place of peace.'

She dabs at my cuts, brisk and efficient, then she rips a plaster from its wrapping and presses it onto the worst of the scratches, smoothing it down with her thumbs in a way that makes me feel small and cared for; a feeling shattered by a sudden memory of the testimony in the witness report: *Parks got the rest of us to ply these girls with food, alcohol, weed and, worst of all, kindness to get them to stay.* I pull my hand away. Hannah rinses her fingers and goes back to her bread-making. I watch as she punches the dough with her knuckles, the way Evangeline used to do it at Molokodi. The similarity is so strong I half expect her to toss me a piece of dough to roll into a grubby little snake.

She glances at the clock. 'Would you like to eat with us?'

'I wouldn't want to put you to any trouble,' I say, careful not to sound too eager.

'It's no trouble.'

'Great. Can I help?'

'You could chop the cabbage. There's a board and a knife over there.' She nods towards a row of sharpened knives lined up on a magnetised rack.

I pick one out, and we work in silence for a while, one on either side of the table. 'So how many of you live here?' I ask when a carefully judged two minutes is up.

'Six at the moment. Plus Jonas of course.'

'Six.' My pulsing heart speeds up. 'That's a lot of people to cook for.'

'Jonas assigns us the tasks that best suit our skills.'

She's been rolling the dough into little balls and now she plops the last one onto a baking tray and scores the tops with a knife. 'There.' She steps back, tipping her head from side to side, admiring her handiwork before she puts the bag of flour away and kicks the cupboard door shut. For a long shocked moment I stare past her at the pinboard now revealed on the wall. Tawdry and at the same time macabre, it's a shrine to Phoebe – snapshots of the same fair-haired, blue-eyed baby whose photo I'd found at Rickman's Farm. In some she's perched on a headless lap, in others she's held upright for the camera by a disembodied female hand. But these pictures are just the framing for the centrepiece – a poster-sized blow up of Phoebe being borne aloft, like a golfing trophy, by a triumphant Jonas Parks. Beneath it a single white bootee hangs – eerily – from a nail. Phoebe, Roz, the car crash, her loss, and her lies. So many thoughts crowd in on me I can hardly get my breath.

I feel Hannah watching me and I say quickly, 'Who's the little girl?'

'She was ours.' She bends down to the oven. 'Jonas's golden child. He named her Phoebe. It means shining one.'

'What happened to her?'

'She died.' A soft clunk as she closes the oven door.

'Is that you in any of those pictures?'

'Phoebe was taken before my time.'

'Her mother was chosen.' The voice comes from behind me. I look round and meet a pair of flat, staring eyes. The woman who owns them stands at the back door clutching a wooden trug overflowing with muddy vegetables. She's tall, thin and accusing, a long grey plait tied with a scrap of twine hangs over one shoulder. Her top lip wobbles as she speaks, accentuating the crags around her mouth. 'She was chosen and she betrayed us.'

'It's alright, Amy,' Hannah says, soothingly.

So this is Amy. The owner of Rickman's Farm, the funder of Jonas's bizarre delusions, the accomplice who helped him snatch Phoebe from Roz. I feel suddenly drained and sick. 'Um, could I use the bathroom?'

'Sure,' Hannah says lightly, as if we'd been chatting about the weather. 'Down the hall, door at the end.'

I get up, unsteadily.

'Who are you?' Amy hisses as I pass her in the doorway, spittle in her breath.

'Clara,' I say, quietly. 'My name is Clara.'

I hurry down a narrow passageway to a dank little cloakroom, throw the door shut and stare around me at the stained grouting and hideous, flower-patterned tiles. *Stay calm. You can do this.* I take a couple of minutes to steady my breath, then I slip out into the hallway and test the latch on the front door. The knob turns but, as I suspected, the door is locked and there's no sign of a key. When I get back Amy has gone and Hannah is setting the kettle on the stove, all bustly housewife again. 'Would you mind laying the table for me and putting the cabbage on once this water boils? I need to speak to Jonas.'

'Of course.'

She goes upstairs and I scoop a handful of tinny cutlery from the drawer by the sink and stare out at the back garden. I think of Roz at Rickman's Farm; young, pregnant and harbouring a secret so awful it made Jonas's grotesque no man's land feel safer than the real world. The kettle screeches. I put the cabbage on to cook and walk over to take a closer look at the photos on the pinboard. I study the shortened finger on Phoebe's left hand, the look of Roz around her nose and mouth and try to picture what this fair-haired, pink-cheeked toddler whose life I'd lived would look like all grown-up; what she'd be doing right now if she'd been pulled from that car crash alive.

A jostling at the door. It's Amy coming back with three others – the blonde I saw earlier, who ignores me, and two much older, whey-faced redheads – disarmingly similar, possibly twins – who glance nervously in my direction and murmur a welcome. So far I've seen five women, none of them Maya. But there's one more to come. 'Hi, I'm Clara,' I say chirpily. The blonde murmurs 'Caroline' and one of the redheads tells me that she is Beatrice, 'call me Bea', and her sister – a slightly thinner and blanker version of herself – is Martha. I circle the table setting down knives and forks. Beatrice fetches glasses and a jug of water and Amy pokes about in the oven. The room grows steamy with the smell of baking bread and the hiss of the cabbage pan. I look around me at these ageing remnants of Jonas's flock, the rejects who weren't 'chosen' to bear his children, and wonder how long it's been since they've had the chance to recruit a stranger to their ranks.

The door opens again and in comes Hannah, bright-eyed and breathless, followed by a slight, stooping man with gold-rimmed spectacles and soft waves of grey hair who walks with a stick and gives off no hint of the abusive, arch manipulator who has destroyed so many lives. But it's not his ordinariness that takes me by surprise, it's the red and white scarring that puckers the left side of his face and gives a quizzical slant to his upper lip.

'Jonas, this is Clara,' Hannah says.

CHAPTER TWENTY-EIGHT

I return Jonas Parks' gaze, searching for – and maybe finding – a flicker of five-year-old Maya Duncan in the set of his eyes and the tilt of his head. His stare doesn't waver. I count the seconds. Get to ten. I'm guessing his silence is designed to unnerve me. 'Hello, Mr—' I catch myself just in time. 'Jonas.'

'Clara,' he says at last, rolling the name around his mouth. 'Hannah tells me your car broke down.'

'Yes, and stupidly I'm out of credit so I was hoping I could borrow your phone to call a garage.'

He shuffles stiffly towards the chair at the head of the table, extends a beckoning finger and points to the empty seat beside him. I sit down gingerly. The others are bowing their heads, folding their hands together. Embarrassed, I do the same, only unlike them I keep my eyes open. I'm hoping we're going for a moment of meditative silence but no, Parks is raising his head, gearing up to say grace.

'Why must I lead?' he asks.

The answer comes back low and reverent. 'That we may follow.'

'Why must I cast light into dark places?'

'That you may destroy the evil which has been planted against us.'

'Why must I punish?'

'That you may save.'

If this deluded twaddle weren't so destructive it would be funny. He catches my eye and my scalp crawls as he studies me and taps steepled fingers against his lower lip. Hannah, at the other end of the table, is doling out dollops of lentil bake while the others hand around the bowl of cabbage and a basket of hot rolls like it's mealtime at the Waltons. I poke a fork around my plate, listen as they discuss the merits of various dog breeds – their last one, it seems, has just died – and wait for the final place at the table to be filled. There's a strange dynamic at work among these women. Martha bends low over her food, leaving Beatrice to speak for them both – '*we* want', '*we* think'; Hannah seems increasingly hyper, bossing and scolding; Amy watches me through lowered lids exuding sullen suspicion; and Caroline stays aloof, addressing herself only to Parks. The empty plates are taken away and replaced by baked apples, scorched at the tops and served in pools of floury custard, and still the spare place stays empty. After a couple of bites of apple I put down my spoon and say to Hannah. 'Sorry, it looks like I laid for too many – I thought you said there were six of you.'

A ripple of unease. Suppressed, yet unmistakable. The women glance at Parks, and then at Hannah, who flashes me her ever-ready smile. 'Annie will have hers later. She's just finishing off some work for Jonas.'

Annie? Of course they'd have changed Maya's name.

When I start to breathe again, Parks is studying me. Finally he speaks. 'Tell me, Clara, is it loneliness or something else that throws such a cold dark shadow across your aura?'

I'm ready for the portentous language, the unblinking eyes, the 'psychic' insights, and the lowered voice designed to draw me close. It's an act. I know that. Even so, it's a polished one and it leaves me faltering.

'I'm… sorry?'

His finger rises slowly, as if lifted by an invisible string, and points to a spot between my breasts. Something changes in the room. The women grow still. 'I sense a wound inside you, Clara. Just… there. You poor child. So much death around you; so much guilt and confusion inside you. Sometimes the pain gets so bad you'd do anything to stop it.' My eyes are burning, my jaw quivers. His arms pull apart, opening wide, and in that moment all I want to do is fall into them and tell him what I did to Kay, how conflicted I feel about Roz and how the shock of Vicky's accident haunts my dreams. I pull back hard. This creep's not reading my pain. He's a trickster, using the information I fed to Hannah to fish for tells. I dig my nails into my palm and tell myself I'm in control, that this is all part of my plan.

Then I give him what I hope is the strained, hurting smile of an innocent ripe for the plucking. 'Things have been difficult since I lost my mother.'

Hannah, who's appeared behind me with a jug of water, lays her hand on my shoulder. 'We were all in pain before we came to Jonas. Why don't you stay for our gathering this evening and hear him speak? It might help you to find some peace.'

'I have to sort out my car.'

'You can do that tomorrow. Stay here tonight and let Jonas heal your wound. Would you like that, Clara?'

I look around me at the bland watchful faces. It feels as if I'm sinking to the bottom of a deep stagnant well and though I can just about see up to the surface the pressure of the water is closing in. 'Yes,' I hear myself say. 'I'd like that very much.'

'Good.' She clasps her hands together. 'And this afternoon we'll find you a task.'

'I'm up for that,' I say.

And then begins the carefully choreographed dance of clearing up. The twins collect the plates, Caroline washes up, I – when passed a tea towel – start to dry and Hannah and Amy put away. No chatter, no music, no laughter. Just six women moving like silent cogs in a well-greased machine. I'm doing my bit as diligently as I can, polishing each piece of cutlery before I lay it in the drawer, when it strikes me that I must be doing the task usually allotted to the absent Annie.

When order has been returned to the kitchen, Hannah invites me up to what she calls the workroom. I follow her up stairs carpeted in bumpy swirls of orange and brown. Half-open doors painted in yellowing white gloss offer glimpses of Blu-Tack smeared walls, mismatched bedding trailing from wooden bunk beds and wardrobes stuffed with crumpled clothes – dorm rooms for the lost and lonely who forgot to grow up. She takes me along the landing and through a door that leads into the extension above the garage. It's hot and stuffy. The ceiling, speckled with browning blobs of tile adhesive, is oppressively low and the narrow louvers at the top of the double-glazed windows block all but the feeblest trace of air. A large photocopier sits in one corner, beside it a couple of trestle tables laid out with stacks of green printouts arranged in rows. I watch carefully as Hannah shows me how to gather up the numbered pages, screw them into a wooden press and paint layers of glue along the spine to bind them together. I pull up a stool and pick out fragments of clichéd bullshit as I square up the papers I've collected – *darkness, light, false teachers, true paths* and, of course, *ways to donate to the world-saving work of Jonas Parks.* After a while we're joined by the twins, and Hannah leaves us to it. The smell of glue grows heady in the stifling warmth. Of course it's Beatrice who answers when I ask how many 'books' Jonas has written. It's all part of one great work apparently, of which there are ten completed volumes and – lucky, lucky world – another ten in the planning. All the while her sister works on silently, only looking up when, with a nervous glance at the door, I ask if they ever met Phoebe's mother. She slides a sideways look at Beatrice who – as ever – is the one who speaks.

'Yes, we came to Jonas three months before Roz arrived.'

I give an involuntary gasp. That makes nearly twenty-three years! These two have been living this life, feeding Parks' delusions, for longer than my lifetime! No wonder they've decamped to another planet.

'Roz,' I say slowly, as if I'd just heard the name for the first time. 'Did you know her well?'

'Well enough.' A shutter descends. 'Jonas gave her refuge. She was chosen to bear his child and she betrayed us.'

'I don't understand. What did she do?'

'She stole Phoebe away.'

'No,' I say, losing patience. 'Why did she need refuge?'

Beatrice shakes her head. 'Only Jonas knows that.'

I keep my tone as chatty as I can. 'Does he have any other children?'

Her sister's brush pauses above the glue pot. She looks at Bea. A shiver of something darts between them. 'One other vessel was chosen,' Bea says quickly.

'What happened?'

'Roz saw the light in her,' Bea says. 'She grew jealous and sent her away.'

'What happened to the baby?'

'The vessel miscarried.'

She's clearly reciting from a script – learned lines that make it impossible to tell if she believes what she's saying or knows it's a lie. She leans across the table to her sister and murmurs, soothingly, 'It's alright, Mouse. Don't upset yourself.'

Mouse. The nickname catches me for a moment, a half-forgotten memory. I run the sound through my head. It catches again. I draw a sharp breath. The hot acrid air scours my throat. This sad husk of a woman was the girl mentioned in the witness report – the newcomer who cracked under Jonas's finger-circling interrogation the morning after the rape and told him she'd seen Roz dragging Kay away from Rickman's Farm.

Several silent minutes pass by as I get progressively more sweaty. I scrape back my hair and try to question Bea about life with Jonas, asking – I hope – the kind of things a would-be convert might want to know, only to be met with evasion, especially when my enquiries veer towards their time at Rickman's Farm. I'm struggling to work out a way to get the answers I need without raising suspicion, when Martha announces in a querulous voice that she's thirsty. It's the first time I've heard her speak.

'Me too,' I say. 'Shall I fetch us something to drink?' I push back my stool but Beatrice is already at the door.

'I'll do it,' she says firmly.

That's fine by me. This could be my only chance to get Martha on her own. I lay down my brush and edge my stool towards hers. Her fingers are moving quickly, layering perfect lines of glue along the papers. 'You're so good at this,' I say. 'I seem to get more glue on my hands than on the paper.'

She dips her brush mechanically into the glue pot and her wide set eyes stare glassily at the wad of printouts in front of her. 'Jonas assigns us the tasks that are best suited to our skills.'

Resisting the urge to slap her, I say gently, 'I'm sorry if I distressed you.'

She doesn't answer. I lean in a little closer. 'Just now, when I asked about the girl who miscarried Jonas's baby, Bea thought you were upset.'

A pause while she considers this, then she lifts her head and says, 'It's because I'm the one who did the bad thing.' Her voice is weak, but her words send a jolt through my limbs.

'What bad thing?' I whisper.

'I…' She screws up her crêpey eyelids as if trying to get control. When she opens them again her voice is a monotone. 'I allowed the chosen vessel to leave the farm. If I had obeyed Jonas's rules and raised the alarm, his child would have lived. But I did nothing and the powers of darkness took her away.'

It's clearly her party piece, polished up by Jonas to keep unruly realities at bay. I have to lure her off script. Gently though. 'Why did you let that happen, Martha?'

'The forces of darkness filled me with jealousy.'

'Of this special girl?'

'Yes.' Her breathing deepens. 'I was blind to the light that Jonas saw in her and angry that he had honoured someone who seemed so worthless. I should have seen that the forces of light were trying to keep her at the farm. They made her so floppy she couldn't walk. But the darkness made Roz strong. She carried her to the gate. Then she lifted her onto the other side and dragged her into the woods.'

'Did you follow them?'

She's looking at me but her pupils are fixed, seeming not to see me. 'I wanted that girl gone.'

'Where did Roz take her?'

'To the main road. When they got there the girl collapsed and Roz waved down a van. A woman got out. They lifted the girl inside, the van drove away and I just stood there, in thrall to the powers of darkness. But I confessed my sin to Jonas and I took my punishment and now I am cleansed.'

Recitation over, she lets out a long breath and re-dips her brush. But I'm not done with her yet. 'That's right, Martha,' I say soothingly. 'You did a bad thing but it wasn't your fault. It was the darkness that kept you silent.' I glance behind me and plough quickly on, hoping I'm on message with Jonas's bullshit. 'But I believe that the forces of light are stronger than the powers of darkness, don't you?' She nods uncertainly. 'So maybe this girl didn't miscarry at all. Maybe a few years later Jonas found out that his second golden child was still alive. Maybe he went and fetched her so she could be brought up by people who realised how special she was.'

Her mouth opens and closes and her lips tremble. 'It's OK.' I raise my hands to calm her but what I took for alarm has been replaced by a small, knowing nod.

'A triumph for the light,' she says, in her reedy voice. 'A defeat for the darkness.'

'That's right. But she'd have to be kept out of sight and her true identity would have to stay hidden in order to keep her safe.'

'Martha!' I look up. Beatrice stands in the doorway. 'Jonas wants you.'

Martha gets up from her stool and shuffles away, bony white feet in beaten down pumps. Bea looks over at me, brisk and in control. 'Will you be alright on your own?'

I stifle a pretend yawn and try to look suitably dead-eyed. 'Yes, fine.' I take the glass of lemonade she hands me. It looks cloudier than the last lot and as soon as she's gone I set it down. My eyes travel around the boxes of crackpot outpourings, the rickety tables and sealed-up windows and I feel the dreary claustrophobia of this place crunch in on me; a world squeezed bloodless by the steely grip of Jonas Parks. But if pandering to his warped ego and hanging out with a bunch of middle-aged zombies is going to lead me to Maya, it's a price I'm willing to pay.

CHAPTER TWENTY-NINE

I'm deep in a fantasy of bursting into Will's flat with Maya at my side when Caroline comes in to tell me it's time for the evening gathering. Closed and silent, she leads me downstairs, turns the handle of the door to the living room and stands back to let me enter. The air is stale and dim, the floorboards bare. Thick curtains pulled across the windows shut out what's left of the sun. As my eyes struggle to adapt to the gloom, I'm seized by a fear that part of me will never leave this room. Jonas is seated on an oversized armchair – wide back, padded arms, stretched brown nylon cover – a small wooden table to one side of him, a low footstool in front; a tinpot throne for a tinpot emperor. The women sit around him in a semi-circle, cross-legged like eager pre-schoolers. He raises a hand as I enter, points to the footstool and calls in a warm, welcoming voice. 'Ah, Clara, there you are. Please, join us.'

The room is stifling. A fly frets beneath the curtains, thumping against the glass. I lower myself onto the stool.

'Today I want to talk about severing the bonds that cause us pain…'

Jonas's head bobs up and down as he speaks and a buzzing starts in my head as if the fly has left the window and entered my skull. It takes me a moment to realise it's the women, humming and nodding, a sway to their bodies that matches the rhythm of his words. I close my eyes and tell myself it's not charisma that this paunchy little man exudes, it's a sense of self-importance so strong I can almost smell it. But the heat and the semi darkness make it hard to think and I find myself being borne along by the drone of his voice.

'… by embracing the forces of light we empower ourselves to destroy the darkness that seeks to hurt us… darkness that descends in the form of ignorance, selfishness, lies and betrayal… darkness which could not stand to see the birth of my golden children.' I tune out and let this bilge wash over me. 'One killed when she was just a child, the other taken from me before it left the womb. Both lost to the world because of the betrayal of one woman.' The humming grows louder, strumming and juddering like a hive of maddened bees. 'The woman who raised the stranger who now sits in our midst, a stranger to whom she gave my dead daughter's identity.' The humming stops. My brain stalls and then, with a suck of horror, the meaning of his words crashes in on me. I see myself from above: sitting there stunned, foolish and exposed.

'Did you think you were dealing with an idiot?' Parks says evenly. 'It's true that after she left Malawi Roz made a pretty good job of going to ground again. I wasn't overly concerned. After all, my only interest in her was knowing how and when the forces of light would punish her for causing the death of my child. But after she died an obscure conservation website published an obituary of her, praising her selfless work with endangered species in Botswana. Imagine how bemused I was to read it and discover that she had been survived by her only daughter, Phoebe.'

I hear the door open and shut behind me. Someone has joined us. Is it Maya? Even as the icy backwash of exposure rolls over me, my brain is scrabbling for a way to finish what I've come to do and get us both out of here. I ache to turn around and look at her, to let her see that I'm on her side, but I can't tear my eyes from Jonas's hypnotic stare.

'And then out of the blue, just a few weeks after Roz's death, a girl from Botswana turns up on my doorstep, steeped in lies.

Naturally I was suspicious.' He glances past me, releasing my gaze. 'So I sent Annie to look for your car.'

I whip round to take my first look at Maya. My brain struggles to reset. The woman at the door is dumpy and somewhere in her fifties with a head of grey-frizzed dreadlocks. The beaded ends click as she crosses the room to stand at Parks' side.

'She broke into the boot, went through the bag you'd locked away in there and found this.' The woman holds up my passport and tosses it to the floor. 'A passport, in the name of Phoebe Locklear, with your photograph in it, giving my dead daughter's date of birth and Roz Locklear as her next of kin.' An eternity passes in the sticky gloom before he speaks again.

'Why are you here? What is it you want from us?'

I struggle to my feet and after a moment of desperation fall back on the truth, or at least a piece of it. 'I want to know why Roz went to Rickman's Farm. Why she was hiding from the police.'

He pushes a thumbnail between his lower teeth. 'Were you fond of her?'

'I loved her.' His nod is bland, so why do I feel as if he's tripped me into a trap? 'What did she do that was so terrible?'

He strings out the silence, feeding on my dread. 'She was an animal rights activist,' he says at last. 'Hardcore. Leader of an underground militant cell. She organised a masked raid on a lab that was using beagles for live experiments. They freed the dogs and set fire to the building. Burnt a multi-million pound facility to the ground.' He smiles, as if he's enjoying my relief, seeing into my brain as it leaps from image to image – juddery frames of Roz, fearless in the face of armed poachers, up all night nursing an injured cheetah, railing at government officials who tried to keep her in line, preaching militant vegetarianism in a country of hearty flesh-eaters. His timing, when he speaks again, is exquisite; the stab of an unseen blade. 'A man died. He was burned alive, trapped beneath falling debris. A night guard.

First week on the job. Twenty-six years old and newly married with a baby son.'

My knees buckle. I drop back onto the stool. He watches me with interest as if I'm a curiosity flapping in a petri dish.

'The tabloids were howling for blood, the pressure was on to find the killers and the police were pulling in known activists for questioning. So they disbanded the cell, cut all ties with each other and went into hiding. Some went abroad. Roz joined our community at Rickman's Farm.' He takes a bottle of tablets from the table beside him, shakes a couple into his hand and swallows them with a mouthful of water. 'She was in a bad way; frightened and wracked with the kind of guilt that a hefty donation to the fund for the grieving widow did nothing to alleviate. But she found solace with us and after a few months she conceived my child.' The audience ripples in response; a collective sighing and twitching of muscles. 'A golden child who needed my guidance to become the very special woman she was destined to be.' A muscle jumps in his cheek. 'I warned Roz to stay on her guard against forces bent on the destruction of such children. But she was weak and in the end she succumbed. As soon as she removed my daughter from my protection I feared her death was inevitable. When it happened it was a devastating loss for me' – theatrical pause – 'a far greater one for humanity.' He looks at me and blinks slowly. 'But you didn't lie your way in here just to satisfy your curiosity about Roz's past.' I feel a shift in the women, a suppressed excitement. He pulls out my notebook and holds it high. 'You came here looking for Maya Duncan.'

I hear my breath catch in my chest. The fly buzzing against the window. The circle of angry upturned faces and the painful punch of my heartbeat against my ribs. 'Your notes made extremely interesting reading, though I have to admit I was a little confused by some of your lines of thought so I left you with Martha. Once she'd reported your conversation back to me it all made perfect sense.' He cocks his head a little, that crooked smile tugging at one cheek. 'Sorry. Did you think it was luck that threw the two of you together? That she was so dull-witted she would answer your questions and not tell me everything you said?'

A blast of rage rattles through me. 'Stop this! You saw the photos of Kay Duncan at Maya's birthday party, you worked out that she was Kaitlin Burney and that Maya was yours and you took her.' The words come out in sharp little jerks. 'Which one of your fucked-up followers did you get to help you? Was it Martha? The desperate act of a crushed, guilt-ridden woman, ready to do anything to redeem herself in your eyes? Or was it Amy? Why not? She was with you when you killed Phoebe. Where is she, Parks? What did you do with Maya?'

He's on his feet, stumbling sideways, knotty fingers reaching for something on the table – a brass hand bell – the next instant an ear-splitting clang tears through my head. I scream through the sound. 'Is she here? Locked away in that shed out there, poisoned by your sick bullshit, or were you responsible for her death as well as Phoebe's?'

A hand – not his – slaps me hard across the mouth. I gulp for air. Eyes shining, Parks wags a single, scar-reddened finger in my face. 'You're wrong. I didn't take Maya Duncan. But I've known for fifteen years that she was mine.' The women gasp. Five pairs of astonished eyes stare at him in wonder. Only Amy stays stone-faced. 'You see, I'd believed the story about Kaitlin Burney's miscarriage right up until the day Maya was abducted. And yes, when I saw the news coverage and realised that I had been lied to for five years I yearned to bring my golden child back where she belonged. But unlike Phoebe, I had no idea who had taken Maya. If the police with all their resources couldn't find her, what chance did I have? For a while I felt abandoned, thwarted, powerless, but I said nothing of Maya Duncan's true bloodline for fear of distressing those who looked to me for guidance. However, over time I began to see that, far from abandoning me, the forces of light had used my daughter's abduction to inform me of her existence and that one day, when her soul was ready to embrace the truth, those same forces would find a way to lead her back to me.' The room erupts; sobs, hugs, kisses.

'That's not going to happen,' I gasp, a giddy slur to my voice. 'Because if she's ever found I'm going to tell her that her two-bit freak show of a father raped her mother when she was fifteen years old!'

More hands jerk me back. I lash out at arms and faces. They're pulling, shoving, twisting me round, pushing from behind. A rug rucks and skids beneath my feet. With a jolt, I stumble. Beatrice – surprisingly strong – grips me by one arm, Hannah – not placid or smiling now – clamps both her hands around the other. With a crazed angry strength they fling me against the wall. A bolt of shock. A flash of pain. Then darkness closes in.

CHAPTER THIRTY

I'm lying on a thin rubbery mat, heaving hard for breath. My mouth is dry, my head throbs, half my ribs are on fire and my right arm feels as if it's been wrenched from its socket. I can use my fingers but any attempt to lift the whole arm makes me whimper with pain. I touch the throbbing bump on my temple and look around me, dazed and disbelieving. In the pale moonlight coming through the barred skylight I see a cramped space lined with metal shelves piled up with hand-bound pamphlets, hundreds of them arranged in colour-coded stacks. Orange, blue, pink, green. The walls behind them are windowless slabs of grey breeze block. My gaze moves from the tin bucket sitting in one corner to the small bottle of water lying next to the mat. A scratchy realisation takes shape. I'm in Parks' shed. Pretty ironic considering who I thought I'd find in here.

Wincing, I crawl to the door and try the knob. It won't budge. I slam my left palm against it, look up and see a basket wedged at the top of the shelves. Almost smiling, I stretch up and take my burner phone from its nest of detoxifying crystals. *Fuck you, Parks.* I switch it on. A message flashes onto the screen. *Insert sim.* I snap off the back of the phone. No sim card. That psycho bitch Hannah must have taken it out. A plunge of panic. I stand on the upturned bucket and inspect the skylight. The glass is sealed and the metal bars are bolted into the frame. In a drench of sweat I beat my fist against the door and howl for help until the walls begin to ripple and sway. A flicker of calm thrums and catches. I tell myself I'm concussed, that it will pass and I have to save my strength and make a plan. Blearily, I inspect the seal on the bottle of water, find it intact and twist off the cap. I take a mouthful and swallow it slowly. It moistens the sandpaper surface of my tongue but does nothing to ease the hunger. Thoughts flare and drift. This is madness. Parks can't keep me here. Why would he even want to? He can't break me. I won't let him. *Stay angry. Treat him with contempt and whatever he says, don't let him get inside your head.*

The square of sky framed by the skylight is blue and bright when I hear the scrape of footsteps outside. I blink myself alert. I'm starving and my whole body aches but my head feels clearer. The door opens. It's Parks with Hannah and Beatrice in tow. The two women stare at me, eyes full of hatred and – far more disturbingly – pity. He props his cane against the shelves and tells them to wait outside. They step back, leaving the door very slightly ajar. I weigh up my chances of forcing my way out. Even bruised and one-armed I could easily overpower Parks, but I'd be no match for Hannah and Beatrice, so I stay where I am and crumple forward like I'm in too much pain to get up. 'You've made your point, Parks,' I say. 'Now let me out.'

'I'm sorry you got hurt,' he says mildly. 'But you have to understand that our community here at Oak Bank is built on loyalty and obedience. Without them we are nothing.'

'You *are* nothing, Parks. And without your gang of swivel-eyed harpies you're less than nothing. How about you do us all a favour and let me take them back to sanity?' I glare up at him.

'Try to put your anger aside,' he says, smoothly. 'Embrace this opportunity to fast, contemplate and renew your spirit.'

'Oh, please, cut the crap. Roz saw you for the fucked-up charlatan you really are and so do I.'

'You think Roz loved you, but you're wrong. She tried to destroy your life, just like she tried to destroy mine.'

'You're the destroyer. You killed Phoebe. Roz was trying to save her.'

'Look at what she did to you.' He takes out my notebook, holds the cover between his thumb and forefinger and waves it in front of me. 'It's all here in your own words. Her lies and manipulation. All the secrets she kept. She's a force of darkness whose every move is designed to cause pain and destruction to those who carry the imprint of light. Higher beings like me' – he looks me in the eye – 'and you.'

'What is this? Lesson two of some online hypnosis course? String out the pauses and waggle stuff around?'

'Can't you feel the light glowing inside you? It even guided you to the false name you chose. *Clara.* It means shining and bright. Did you know that?'

'I picked it out especially for you because I once knew a Clara I despised.'

He steps forward and grasps my shoulder, sending a judder of pain down my arm.

I pull away. 'Don't touch me.'

'Roz's death has left you rudderless and alone with no idea who you are.' He pauses, savouring my distress. '*That's* the real reason you came here, isn't it? You're trapped in a limbo of uncertainty and you thought *I* could set you free.'

'You know nothing about me.'

'You were right to seek me out. Don't fight it. Stay here and let me sever the toxic ties that bind you to Roz.'

'So you can cut me off from reality and jerk my strings till I sign over all her money? No thanks.'

'This isn't about money.' His voice has dropped to a soft, insistent purr. 'When you've been purged of darkness and your heart is open you will see that it's about belonging.'

'You can't keep me here.' I swallow down the panic. 'My boyfriend knows where I am. If I'm not back by tonight he'll come and get me.'

'I think not.' He flicks through the pages of my notebook. 'Poor Will. As far as I can see you've gone out of your way to keep him in the dark about your search for your identity. But I can't blame you. A journalist who's built his career on covering the Maya Duncan case is the last person you should trust with the awful truth about her mother's death.'

I look away so he won't see the effect of his words. 'False imprisonment is a crime,' I murmur.

He shakes his head. 'The powers of light drew you here so I could mend your broken spirit and fill the emptiness in your heart. I know it, and beneath all that anger and guilt, so do you.'

I feel dizzy and sick and dig deep for a way to hit back. 'You're pathetic, Parks. A sad little man who never got over being thrown out of the Breakaway Brethren.'

His mocking smile falters, just for a second, before it settles back in place.

'You're trying to fight what you feel. Don't. Just accept that from now on whatever you do and wherever you go there will always be a little piece of me in here.' He presses a finger into the centre of my brow and leans in so close that his face almost touches mine. 'Always.'

I strike his hand away. 'You deluded fuck! Your mind games are a joke.' But as he backs towards the door, I can still feel the intrusive pressure of his touch.

A scuffing noise pulls at my threadbare sleep. I open my eyes. For a moment I think I dreamed it. Four faint taps on the keypad tell me I didn't. I lift my head. A hand appears at the edge of the door and slowly pushes it open. Enough moonlight seeps through the skylight to make out a crouched figure. With soundless steps it moves across the room and squats at my side, a rustle of clothing as it leans over me. I close my fingers around the burner phone and flick on the torch. Two fierce unblinking eyes stare down at me through the beam.

'Amy!'

Her eyes travel over my features as if she's searching for something hidden beneath my skin. I shift the torch. The beam catches something wedged in her belt. I realise, cold with terror, she's got a hammer and one of the knives from the kitchen. *Stay calm. No sudden movements.* 'Does Jonas know you're here?' I say, my voice as steady as I can make it.

'I nursed him.'

'What?'

'After the accident.' She sits back a little, her unfocused eyes staring off at the shelves behind me. 'It was me who brought him back to health. Me who comforted him for the loss of Phoebe.' She grinds her bunched knuckles into her chest. 'Me who told him our golden girl could never be replaced and that his legacy must be his writing.' She wrenches the phone from my hand and drops it on the floor.

'Why are you here, Amy?' I say, my voice hardly more than a whisper.

She dips in and out of the torch beam, her mouth trembling like a child's. 'He says he feels a bond between the two of you. He says once he's set you on the true path and opened your mind to the light, you'll feel it too.'

I glance past her to the half-open door. 'That's not true, Amy. There'll never be a bond between me and Jonas.'

'He says you're *special*.' Her lip curls. 'Just like that slut Kaitlin. His *special* girl.'

The word makes me jittery and sick. 'I'm not special, Amy.' Teeth gritted against the pain, I press both my elbows into the mat and make a slight move to sit up. 'I'm not special in any way.'

Her eyes drift off to the shelves again and almost dreamily she pulls the knife from her belt. The torchlight catches the sharpened edge of the blade. Wondering how much damage I can do with my keys, I edge my fingers towards the pocket of my jeans. She looks up sharply and thrusts the knife into the space between us. I freeze.

'I know exactly what you are.' She lifts a strand of hair from my face with the tip of the blade. 'All that pretty hair he likes so much, those big green eyes.' She circles my face with the knife. 'You're a tool of the darkness, a pretty puppet being manipulated by demons to rekindle his hunger for progeny.'

I hear my breath speed up. I try to slow it down. 'Jonas will be angry if you hurt me,' I say, softly. 'He'll punish you.'

'You think I care about punishment? I have to rid him of temptation.' She's moving oddly now, rocking back and forth as if she's trying to ease some inner cramp. 'If I don't it will turn out like before. All the true believers pushed aside to make way for a fiend cloaked in borrowed flesh. I won't let that happen. Not again.'

Sweat prickles my spine.

'Jonas isn't Maya Duncan's father,' she sneers.

'How do you know?' I whisper.

'Because that slut Kaitlin wasn't worthy to bear his child. That's why she miscarried. When she lost her tainted brat it was a blessing.'

'A blessing?' I ease my finger deeper into my pocket.

Her voice softens. 'Of course. It forced Jonas to focus on his true calling, his writing. That made the bad seeds fall away until only six of us were left. The truly worthy. We found peace. We were happy.' Her focus snaps back to me. 'And then you turn up with your filthy accusations and your lies about a living child.' She raises the knife, digs her other hand into the pocket of her cardigan and pulls out a loop of plastic. A beat of confusion. Then I realise. It's a zip tie.

'Hold out your wrists.'

My finger finds the edge of my key ring. She stabs the knife into my arm, three swift, impersonal punctures like she's pricking sausages. 'Do it.'

More shocked by the callousness of her brutality than the sudden pain, I pull my hand from my pocket and raise my clasped hands, keeping my wrists as far apart as I dare. One handed, she drops the zip tie over my wrists and yanks it tight. Never taking my eyes from the knife, I bring my arm to my mouth and suck off the blood. 'Amy, please—'

'Quiet, demon!' She drops her knee onto my hip, grinding it into my flesh, and pulls the spotted scarf from her neck. 'I am strong against the wiles of darkness.'

She clamps the knife between her teeth and pulls my head up. I thrash and buck. She smacks her open palm against the side of my neck, leaving me limp and stunned while she winds the scarf around my mouth and knots it tight. 'Get up.'

She sees me struggling, grabs my bound wrists and hauls me to my feet. White-hot pain shoots through my sprained shoulder. With a jerk, she spins me around and pushes me out into the night. A distant glimmer through the trees. There's a light on in one of the bedrooms. I turn and make a bolt through the undergrowth. I nearly make it to the lawn when my foot catches in a knot of ground ivy and twists sharply. I smack forward into a bed of nettles. Within seconds she's grabbing me from behind. Winded, stung and gasping through a sweaty mouthful of scarf I roll over and kick out with all my strength. She dodges my feet and with one hand clutching a hank of my hair and the other holding the knife to my ribs she yanks me up. Pain pulses through my ankle but she forces me through the trees to the back of the shed, nicking my skin through my shirt when I stumble or try to resist. There's a smell of newly dug earth. In the moonlight, I make out vegetable beds and neat lines of bean poles. This is her fiefdom. Her vegetable garden. The perfect place to bury a body.

Moist soil sucks my feet and my gaze swings wildly as she marches me over to the far wall. *Fight back, kiddo.*

'Down.' She pushes me onto my knees and with the same casual violence she'd used to stab me in the arm she shoves me onto my side. I hear her step away. I rock my hips, roll over and see her outline in the shadows. She cries out, 'I am strong against the temptations of darkness.'

A thud as she drops the knife, a squelch of soil as she pulls a spade from one of the vegetable beds and raises it high. I tense my muscles, ready to hurl my bound hands at her legs and bring her down as soon as she comes for me. Muttering the same line over and over like a mantra, she turns, swings the spade at the wall and with a crazed determination smashes the blade at the creeper, hitting the same spot again and again. Knowing I can't outrun her on my throbbing ankle I wriggle forwards, aiming for the patch of earth where the knife fell. My fingers touch metal. I strain to work my palms around the handle but they're shaking so violently I cut my thumb on the blade. Finally I have it in my grip. Braced against the pain I heave myself onto my feet and hobble towards her. She glances back, sees me coming and takes a kick at the creeper. With a crash a door swings open in the brickwork. I look from the gaunt triumph of her face to the shadowy wasteland beyond. She throws down the spade, raises both hands like a grotesque parody of a flapper and shoves me hard through the gap. I skitter forward and go down with a grunt. Painfully I twist my head. 'I thought you were going to kill me.'

'And do what the demon wanted?' She makes an odd gurgling sound. 'It sensed your weakness. It wanted me to set it free so it could enter a bolder, wilier vessel. I almost succumbed, but at the last I proved strong against the temptations of darkness.' The door slams shut behind me. Pressing my cheek to the cold ground, I curl up like a beaten dog, cringing with the clang of each blow as she nails up the door from the other side.

My wrists are raw when the knife finally snaps through the zip tie, my arm throbs and my shoulder and ankle are on fire. Ignoring the pain, I limp to my car and screech my way up through the gears, my only thought to get away. Away from sad demented Amy Rickman, away from the penetrating stare and insidious voice of Jonas Parks, away from my crushed hopes of finding Maya Duncan alive at Oak Bank. I hit thirty, forty, fifty, sixty and still can't shake off the burn of Parks' finger on my forehead or the sudden loathsome longing to turn the car around and beg him to take away the gut-wringing emptiness inside.

CHAPTER THIRTY-ONE

I fall through the front door and collapse in the hallway, the last few hours coming back to me in waves of sensation – shock that I'd got it so wrong about Maya, metal piercing my flesh, wet earth squelching underfoot, the stone-cold certainty that Amy Rickman was going to beat me to death with a garden spade, fury that Parks still has my notebook. Two, three, maybe four hours later I watch a letter drift through the letterbox and land at my side. Through half closed eyes I peer at the perky red envelope. It's an offer of cheap, super-fast broadband addressed to Ms P. Locklear, a dead girl whose identity weighs me down like a sodden shroud. Slowly and painfully I crawl up the stairs, telling myself to accept that I've hit the end of the road, that I'll never find Maya or discover who I am. I unlock the door. A bleak silence hangs with the plaster dust. I fill it by thrashing around in search of paracetamol. I take two, stare at the packet and swallow a third, then I turn on my phone and spool through the messages. The texts from Will petered out six hours ago. The last one says, simply, *Miss you. xxx*

I limp to the bathroom and lean over the sink. Slowly I lift my head to the mirror. A bloody, blank-eyed stranger stares back. I finger the purple swelling on my cheek, pick a piece of grit from the mess of blood crusting my hairline and touch the angry wounds on my arm. Tears run down my cheeks, scoring runnels in the grime. I step into the shower, turn the water on full blast and try to scrub away the horror of Oak Bank.

*

I sleep for several hours but still wake up exhausted. I check the time. It's far too late for the builders to come. They must be working on their other job. I'm used to it now. Maybe it will always be like this. Maybe I'll go on living my wrecked limbo of a life in my wrecked limbo of a flat forever. I take more painkillers and pick up the thriller I bought at the airport on the way to France. It's useless. I can't focus on the plot or remember who any of the characters are. All I can see is Parks poring over my notebook, and the thought of him violating my deepest hopes, fears and confusions while devouring everything I know about Kay makes me hotter and hotter and twitchier and twitchier – a top spinning out of control. What if he sees something I've missed and uses my research to find Maya? For all his bullshit about the powers of light bringing Maya back to him when her soul was ready, I don't believe for one minute that he wouldn't go out and find her if he could.

Like an addict in search of a fix, I toss down the book and rummage around for the folder of Roz's cuttings. A sense of purpose as I hold it in my hands, an easing of the restlessness as I redraw my compass of names on the cover: Roz, Kay, Phoebe, Maya. North, South, East, West. Calmer now, I sift through the articles one by one in a bid to piece together my lost notes. Deep in the task, I unfold a rare interview Kay gave to mark the fifth anniversary of Maya's disappearance. My eyes pull away from a photo of the house in Stanford Street and snag on one of the few direct quotes the interviewer managed to squeeze out of her: *'Every night I dream that Maya comes back to me and she's still a little kid and I get the chance to start over and make things right.'* I falter, choked by a loosening hold on what's real. Did I remember reading those words and only imagine that Kay said them – or something very like them – to my face? A thought creeps up on me, slowly at first and then in a wretched sort of rush – in all the time I was with her she told me almost nothing about herself or the day of the abduction that hadn't been in the papers. No unburdening of secrets, no flesh to hang on the bones of the story laid out in these cuttings, no private memories of Maya. Maybe stock responses were the only way she'd been able to deal with the horror of losing her child – but the thought of the spaces where those intimacies should have been lodges in my brain, unsettling me in ways I can't describe.

I reach for my phone and swipe to the selfie of the three of us in Toulon. Even here there's no hint of the real Kay. Behind the designer sunglasses and floppy hat, the woman hanging onto David Duncan's arm could be any petite, mid-thirties brunette. I glance at Vicky's promo shot of the band pinned to my wall – dyed black hair, kohl-smeared eyes, red-painted pouts. I turn back to the circled names on the front of the folder. In the balloon of emptiness around Kay's I write *Anger? Memories? Pain?* Fired up now, I fetch my trusty teacup, a bottle of vodka and a reel of tape and kneel on the bed arranging articles, photos and hastily scribbled Post-it notes around the picture of the band. As I work I scrub at my forehead with the back of my wrist trying to erase the memory of Parks' finger but the imprint is still there, pulsing and poisonous, when I flop down onto the pillow and fall into a deep, drunken sleep.

The Doxettes are singing, skinny bodies gyrating in the aquarium judder of strobe lights, voices in the crowd screaming out their names.

Hot and hungover, I wake to the shrilling of brakes in the street below and sunlight stabbing my brain through a crack in the breeze-blown curtains. It's late morning. I pick my way around the packing cases, make a coffee and carry the mug and a packet of custard creams back to bed. I wriggle forward to inspect the picture of the band. The edges of the image are dark, the scrawl of felt-pen signatures and kisses half visible against the light-fringed outlines of raised fists and bobbing heads. I dunk a biscuit into my coffee and imagine those hands – black nail polish, cheap flashy rings – passing round the magenta felt tip to write their names: Vicky, Krissi and Kay. The I's dotted with tears – or maybe they're droplets of blood, the strokes of the initials slanted and bold. I drop back on my heels, dump the coffee and the custard creams on the floor and slide back under the duvet. I close my eyes and stare out across a rubble-strewn space-scape of dead ends and discarded dreams, reaching for thoughts that flit and tumble with the queasy turns of my stomach. Slowly I push myself upright and blink at the signatures on the photo. Krissi with a K. Was that a teenage affectation or a shortening of something German chosen by her au pair mother who abandoned her as a baby? I'm back in the salon, Vicky's fingers massaging my scalp.

'She even stopped spelling her name the German way because she hated being reminded of her mum.'

Thought-beats pulse with my heart. Prescriptions, passports, anything official – they'd still have used the original German spelling, wouldn't they? I reach for my keys and hobble barefoot into the street.

'Overslept love?' A red face leers from a passing van. I let go of my not quite long enough T-shirt and raise a finger as I make a wobbly dash for my car and unlock the door. I throw myself across the seats and wrench open the glovebox, scrabbling with both hands, tossing the logbook, lipstick and a crumpled paper cup to the floor. *Please* let it be here! I shove my fingers into the corners. A greasy ooze as they close around the metal tube of ointment. That smell of tar as I hold it up and read the half-concealed printing on the chemist's label. Kristin Mül—. Carefully, I unroll the flattened end. And there it is: *Kristin Müller*.

I gaze at the letters, as sure as I've ever been about anything that this is the birth name of the Doxettes' lead singer, the woman who now calls herself Chrissie Miller. I flash back to my first night at the Villa Rosa. The sun is sinking, a big fiery ball dripping gold across the bay and I'm smiling when I ask Kay if Chrissie ever forgave her for signing a solo deal with David Duncan. A moment of silence, then she snaps at me so sharply I flinch away. *'Why the big interest in Chrissie? I haven't seen her for years.'*

My eyes lock on the date the prescription was filled – 2 February last year.

Were you a liar, Kay? If you lied about Chrissie Miller, did your lies extend to the life you'd lived and the child you'd lost? If you weren't, then what the hell is Chrissie's medication doing in your glovebox? A startling possibility flickers through my head, like something glimpsed from a speeding train before it pings out of sight.

I hurry back to the flat and try Chrissie's number again. It's still unavailable. I look up the address Vicky sent me. It's in Shoreditch. Flat 8, Rysedale House. I dress quickly, dab layers of concealer onto my bruises and try to concoct a story to explain my injuries that doesn't involve the unscratched Healey. After twenty minutes I've got a face the texture of newly laid cement and a half-baked story about a manic Deliveroo biker ploughing into me on the pavement. I'm strapping a bandage around my swollen ankle when my phone rings.

'Miss Locklear?' The voice is young and eager.

'Yes.'

'This is Emma Waters. I'm an intern at Edgecombe and Harris.'

My distracted brain takes a second to place the company. Then my heart sinks. It's Roz's broker.

I squeeze the phone under my chin and tug the bandage tighter. 'Hi, Emma, I'm a bit busy, is there something I forgot to sign?'

'Mr Edgecombe asked me to look into the Circle Trust for you.'

'Oh.' She has all my attention now.

'I'm not getting very far. Could I just check the information you gave him?'

'Sure.'

'You said the trust funded the building of a gospel hall in Northamptonshire, dedicated to the memory of a pastor in the Breakaway Brethren. A man called George Burney.'

'That's right.'

'Anything else?'

'Sorry. That's all I know.'

'Well, I've found a number of trusts registered under that name but the one that best fits those details is private *and* offshore, so unfortunately there's very little information in the public domain.'

'Anything you can tell me would be helpful, anything at all.'

'Well, I did come across an accounting document leaked in 2008 that suggests the majority of its assets trace back to a batch of shares in a long defunct company called J. P. Dutton & Co. Manufacturing.'

'Dutton's?' I let the half-unrolled bandage drop to the floor. 'Burney was one of their bookkeepers. How many shares are we talking about?'

'Ten thousand, bought in the 1980s when the company was offering them to their employees for a penny each. The take-up was small but the company got bought out in 1999 and over the next ten years its assets became a counter in a chain of takeovers, eventually ending up in the hands of a big German conglomerate. By which time those original Dutton's shareholders would have made a killing.'

'So was the trust set up by George Burney?'

'There's no way of telling. This kind of trust is specifically designed to hide the identity of the trustor.'

'Any idea who the trustees are?'

'No, sorry.'

'How about the beneficiaries?'

'It's usually direct descendants but the trustees made a one-off grant of one point five million to a religious foundation a couple of years ago, which I'm guessing was the money to build that gospel hall.'

'What's the trust worth now?'

'Impossible to say, but we're definitely talking serious money.'

'Did you find out anything else?'

'That's it, I'm afraid.'

'Thanks, Emma.'

She says she'll report anything else she finds and hangs up.

My brain spins wildly and stalls on the image of miserly George Burney raking in massive returns on his thousand pounds' worth of one-penny shares while forcing his wife and child to live like paupers. Seems like the devil really does look after his own.

CHAPTER THIRTY-TWO

The day is clouding over as I squeeze into a parking space behind
Shoreditch Town Hall. Disconcerted that I'm only a mile or so
from Will's flat, I keep my head down as I drop into a corner shop
to buy a new notebook. The only one they have is small and flimsy,
a poor substitute for the leather-bound beauty I bought in Cassis
but it will have to do. I stuff it into my bag and cut through a maze
of back streets: shabby warehouses, stripped-down bars and cafés,
boarded-up shopfronts splattered with graffiti – *UFO, SWANK,
TWEAK* and, disconcertingly, *WHERE IS LOVE?* Rysedale House
turns out to be an ugly concrete building wedged between a
second-hand furniture warehouse and a printworks. A skinny
man in full-body lycra noses his bike through the front door. I
hurry forward with a smile and slip through the door while he's
fastening his helmet, step over a couple of folded buggies and a
half-dismantled bike and set off up the concrete stairs. I get to
the top and press the bell of number eight. The ring echoes into
silence. I press again, glance up into the eye of a tiny camera, and
down at the pale strip of light beneath the door. After a couple
more presses a door opens downstairs. I lean into the stairwell. A
harassed-looking woman is crossing the landing, baby under one
arm, shopping bags over the other.

'Excuse me. I'm looking for Chrissie Miller.'

The woman shrugs, barely curious as she settles her baby onto
her hip.

'Do you know if she's around? She works abroad a lot.'

'Short, skinny, changes her hairstyle every five minutes?'
I nod.

'Saw her yesterday,' she says grumpily. 'Stuck-up cow.'

I try Chrissie's bell again and listen to the silence. Then I tear a sheet of paper from the notebook, scribble my number and write:

Can we meet? I need to ask you about Kay Duncan. It's personal and important. I'm not a journalist.

Phoebe Locklear

As I crouch down to slip the note under the door a shadow twitches across the strip of light. The movement is so fleeting I might have imagined it. I glance up at the camera, and push the folded paper beneath the door. I head back to my car, glancing at my phone every ten minutes, convinced that Chrissie Miller had been standing behind her front door, watching me on her camera feed. Why wouldn't you let me see your face, Chrissie? What were you afraid of? Answers spin off in such wild directions I have to stop at a bench on a littered patch of concrete and sit down, head between my knees, looking – I'm sure to the passers-by – like some hungover party girl struggling to make it home from a drunken night out. I close my eyes, unable to stop my brain hurtling from image to image, all unsettling. Chrissie's medication in Kay's car. Kay's canvases and brushes sitting dry and untouched at the Villa Rosa, even though she'd gone to France to paint. Kay suddenly switching from prosecuting her abusive father to offering him forgiveness. Kay cancelling the rented studio in the centre of town in favour of an isolated villa. Kay and Chrissie, Chrissie and Kay, and the only friend still in touch with them both, dead in a freak accident. Why were you so upset when you left the salon, Vicky? Who did you call? Were they there in your flat when you died? I take the tube of ointment from my bag and I'm re-examining the label when my phone buzzes. It's a pin from an unknown number, marking a spot way out of town, and a text.

Tonight 9 p.m., C.

It's Chrissie. I let out a blurt of laughter. I really must have been losing it to think what I'd been thinking. I read the message again. It's a bit curt and it would have been nice to meet somewhere closer but at least she's agreed to see me. This time though, just to be on the safe side, I should tell someone where I'm going – pretend it's a Tinder date and I'm following the safety tips. I run through everyone I know in the UK. The list is depressingly short. Will – hardly. Tim Edgecombe, Roz's broker – weird. Tomas, my builder – even weirder. Delphine Lomas – she'd guess I was lying. I'm spooling back through my contacts when my phone buzzes again.

Sorry, I was texting in the car. Let me know if you can make it. If not I'll be in town tomorrow lunchtime.

I text back.

Tonight's fine. See you there.

I re-wrap the tube of ointment in a tissue, zip it back into my bag and walk quickly to the car. I glance back as I unlock the door, a reflex I don't seem to be able to shake. Annoyed at how jittery I've become, I pull open the door and go rigid, halted by a smell – stale sweat and the unmistakable taint of weed. The scent of the intruder who broke into my home. I shrink back and see a thin white scratch beside the lock. Furious, I spin round again. I can't see anybody watching me and there's nothing missing when

I check inside, but the sting of violation is still burning as I start the engine and race away.

By seven thirty I'm heading east out of London, drab flyovers, graffitied concrete, fine rain misting the windscreen, excitement building in my head. Blasts of Bob Dylan – Roz's favourite – bring back bursts of childhood: the sudden black of the African night, playing marbles with a boy called Blessings, the scorched earth that leaves a dappled pattern on my knees, Roz slowing the jeep to skirt a roadside preacher in full flow, the rapt faces of the passers-by who have stopped to say 'Amen'. I take the turning off the main road and peer through the darkness, searching for a pub or a house, surprised when my destination turns out to be a picnic area in a patch of woodland. I pull into the parking area, keep the engine running and look around me. Nothing but trees. I check the time. I'm early. I turn on the heater. Flick the knob first one way, then the other. No comforting whirr, no whoosh of warmth. I rub my arms to keep warm.

Movement in the bushes. I switch on the headlights. A floodlit outline appears. It's not a woman. It's a man, hurrying full tilt towards the car. I twist the key and ram my foot on the accelerator. The starter grinds. I twist again. It coughs and stops. I fling myself across the passenger seat, reaching for the lock. The door jerks away from my hand. Dark mac, soft grey trousers, black leather gloves. I kick open the driver's door and swing my legs onto the mud. A hand grips my shoulder. I twist around and look into a face – familiar, chubby, soft-lipped.

'David!'

He pulls away, squinting at my bruises in the light from the dashboard. 'What did you do to your face?'

'Doesn't matter. What are you doing here?'

He squeezes into the car, jams his briefcase onto his lap and slams the door.

'Chrissie Miller called me.'

'Chrissie rang *you*?' The patter of rain, the hum of distant traffic, and a creep of doubt. 'What, she just happened to have your number on speed dial? After twenty years?'

'She asked if I knew who you were. When I told her what happened in Cassis she changed her mind about talking to you.'

'You're lying.'

He runs a hand through his wet hair. 'Phoebe, listen to me.'

'Why didn't she open the door?'

'What are you talking about?'

'When I went to her flat. She saw me on the security camera but she wouldn't let me in.'

He shrugs. 'How should I know? She probably had a man in there or maybe she'd just got out of the shower.'

'Bullshit.'

He lays his hand on my arm. 'You've got to stop this, Phoebe.'

'Stop what?'

'Hounding people.'

'I'm not hounding anyone. I just want to talk to her.'

His grip tightens. I look down at his expensively gloved fingers then up at his face and flash to the photo of the band. Chrissie and Kay, two lookalike teenage brunettes gyrating on stage, vying for his attention. 'They shared each other's secrets, and they wore each other's clothes.' Vicky's words slip from my lips and detonate an explosion of half-framed thoughts that flare and turn in stunned slow motion silence, twisting and falling into an electrifying pattern that fuses all my doubts and suspicions into a single cold certainty. 'That's why Chrissie wouldn't let me see her face. That's why she called you.'

'What are you talking about?'

'That woman at the Villa Rosa. She wasn't Kay. She was Chrissie.'

I jump from the car and run.

'Phoebe! Come back!'

I plunge into the trees, letting the branches tear my face and legs.

'Phoebe!' David's voice gusts through the leaves.

'You killed her!' I shout. 'You killed Kay. That whole charade with the DNA test and the crap about protecting her was just a ploy to throw me off the scent.'

'For God's sake! What's the matter with you?'

'You and Chrissie. You killed Kay then you hired some creep to follow me around and break into my flat and my car to find out how much I'd worked out.'

'Oh for God's sake, I've had it up to here with your fantasies. I never hurt Kay and I haven't come here to hurt you.'

I keep moving, trainers skidding on leaf mould, searching for a path in the misty gloom. 'No? Then why *did* you come?'

'To tell you who your mother is.'

The shock trips me up. I throw out my hands and slam my palm against a tree. 'Go on then. Who is she?'

'I'm not going to shout across a goddamn car park.'

I turn back, limping through the trees till I can see him. He's leaning back against the car, arms folded in exasperation.

'You're lying.'

He looks up, head straining towards my voice. 'Why would I lie? You were right about Chrissie. She knows things about Kay's past that Kay never told anyone else, not even me. When I told her about Roz and that bizarre letter she wrote about you being Maya, she put the pieces together and worked out who you are.'

Still wary, I take a small step closer. 'Why didn't she tell me herself?'

'She thinks you're better off not knowing.' He blots his forehead with a folded handkerchief, his voice so low I can barely hear him. 'I didn't agree, so I told her I'd come instead.'

'Why?'

'*Why?*' His voice catches, hoarse and throaty. 'You've got the gall to ask me *why?*' He stuffs the handkerchief into his pocket. 'After Kay killed herself I asked you, no, I *begged* you, to let her rest in peace. But you just went on and on with your obsession; buying her car, stalking her friends, trampling on their grief and mine. It has to end. This is the only way.'

I step from the shadow and hurl the tube of ointment at his feet. 'What was this doing in Kay's car? She told me she hadn't spoken to Chrissie for years.'

He bends down, picks it up and holds it to the light of the headlamps. With the other hand he pats his top pocket for his glasses, works them over his ears and reads the label. 'Jesus, so that's what this is about.' He takes off his glasses, folds them carefully and with a sigh slips them back into his pocket. 'Chrissie came to my office – I don't know, eighteen, nineteen months ago. She wanted me to relaunch her career. I told her it wasn't going to happen. She got upset. I calmed her down and gave her a lift to the station.'

'In Kay's car?'

'I drove it sometimes, OK? Maybe mine was being serviced, maybe I just fancied driving the Healey that day. Who knows? It's no big deal. Check with my secretary.'

I stand there, not moving, water dripping down my neck from the branches above.

'Look' – he sighs – 'I don't blame you for what Kay did. I did at first, but I was too angry to think straight. Since then I've had time to think about it and now I realise that you're just as much a victim of Roz Locklear's warped mind games as she was. So if you want you can get back in your car and drive away. But for Kay's sake I'd like you to come with me right now to get the answers you need and put an end to this nightmare, once and for all.'

I walk towards the car, tears of release stinging my eyes. He pats my shoulder and opens the passenger door. 'Come on. I'll drive. It's time you knew the truth.'

I get in. One hand across the back of my seat he reverses the car, swings it around and heads back to the main road.

'Why does Chrissie think I'm better off not knowing who my mother is?'

Tight faced in the crimson tail-lights of the car in front he slams his foot on the accelerator and veers into the wake of a lorry. 'I think her actual words were "better a rosy dream than a shitty rejection".'

'Because her own mother rejected her?'

He turns to look at me. 'How do you know about that?'

'Vicky Bunce told me.' I look away to the passing dark. 'Is that what I'm heading for? A shitty rejection?'

'I honestly don't know.' Headlights sweep past, rain hits the windscreen and drums on the soft top. 'What else did Vicky tell you?'

'Just stuff about the band.'

'Did she mention she used to go out with a tattoo artist?'

'No.'

'Just for a while. He was training her up. By all accounts she was getting quite good at it then he dumped her and she went back to hairdressing.'

I don't answer. Too wound-up for small talk, I sit there shivering, my heartbeat quickening with the double speed of the wipers, my thoughts flipping between dread and excitement.

'You're cold,' he says. 'I kept telling Kay to get the heater fixed.'

'I'll be alright.'

A hand-painted sign flashes past in the darkness. He's slowing down, pulling into a lay-by, headlights sweeping across hedgerows, tires crunching on uneven ground. Ahead of us, a rack of lights glimmers through the rain. He draws closer. It's a tea truck, the edges studded with carnival bulbs, a torn awning flapping above the serving hatch.

'Wait here. I'll get us some coffee,' he opens the door. 'It'll be disgusting but it'll warm us up.'

I watch him at the counter, leaning in to speak to a server I can't see. He hurries back, collar up, head down through the rain, and hands me a polystyrene beaker with a badly fitting lid, sucking breath through his teeth as hot coffee splashes onto his hand. I take a sip. He's right. It tastes like swill. I'm about to put the lid back on when he drops a Kit Kat into my lap. 'That should take the taste away.'

I smile. Suddenly aware of how hungry I am, I tear back the wrapper, the smell and snap of childhood as I break off a finger and offer it to him, a momentary ache of longing to look up and see Roz at the wheel, shorts rucked across her sunburned thighs, a thermos squeezed between her knees. He bites into the chocolate, takes a gulp of coffee and sets off again, hitting the accelerator hard as he pulls back into the traffic.

'Why does Chrissie think this woman is my mother?' I say.

'I don't know. All I could get out of her was a name and an address.' He's speeding around a roundabout, taking a turn-off. Overwhelmed by adrenaline, I nibble my Kit Kat, sip my coffee, and watch the raindrops slide down the windscreen in soft grey blobs.

I jolt awake. David must have got the heater to work. I'm warmer now and the tension inside me has loosened. It's dark outside. Branches scrape the windows and claw the soft top. A siren pulses behind us, or maybe it's my phone. I lift my hand to check it. My coffee cup tips over. David is speaking. Words spill into my lap, warm and wet, dregs of meaning dripping down my thighs.

'... designed a tattoo for the band... that bloke of Vicky's finished hers... did the outline of Kay's and Chrissie's... and left Vicky to fill in the rest.' I scrabble to catch each sound before it trickles through my fingers. '... she didn't quite get them all matching... something to do with the teardrops... or was it the thorns?' Cars whoosh past, brushing my skin with light, blood roars in my ears. 'Don't get me wrong, she made a pretty good job of it. In fact she was probably the only person in the world who'd ever noticed the difference.' My eyelids flicker and droop. Dark shadows spread like treacle, the dirt at my feet grows sticky with sound. 'I usually pride myself on attention to detail, but that one just passed me by. So when Vicky saw the photo she got herself in quite a state… called me to ask what the hell was going on… I had no choice… you do see that, don't you? I had to makes sure she never told anyone else.' Nausea coils around my stomach and pitches me forward. I want Roz to hold back my hair and lay her cool firm hand on my neck while I retch – *Come on, kiddo, spit it up.*

The car is stopping. We're back where we started. In the picnic area in the woods. I was right. David killed Kay *and* he killed Vicky and now he's going to kill me. Maya Duncan calls to me through the darkness, a naked bulb throws discs of light around a soot-caked cellar. Something injured howls in the dark, a cry of pain. I lift my head. It's not an animal. It's David. 'I never wanted it to come to this. I warned you off, I offered you money but you just wouldn't stop… poking and prodding, digging into Kay's past, her friends, her life. Pestering her family, even her father's carer.' A monkey screech drowns him out, sharp piercing whoops that bounce around my skull as my phone flashes on the dashboard.

Blood thuds in my head, my limbs are heavy. I flop against the door. He grabs me hard – too hard – and grapples me into the driver's seat. He's shaking pills onto my lap, pressing my fingers around the bottle. His voice is low and insistent. 'It's alright. Just relax.' The door slams. I screw up my eyes. He's dragging a bag from the bushes. Hyenas rustle the leaves outside the tent, circling, sniffing, scratching, brushing their bodies against the canvas. I open my mouth to call out to Roz. With a stab of pain I remember. She's gone. So much death. It's alright. If I shout for Will, he'll come. Kind, clever Will who knows how it feels to be betrayed. I open my lips. My tongue is numb. I have no voice. I have to get away. I'm running, panting, stumbling over rocks. I can see the sea, dark and choppy beyond the cliff edge. My legs won't stop. I kick out and plunge into nothingness.

Jonas Parks floats towards me, a circling finger points at my brow. I push him away and go on falling, falling, falling. Kay and Chrissie, Chrissie and Kay. They wore each other's clothes and they shared each other's secrets. There's a body beneath me, rocking on the water. A wave rises up and rolls it over. A bloated face blinks up at me. It's my own. A screech shakes the darkness. A pause. The sound comes again. The volume rising in pitch with each ring. Hope flickers inside me. I see David at the car window. I will my hands to reach down and grab my phone. They won't move. My whole body is leaden. He wrenches open the door. His gloved fingers grab my phone. For a second the glow from the screen sharpens the pudgy curves of his face into a mask of crags. He frowns as he taps the keys then he twists abruptly and hurls the handset onto the back seat.

CHAPTER THIRTY-THREE

A woman stumbles towards me, bent as if in pain, gasping into her phone. Images just strong enough to carry through the hazy confusion of black trees and purple sky. 'I need an ambulance.' It's a voice from my dreams, only strained and tearful. A screen-lit flash of eyes, nose and chin framed by a hoodie. The woman from the Villa Rosa. The woman who wasn't Kay. Half-formed thoughts hold for a heartbeat before hardening into leaden lumps of loss.

'Chrissie.'

I mouth the name but no sound comes out. A blurred outline of trunks and branches wavers in the moonlight. She's seizing me under the arms and dragging me clear of the car. Her hood flops back. A few seconds of bleach-blonde hair dyed pink at the tips. As she lays me onto the cold wet ground something white drifts into focus, shuddering with the thrum of the engine. It's a piece of rag wrapped around the end of the exhaust pipe. It seems so strange. So unlikely. And then I realise why it's there. It's holding a rubber hose in place.

A heartbeat beep of monitors, softness beneath my skin. A flicker of fear. Someone is leaning over me. A woman. I feel her breath, traces of shampoo and skin cream beneath the smell of earth and cigarettes. She puts her lips to my left ear. Is it her? Is it Chrissie?

'The doctor says you can hear me, Phoebe. I hope that's the case. By the time you wake up I'll be long gone and I'm going to tell you the truth so you won't come searching for me, looking for answers or revenge.'

There's a patch of light beyond her voice. I drag myself towards it but there's nothing to catch hold of and I'm so tired and heavy I drift back into the murk.

'I've done some bad things. I know that. But I saved your life. All I ask in return is a chance to live mine. You wanted facts. Well, I'm sorry, Kay's death doesn't change anything. You're not Maya Duncan.' Her voice grows cold and flat. 'Maya Duncan is dead. If Kay had allowed herself to accept that, she might have found peace a long time ago. Fact number two, whatever David told you, I've got no idea who your mother is or why that Roz woman lied to you.' She pauses. 'Fact number three. David didn't kill Kay. I did.' Shock shoots me back to the surface. I hover for a moment, struggling to cry out as the black sucks me back. 'Everything he's done to cover it up, he's done to protect me.'

A wave of nausea rolls through me. A chair creaks. The smell of her retreats, just a fraction. She must be sitting back, looking down at me. If I could open my eyes what would I see in hers? Regret, triumph, contempt? I imagine the priest in the little church in Cassis trapped in the dark of the confessional as the faithful unburden their guilt and their secrets.

'It started with Lila Mendez. Her new husband was suing David and the settlement was going to bankrupt him. David had found out years ago that Kay's penny-pinching father was in a fact a very wealthy man. I know, difficult to believe, isn't it? He'd got lucky with some shares he bought for nothing back in the eighties then discovered he'd got balls of steel and a knack for playing the stock market. But for Pastor George, making money was never about bringing joy into anyone's life. Like everything else he did, it was about winning, beating the odds, being in control.'

She stops for breath. 'When he knew he was dying he got fixated on using the money to make Kay accept that he'd done the "righteous" thing by trying to beat the devil out of her when she was a kid, and he wanted her to admit that it was her evil that had forced him to throw her out when she fell pregnant. All she had to do was swallow her pride, beg the twisted fuck for forgiveness and all his millions would have been hers. Like David said, it should have been easy. But she said she'd rather die than give in to that old bastard's demands, because saying no to him was all she had. The only way to make him pay for what he'd done to her and her mother.'

I hear the soft click of her swallow. 'So David got me to help him fake a reconciliation. It wasn't hard. George Burney was on his last legs and I was telling him exactly what he wanted to hear. Kay was all wrapped up in her plans to go off to France so we thought she wouldn't find out till it was too late. But she did. David was on his boat and she went tearing down to Brighton to have it out with him. He'd gone into town. But I was there. We argued. I told her to get over it and stop being such a fucking idiot about the money. She slapped me. I pushed her. She fell back and hit her head on the wheel.'

Her voice loses its hardness. 'She just lay there, eyes closed, head tipped to one side. Jesus – I can still see her. I panicked and started to scream. I couldn't stop. Then David came back. He checked her pulse then he took me down to the cabin, gave me a pill to calm me down and told me she was just concussed, and that I had to keep out of the way while he called the ambulance.' I try hard to hold on to her words, to picture the scene, to imagine her panic. 'An hour or so later he woke me up and told me he'd found her dead when he went back on deck. Then he sat me down and said he'd worked out a way to keep me out of prison. He was very calm, very composed. He said he'd put her body in the on-board freezer, sail to France and keep her frozen until George Burney died and his estate had been settled in Kay's favour. I'd just have to drive to Cassis and live as Kay until the trust had agreed to name him as the next beneficiary. Then I'd get overcome with grief and walk into the sea. A week or so later he'd plant Kay's sea-ravaged body in one of the creeks. He made it all sound simple. I wouldn't have to do much acting, just keep my head down and sit it out at the Villa Rosa.'

I hear the soft in and out of her breath. 'I never meant to kill her. I was distraught when I realised what I'd done but like David said, me going to jail wasn't going to bring her back. This way he could save his business, set me up in a new life somewhere far away, and Kay – Christ, I know I sound like a bitch whenever I talk about her – but she hated her life. Hated it like she'd give anything for it to be over. No more trolls, no more tabloids, no more fake psychics stirring up her guilt about Maya, no more passers-by spitting in her face.'

She's so caught up in her justification it's as if she's actually convinced herself that Kay is better off dead. 'So we switched her rental from a studio in town to that hideaway on the hill and I went to live there as her. It was creepy up there all on my own with that damn generator whirring on and off all the time, reminding me that her body was in the freezer in the outhouse. But I just kept counting the days and telling myself it was the price I had to pay to stay free. It was all going to plan. Burney was dead, the trustees had agreed to name David as the next beneficiary and we were just waiting for the dust to settle, when you knocked on the door.'

I can feel her anger. It's like something hot and acrid filling the room. 'So we brought the suicide forward to get you off our backs. I thought it would work, that once you thought Kay was dead you'd just walk away. But David wasn't convinced, so when you went back to the UK he had you watched. And he was right to be worried, wasn't he? You just wouldn't stop digging and you were getting too damn close to the truth.' She stops to calm her breath but it goes on juddering in and out. 'Then Vicky died.'

She's crying now, sobbing quietly. 'At first David swore her death was nothing to do with him but when he finally admitted it I realised that things were spinning out of control. When you came to the flat he was with me, watching you on the security camera. So when he arranged to meet you I followed him. He said he was just going to talk to you, fob you off with some bullshit about your real mother and offer to pay for a private detective to send you off on a wild goose chase to find her. But when he left that coffee stall on the bypass and drove back towards the woods I knew he was going to kill you. I tried and tried to call you but you didn't pick up. So I waited till he'd gone, pulled you out of the car and called an ambulance.'

I hear the rustle of paper. She's folding something, putting it on the bedside table. 'Once we got to the hospital I called David and I told him you'd survived.' She lets out a long sigh. 'I had to let him end it his way. I owed him that. He can't hurt you now. You're safe. Free to start over and find your real mother. Free to go public with the truth. But before you do, just ask yourself if you really want to live out the rest of your life as the girl at the heart of the Kay Duncan scandal. Hounded, lied about, suspected? A new victim for the tabloids to turn on? They'll say you were after Kay's money, that you were part of a conspiracy to hide what really happened to Maya, that you and David were lovers, that you only went to the police when the affair went sour. So for both our sakes, I'm begging you to just walk away from this and let me do the same.'

White. Pure white through the hush. She was here, standing by my bed. Now she's gone. Though the phone and the folded newspaper that have appeared on the bedside table tell me she was real. Drifting and nauseous, I tug at the paper until it falls onto the bed. The headline takes a while to stumble into focus.

Double tragedy as music mogul David Duncan dies in car crash weeks after suicide drowning of troubled wife Kay

Duncan's car left the road late last night and crashed into trees on the A12 near Colchester. No other vehicles were involved in the incident. Initial tests found high levels of alcohol and benzodiazepam in his bloodstream. Police are treating the incident as a suspected suicide.

The effort of lifting the paper has taken all the energy I have. I lie back and try to accept that I'm alive.

CHAPTER THIRTY-FOUR

When I wake again, most of the fog has gone. I fumble with the keys on my phone. Eight missed calls from Chrissie Miller. Four frantic texts telling me not to go to our meeting, a voice message shrill with panic. I play it again. And again. Memories bleed through: Chrissie bending over me in the darkness, feeling for my pulse, gasping that the ambulance is on its way, her breath on my cheek as she whispers her confession. Words and images hurtle around my head, flaring and fading as I try to hold them down. George Burney, Kay, David, Chrissie, the money, the boat, the slap, the fall, the body slumped on deck. Hand trembling, I press the red button beside the bed. A nurse appears, middle-aged, red-faced, crisp-haired.

'Hey, what are you doing? You shouldn't even be awake.'

'The woman who brought me in,' my voice is a rasp, the sound of a stranger, 'is she still here?'

'She left hours ago.'

I struggle onto my elbows. 'I need to see her.'

Firm hands clasp my shoulders and ease me back onto the pillows. Her name tag, 'Maureen' hovers above my face. 'Come on, lie down. I'll let the mental health team know you're awake.'

'*Mental health?* I don't need—' Then it hits me. They think I'm a failed suicide.

'Pretty girl like you with your whole life ahead of you,' she says, her mouth puckered and disapproving. 'What on earth were you thinking?'

In a different mood I might have smiled. Maureen is definitely not what Roz would have called a pussy-footer.

'Please… in my bag. There's a notebook.'

'Is there someone you'd like us to call? Someone who'll be worrying about you?'

'No. No thanks. Look, I will rest, I promise… I just need to get my thoughts straight before I see the counsellor.'

She harrumphs but rummages in the bedside locker and hands me my notebook and pen.

I hold them tight and lie back while she bustles about, a small eternity passing as she checks my pulse, smooths my pillow and changes the IV drip. The minute she's gone I open the notebook and scribble down everything I can remember of Chrissie's confession.

Twenty minutes later, Maureen is back. This time with an iPad. 'I need to check the details we got from the documents in your bag.' She consults the screen and reels off Phoebe Locklear's name, age and address. 'Is that correct?'

I nod. 'When can I leave?'

'Not for at least twenty-four hours. They need to assess the damage to your lungs and at some point the police will want to talk to you.'

'Why?'

'Incidents like this, they like to make sure there was no one else involved.' She pats my hand and backs away through the curtains.

I can't face the police. Not till I've worked out a watertight cover story, but if I go home they'll probably turn up at the flat. There's only one other place I can go. I pull the oxygen tube from my nose and the drip from my hand. Though the trembling won't stop and the nausea makes me weak, I twist my legs off the bed and plant my feet on the linoleum floor. Yesterday's clothes are in the locker. They smell of exhaust fumes. I loosen the ties on my hospital gown and call a cab. The corridor is busy. As I slip past the nurses' station Maureen is nowhere to be seen.

*

I hit Will's bell and look up at the security camera.

'Phoebe!' His voice through the speaker sparks tears of relief. I slump forward as the door clicks open. I hear the thump of his feet on the stairs and then I feel the pressure of his arms.

'What the hell happened?'

I lean against him, barely strong enough to shape my lie as he helps me up the stairs.

'They took out the old boiler in my flat. There must have been a gas leak.'

'You should sue the builders. You could have died.'

'I'm alright.'

'You need to see a doctor.'

'I just felt a bit spaced out, so I got a cab and came here.'

He turns my hand and looks pointedly at the bruise and the shreds of sticking plaster left when I ripped out the drip.

'I… went to A&E first. I just got discharged.' I catch what's left of my breath.

'They should have kept you in. Carbon monoxide poisoning is no joke.'

He half carries me across the living area, sweeps aside a pair of socks and a magazine and lays me on the sofa. I slip my arms around his neck. He leans in, kisses me on the forehead and whispers, 'Take off your clothes.'

'What?'

He pulls a leaf from my hair. 'They're covered in mud.'

'Oh.' What else can I say?

I sit like a little kid while he eases off my shoes, pulls off my jeans and tugs my shirt over my head. I shiver a little in my bra and pants as he looks down at my body. It's a mess of cuts and bruises. Souvenirs of my visit to Oak Bank, which seems like a lifetime ago. He lifts my wrist and runs a finger down the three puncture

wounds made by the tip of Amy's knife. I wait for him to explode
with questions, almost willing him to berate me for blanking him
for days then turning up half dead on his doorstep. But he doesn't
say anything, just goes into the bathroom and turns on the taps.

'All yours,' he says as he reappears.

'Thank you.' I shuffle past him and close the door.

Gasping and wincing, I strip off my underwear and lower myself
into the steamy water. As my tensed-up muscles relax, I close my
eyes and let my mind rewind to Chrissie's voice in my ear. '*I saved
your life. All I ask in return is a chance to live mine.*'

I open my eyes. The water is tepid and Will is standing over me
clutching a big white towel. I hold myself still, unnerved by this
casual intimacy, yet surprised how natural it feels to step out of
the bath, let him wrap the towel around my naked body and tuck
the end between my breasts.

'I dug out some clean clothes for you,' he says.

I make my way to the bedroom, damp feet padding on bare
wood, worried that I'm going to be presented with his ex-wife's
skinny jeans or his last girlfriend's bathrobe. Is it tempting fate to
feel this pleased when I see that the worn flannel shirt and baggy
jogging pants laid out on the bed are definitely his? In the sitting
room there's a mug of soup and a spoon waiting on the glass coffee
table. I curl up beside him on the sofa and take a sip. The taste
shocks my system, jolting my starved senses. 'It's good.'

'Handsome, solvent *and* I can use a tin opener.'

'Modest too,' I wheeze. 'My kind of guy.'

There's a lost, searching look on his face. 'Am I?'

I nod hard.

'So why the radio silence?'

'Because I'm… rubbish girlfriend material?'

'You're not rubbish.'

'Hey. I said rubbish girlfriend material. In every other way I'm borderline spectacular.'

He smiles for the first time since I got here. 'I know.'

I say in a rush, 'I went to see Jonas Parks.'

'You should have told me, I'd have come with you.' He tucks a cushion under my head. 'Was he as creepy as he looks in the photos?'

'Creepier. And he's got these six women living with him who hang on his every word and act like he's some kind of god.'

'Lucky Jonas. Some of us don't even get a text.'

'You were right about his connection to Roz,' I say quickly. 'She hid on his commune for a while about twenty years ago.'

'Hid?'

'From the police. She was involved in an animal rights raid on a lab. They set fire to it and a young night guard died.'

'Jesus.'

'He'd just had a kid. I think the guilt hung over her for the rest of her life, affected everything she did.'

'Secrets can do that to you.'

'I know.'

He runs a finger along my jaw. 'Why do I get the feeling there's more to this story than you're letting on?'

'Maybe you've got a suspicious mind.'

'Could be.'

'What are you working on?' I say, as if my voice isn't straining like a faulty piston, and there isn't a herd of elephants stomping around the room.

He's so quiet for so long I think he's not going to answer, but then he sighs. 'Another magazine feature about Kay Duncan. It's way overdue but I've been a bit... preoccupied, and they wanted a new angle.'

I take another sip of soup. 'What did you come up with?'

'You really want to know?'

'Yes,' I say, nervous about what this new angle might be.

'OK then: "The role of the media in making myths around the story. Fifteen years of cruel speculation and shadow chasing, masquerading as journalism".'

'I haven't seen any speculation about her actual death,' I say carefully. 'Just… stuff about why she did it.'

'Well, a corpse and an autopsy tend to get in the way of a good conspiracy theory, but imagine the feeding frenzy if they hadn't found her body or there'd been the slightest doubt about the cause of death.'

I stir my soup, let the spoon clink against the mug. 'Did you see the report?'

'Yes, they sent me a copy.'

'Can I have a look?'

'Why?'

'I'm… interested. You forget, you're talking to a soon-to-be medic.'

'Who was too squeamish to look at photos of the corpse.'

'You shoved them in my face. I wasn't prepared.'

'Tell you what, I'll let you read the report if you promise to get some rest and let me work.'

'Deal.'

He takes a file from the papers on his desk and drops it into my lap.

I reach up and take his hand. He squeezes my fingers very gently before pulling away. I watch him walk back to his desk and then I open the report. Inside are two diagrams of a body, front and back view, studded with circles mapping wounds and abrasions, a whole cluster of them indicating the damage to the face and skull. Google translate confirms that they were all inflicted post-mortem; some by aquatic predation, others by impact with coastal rocks. I turn the page. I don't need help to translate 'Cause de décès: Noyade' – Death by drowning. The print blurs. My heart speeds up. I looked up the effects of carbon monoxide poisoning in the cab on the way from the hospital. Headache, weakness, dizziness, nausea. Nothing about making the world feel like a puzzle I don't have the brain power to solve. I feel Will's stare. I look up. 'What's wrong?'

'Check your Facebook.'

I take my phone from my bag and click the app. There's a string of fresh comments.

You OK, hon?

What's up Pheebs?

Call me.

The senders are all old classmates, people I haven't spoken to since I left Botswana.

I swipe up to the post they're commenting on. There it is. Posted fifteen hours ago.

This was the only way. I told too many lies and I hurt too many people.

A suicide note I never wrote. I see David Duncan hovering at my side when I keyed in my password before calling the clinic in Toulon, David Duncan typing in the darkness before hurling my phone onto the back seat of the Healey, David Duncan slamming the car door as he leaves me to die.

Will swivels round in his chair, crosses his arms and exhales. A long hard gust. 'Do you want to tell me what the hell is going on?'

'I must have been hacked.'

Silence.

'Oh, come on. If I was going to kill myself do you think I'd post a suicide note on bloody Facebook? Some joker at the hospital must have nicked my phone when I was asleep.'

He pushes himself up to standing and crosses the floor in four long strides.

'Will—'

'I need some air. If you decide you want to tell me the truth, give me a call.' The door shuts hard behind him.

Filled with hopeless, choking anger I stab at my phone, swiping through my WhatsApp messages and backed-up emails to see what else David Duncan hacked to make me look suicidal. I blink down at the screen. A name drifts up at me from another world, one where I'd felt trusting and safe. I click it open and read the message. I read it again and stare at the screen for a long, long time. I close my eyes. When I open them the words are still there; a block of black letters, stark against the blue-tinged white.

I make a call. But not to Will. The number I dial is in France.

CHAPTER THIRTY-FIVE

I haul myself up the concrete steps, kept upright only by fear that I'm too late. Four floors of agony, lifting and lowering each foot and clinging to the handrail. A teenage boy comes running down, eyes on his phone, a careless thump with his elbow as he barges past me. Sweaty and straining, I reach the top, kick off my trainer and throw it at her door. I wait, imagining her checking the security feed, looking to see who's there. Slowly the door opens. She steps out. Turns her head.

Her eyes lock on mine. The shock of seeing that face is real but I'm gripped by panic that this pink-haired, hollow-eyed creature is a phantom, conjured up by the after-effects of sedation and the lack of oxygen in my veins. Her features contort. 'You're supposed to be in hospital.'

'You're supposed to be dead.'

'Are you going to the police?'

'Not if you give me what I want.'

She closes her eyes and shakes her head, like if she wishes hard enough I'll be gone when she opens them, then she turns and walks back inside. Slowly I shuffle across the hallway and follow her into a small, tired room, my heart beating fast as I try to fill my damaged lungs. I look around me. Beige walls. A single half-packed suitcase open on the stained carpet. On the table a passport, a wad of cash, a scatter of cosmetics and a lit cigarette balanced on the edge of a saucer. My face in her mirror, white as raw fish, rolling in and out of focus. I drop onto the edge of a chair.

She finds the smouldering cigarette and mashes it to a pulp, 'If it's old man Burney's money you're after you can forget it. Now David's dead the Breakaway Brethren will get the lot.'

It's an odd combination of indifference and aggression. I can't work out how much of it's a front and how much is the real her. 'I don't want money,' I say.

'Then what *do* you want, Phoebe?'

'The truth.'

She sighs wearily, picks up the passport and slips it into the pocket of her jeans.

'Look, I'm sorry you got caught up in this. I'm sorry that madwoman Roz filled your head with lies and I'm sorry you nearly died. But like I told you in the hospital; I have no idea who your mother is. So let's not waste each other's time. I've got a plane to catch.'

'I don't want to drag this out either, Chrissie. I'm sick of dead ends and false leads. But there's a couple of things I need to get straight in my head.'

'Like what?'

I take a sip of breath. 'Like what David did with the body between taking it out of the freezer at the Villa Rosa and planting it in the creek.'

'For God's sake—'

'I've been asking myself how he managed to keep it immersed in the sea for nearly a week without it getting found or swept away.'

'What does it matter?'

'He must have had some kind of container that let water and predators in but stopped the body getting out.' I pause for a beat. 'Something like that big old lobster trap he'd got locked in the store of his boathouse.'

The fight goes out of her and she gazes at me with a weary misery. 'He bolted it to the hull of *Serenity*.'

'So all the time he was chugging around the bay playing the grieving widower, her body was right there under the boat, rotting down in real time. That takes some nerve. Nearly as much as it must have taken to bash her rotting face against the cliff to obliterate her features and make it look like storm damage.'

She looks away and runs tense fingers through her butchered hair. 'I told you. He did it to protect me. Are you done?'

'Not quite.' I cough hard into my fist and wince at the pain. 'When you and Kay were arguing on the boat, was the deck wet?'

She gazes at me, a little tick of impatience lifting her lip. 'What the hell are you talking about?'

'If she landed on the back of her head there'd have to have been about a foot of water to cover her mouth and nose.'

'No,' she says, getting annoyed. 'The deck wasn't wet.'

'The autopsy said Kay drowned.' I drop the report onto the table.

She raises a dismissive hand. 'Her whole body was a mess, it had been decomposing in warm water for nearly a week.'

'So what? You can't put saltwater into lung tissue after death no matter how decomposed it is. David's no fool. He'd have known that.'

It's getting windy, a rain-spattered breeze rattles the window. 'What's your point?'

'My point is, Kay drowned. Which means that you didn't kill her.'

She sits silent for a minute, a little crease forming in her forehead dead between her eyes. She puts a finger on the autopsy report and drags it towards her.

'David was right. After you hit her she was just concussed, but once he'd taken you down to the cabin I think he must have lowered a bucket over the side and filled it with seawater. Then he lifted her up and shoved her head in it. It would have been awkward but he's a big man and she was no size. All he had to do was hold her face under until the bubbles stopped. He'd have been a bit messed up, soaked through. He wouldn't have liked that. He's so careful about his clothes. So he probably put on fresh ones, maybe he had a shower. How did he smell when he woke you up? And his clothes? Were they different?'

The crease in her forehead deepens.

'He saw his chance to put an end to all his problems, and he set you up.'

She lifts her head and it's as if I can see the truth take hold. When she speaks it's slowly, like someone emerging from a dream. 'I didn't kill her.'

'No, David did.'

Her stare is lost, fixed on the far distance. 'I didn't kill her,' she says again and fumbles for her cigarettes.

'Once the body had been found I'm assuming it was David who graffitied the walls of the boathouse to make it look like he was being harassed by vandals and then set fire to it to destroy the evidence.'

She nods slowly.

'That was smart thinking,' I say, and for a moment I see the reflection of that hot bright blaze dancing on the water and feel the sting of smoke in my eyes. 'But why did he go to all the trouble of destroying the evidence in his boat and his car and not bother with the Villa Rosa?' I draw a scratchy intake of breath. 'I mean, what if the police had got suspicious and found Chrissie Miller's prints and DNA all over the house and no sign of Kay's?'

A pulse flickers fast in her top lip. She touches it with her fingertip then drops her hand.

'The day after the fire, I went up to the villa. Shelley Morton was there clearing it out and she mentioned that the only thing in the whole place David disposed of personally was the freezer.' She blinks just once and takes a cigarette from the pack. 'I remembered that and I thought, what if Chrissie Miller had never set foot inside the Villa Rosa? What if the only time she'd spent there she'd been sealed up in plastic in that freezer in the outhouse?' I want desperately for her to look up but her gaze stays fixed on the cigarette, turning it backwards and forwards, like she'd forgotten which end to light or even what she was meant to do with it.

'That story you told me in the hospital wasn't quite right, was it?' I say, rationing my breath to ease out the words. 'It wasn't Chrissie who pushed Kay on the boat. It wasn't Kay who David drowned. It wasn't Kay's body they found shoved in those rocks with her face bashed in and it wasn't *Kay's* Doxettes tattoo that sent Vicky Bunce into a tail spin when she saw the photos of the corpse. So tell me, if the woman in the water was Chrissie Miller, who the hell does that make you?'

A car pulls up in the street below, sloshing through the puddles. A door slams. Someone drags a suitcase along the pavement, stuttering the wheels over the cracks. She starts to shake, little tremors like she's shivering from cold, though her voice, when it comes, is steady and devoid of emotion.

'Well, one thing we know for sure. I'm *not* your mother,' she says, staring me down 'Other than that, take your pick. The monster who killed her kid and used her husband's money to cover it up? The rich bitch junkie who was too stoned to notice that her five-year-old had gone missing? The bad mother who's been trapped in her own small corner of hell for the last fifteen years? Or what about the never-ending source of tabloid fodder whose every move sparks an outpouring of self-righteous venom?' She lets out a small sour laugh. 'Oh, yes, and if they ever find out that I faked my own death I'll be the she-devil who finally showed her true colours by murdering her husband's lover.'

'Is that why you hit her?'

'Because she was screwing David?' Her eyelids fall and rise with the shake of her head. 'I never cared about his other women. They came and they went. I was the one that mattered. His life's work. The broken bird he loved to keep on saving from herself.' The trembling travels up her body, tensing in spasms. 'I hit her because she was the same fucked-up, jealous Chrissie she'd always been. She taunted me. She told me how pathetic I was. How I'd failed as a daughter, a singer, a mother and a wife. Stuff I'd told myself a thousand times, so when she got no reaction she fetched a bundle of letters from the cabin and threw them at me. "Here's what your husband really thinks of you, Kay-babes," she said. "All these letters about Maya. He keeps them from you but he shows them to me. They're always good for a laugh. There's one there that's better than most. Some crazy bitch who's come up with quite a story about snatching her off the street. I said to him, once the old man snuffs it we should let you see it – maybe it will push you over the edge and we'll finally be shot of you".'

She screws up her eyes and bites her lip. 'I couldn't bear it. I slapped her hard. She fell back and hit her head. I watched her crumple to the floor, and I panicked. Then suddenly David was there pulling me down to the cabin, giving me a pill, telling me he'd call an ambulance and she'd be alright. When I woke up and he told me I'd killed her I was terrified.' She lifts her head to look at me. 'What jury on earth would let Crazy Kay the child murderer walk free from a charge of manslaughter? Even if I'd only got a few months, how long do you think I'd have lasted in prison? The monster who got away with killing her own daughter? All those thieves, drug pushers and people traffickers making themselves feel good by torturing someone further down the scale of filth? I told David I'd kill myself before I'd let them put me in jail. That's when he told me he'd worked out a way to save me.' Her head nods while she bites back tears. 'That's what he always did. He dealt with the bad stuff and he made it go away.'

'For Christ's sake,' I wheeze. 'He drowned her and then he set you up so you wouldn't tell your father your reconciliation was fake.'

She stares away, as if she hasn't heard me. 'We had all Chrissie's things; her phone, her passport, the keys to her flat, and it's not as if she had any family to worry about.' She turns her head and gazes at my face, but she's not seeing me. She's back on that boat, zonked out on Xanax, listening to David Duncan whisper bullshit in her ear. 'He said we'd keep her frozen until the old man died then do a body swap. I'd be dead Chrissie and dead Chrissie would be me.'

She puts the unlit cigarette between her lips then takes it out and teases a shred of tobacco from her tongue. 'I went to France and swapped the little studio I'd rented in town for that isolated house on the hill, so that when it came out that Kay Duncan had been living there no one would have more than a fleeting memory of the dark-haired Brit who'd always kept herself to herself.'

'And you abandoned your plans to expose your father's abuse.'

'I should have had the guts to do it years ago. As it was, I had to let him win.' Her voice slides into bitterness. 'He died with his reputation intact, smug in the belief that I'd admitted it was my evil that had forced him to punish me.'

'Is that why you stopped painting?'

'Partly. But there's nothing like thinking you're a killer to crush the creative urge.' Tears are running down her face, and her lips quiver. 'The only thing that kept me going while we waited for the old bastard to die was the thought that I was going to finally escape from being Kay Duncan. The end was in sight. The Circle Trust was sending me money and, in the "absence of issue", they'd agreed to name David as the next beneficiary. I'd even bought myself a ticket to Costa Rica. And then out of nowhere, you appeared.' She glares at me, hurt and accusatory. 'For three whole days I truly believed you were Maya. I'd never been more certain of anything in my life. Have you any idea how wonderful that felt? All that hope and energy flooding back, wiping out the nightmares of what might have happened to her? I called David and I told him we had to find some other way to dispose of Chrissie's body because, for the first time in fifteen years, I *wanted* to be Kay Duncan. He tried to force me to be realistic. He said it looked good but it had looked good before. So we did the DNA test and he kept saying,

"Let's not celebrate till the results come through." I didn't listen. I couldn't. And when he was proved right it was a plummet back to hell. I couldn't face that again, not ever. So I agreed to bring the "suicide" forward.' The rain is falling harder, pounding against the window. 'And David... David did the rest. He thought he'd got it all worked out, every tiny detail.'

'Right down to the toothbrush.'

'What?'

'Keeping Chrissie's toothbrush for what? Over a year? Then giving it to the police and telling them it was Kay's.'

She grimaces. 'It worked though, didn't it? Scotched any doubts about the identity of the body.'

'Does anyone else know you're alive?' I say.

She drops her head. 'Not now that Vicky's gone.'

I turn this over, finger the shape of it, the dents and pitfalls, and feel a queasy sense of power. 'So if I keep quiet you get to start over as Chrissie Miller. No more Kay. No more trolls, no more hoaxes, no more dashed hopes. No more Maya.'

'That's right, Phoebe. A chance of freedom I don't deserve.'

Unable to breathe, I shake my head to loosen the words. 'What if Maya's alive?'

A grimace of pain, then her face hardens. 'Is this your revenge? Wind me up so you can watch me fall apart all over again? Well, it's not going to work. Not this time. My daughter is dead. Bones in a ditch. Probably has been since the day she went missing.' She looks at me with a mixture of hurt and misery. 'Are we done?'

'Not quite,' I say, though every word burns my lungs. 'I want to read you something.' I press a couple of keys on my phone. She tightens her lips and starts counting the bundle of cash on the table into neat little piles.

'"Hey, Phoebe, sorry it's taken me so long to get back to you."' The words come feebly, tiny wisps of sound. '"Things just aren't the same without Roz, so I've been job hunting in South Africa."'

Her head twitches with impatience. 'What is this?'

I press my chest to ease the tightness, but I feel like I'm suffocating. 'It's from the vet at Molokodi. Rob McClennan. He runs the breeding programme for endangered species... tracks family groups, analyses genetic material, makes sure we don't breed from—'

'I get the picture,' she says.

I wait for the words on the screen to steady, though I know them by heart. '"I just ran the tests on those samples you sent me – a bloody T-shirt? Very dramatic! Hope everything's OK."'

'What samples? What T-shirt?'

'My hair and your blood. On my T-shirt from that time you cut yourself. You remember – you were slicing tomatoes at the Villa Rosa?'

She stops fiddling with the money.

'I'll spare you the in-depth science, but he says the DNA sequences they generated bear no relation to the ones I forwarded to him from the clinic.' Her eyes find mine. I hold her gaze. 'He says the samples I sent him were slightly degraded, but his tests show a 98.976 per cent probability that the cells from your blood and my hair are from a mother and daughter.'

So many tiny noises; water dripping in the cistern, murmurs from the next-door flat, a hiss of contempt from her lips that bubbles into a mirthless snort of laughter. 'Well, ten out of ten for persistence, Phoebe. But if you think I'm going to take the word of some bush vet over a state-of-the-art clinic that guarantees legally certified results, you must be even crazier than I thought.'

I close my eyes. 'It didn't make sense to me either, so I called the clinic. I asked them to see if our samples could have got mixed up with someone else's. The receptionist was polite, like she gets this all the time.' My voice dwindles to a sigh. 'She insisted there was absolutely no chance of a mix-up with the samples but she promised she'd investigate anyway and get back to me. I asked her to make sure she still had my email address.' I gasp in more air. 'When she checked her system the only contact details they had for our case were David's. He must have deleted yours and mine before he sent off the application.'

She throws up her hands. 'What the hell is wrong with you? You were sitting there, right next to me, when the results arrived in my inbox. I can show you the message.'

The rain on the window and my voice – thin and shredded – from far away. 'The emails you and I got weren't sent by the clinic. They were sent by David.'

'Oh God. Is this the exhaust fumes talking or just another of your paranoid fantasies?'

'It's called spoofing, Kay. Spammers do it all the time. They send you messages that look exactly like they come from someone you want to hear from – your friends, your bank, your employer.' My lungs are burning up. 'David couldn't risk that DNA test coming out positive. Your daughter turning up would have destroyed his whole plan to get you out of the way and his hands on your father's money. So he deleted our addresses from the application form before he even sent it off. Then he spoofed the clinic's account and sent us a set of test results he'd cut and pasted from the internet. The ones he picked come up fifth in images when you google "negative maternal DNA test".'

'You're lying. David would never have kept me from Maya.'

'I think we've all been surprised at what David Duncan was capable of.' Fire tears through my chest but I won't let it silence me. 'He didn't set you free, Kay. He made you an accessory to murder and sent us fake results from a fake email so he could pay off Lila Mendez.' I hold out my phone. 'The clinic sent me the real results. A 99.347 per cent certainty of a maternal link.'

She stares at the screen, her gaze loosening as the enormity of what she's seeing sinks in.

'Fake results from a fake email,' I say. I think I'm going to cry but suddenly space makes a leap and she's clasping me close. Her face in my hair, her arms tightening around me, my heart beating hard against her ribs as all the wanting, hoping, anger and uncertainty erupt in choking sobs of relief, great heaving gasps at the earth-shattering, life-altering simplicity of what David did. She pulls back a little, closes her eyes, touches my hair and pushes her fingertips to my nose and cheekbones, like a blind woman feeling for a face she once knew.

'It's you,' she whispers. 'My baby. My Maya. You came home.'

That name in her mouth gives me a tender thrill and strips away another layer of the false Phoebe I've been for so long. Her hands grow still, cupped around my cheeks, and we stay like that for a long time, holding our breath as if we're in some kind of trance. And then her body slackens. She lets go. All the joy sucked from her.

'What's wrong?'

'It's too late.'

'For what?'

'To be your mother.'

'No.'

'Kay Duncan's dead, cremated. That's the way she has to stay.'

We stand there in Chrissie Miller's dull shabby room, looking at each other, full of relief, regret, happiness, fear and longing for what might have been.

'You and I know the truth,' I say, and I tell myself it's enough.

EPILOGUE

It's two years since that day at Chrissie's flat, eighteen months since I started medicine at UCL and a year since I broke up with Will. I tried to make it work, God, I tried – but there are only so many lies I can live. Only so many nights I can stay awake in case I murmur Kay's secrets in my sleep, shrugs I can give when the tabloids churn out a new sighting of Maya Duncan and excuses I can come up with for not inviting him along on my trips to see my 'aunt' in Costa Rica.

We have a house there – a creeper-covered cabin on a hill overlooking the sea where she paints; bright images of flowers and trees and sky. No people. She never paints people and beyond those four, whitewashed walls I never call her Kay, only Chrissie – though the name turns my stomach. As for me, to keep her safe – I must be forever Phoebe.

Every time I hear or say or write that name I think of Roz; how much I hate her for everything she took from me, how much I love her for who she was and everything she did to save me from Parks. Looking back on the time I spent in his warped little world, I'm pretty sure that by the end he'd guessed I was his daughter – all that talk about higher beings and belonging, that possessive finger drilling into my brow – but I have no interest in finding out if my hunch was right. Neither has Kay. In fact, she has no interest in discussing anything to do with the past and she refuses to even think about the future.

When we're together, she cooks for me, usually badly but with gusto, paints my nails, takes me down to the sea to watch the dolphins or to the lagoon to look for turtles. In the night, when I have nightmares of her exposure and arrest, I pad across the verandah to her room and she holds me close until the panic subsides. Six months ago I asked her how she managed to sleep so soundly and she said very quietly, 'For the first time in my life I'm happy. I have you, I have all this and I'm free to be myself. Why would I spoil a single second worrying how long it's going to last?' Then she laughed and twisted a loop of my hair through her fingers. 'Anyway, there's nothing in this world worth having that doesn't come with risk.'

When I'm back in London, I fill my days with lectures and lab work. In the evenings I go home alone to my empty, exquisitely decorated flat and immerse myself in *Gray's Anatomy* in the hope that exhaustion will help me to sleep through. Tonight though, it's not a nightmare that wakes me, it's a text from Will. The same one he's been sending me every week since the day I left him.

When you're ready to trust me, I'll be here. x

Usually I delete them. Lately I've been tempted to text him back.

A LETTER FROM SAM

Dear Reader,

Thank you so much for choosing to read *Gone Before*. I hope you enjoy it as much as I enjoyed creating the characters and weaving the twists and turns of the plot. The story sprang from an idea I'd been thinking about for a long time and when I visited Provence and saw the hidden creeks and soaring cliffs of the coastline around Cassis I knew it would be the perfect place to set the opening of the mystery. During my career as a television producer, I covered many strange real-life stories but none were as compelling as those that centred around family secrets. I think this is why, as a writer, I am so intrigued by the tensions that smoulder behind closed doors. If *Gone Before* had you hooked I hope you go on to enjoy what comes next.

If you want to keep up to date with all my latest releases, just sign up at the following link. Your email address will never be shared and you can unsubscribe at any time.

www.bookouture.com/sam-hepburn

If you liked *Gone Before*, I would be very grateful if you could write a review. I would love to know what you think and sharing your thoughts in a review is a brilliant way to help other readers to discover my books. Thank you!

I always enjoy hearing from my readers – you can get in touch on my Facebook page, through Twitter, Goodreads or my website.

All my best,
Sam

SamHepburnAuthor

@Sam_Osman_Books

www.samhepburnbooks.com

ACKNOWLEDGEMENTS

A big thank you as ever to my agent, Stephanie Thwaites, for her brilliant guidance and support, to Beth Holgate for being the perfect companion in Cassis, to Sarah Curtis for feedback on early drafts, to John Willis for his advice on all things nautical, to everyone at Bookouture, in particular my editor, Lucy Dauman, whose sharp editorial eye was crucial in creating this book, and to my husband, James, for pretty much everything.